The Beckett Cypher – The Case, is a novel of passion, love, intrigue, mystery, crime, corruption and conspiracy. Readers may find that some details in the investigation, although fictional, bear striking resemblance to current events that have unfolded and are still developing throughout the world.

Shane Beckett is a highly trained undercover operative, working under contract for the Carson City Sheriff. His mission, to investigate an organized crime family that controls drug cartel distribution in the area, is about to take a turn that will alter his life, his family and his future. Shane is investigating king-pin Franky Magadinno, who for decades built a powerful crime syndicate, protected by corrupt government officials and the violent criminal underworld.

Less than 2 hours' drive from Carson City, Shane's brother, Heath, is working hard to restore his new life, as a federal parolee, now free from prison, and a drug trafficking conviction. But Heath soon discovers that leaving the drug world he now hates, will be impossible, due to prison debts that have followed him outside. Heath is once again forced to choose between family and drug-money, as he is pulled in to the underworld Shane is investigating. Whether Shane will confront his brother as an enemy, or embrace him as an ally, is now up to Heath.

As the investigation intensifies, Shane finally finds the true love he has longed for, only to discover that she is far more than just his dream girl. He learns that he too, is being followed and investigated. Shane must choose to trust his new love and her family, or reject them, as he struggles with difficult choices.

The Case begins to spiral out of control, as one of the crime family is murdered, and Shane realizes *he* may be the next target. What follows is a twisted, tangled web of corruption, lies and betrayals, mixed with criminal investigation and political maneuvering, that leads to the ultimate discovery for Shane and Heath…the discovery of why their parents were murdered, and who was ultimately responsible.

The Case becomes the preoccupation that will take Shane, and those who love him, through a series of unpredictable twists and turns, in *The Beckett Cypher* novels. Love, passion, romance, crime, politics, corruption, and money all play their parts, leading to the final conflict involving a shadow government. The conflict will become an all-out cold war, with explosive and deadly results, as love and hope develop for some, while despair and failure unfold for others, and everyone's alliances are put to the test. But to unravel the mystery and solve *The Case*, Shane needs to find the key – *The Beckett Cypher*.

The Beckett
CYPHER

The Beckett CYPHER

Book 1—The Case

LEE CUNNINGHAM

ISBN Paperback: 978-1-7320055-0-1
ISBN eBook: 978-1-7320055-1-8

Printed in the United States of America

Cover and Interior Design: Ghislain Viau

1

"A Mirror Can't Show What Lies Deep Inside"
(Patrick Shane Beckett)

Shane Beckett sat hunkered down in the driver's seat of a new Ford Focus outfitted with dark tinted windows and paper plates that advertised a Reno, Nevada Ford dealer. He peered through binoculars 150 yards up the road to a driveway that led to the suspect's house. A streetlight illuminated the target driveway, garage, and front porch. Thanks to the lighting Shane could clearly see everyone coming to or leaving from the house, even though it was 2:00 A.M.

The neighborhood was quiet, due to the early morning April cold, and a light rain which had begun earlier in the evening. Shane liked rain during surveillance. It provided him one more layer of cover, the wet covering the darkness over his location. And he liked the feeling of watching crooks without worrying too much about *being* watched, himself. After all, the purpose of any surveillance was to see, without being seen. And Shane was very good on surveillance.

The subject of Shane's surveillance tonight was Hector Alverez, and Hector was one of Shane's favorite targets. Hector was a shadowy figure, a recently surfaced lieutenant in a drug cartel known as the Mexican Gulf Cartel, who also had deep ties to the American prison-born Mexican Mafia. And although Shane had only been on this case for two months he had already identified the key players in Hector's new life in the United States, and most of these associates' routines, habits and acquaintances.

Shane had been hired under contract by the Carson City Sheriff to work just one case, a case that required a deep cover operative unknown to the staff and deputies of the Sheriff's Office or any other local, state or federal official in the area. Shane was working this assignment alone, gathering intelligence on the last major organized drug crime family still active in Nevada's capital city. And he was identifying the family's methamphetamine and heroin distribution network. That was where Hector came into play. He was now working directly under the family crime boss, Franky Magadinno.

Even more importantly, Shane was charged with identifying the Magadinno ties to all the Mexican drug cartels that now supplied illegal drugs to the area, and all the people who protected that network. And *that* list was much longer and more interesting than a handful of drug dealers with Hispanic surnames. *That* list had led Shane to discover economic and political ties Hector and Franky had with both private businesses leaders and government officials.

As he continued to scan his surroundings, Shane sat in thought about how he had arrived at this point in his life, and in American history. Drug distribution didn't just involve drugs. The criminal element that controlled these drugs spilled over into political corruption and power alliances, involving prostitution, money laundering, fraud, kidnapping, extortion, bribery, and when it was beneficial, murder. To accomplish all this successfully without incurring major losses to the crime organization, corrupt officials were needed to provide high level protection, insulating the crime syndicate from law enforcement and prosecution.

Shane knew this all too well from his former days as an undercover agent with Drug Enforcement Administration, working in a federal task force. His years at DEA, although few, had been packed with action, intrigue and surprise. Shane's "street education" had taught him that people working in the powerful criminal justice system *could* be bought, corrupted and controlled at all levels, including the local, county, state and federal systems.

The highest profile case that Shane and his team worked in his federal career cost millions in tax payer dollars, in addition to the ultimate sacrifice of the lives of two dedicated agents. Both agents had been Shane's closest partners, and friends. After months of legal wrangling, warrants were finally issued that culminated in twelve arrests. But by the end of many well-orchestrated delays in prosecution and the lengthy trial that eventually followed, a mountain of evidence had disappeared from its temporary holding safe in the court system, and what little evidence remained was then deemed "tainted" by a judge who was on-the-take. The case was dismissed by the judge with prejudice, barring any later attempt at prosecution.

To add insult to injury, the higher-ups in Shane's agency wouldn't authorize an investigation into the judge's behavior. The topper was that the crooks that evaded prosecution were later labeled "untouchable" when they returned to their life of crime. They had been effectively insulated, through law suits and political correctness issues related to their ethnic minority and illegal immigration status. Corruption had triumphed over justice, and once again evil laughed in the face of law and order.

Shane's four-year task force experience had shown him first hand that the criminal justice system was in part corrupt, infected with crooked politicians, lawyers, judges and even a few bad cops. Shane knew he couldn't continue to work in a corrupt and broken system, and he had simply walked away from a promising career. He now worked by himself as a contract operative, conducting specialized investigations for agencies trying to rid themselves of the ever-spreading and contaminating corruption.

To successfully navigate and survive in the solo undercover world in which he now lived, Shane was forced to learn quickly how to identify and follow only the real leads…and of course, always the money. He had also learned how to rapidly distinguish the good guys from the bad guys, on both sides of the law. Working as a private investigator, Shane developed the ability to use people from all walks of life to expose the truth. *Truth* had now become all important to Shane. He would expose it, turn it over to authorities, and then leave, not worrying about how or where the information lived or died, or how it was used when he was gone.

During the first years on his own, Shane had also developed and honed unique specialized skills, making him the perfect choice to work this one particular case in Carson City. And the case was perfect for him, allowing him to use *all* of his unique abilities. Plus, it allowed him to work alone just as he liked it, not dependent on or responsible for anyone else. Shane didn't ever intend to lose a partner again.

So, when the newly elected Carson City Sheriff explained the case to Shane at their first meeting, Shane immediately accepted the offer. This Carson City Sheriff had been in office less than a year, but he was well versed on corruption in the state capital. After his election Sheriff Mark Roberts had met with agents from the DEA and Nevada Division of Investigation to inquire about a series of murders that had plagued him during his previous twenty-year career with the FBI.

Roberts had been blocked and delayed in working these cases for nearly two decades at the Bureau. When he retired from the FBI to run for office, he promised himself that someday he would solve these mysteries and discover who in his organization had been responsible for impeding the investigations.

Although Roberts himself could never identify all the players and make all the connections, he was certain that this drug cartel and some high-powered politicians had worked together to orchestrate these particular murders. But when Roberts was closest to making progress on the case, using a Confidential Informant it took years for him to develop, Roberts' wife, Lisa went missing, and the CI suddenly got cold feet. Lisa was never located, and Roberts knew that foul play had to be involved, even though his own bosses suggested she had voluntarily left him.

Most of his close friends at the FBI knew that Mark's wife was troubled by the long hours her husband worked, and that she had been unhappy during their last year of marriage. She had even left Mark and rented an apartment close to her work in Gardnerville, south of Carson City. But what they didn't know was that for the three months preceding her disappearance, Lisa and Mark had been meeting at a secret hideaway in Nevada City on their weekends. The couple had rekindled their romance, and Lisa was planning on moving back in with Mark just before she disappeared. In fact, she had already sublet her apartment.

Roberts' motivation to move to Carson City and run for Sheriff was in part to solve these crimes. He remained committed to uncovering the dirty little secrets involved in these connected murders, and his own wife's disappearance, which he adamantly believed was entwined with the unsolved cases. He had become obsessed with knowing the truth once and for all. Wisely, he had kept this obsession to himself.

Mark Roberts was a smart, politically savvy man. He knew that solving these cases would make many powerful people with something to hide, very uncomfortable. And he knew he had to limit the knowledge of the investigation to the fewest number of people possible in order to succeed and to survive…and in order to give his investigator a real chance at uncovering the truth. Roberts decided that only he and one other person in his department would know anything about the investigation. And he decided he needed one of the best undercover operatives in the business for this sensitive assignment.

Mark Roberts' first decision was selecting and recruiting Shane Beckett. Shane had been suggested by Bryan Holland, Roberts' longtime friend and a fellow Quantico graduate. Roberts trusted Bryan Holland with his life and Bryan trusted Shane with his own. Plus, Bryan Holland knew Shane's abilities from task force work *and* a lifelong friendship. That recommendation alone had been good enough for Roberts.

Secondly, Roberts had appointed one of the only people he believed he could trust, longtime acquaintance and former California Department of Justice agent Brian Grant, as his Undersheriff. After leaving the DOJ, Grant had worked himself up through the Carson City Sheriff's Office ranks, starting as a patrol officer, and finally serving as the Undersheriff in the previous administration.

Mark Roberts and Brian Grant had met at Quantico, Virginia, when Brian was a new lieutenant and attended the FBI National Academy. They had become distant friends and stayed in touch throughout Grant's rise to Undersheriff and while Roberts left the FBI to run for office. Grant had even managed to secure high level donors to assist Roberts, in his bid for office as a first-time candidate.

Roberts understood that Brian knew the department intimately. And Mark Roberts thought he needed someone with intimate knowledge of this historically political Sheriff's Office. While many people advised Mark against keeping a manager from a previous administration, Roberts believed he could trust Grant, so the job of Undersheriff was offered and quickly accepted.

Although Roberts alone had recruited Shane and was the only person to know Shane's true identity, and more importantly his true mission, he had placed Grant in charge of managing the finances of the undercover operation. Roberts had secretly commissioned Shane a "special deputy," and had arranged to cover all expenses of the investigation, using federal money awarded the Sheriff's Office through a grant to increase drug awareness and impact illegal drug sales.

Roberts set up a special account that Brian Grant would manage personally, making payments to a consulting corporation created for this case only. No one but Roberts, Grant and Shane would know of Shane's existence until the investigation was complete. And only Roberts and Shane would know the details of the case and the identity of the targets. Shane was free to move about and work unrestrained. Only Roberts knew the location of Shane's Carson City apartment. Both Roberts and Grant had Shane's undercover phone number, but Grant was directed to use the contact only in case of an emergency involving Roberts, or under Roberts' direct order.

∾

Coincidently, Shane's target, Hector Alvarez, had also been recruited to fill a specific assignment. Hector had been selected by an organization known to law enforcement as the Magadinno Family Crime Syndicate, to allow the family to affiliate more deeply with the various Mexican drug cartels. Hector was Mexican by birth and had been Franky's personal choice for his Number Two in command to fill this void.

Hector was well versed with both Colombian and Mexican drug cartels and worked effectively with most of them, importing all the various drugs the cartels supplied to different locations. While Hector was from Mexico, benefactors had recognized his talent at an early age. They had sent him to be educated at an expensive private university in the United States. Thereafter he was prepped for service as a high-level facilitator in the drug world.

Shane had spent sleepless nights trying to figure out who had selected and groomed Hector for his current role. It didn't make sense to Shane that Franky would spend the time and money to invest in a poor boy from the streets in Mexico. Shane felt another explanation was more likely, but that explanation had so far proved elusive.

Franky had started in the family business decades earlier, primarily importing cocaine and marijuana. In dealing with rival cartels, he found out quickly that he needed a facilitator to keep hard drugs flowing to his warehouses. This was especially true after meth had overtaken the cocaine market and cocaine supplies became expensive and unreliable.

The public demand for cocaine grew exponentially in the 70's and 80's. But coca leaves don't grow naturally in the States, so it couldn't be produced locally. It came to the States initially from

Peru and Colombia. The problem for the Colombian drug lords was that cocaine was produced far away from their American market on a different continent. The drug had to be transported thousands of miles, through, around or over several different countries, to its U.S. destination, making the business very expensive and risky. The Colombians gave the risk to the Mexicans.

For decades, Colombian drug cartels had ruled the drug trade supplying tons of Colombian-produced cocaine to a voracious market in the United States. The Colombians used their Mexican counterparts to smuggle product through Mexico and into the United States to safe houses for distribution. But while the Colombians got substantially richer, the Mexicans took all the risk in Mexico and the U.S., and often were arrested, robbed or killed in the process, all while making only a small fraction of the huge profit.

But while they worked for the Colombian cartels, the Mexican drug runners gained a great deal of experience in the States, and soon understood both the cocaine distribution business *and eventually* its more lucrative rival, the methamphetamine trade that American outlaw biker gangs had previously controlled in the U.S. And as Ronald Reagan's "War on Drugs" took its toll on the cocaine supply, the "coke" price sky rocketed, creating a very timely opportunity.

Methamphetamine, although a totally different drug, produces many of the same psychological and physiological effects on the body as cocaine. And it doesn't come from the coca plant, but rather, is made from precursor chemicals. The Mexican drug cartels were soon producing meth or "crank" by the truckload from cheap, easy to come by chemicals they "cooked" just south of the U.S. border in Mexico.

Using already established cocaine distribution routes and safe houses in the U.S., they simply flooded the U.S. market with cheap meth. The Mexican drug cartels had adapted, and as a result, they became increasingly organized, wealthy and powerful.

As their power grew, the Mexican cartels took over the meth market so quickly, ruthlessly and efficiently, that the biker gangs could do nothing about the loss of their business. American drug dealers producing crank found it much more difficult and costly to obtain meth precursor chemicals, and in the end, they just could not compete. One more American industry moved south to Mexico, due to economic pressure. Mexican and hybrid gangs flourished as a result.

Adding to law enforcement's already huge drug enforcement problem, was the fact that the Mexican cartels had developed influence and power through decades of cultivating corruption at all levels of government in Mexico and the United States. The cartels were well connected, well-armed by the Mexican Army, and protected by elected officials and law enforcement on their payroll in both Mexico and the U.S.

Mexican cartels also proved more ruthless than the Colombian cartels. They commanded well-deserved fear on both sides of the U.S. border. Mexican cartel drug murders were legendary, and local law enforcement seemed powerless to stop the terror from spreading. Inevitably, the terror also spread to the U.S. side of the border, and then marched inland.

U.S. law enforcement soon figured out that the Mexican cartels were here to stay. The cartels' corruption of U.S officials and law enforcement tracked with cartel movements within the U.S., beginning with the Border Patrol and pushing inward toward the heartland. As cartel profits increased, influence followed, and a growing number of politicians and officials were added to the cartel payroll.

And then, as heroin use increased rapidly in the late 90's, that additional revenue source vastly increased cartel profits, and further exacerbated the situation for American law enforcement. Politicians around the country took notice of the vast amount of money controlled by the cartels...and available to *them*...at an arm's length of course.

And as Americans grew more addicted to prescription drugs, prescription opioids became increasingly difficult to obtain, as law enforcement focused on yet another addictive source. When demand exceeded supply, Mexican drug cartels offered up cheap heroin and opioids as readily available alternatives, and demand spread like a wildland fire through a windy American prairie.

By the time Shane had taken this case, the Mexican cartels were also controlling the expanding methamphetamine, heroin and opioid trade and most of the illegal marijuana trade. They laundered their illegitimate money through legitimate businesses spread out along the U.S. interstate highway 'trade routes' they had used to smuggle drugs for decades.

And as cartel influence in the United States grew, violent gangs like MS 13 flourished and became powerful beyond most Americans' comprehension. Addictions, overdoses and deaths among drug abusers skyrocketed, keeping pace with the growing numbers of illegals crossing the southern border, and accelerating violence from cartels and organized gangs. While America slumbered, and its citizens became more politically correct, crime syndicates like The Magadinno Family Crime Syndicate, took advantage of the lack of security, and became politically and criminally entrenched in all 50 states.

As time marched on, cartels invested heavily in corrupting local, state and federal U.S. politicians and law enforcement officials when they could, to protect their empires and wealthy bosses, who ran cartel business north of the border. Corruption was run like a well-managed business. Soon anyone who wanted to sell their drugs had to do business with the Mexican cartels or gangs like "MS 13, whose motto was, "kill, rape and control."

And anyone who wanted to succeed in politics was a target of control for this new underworld. Within half a century many members of the American political elite were partying with millionaire cartel bosses, just as they had with the Hollywood elite, the voracious wolves of Wall Street, big bank CEOs, arms dealers supplying third world war lords, and infamous, rapacious dictators, in the past.

After decades of fighting drug abuse and paying for the treatment of millions of offenders, American citizens had grown weary of fighting the War on Drugs. Activists in all states began to organize and push to decriminalize drugs, beginning with marijuana. And as marijuana was legalized in state after state, the growing number of ethnic minority drug dealers in prison became an issue for the first ethnic minority U.S. President, who began pushing for early prison releases for those imprisoned on drug charges. Those released who returned to crime poured more fuel a growing blaze.

The aggravating problem American families faced alone, was that both meth and heroin were highly addictive. And Shane understood this only too well. Shane's own younger brother Heath had used crank for years, first socially, then as an addict, and finally as an addict in complete denial. Heath's addiction had cost him his successful landscape architect business in southern California, his freedom, and finally his wife and twin daughters.

Shane knew how an addict's family becomes disposable, replaced by meth buddies craving the drug. Heath's "party" friends had quickly taken priority over his real friends and family, as Heath grew more dependent on drugs. And, as the dependence grew, and he became less committed to his responsibilities, Heath's lucrative landscape business and real friends began to slip away. When his business left, and the money dried up, all of Heath's "druggy" friends also vanished. Heath sold meth to make up the loss.

As for Shane, he had discovered Heath's crank problems too late to intervene and help prevent his brother from going to prison. Heath was eventually convicted and sentenced for sales of meth and sent to a federal prison in California.

Shane had not seen his brother regularly, at other than prison visitations during the holidays, for nearly three years. As he now sat watching the rain and flickering shadows during the surveillance, Shane thought how he hated the pain and misery these lethally addictive hard drugs inflicted on their victims and their families. And he hated the monsters who dealt these drugs, spreading death and suffering, with no remorse.

Heath's wife had tried to be supportive for the first year after he was sentenced to prison. But eventually she met another man, divorced Heath and remarried. She moved on with her new life. After his release from prison, Heath rarely had the opportunity to spend time with his young daughters. And when he did, he was too embarrassed to play the loving, remorseful dad.

Shane sat in the driver's seat thinking about his beloved little brother. Heath's story was common in the drug world. It was sadly repeated over and over...a good life thrown away chasing the elusive methamphetamine high at all costs. No one was left to care for Heath except Shane, who had visited Heath in prison, sent him care packages, supported him financially, and finally helped him obtain parole.

After his release, Shane paid for Heath's apartment while he got established in his new life. A few months after Heath's parole, Shane convinced a friend with a brother in the landscape business to make a pitch to hire Heath as a laborer. Almost immediately, Heath's new boss recognized his talent, and eventually took him on as a full partner. Heath began to reclaim his life, one sober day at a time.

Heath had learned the hard way to hate the world of meth, and all the pain and misery it held. Now he could often be found at the gym or jogging on the beach, if he wasn't working. When Shane last saw Heath, he could see that Heath had lost the "crank" look. Heath had regained his muscle tone and his youthful good looks. And although Heath knew his struggle in the years ahead would prove challenging, he also knew he was well on his way to recovering his appearance, a healthy attitude for life…and most of all, hope.

After the demise of the cocaine trade, Franky Magadinno recognized the future in methamphetamine, and brought in Hector Alvarez as a liaison between the Magadinno Family and the Mexican drug cartels that controlled the meth supply to Nevada. Hector had been the trusted adjutant to a cartel lieutenant Franky knew from years of "working vacations" spent in Mexico.

Franky had been wined and dined by the Gulf and Sonora drug cartels and had developed relationships with both while in Mexico. It was in Cancun he first met Hector, a young, well-educated, handsome, gregarious, problem solver who "fixed" everything during Franky's Mexico visits. Each time Franky arrived for another "meeting," Hector was waiting as his facilitator to "recreation" and negotiations with both cartels. It was as if Hector's position had been created just for Franky, the man who could move mountains of dope into the U.S.

Franky never had to go through Mexican customs, was always treated royally during his stay in Mexico, and never paid for anything on his "vacations." The truth was that the cartels wanted Franky to distribute their product as much as Franky wanted their product to sell, and they were competing for his loyalties. Franky was protected, connected and established within his U.S. marketplace, and the cartels could walk their product into the Nevada, Lake Tahoe, and Sacramento marketplace with no risk to them as they expanded *their* marketplace.

There was an astronomical amount of money to be made with very little risk for anyone. It promised to be the perfect marriage of crime families at a time when warring cartels had ravaged each other south of the border. And Franky had played a hand in those wars and was feared as much as he was needed. With Franky on board, all that was required for continuing cartel success in the States were a few well connected law enforcement and political figures who could be owned by the cartels...and they were not hard to find. Franky had courted them for more than a decade in other ventures and was already well established in influence peddling.

Hector had quickly become Franky's favorite contact in Mexico and the feeling seemed mutual. While his father had reportedly worked for a cartel in the past, Hector had connections and trust in both of the competing cartels and managed an uneasy truce between them. Hector visited Franky on many occasions over the years. He seemed to love life in the States and jumped at any chance to stay in the U.S. with Franky, and work in the business north of the border.

Franky arranged for all of Hector's visa paperwork through his attorney, while his "pocket politicians" expedited the process. When Hector arrived in the U.S., he did so under the guise of being employed as an "engineering consultant," allegedly to work on a government contract secured by one of Franky's businesses, a concrete and concrete products company.

In the past, this company, Silver State Concrete Products, LLC, had bid on a lucrative contract to supply cement and concrete work for the Yucca Mountain radioactive dump and storage site. This controversial site was the Department of Energy's proposed radioactive waste storage site near Nellis Air Force Base, and had been placed inside the Nevada Test Site near Beatty, Nevada. More importantly, it was close to one of Franky's cement plants. "Probably just coincidence," Shane thought, sarcastically.

There had been large-scale organized public opposition to the site selection, due to volcanic activity, fault lines, earthquake activity and ground water problems at the site. There had also been a great deal of competition for the contract, which was likely to make the winner very wealthy, if he wasn't wealthy already.

But as usual, the public outcry was subdued by the lapse of time and mounting reams of costly government study, paperwork, bureaucracy and legalese. Finally, the public outcry diminished to the point that just a few people noticed that the contract was ready to be awarded, and by that time, Franky's competition was down to one well known out-of-state bidder, Northern California Concrete Corp., owned by wealthy businessman, Harold O'Leary, and his father, Walter O'Leary.

Suddenly, with just days to go during the final period of revised plans and re-bidding, Harold O'Leary and his assistant vanished with no explanation. The Department of Energy, through the FBI, conducted an inquiry over the disappearance, and local law enforcement opened a missing person's case, but there was no obvious evidence of foul play, and the case soon grew cold.

The FBI investigation concluded that, after leaving the test site prior to submitting their final bid, O'Leary and his assistant just disappeared. They were never found. The case was placed in the inactive file more quickly that it should have been. There was nothing tying the disappearance to Franky, and soon a senior U.S. Senator from Nevada was pushing for a resolution "to promote jobs for his constituents." The huge contract was awarded to Franky's company. As usual, Franky was the last man standing and the financial winner.

The Senator received his reward a short time later in the form of a Lake Tahoe home, quietly transferred from one of Franky's LLCs to a holding company owned by the Senator's closest friend. Just as quietly, the home was transferred to the Senator some nine years later.

The lead FBI special agent on the O'Leary case retired, with a very large and very secret cash bonus, and the file was turned over to a relatively unknown junior agent, named Mark Roberts, who had recently been promoted and transferred to Reno, Nevada. It was to be Roberts' first big case, one he would never solve, and one he could never forget. Roberts always suspected Magadinno and believed he had received protection from high up in the bureau…but he could prove nothing. It was the first in the series of disappearances and murders Mark believed were connected, that would, collectively, torture him during his career.

Franky Magadinno, the Don who ran the Magadinno Crime Family Syndicate, did so with an iron fist. He brought Hector up in the organization as fast as possible. When Franky's oldest daughter, Anna, started seeing Hector, she did so with Franky's complete blessing. He knew the union would provide him even more control and loyalty.

Shortly after Anna's old college sweetheart returned from some graduate work the following summer, and surprised Anna with a visit, the young man found himself in a Sacramento hospital recovering from injuries sustained in a hit-and-run traffic accident.

After a small payoff, combined with a large threat, the young suiter never called Anna again. More importantly he never called the police. The rumor was that the young student had jumped at an opportunity for graduate study abroad in Europe after he had been awarded a scholarship by an anonymous donor. He was anxious to travel and study far from Nevada, and far from Anna.

Whether the plan was arranged by Franky or by Hector made no difference to Shane. They were both cut from the same cloth, he thought, and they both appreciated the result. Always the opportunist, Franky saw dollar signs and security, with both Hector and Mexican drug cartels in his family and business future. "A better investment than real estate or the stock market by a hundred times," Franky had bragged to friends.

And it seemed Hector saw his future just as bright. He would be a good family member to both drug cartels and the Magadinno Family Crime Syndicate, have babies with Anna, and someday sit on the throne of the Syndicate, and maybe a cartel or two. It seemed to outsiders that Hector was truly blessed.

Franky was known as handsome and charming, but he was infamous for being lethally ruthless with his enemies, all of whom simply disappeared without a trace. Franky was known in mob circles as "The Silencer." He liked to say his critics were "permanently silenced by their absence from life," as he laughed a loud and long series of belly laughs.

None of Franky's victims were ever found, and no witnesses had ever come forth. The result of this often-reinforced reputation was that Franky's competition slowly became non-existent during his 30-year reign in Carson City. Franky ordered no visible blood baths and no messy shootings, yet he managed to maintain control over the cocaine, and finally all the meth and heroin markets in Nevada and Sacramento, distributing all the drugs the Mexican cartels could deliver.

His most lucrative territories eventually included Lake Tahoe, Sacramento, Reno, Carson City, Las Vegas and all the small towns and villages along the highways that connected the routes. And the topper on the cake was that Franky's "legitimate" businesses grew and grew, many assisted by government contracts, affording him a legal dumping ground to launder his dirty cash. These contracts became more and more numerous each year, as they were pushed his way by the growing number of pocket politicians on Franky's payroll.

Hector had married Franky's daughter, Anna, less than a year ago, in a wedding gala most stars could only dream about. A typical new age Mafioso, Franky was so well connected with local, state and federal politicians and socialites, that the well-publicized event was billed as "Nevada's Social Event of the Year" in all the local newspapers and the most important west coast social elite circles and magazines.

Radio and television personalities and stars flocked to the wedding, if they were lucky enough to be invited. "Everyone who is someone should do anything they can to get invited," cooed one reporter. Shane nearly gagged when he read that line from a newspaper article Roberts had included in the background material. "If only they knew the truth," he had said out loud. But on second thought, Shane believed knowledge of the truth wouldn't make a difference to many of the Hollywood elite.

Sadly, the public didn't know the truth and probably never would. They saw Franky as the epitome of success, the hope for the working masses, the self-made man. Besides the Silver State Concrete Products, LLC, Franky owned several other companies, LLCs and corporations, all of which appeared to be legitimate on the surface.

Collectively, these companies employed more than five thousand people. Franky filtered his drug-made-millions to all his businesses. And all this raw, untaxed, illegal capital provided Franky a huge advantage over truly legitimate competitors who didn't have secret illegal funding sources.

The result was a complex crime machine that produced untold amounts of cash on both sides of the law, and both sides of the border. And, a calculated percentage of that cash made its way to local, state and federal politicians and officials, who all owed much of their political and financial success to Franky's political influence, and tax-deductible donations to their campaigns and private lives. In turn, they repaid Franky with lucrative contracts and protection from law enforcement and inquiries. *And* best of all, they provided him an air of legitimacy.

They were bought and paid for, Franky's "pocket politicians." The icing on the cake was a few deeply-owned law enforcement officers and agents, none of whom could ever afford to go to prison. They would do anything Franky ordered, both for the cash and to protect their own dirty little secrets.

Franky had personally collected an impressive group of corrupt officials over the years. Among their number were two U.S. senators, more than a dozen state legislators, three mayors, several law enforcement officials, one FBI agent, and two DEA agents. These "resources" were frequently called on to assist their crime boss with small favors, for which they were paid outrageous sums of money. But, as Shane's dad had always said, "There are no free lunches." Shane knew every one of them eventually either paid Franky back many times over, or owed Franky big, an "obligata," as it was known.

Franky's influence mushroomed. The more men and women he helped make in politics and government, the more influence Franky acquired, and the more money he made with their help. The more money Franky made, the more his tentacles spread out across the States, and the more influence he acquired. Shane often wondered if anything less than a bullet to the brain could kill the horrible beast that Franky had become. He grew and spread through society like an aggressive cancer.

Franky Magadinno and his way of life represented everything Shane hated about politics and corruption. It was an evil that lived and spread like a malignancy of "quid pro quo," Latin for "something for something," "give and take," "a favor for a favor," and "you scratch my back and I'll scratch yours."

This concept of "your favor to me, for a favor to you, now or later" had corrupted more people in politics than anything else. In the world of corruption, it was *the* immoral arrangement, never a goodwill gesture. It was also the reason Shane's parents had been killed, the reason he had been driven into and then out of police work, the reason he trusted few people, and the reason he was always alone.

The underworld's "quid pro quo" was the vile currency of politics and corruption, and Shane loathed it in these people. These tainted servants of the people quickly stopped serving the people who had elected them and instead, served themselves and their cronies, to all types of dirty ends.

Franky's life may have looked good on the face of it, but "a mirror can't show what lies deep inside," Shane thought. Franky Magadinno was a pus-filled pimple on the asshole of society. And Shane wanted to pop him to relieve the swelling, infection, pain, contamination, and death he spread to others.

Suddenly, a brief flash of light interrupted Shane's thoughts. He thought he heard an engine on the far side of the Magadinno compound. His adrenaline surged. But when no headlights or car appeared, he went back to his thoughts and his visual surveillance circuit.

Tonight, most of the members of the Magadinno and Alvarez families were gathered in Franky's home, anxiously awaiting a call from Carson Tahoe Hospital that would announce the arrival of Hector and Anna's first baby, rumored to be a boy.

Franky and his entourage would be leaving for the hospital as soon as they got the call. Anna and Hector had already arrived at the hospital about 12:00 p.m. Shane had immediately received a call from his hospital informant, and shortly thereafter he had arrived on location at the compound at twenty minutes after midnight to set up for his entry. He was now waiting for a call from his floor nurse contact to advise him of the birth.

Once the family received the call, they would all rush to the hospital to greet the newest little addition to the mob, leaving only be two guards remaining in the compound. Shane would have plenty of time to enter through the unlocked door off the second story master bedroom balcony, and plant the bugs, phone, and cameras he had prepared to complete his surveillance set-up.

Shane would then have much deeper access to the Magadinno network, and most of the intelligence could be gathered from the safety of Shane's home computer. "Much safer and certainly more comfortable," he thought, as he shivered in the cold. He couldn't take a chance on the engine running to keep the car warm, and the temperature had dropped to a chilly 36 degrees.

It was times like this Shane felt best with adrenaline seeping into his system and ready to kick into full production. His mind was already at a heightened state of awareness as he went through his final equipment check. He loved the feeling of blood surging through his arteries and veins, being pushed faster and harder than normal. He could feel the rush beginning to warm his insides. He relished the pounding and surging that gave him added quickness and increased strength.

Over the years, Shane had learned to control his breathing and outward appearance, so others would not suspect his condition and know something was about to happen. Shane always looked calm, even with the adrenaline on board and the ringing in his ears it produced.

It would be a good night if Shane's informant called quickly. But if he had to wait too long, the euphoria would eventually wane, and his mind would become dull as the adrenaline was metabolized. That would leave him drained, subdued, colder and stiff. Then Shane would tire and lose his edge as his body recovered and calmed, and when the call came, he would be "low and slow," as he liked to say.

Shane silently prayed for the little mobster to be born soon. Not a nice thought, he suddenly realized, but with family like this and the kind of training the little guy would receive, Shane knew he would have no chance of normal development. In a brief 18 years, the newborn would be watching his dad kill someone, in a "hit" made to bring the kid along and solve a problem at the same time.

A few months or years later, "Junior" would be inducted into the crime family hall of fame by "proving himself" to the family, when he became a "hit-man." Shane had once heard Franky boast, "When you're connected by murder, all mouths are sealed, and the relationships last forever. Better than a marriage by far. No possibility of divorce!" Franky always laughed at his own maxims. His audience *always* obediently followed with their own expected laughs.

Time drug on for another hour, and Shane's mind began to wander more and more. He could now complete the surveillance circuit with his eyes, warily watching and double-checking every point of potential danger, and still think about something else.

But, as the loss of the first rush of adrenaline began to take effect, Shane went into maintenance and self-preservation mode, to keep his mind alert and his body as warm and limber as possible. He began slow movements to extend his muscles.

As he stretched and rubbed his hands, legs and face, he thought about the morning's events as the cold fought to set in further. In his mind, Shane saw the woman he watched every weekday morning at his favorite espresso café. He knew she had noticed him too, and Shane liked that every time he saw her, she looked at him longer and smiled more freely than the time before.

She had become a welcome change to Shane's lonely existence when, one morning (12 weeks and three days ago, not that he was counting), he had first seen her. She was so beautiful that Shane couldn't help but stare. But it wasn't just that she was beautiful, there was so much more.

This woman had it all. She had fantastic legs, a lovely slender waist, sumptuous breasts, and an angel's face framed with thick, flowing dark brown hair with red highlights. She had the most superb curves and body he could ever recall seeing. And her beautiful face was complemented by a smile that melted his heart. To him, even her feet and hands were the stuff that dreams were made of…graceful, long slender digits in perfect proportion to the rest of her body. She was a masterpiece.

Shane had seen her in tight Wranglers and a clingy sweater one day, and the sight cost him concentration for days. Shane couldn't even think about her without butterflies filling his stomach. But it was her friendliness, manners, classy personality, easy laugh and exuding warmth that kept Shane returning each day anticipating another sighting, and then, wanting more. He now found himself smitten with a perfect stranger. "Perfect indeed," he thought with a wide smile.

Shane had overheard the waitress call the woman "Kate," during his second sighting. Kate didn't just walk into the coffee shop each day; she virtually floated in and across the room. As she moved, long, curly, dark brownish-red locks of hair gently caressed her cheeks, as if paying homage to her exquisite complexion. Kate's skin bore the faint telltale freckles of a redhead, appearing like tiny leopard spots, accenting her creamy flawless skin with a regal effect.

When Kate walked, her firm body bounced ever so slightly, revealing that she was in great physical shape. Shane liked everything about Kate. He liked the way her mouth moved when she spoke, how she tilted her head when she read the newspaper or her tablet, and the genuine goodness she radiated. He even liked her taste in clothes. Kate always looked like a model, even in tennis shoes, jeans and a T-shirt.

Kate always wore a unique deep red nail polish and matching lipstick, which Shane found mesmerizing on her. But one day, when Kate walked into the shop wearing four-inch high-heeled sandals and a short black dress, Shane thought he was going to pass out. This was a rush even he couldn't conceal, and he suspected he was beet red, boyish and obvious. Although Shane's eyes usually never gave him away, he felt they called out now to all who saw him, "Look at me, I'm a mess around her!"

He was like a silly schoolboy with his first crush. That day, Shane realized he wasn't breathing as Kate looked at him, and he grinned widely. In the hour that followed, he couldn't keep his eyes off her, and time and time again, she caught him staring. And each time she caught him he felt more and more out of control and embarrassed. Kate sat facing him and crossed her legs, revealing the tops of sheer barely black nylon stockings secured by a garter belt outlined by a lacy slip. She was obviously having fun tormenting him, and finally, he could take it no more.

He felt he had to leave and made his exit as dignified and controlled as he could, although he bumped loudly in to a table on his exit. But once outside, he regretted leaving. "What will she think?" he questioned. Shane, the iron man, was walking away, defeated by a woman who had never spoken to him, who probably now thought he was uninterested!

But nothing could be further from the truth. He was hopelessly interested. And even though he spent the rest of that day working out and listening to music turned up a little too loud, it didn't help him a bit. He couldn't stop daydreaming about Kate. He had become obsessed with this raving beauty, who didn't even know his name.

He wondered each day, "What will Kate wear this morning? Will she be alone again? Does she have a boyfriend? Does she live in Carson City? What does she do?" Shane asked himself a thousand questions about Kate. He thought that, with enough time, he could find the courage to approach her and ask her face-to-face, at least what her name was…even though he already knew that much.

But life is always about choices. Shane knew he could *make* the time, if he could only muster the courage. He thought he should be able to approach this woman. Women had never been a problem for him before. But, he admitted to himself that he had never felt this way about a woman before, not even in a relationship.

Each day Shane found it more and more difficult not to stare when Kate was in the room. He would force his eyes to lock on to another person just to give his stomach a break from the butterflies. He felt like he was in high school again and hated that he loved that lost feeling.

Sitting on surveillance now Shane wondered how soft Kate's lips were. He fantasized about kissing her sensuous mouth, as she smiled at him, like she often did when she looked at him from across the room. He once thought maybe he just needed a vacation, but then, he knew he wouldn't want to go anywhere that he couldn't look forward to seeing his beautiful Kate.

In the 12 weeks and three days that Shane had been watching Kate, he had memorized everything about her. He thought about her constantly, and even dreamed about her in the few hours he slept each night. No woman had ever had this effect on Shane and he wondered, "Why this woman and why now?" Was he just too lonely or was she really something special?

He recalled that one day Kate didn't arrive at their espresso café, and Shane spent the better part of the day depressed, wondering if he would see her again. He was angry with himself that he hadn't approached her, gotten to know her, and asked her out. Now he feared he might never have the chance.

Shane's life in deep cover had been solo, always alone, always void of communication, other than now, when he reported to Sheriff Roberts once each week. He shadowed his targets, took his surveillance photos, recorded conversations, monitored activity, and wrote his computer entries, all alone, all the time. He worked out alone in his apartment before and after work, and he sat alone at night. He nearly always spent his days on and off the job alone. He called no one, except his uncle Pete. He had forsaken most of his old friends for his career, many years ago.

But Shane was tired of being alone, and now he longed to share his life and love with someone. Maybe Kate could be that someone, even though he could only look at her for now. He just couldn't talk to her yet, and for sure he couldn't touch her. But, for now, Kate had given Shane the excitement, dreams, and hope for passion he had desperately needed for a very long time.

As he again completed the visual surveillance with his eyes, Shane yearned for tomorrow morning when he could possibly see Kate again. As he thought about her, he suddenly found it interesting that they had both chosen the same small, mom and pop espresso shop, rather than the trendy chain stores most of the locals frequented. Another coincidence maybe. They seemed to share so much in common. He had gleaned some information from listening to her conversations with friends or coworkers she met.

He wondered what she was really like. Could she be as wonderful and exciting as she looked? Shane imagined that maybe they had more things in common than good fresh Italian-roasted espresso. He could only hope that one day he would find out. But when would that be, and how?

Shane's dream was to have a wife and best friend, like his own dad had in his mother, when they were alive. Theirs was a relationship that had stood the test of time and all the trials that life had thrown at them, and they had only grown closer and more in love through the years. If only someone like Kate could hold that future for Shane, there was hope for him, he thought.

But in this throw away time in which we live, Shane wondered, "Do people still love like that? Are there still men and women out there that want a partner for life? Are there still women out there that are as beautiful on the inside as they are on the outside?"

Shane's thoughts continued to drift as his eyes completed another patrol of his surroundings. "Is Kate as beautiful on the inside as she looks on the outside?"

Shane's dad had always told him, "A mirror can't show what lies deep inside. But what lies deep inside is what's most important." He used to say, "You can look at incredible beauty, but you will only see the ugliness beneath…*if* you know it's there."

And his father had been right. Shane had known some beauties in his last assignment in Newport Beach, and most of their beauty *had* been only skin deep. Some were downright ugly on the inside, with hearts as dark as the ace of spades, self-absorbed narcissists, void of the ability to love. "What a waste of beautiful skin," he had thought.

As Shane completed the last surveillance circuit with his eyes, he rolled down the front windows on both sides of the vehicle to focus on a sound he had heard. Then he heard it again, car engines starting in the garages, as lights flickered on and then off in several rooms of the house. The front driveway motion detector light activated, and Shane saw figures coming toward one of the cars parked outside.

He began counting bodies moving outside. His phone suddenly vibrated in its case on his hip, and he jumped. Adrenaline surged again. He answered quickly and quietly. His nurse informant told him the baby boy had arrived. The family had been notified and were on their way.

Shane felt the adrenaline rush returning, this time faster in a much larger and needed dose. The effect on his body would be more dramatic this time. A vehicle drove out of the driveway toward him, the wrong way to the hospital, surprising him, and the adrenaline surged again. His ears began to ring. He slumped down more deeply into the seat, and by the time the vehicle neared him, his windows were back up and the vehicle ignition back off, so no dash lights gave away his presence.

Even though Shane had placed a cardboard cut-out over the dash to block the red lights on the dash display that illuminated when the ignition was turned to "accessories", other interior LED lights also activated, and could still call attention to him if someone was looking closely.

Shane was always prepared for someone to be conducting counter-surveillance. He had been trained by experts and had spent years perfecting that training through his own experiences, and trial and error. He knew to expect the unexpected, plan for the worst, and quadruple check all contingencies, so there was never a problem he couldn't handle. So far there had *never* been a problem he couldn't handle. He had always been successful and had overcome the odds.

Normally everything went off without a hitch. Most people were oblivious to what was happening around them. But crooks, cops, and people playing both sides, or playing an unknown side...they were the wild cards that got people caught, injured or killed. Shane was always prepared to make sure he was not one of these statistics.

Shane's perfect case was one that he worked long enough to gather all that a department needed to solve a case and advance an investigation to the desired point, and then he disappeared, with no trace, leaving the target wondering what had happened. Then he would be off to the next department and a new assignment. He was a special contract operative, a unique professional with no permanent roots or baggage…and no real life.

He heard a screech of rubber, and suddenly another car left, and then another. Both drove out and stopped on the street, facing the correct way to the hospital. There should be one more car, and Shane was getting anxious. He was still thinking about the car that had left the wrong way, when he saw lights in his rear-view mirror. He was slumped down again, ready to go, backpack in hand, as the car drove slowly by him and he got a look at the driver and passenger. It was Franky's personal bodyguards, Vick and Bobby, checking the neighborhood

Shane had assumed that, prior to leaving for something this important, these two would deviate from their normal M.O. (Method of Operation) of counter-surveillance neighborhood checks, as they had in the past. But this time, they had *not* deviated, and Shane promised himself he wouldn't expect they might deviate from a standard routine again. As Vick drove close to the driveway, Franky's limo pulled out in front, and all four cars drove out of sight toward the hospital in a small orderly caravan.

Shane believed that there were two guards left in the house now. This was not just guesswork, but the result of weeks of surveillance to identify the members of the family and organization who lived and worked on the grounds and in the houses, and their routines. He had also learned where the compound's security surveillance cameras and motion detectors were located.

He had previously obtained the plans for the alarm system from Sheriff Roberts, who knew the contractor who installed the system before Franky purchased the property. Shane had carefully planned his entry. He had painstakingly rehearsed all the details of this night several times, all while patiently waiting for this one night of a planned major distraction.

Shane had even identified the nanny who had been hired to help with the new little Mafioso, and he had conducted a separate surveillance to learn about her life and connections. His hospital informant had recognized a photo he had taken of the nanny, and told him in her first phone call earlier, that the nanny had arrived at the hospital with Hector and Anna.

Shane had done all he could to prepare for his entry into the Magadinno compound. It was time to go. One last surveillance circuit check, a deep calming breath, and he was ready.

Shane opened the door of his car, but no interior lights came on, as he had removed the bulbs from the doors and overhead lamps in advance. He pressed the door firmly, but gently, and closed and latched it with just a click. He slung the large backpack over his shoulders as he slipped both arms through the straps. He then walked quickly to Franky's west side neighbor's yard. He effortlessly vaulted the six-foot fence into the neighbor's yard. He turned completely around to check the grounds and the house. This neighbor had no dogs, but Franky had three.

Shane retrieved the baggie from his jacket inside pocket that contained the steak pieces laced with a tranquilizer. Once consumed, they would put the dogs to sleep for at least an hour. Even though he had spent many nights feeding the dogs, and making friends to avoid the possibility of barking, he was not about to take any chances. The dogs presented a problem, friends or not.

He had tested the tranquilizer on other dogs to prepare for other assignments, and he knew these dogs would recover normally, completely unharmed, so no one would be the wiser. He also had previously tested a quarter dose on these dogs, just to make sure the tranquilizer worked.

Shane vaulted the neighbor's fence into the Magadinno compound side yard at a blind spot to the security surveillance cameras. In his few nights with the dogs, he had trained them to come to a cricket clicker he had purchased at a toy store. Three clicks and the nameless dogs were at his side, eating the specially prepared steak. He delayed a few minutes to stroke the last dog gently as he lay down to nap. Shane liked dogs a lot, and he was sure this one was just a crime family tool, and not the pet he deserved to be.

The west yard surveillance camera made its run to the front driveway, and with his canine friends asleep, Shane moved quickly and silently from the cover of the bushes near the fence to the tree growing just off the master bedroom balcony. He could hear the two remaining guards laughing loudly, as they watched a movie on the television in the kitchen downstairs. He delayed, as he listened for anything unusual and watched the dancing lights from the TV screen move around the room and ceiling.

Using a technique learned from a burglar he had surveilled in his earlier police years, Shane scampered up the tree and stepped up on to one of the two tree steps he had previously placed in the tree, a week earlier. They were both small camo steps, and easily concealed from view, once in the tree. He reached up and checked the second step, he had placed at a higher and offset position, to make sure it was still securely attached.

After the camera passed the location, he then moved to a large limb above the lower step and reset that step to a position higher than the top step. He then climbed from one step to the other, removing the lower step as he moved. He moved carefully and quietly up the steps and limbs. He repeated the process, until he finally stood on the upper step, at the final position. He had planned his ascent to avoid the lone tracking surveillance camera. His final destination was now above and in clear view of, the master bedroom balcony. He positioned himself for the jump.

Now, both he and the step were totally out of view of all the cameras. From the higher step he stepped out on to a solid limb, and in one motion, immediately leapt out and down, landing on the second story master bedroom balcony.

Shane's soft sole shoes didn't make enough noise on the landing to alert the guards over the TV and their own laughter. All his equipment held silently, fast in place, due to his diligent packing. He had practiced the jump from a tree onto his own apartment balcony and knew the equipment would not betray him with noise or movement.

Shane had packed the oversized backpack with all the surveillance equipment he needed and had wrapped all individual parts in dish towels to muffle any noise of movement. The various components were stacked in the exact order he would need them as he moved through the house.

Shane entered through the unlocked master bedroom sliding glass door. Once inside, he began to make his way through the house, placing miniature wireless bugs and video cameras in places they would never be detected. First, he finished the master suite and adjoining office. Then he began his work in the other upstairs bedrooms, before heading downstairs. These devices could be turned on and off by a remote master.

Turning the remote master off, would allow Shane to make all devices silent, and even more difficult to find if a "sweeper" or bug detector was employed. The remote master itself, was already in place, located on a telephone pole near the compound, with a direct line of sight to the master bedroom primary unit. The master bedroom primary unit would send signals to all other bugs and cameras in the house.

Shane had programmed the remote master, so it could be activated and controlled by his cell phone, using a 13-digit code. At the first hint of a check for devices, he would turn off all his bugs and cameras. Only the most sophisticated equipment and personnel could then find any of his devices.

The best part of the system was that Shane could monitor conversations and video digitally from his remote computer, linked by phone to the remote master. In addition, all the conversations and video feeds from different rooms could be selected and recorded, and later separated and viewed individually.

Both remaining guards sat in the kitchen, drinking and laughing loudly at the movie during Shane's movements in the house, making his task much easier. The last downstairs bug Shane planted in the dining area off the kitchen had an extra directional microphone that would pick up all kitchen conversation.

But Shane missed no opportunity and had one more ace in the hole. Earlier in the week, he had watched Franky buy a new "smart" cell phone at a local store. The phone would be a gift to Hector to celebrate the birth of his son.

Now, as he went through the house setting up his devices, he looked for the phone to switch it out with a "special" replacement phone of the same model and color he had pre-programmed and brought with him. He didn't find the phone until he entered the offset upstairs room he had saved for last. It was in the maid's room, still in the box, sitting on wrapping paper on a night stand, next to a card addressed from Franky to Hector.

"The gift for Hector isn't even wrapped!" Shane thought, "This couldn't have gotten much better." He quickly checked the phone to see if there were any contacts inputted, and seeing none, switched the phones and placed the programmed gift phone in the box. When Hector used the phone Shane had provided, Shane would be able to receive a computer print-out identifying all incoming and outgoing calls, and he would be able to monitor all the conversations remotely, as if on a conference call. The software installed in Shane's computer would also record all this information automatically in his absence.

Shane was just about to leave the room when he heard voices and steps coming quickly up the staircase not far down the hall. Shane was trapped in the maid's room near the top of the stairs, and one of the voices was female. Shane felt another quick adrenaline rush. There were no open windows, and there was only one door to the room. Shane had little time, and he had no way out!

2

"These things gotta happen every five years or so.
It helps to get rid of the bad blood."
(Peter Clemenza, in the movie, *The Godfather*)

Shane froze only briefly while he chose his path of retreat. He had read the room on entry, and once again scanned the room to confirm his choice to hide in a closet next to the small window. In a moment, he was inside, the door closed, and safely concealed between some very large, long dresses and the wall. A few seconds later, two subjects entered the room. Shane recognized the voices, and knew immediately it was the new nanny, April, and Franky's Chief of Security, Big John Galliano.

If Shane's guess was right, April was rooming with the live-in maid, Lucinda. When he placed his bug in the room, he had seen suitcases on one of the beds and clothes laid out on both beds, in two very different sizes. Lucinda was a good-sized girl, while April was 5-foot nothing and maybe broke 100 pounds soaking wet.

The light flicked on and Big John ushered April into the room, chastising her for forgetting the bag of baby accessories that included a handmade blanket from the baby's paternal grandmother. April searched around frantically, and finally found at least part of what she was searching for, a small tote with a baby's blanket protruding out the top. She then opened one of the closet doors, reached in and grabbed a raincoat (fortunately placed on the far side of the closet), and closed the door. April walked out of the room first, but Big John's footsteps did not follow.

Shane's Glock .45 was already pointed at the door. As seconds seemed like minutes, Shane heard movement in front of the closet. He then heard a rubbing sound on the carpet, coming closer to the closet door, and he prepared for the worst.

"This could be the shortest assignment I ever worked," thought Shane, as he prepared to pump a round into Big John if he was discovered. Sweat began to form on his brow as Shane focused on recalling details from Big John's police profile.

When he had been hired for this assignment, Sheriff Roberts had provided him all the intelligence files he could gather from the combined resources of several agencies, including the FBI, DEA, Reno PD, Washoe County Sheriff's Office, and Carson City Sheriff's Office, just to name a few. Shane had spent his first week just reading intelligence from these cases that had been gathered over decades, by dozens of agents and officers. It seemed every law enforcement agency in a five-hundred mile radius knew about the Magadinno Family Crime Syndicate, in one way or another. Even so, none of them had been able to prosecute a case against Franky successfully, or against Franky's father before him.

Franky had initially been linked to drugs, prostitution, gambling and extortion, typical for an organized crime boss. But his resume had grown through the years and was now much more impressive. In time, Franky had diversified into robbery, theft, international transportation of stolen property, kidnapping, murder-for-hire and, of course, plain murder. The totality of all the intelligence left Shane amazed that he was working this assignment alone. But he had initially accepted the reasons and the risk.

At this very second he wondered again why he hadn't been hired to augment a 20-man interagency task force. But, by the time he had a feel for whom and what he was dealing with, Shane had been on the job a week, and it was too late to reconsider. He was no longer sure he could put a major case together against the Magadinno Family, working alone. Right now he wasn't even sure he could survive a solo investigation.

The one thing Shane *was* sure of was that he could not allow himself to be discovered or captured by the Magadinnos, or life, as he knew it, would be over. Shane took all this intelligence he had digested very seriously, and he knew that if he were discovered and captured, he would likely be tortured, slowly and painfully for information first, and then killed. He would "simply disappear," as Franky would say.

But, what was worse, was that Shane had learned that Franky and Big John approached the violent side of their business with equal fervor. The reports he read gave Shane a window into the souls of these two dirt-bags, and the scene wasn't pretty. It appeared that Franky and Big John often competed to see who could be more violent, brutal and fearsome. Informants, over the years, had reported almost unbelievable tales of tortures and killings that took on a party-like atmosphere for these two maniacs.

While these thoughts raced through his head, Shane strained over the surging adrenaline and ringing in his ears to hear more, and wondered what Big John was doing on the other side of the door. Shane's stomach growled, and he was sure Big John must have heard the rumble. Beads of sweat began to trickle down Shane's forehead to his nose and eyebrows, and, for the first time, he noticed how warm it was in the closet. While the adrenaline raced through his body a rhythmic beating pulse now played drums in his ears to keep time for the ringing. He focused on controlling his breathing as he strained to hear.

Shane said a quick and silent prayer, speaking from his heart directly to God, something he now did more often, the older he got, and the more jobs like this he worked. The silence elevated Shane's fear that Big John knew he was there. He could feel his pulse surge harder and thought Big John might even hear his heart pounding. He heard a brushing near the door, and pressed a little harder on the trigger, as he aimed at where the big man should be on the other side of the door.

As he did, Shane placed his ear gently on the closet door, and tried to decipher every little sound from the other side. Suddenly, Big John cursed loudly at April, just inches from Shane's head on the other side of the door, and Shane jerked back, hitting his head on the hanger rod. Fortunately, it seemed that Big John had covered the resulting "clunk" with his own loud rant. April's quick steps came back into the room, and she apologized profusely to John.

Shane listened as April explained how she must have knocked over the coffee she had been drinking when she placed it on the floor next to the tote, as she grabbed her raincoat. Big John had mopped up the stain with a towel, but made it known he didn't appreciate having been left the task by a lowly nanny.

Within seconds, the pair's footsteps told Shane they were both out of the room and trudging back downstairs. As they hit the landing,

Big John complained loudly and eloquently to April leaving no doubt about how irritated he was by the disruption to his meal and movie.

Shane was left alone, still controlling his silent breathing, and listening to his stomach growl. He thanked God for another prayer answered, and promised both himself and God that, next time he had to come this close to danger, he would eat something more bland and predictable beforehand. Shane chuckled silently as he asked himself, "Did I almost die for two tacos and a spicy tamale?"

By the time April left the house, slamming the kitchen door, Shane was already out of the room, down the hallway to the master bedroom, and headed out on to the balcony. He had placed the downstairs bugs and camera before April had arrived back at the house. After a quick check for anything out of place, Shane prepared for the most difficult part of the evening, the jump from the balcony wrought iron railing back into the tree.

To make the jump easier, Shane had placed the highest camouflaged step on the tree trunk, next to a branch located left of, and several feet lower than, the one he had used before on the entry. The stand had been out of sight of the compound's security surveillance camera when placed there, and was now only partially visible to a keen eye *if* a person was closely looking for it.

Shane knew the jump would be difficult. The stand was small, measuring about 2 feet by 2 feet, and now, the coated aluminum was wet with rain, and bound to be slippery. As Shane was just about to jump, he checked his surroundings while waiting for the surveillance camera to pass, below his location.

He noticed a figure running down the street toward his car. The body movement was familiar to him, agile and quiet, and Shane knew that he should know the person's identity even though he could not possibly see their face. The figure, dressed in black from head to toe, stayed in the shadows as much as possible. He tried to recall ever seeing any of the crime family running. He could not.

Shane didn't like this wrinkle, especially at this moment before his exit, but he had to proceed with his escape from the compound. He checked the path of the lower patrolling security camera, immediately jumped, grabbed the branch, and hit the step with both feet, all at the same time, almost perfectly.

Shane had practiced a similar leap in the forest up in Clear Creek Canyon many times, even at night, but never at night in the rain. Shane seized the limb to his right to stabilize himself while his feet landed on the step. But the metal was too slippery, and he slid forward, his right knee and shin colliding hard with the tree trunk. A jagged remnant of a branch that had been trimmed from the tree, sliced through Shane's pants at shin level, and punctured his skin as it cut its way to the bone.

Shane grimaced in pain, but he had no time to delay, as the lower security camera was making its circuit back. The timing to descend the tree had to be perfect. He wrapped his arms around the tree trunk and stood on a rear limb to remove his weight from the step, as he activated the step's quick release, swinging the step away and into his backpack, in one practiced motion.

When the camera cleared his path below, he reached up, grabbed the second step, repeated the maneuver and placed it in his pack. Upon reaching a branch a few feet lower, he then dropped to the ground. Shane quickly swung the swivel pack around to his back, and stepped behind the tree, just before the security camera completed its track back across the yard and passed the tree. If the guards later checked the video feed they would see nothing.

Shane ran back to the fence, where he had left his canine friends sleeping peacefully. He was careful to take a path that kept the tree and some shrubs between him and the kitchen window. Shane could hear Big John laughing loudly at his movie, and he was thankful the guards were preoccupied. He reached down and felt the dogs to check their breathing, petted the soft muzzles, and assured himself they would recover normally.

Shane placed one hand on the top of the fence, his foot on a frost-free hose bib next to the fence, and with a quick vault up, he was silently over the fence and standing in the neighbor's yard. Franky's neighbor was a single doctor at a local clinic, who was in Las Vegas with his girlfriend for the week, so Shane was safe to take his time as he made his exit from the yard. He quickly felt his shin and immediately recognized the sticky feel and metallic smell of warm blood on his hand.

As he slowly approached the gate leading to the street, Shane's thoughts returned to the jogger. He wondered silently to himself, "Who jogs in the shadows in a cold April rain at 3:45 A.M?" As a general rule, Shane did not believe in coincidences or unexplained mysteries. But the jogger's gait was familiar to him. He struggled to recall all he could about the few seconds of movement he had seen, as he peered through the gate into the street. When he was sure there was no one there, Shane vaulted effortlessly over the fence, rather than using the squeaky gate, and walked quickly to his vehicle.

As his mind raced, still trying to recall who the jog belonged to, Shane checked the street for movement while he walked. He glanced over his shoulder at the compound twice before he arrived at his car. As Shane approached the driver's side door, he froze, his eyes fixed on a small, white, business-sized card resting between the windshield and the wiper blade. He slowly retrieved the wet card, examined it carefully, and read four words that appeared in large type: "BE CAREFUL NEXT FRIDAY." The note was unsigned, and there was not another mark on either side of the card.

Shane scanned the neighborhood again for signs of anything out of the ordinary, as he unlocked the car door. He recalled all the vehicles that had been parked on the street when he first arrived. He saw nothing out of place, and wondered if the jogger was in a car, a yard or a house watching him right now. Shane entered his car, started the engine, waited a few seconds as he completed another scan of the area, and then made a slow U-turn, using no brakes, his headlights off. He drove slowly forward, the way the jogger had been running. When he was down the street a block, he switched on the headlights.

Shane had done pre-surveillance many times in this neighborhood, and had recorded all of the neighborhood vehicles. He had also made both written and mental notes about other items he had seen there. As Shane drove forward, he hoped to find the jogger's car, a dry spot where the car had been parked, or cigarettes on the ground where a vehicle had been parked…anything that would help him discover the identity of the mysterious stranger. He found nothing.

Shane drove slowly toward his apartment, as he searched for an answer. "Who could possibly know he was here, or what he was doing? Was there a leak, a witness, another agent, a concerned citizen?" He wondered in vain. Nothing made sense, as he went over and over the possibilities in his mind. He concentrated on the card, and decided it had to have been left by the jogger. "Who was he and what did he want? What was going to happen next Friday?" His normally quick and intuitive mind offered no plausible explanations.

There was nothing in Shane's intelligence that identified anything specific about next Friday. Shane wondered, "Who wanted to get mixed up with the Magadinnos, or follow me in the early morning hours on a chilly, wet, April morning?"

Surely, he thought, if it were one of Franky Magadinno's boys, there would have been no note, he would not have been allowed to leave, and there would have been more than one person for him to deal with. He abandoned that thought. He frowned as he drove, unhappy about this new development. Shane did not like surprises or problems during an undercover surveillance, and this promised to present both.

As he racked his brain, he recalled that his only confirmed plan for next Friday, was an afternoon meeting with Sheriff Roberts, at their usual meeting spot. He decided he must change the meet location or postpone the meeting. He also decided the jogger's identity was his top priority. First, he had to get the card to Mark Roberts. Due to his deep cover, Shane had no connections to a local crime lab, and Mark would have to get the card to a lab and have a technician process it for latent fingerprints. If the card was void of prints, it was more likely the card giver was a professional, and Shane's problem could be more serious. But, at least he would know that much.

In any event, he would need to change apartments, re-order his routine, and alter his local habits. And then it hit him, and hit him hard. Changing his routine would mean not going to the café, and not seeing Kate, and *that* was too painful for Shane to accept at this point in his life. Shane would have to figure another way to increase his own security, so he could keep the local habits he *needed*.

"I won't give up my one pleasure in life," Shane thought stubbornly. He was deviating from his own practiced security behaviors. He calculated the risks again, but his first decision remained final. He had to have *some* love life, even if it were just the hope of a love life.

Shane braked for a red light as he prepared to turn right on to Stewart Street, and as he did so, a lightning bolt of pain shot up his shin. He winced and reached down to feel his leg. More of the sticky blood had soaked through his pants, and he was suddenly aware this was a more serious injury than he had originally thought. By the time he arrived home, he would be leaving bloody shoe prints on the asphalt next to his car.

Shane drove in to the apartment parking lot and double checked the area for anything out of the ordinary. He saw nothing. He grabbed a cloth he kept under the driver's seat to wipe condensation from the inside of the car windows during surveillance. He stepped out on to the lawn, wiped his shoes off on the wet grass, and tied the cloth around the bloody shoe, so he wouldn't leave a trail to his apartment. He slowly climbed the stairs to his apartment, checking for surveillance. Each step left him in increasing agony. He realized the adrenaline had worn off.

Once on the landing, Shane did another quick outside area check, and slipped inside, gun in hand. He checked the living room slowly upon his entry, while he locked and dead bolted the door behind him. In one smooth motion, he swung the backpack off his shoulder, dropped it silently on the entryway, and moved to one side.

He swept the apartment, going quickly, but carefully, from room to room, as silently as possible. When he had cleared each room, and was sure he was alone, he tended to his wound, undressing in the shower, so there would be no difficult mess to clean.

"What a great life I chose for myself," Shane said aloud, mockingly. Most guys his age were sleeping right now, snuggled up against their wife or girlfriend, or at least their favorite pet. Here he was, undressing alone in a shower at 4:00 A.M., so he could check the seriousness of a wound he had received jumping from a crime figure's balcony, at night, into a tree, in the rain. And now, he was going to have to go to a doctor, which he didn't want to do, for fear of leaving a trail that might lead to his discovery.

Shane checked the wound, hoping he could clean and bandage it adequately himself. But the jagged tree branch had done too much damage. Try as he might, he could not stop the bleeding, and finally he gave up, deciding he would have to go to urgent care to get the wound cleaned…and sealed with an unknown number of stitches. He was tired and in moderate pain. But most of all, he was increasingly more aware of his lonely life than ever before. He didn't even have a *dog* to console him and accompany him on his trip to urgent care. His thoughts returned to Kate.

Shane grabbed his medical kit, a good one, put together by a nurse he once dated in Denver. "Nice girl," he recalled, but far too clingy for his lifestyle or his self-respect. She had called or texted him a *minimum* of twenty times a day, and, eventually started interrogating him nightly about his whereabouts when they were apart. "Eventually" meant for Shane that the relationship had lasted more than two weeks. He couldn't take the building micro-management and suspicious jealousy. He had broken off the relationship after the first jealous rant, in week three.

"Still," he mused, "she was a nice girl and right for him in many ways—just not all the *necessary* right ways." He wondered if there really was someone out there who would be "right" for him, and what she would be like.

While he thought about his life, Shane began the work of stabilizing the injury site with a series of compress layers, held together by pink self-adhering sports tape—Nurse Sherry's playful touch. He would use the urgent care in Minden, Nevada, some 25 minutes south of Carson City, and in a different county, Douglas County. It was far enough away to not draw any attention to his activities, and close enough to get to quickly, should the bleeding continue.

He dressed in his jogging suit and tennis shoes, and, carefully scanning the approach, returned to his car to make the drive. As he turned south on Hwy 395 and drove over Indian Hill, he realized again how tired he was. The adrenaline had worked well for him earlier when he needed it. But now he was drained, in pain and sleepy, left sluggish by the adrenaline void and its corresponding aftermath.

Shane was admitted immediately when he arrived at urgent care, as no other patients were being treated. Bleeding through the compresses on to his shoe and the clinic floor, he bypassed the unmanned front administration desk, and was shown to an emergency room by a friendly, somewhat older nurse, who seemed interested to hear his early morning story. When the nurse produced the standard paperwork and HIPAA form, Shane protected his identity by using his fictitious undercover driver's license and credit card, in his assumed name of Daniel Lester Harrington.

The credit card was good, and the clinic would get paid. Sheriff Mark Roberts had given Shane the undercover "cold" name, driver's license and credit card to protect his identity and the assignment. Only Roberts knew Shane's true identity, and that information was locked in a safe in the Sheriff's home. A trusted DMV employee in

Las Vegas, who provided law enforcement with fictitious "cold" license plates and IDs, had provided the driver's license, one of many given out to operatives at various Nevada departments each year.

After the initial interview the nurse had Shane remove his jogging pants to expose his injury. Soon after, a pretty, young doctor entered and began examining Shane's wound. He noticed she was eyeing him suspiciously. "So you told the nurse you tripped on a bush while jogging?" the doctor asked, with a sidelong glance. Her pretty eyes lit up, as she assumed the look of someone who thought they knew something was amiss.

"Yeah, when it started raining, I decided to leave the hazards of an uneven sidewalk and jog in the street, where it was safer. As I ran, I tried to jump over this shrub between the sidewalk and the street to continue home, but I caught a broken branch with my shin and knee, and the rest is painful history," Shane explained.

As he spoke, Shane leaned back and supported himself with his arms, making his stomach and arms rigid. He also closed his eyes, to avoid any telltale lying eye movements that would invalidate the story to his physician, just in case she knew any tells of lying body language. Normally, he could have focused on controlling his body to appear to tell the truth, but he was tired and in pain, and this was safer and easier.

After a long pause, the doctor asked, "So, who jogs in a cold early morning April rain?" Shane smiled, realizing he had asked the same question about the real mystery jogger an hour earlier. With his eyes still closed, he said, "An idiot like me, I guess." A playful laugh told Shane the doctor believed the story. Self-deprecating statements always bolstered believability. "People tend to believe what they like," Shane thought to himself.

Shane looked down from his seat on the paper-covered table, where he sat clad only in his underwear, and noticed the lady doctor's head was at his crotch level. She was glancing secretively at his crotch, while she inspected and cleaned his wound. He watched her eyes flitting back and forth from his wound to his manhood, as if she were unable to concentrate on the task at hand. Shane suddenly realized he was seated on the examining table, wearing nothing but his "tighty whities." He immediately turned red.

The tight briefs fit Shane snugly, revealing the outline of his male anatomy, leaving little to the imagination. Shane's friend Mike always called the male genitalia a "package," and Shane's new doctor apparently found his "package" alluring. Shane closed his eyes and thought, "There's hope for me...she likes the package."

He glanced down again, noticed the doctor was not wearing a ring, and that she was actually very beautiful. Shane thought to himself, "You must be getting old if you didn't notice until now the doc is single *and* pretty." He smiled again about his strange life.

The doctor had used a local anesthetic to dull the pain, and the drug had finally taken effect. She began to slowly, but methodically, stitch his wound, in no perceptible rush. Other than an occasional twinge of dull pain and the sensation of tugging at the skin, the procedure was no longer uncomfortable. Nearing the end, Shane leaned further back, with his eyes nearly closed, and almost drifted off to sleep.

The doctor suddenly said, "We're done, Mr. Harrington."

Shane opened his eyes, smiled, and said, "Thank you, Miss..."

The doctor reached out her hand, and said, "Leslie...Dr. Leslie Graham."

Shane took Leslie's hand, and said, "Dr. Leslie Graham...I'm Dan, Dan Harrington."

Dr. Leslie squeezed Shane's hand a little too long, and a little too tightly, seeming to convey an interest in Shane, the man, not just Shane, the patient. She smiled and said, "Well, Dan, my nurse, Marjorie, is preparing a home-coming kit for you. Nothing too fancy, just a few extra bandages, some iodine-based cleaning solution and a roll of tape in a *manlier* blue." Dr. Leslie beamed at Shane, obviously flirting and looking for approval.

As Dr. Leslie continued to look at Shane and smile, and Shane returned both the look and smile, Dr. Leslie's face flushed pink. She quickly looked away, and continued then, trying to assume a more professional tone. "I will want to see you back in four or five days to remove the sutures, Dan." Dr. Leslie smiled again and added, "But you can come back earlier, if you want to see me... to look at the wound, to check for infection, or if you have problems with the sutures, or any unusual pain or swelling."

The doctor was now blushing even more, realizing she had been a little too obvious about communicating her attraction. "Once the sutures are out, I shouldn't need to see you professionally again. I mean, I won't be your doctor, Dan, unless you need me in that way." Her red hue deepened to crimson now, as she dug her professional hole a little deeper. Shane noticed aroused nipples, visible through Dr. Leslie's blouse. At that moment, Nurse Marjorie came back in, and the doctor moved away, folding her arms across her chest, while she continued to smile and flash her eyes at Shane. Her complexion continued to flush red.

Dr. Leslie remained as the nurse gave Shane a prescription for antibiotics, followed by the icing for swelling and wound cleaning instructions, and asked him when he had his last tetanus shot. Shane signed some paperwork, said his thanks and goodbyes, and began walking toward the doors. He turned back to wave at Dr. Leslie, and saw that both she and Nurse Marjorie had followed him toward the door. They were both smiling and waving like schoolgirls. He returned their waves flushing a little red himself.

Shane looked in the bag as he walked to the car, and noticed that Dr. Leslie's business card sat on top, with a cell phone number handwritten under her name. He smiled and thought how unpredictable life could be. He had been focused on one girl he couldn't get up the nerve to talk to after seeing her for weeks, and another girl had come along and approached *him* on their first encounter.

As he started the short drive back home, Shane realized again how sleepy and sore he was. He wanted his bed and some rest, but it was nearly 7:00 A.M., in weekday rush hour traffic on Hwy 395 heading north to Carson City, and if he wanted to see Kate, he would have to go directly to the café. He might not even make it in time, he thought, so he drove on a little faster.

As fatigue escalated from the events of the last 24 hours, Shane tried to concentrate on staying awake as he drove. He used all the tricks he knew so well from too many late night surveillances. It had just stopped raining, and Shane's windows were now half open, with the heat turned off, making it as cold as he could stand it. He drove sitting straight up in the seat, with both hands on the wheel. He turned the radio on to loud rock.

But nothing seemed to work, and his head was soon bobbing up and down, like the dog head on a backseat window doll. Shane changed the station to local news. As he approached Indian Hill, the morning news report came on, and suddenly Shane was jolted awake. As he listened wide-eyed, the announcer reported that Carson City Sheriff's Office personnel had responded to a "gunshot with injuries" call at the Magadinno residence. Shane had no trouble staying awake for the rest of the drive.

"Who shot who?!" He wondered aloud. "There were only two guards left, and they were both watching a movie!"

∞

Shane skipped the café and drove straight home. Once he had again cleared the parking lot and his apartment of any potential threat, Shane fired up his computer and began activating the newly placed bugs and devices. He listened intently to voices of police personnel, and the Magadinno and Alavarez families and staff discussing the incident. There had been no witnesses.

According to the other guard, Big John Galliano had walked outside to check a noise, and there was a report of a single gunshot. When the guard got to Big John, he found him dead with a gunshot wound to the head.

Shane made a quick call to Sheriff Roberts, who confirmed quietly that Big John Galliano had, indeed, died of a single gunshot wound to the head. The wound appeared to be from a small caliber rifle. No witnesses had come forth during the initial investigation. Mark said he would call Shane if he learned of anything new. Neither of them wanted to say too much on the phone. They agreed to arrange a brief meeting later in the day.

Shane continued listening to the conversations in and around the house. After a full hour had passed, and it was already nearly 9:00 A.M., he gave up and drifted off to sleep on the couch. He decided he had probably already missed Kate, and he was too tired and beat up to get back in his car and drive anywhere. Besides, he knew he looked like hell, and didn't want her to see him that way.

During the next few days, Shane met twice with Sheriff Roberts. At their first meeting, Shane briefed Roberts about his surveillance, the sighting of the jogger, his injury, finding the card on his windshield, and his whereabouts during Big John's demise. He gave the card to Sheriff Roberts, in a sealed evidence bag, void of any markings.

Mark informed him that Carson City Sheriff's Office was conducting a homicide investigation, with the assistance of the FBI. He said the other guard had passed both a polygraph and Voice Stress Analyzer (VSA), and, that there were no leads in the shooting.

Mark said, "The initial conclusion, after a week of investigation, is that there is no evidence at the scene, apart from fragments of the round in Big John's skull, and the homicide appears to be a professional "hit." The round recovered from Big John was from a 22-250 rifle. This is the first hit I've ever investigated involving that caliber."

Shane knew the caliber. The 22-250 was a small caliber, highly accurate rifle used by shooting enthusiasts and hunters. With a good quality rifle and ammunition, the caliber had tactical applications, and was also used by snipers...and professional "hit-men." The implication of a "hit" made Shane nervous, and even more cautious, especially with Friday approaching in two days.

Shane expressed all his concerns to Sheriff Mark Roberts. "This isn't good news, and makes me rethink the whole investigation, Mark. We already have one set of bad guys to deal with who are, arguably, the most dangerous *I* have ever dealt with. Now we have an unknown in the mix, willing to skillfully kill one of these guys, and we have no idea who he or she is!"

"Shane, you're not the only one nervous. Politicians have begun to come out of the woodwork, calling me at the Sheriff's Office to make inquiries. Most are pressing me for a speedy resolution, trying to make this go away fast. It's very concerning to me that legislators at all levels of local, state and federal government are so anxious to put the incident behind them. Many of them I've never met, and some I had never even heard of until now."

Roberts drew in a thoughtful breath, and continued. "This incident, along with the birth of Franky's grandson, has turned on a spotlight, shining right down on the Magadinnos. And, while the press is turning *up* the light and dying for a story, it seems everyone else is dying to turn the light *off,* and move back into their dark holes, to avoid *any* story and the resulting fallout."

Shane shook his head. "What fallout are they worried about specifically…if you know?"

"That would only be conjecture on my part, my friend. And that conjecture would be all the suspicions intimated between the lines in the pages of the intelligence you read. Corrupt government and law enforcement officials protecting high profile criminals are on par with the seediest and most notorious stories in history. And the reason a lot of these stories are never known, or known completely, is that government has the ability to cover them up or kill them quickly to minimize their impact. I'm afraid I don't know any more than that …*beyond a reasonable doubt.*"

Shane studied Roberts and believed him to be telling all he knew. "Then can I have a list of the people putting pressure on you to bury this quickly? Maybe that will help as we go forward."

Roberts removed an envelope from his inside jacket pocket, and handed it to Shane. He smiled and said, "At least we think alike, Shane. Be extra careful, my friend!"

As he studied the lengthy list of political inquires, and watched Roberts leave, Shane felt less sure of his abilities to conduct this investigation alone, than he had when they had begun speaking.

During the following day, Shane began the tedious business of monitoring phone calls from Hector's phone, which Hector activated the day after Shane's visit. Shane worked from the lounge chair in his apartment living room, while his leg began to heal. He also monitored the surveillance listening devices and cameras on his computer, using high quality headphones and multiple flat screen monitors.

He manipulated the settings on all the devices through the remote master, using surveillance software installed on his computer. When not in his apartment Shane could now monitor events and conversations as they unfolded using his cell phone.

He listened to conversations and watched videos, selecting and recording all that seemed important for 14 long hours the first day. He compiled intelligence reports as fast as he could, knowing that any pertinent information couldn't go to homicide detectives directly, as they didn't even know Shane existed. Any information on the Magadinno shooting would have to be given to investigators through Mark Roberts, and explained as coming from an unknown informant.

At the end of two full days, Shane had no clues about the shooter's identity, because the cartels and syndicate had no idea who had killed Big John. The Magadinno and Alvarez families had pulled in their own informants, interrogated and threatened all their fringe contacts, and finally, in frustration, even offered a reward for any information on the shooter's identity.

But in the end, all they could do was assign more guards and increase security at the compound. The families had developed no leads on who was responsible for the hit on Big John. They eventually settled into an uneasy routine, while Franky continued to press all his underworld sources, pocket politicians and paid-for officials, seeking more information.

Shane's work was exhausting, but after three days, he had identified enough patterns that he was able to reduce his monitoring times, and speed through the editing more efficiently. He now knew the next day's plans of Franky's entire syndicate as well as Franky did. And a picture began to form of how the syndicate operated and interacted with both the Gulf and Sinaloa drug cartels, and how it integrated its business with the Mexican Mafia and MS-13, among others.

Each day produced more details making the end result more predictable. For Shane it was like placing 50 small pieces each day in their places as he constructed a massive jigsaw puzzle large enough to cover a huge living room wall. Eventually the viewer would see the entire scene, and fully understand the picture it painted.

He put the most important pieces of his work together in the form of a pyramid crime organizational chart for each group identified, along with spreadsheets of dates, times, crimes, shipments, personnel and connections between the organizations. Shane hoped the end result would mean the demise of the Magadinnos, and their stranglehold on the underworld of the Nevada State Capital and surrounding areas.

Each night, before Shane went to bed, he copied the entire day's file, including videos, notes and conversations, from his computer onto one of two synchronized external hard drives. Each night he delivered the copied drive to the only person in town Shane *knew* he could trust, an old friend of Shane's dad who was family to him, Pete Harrington.

Pete was now a practicing corporate and defense attorney, who owned a small practice in Carson City. Pete, and his wife, Claire, had been so close to Shane's family when he and Heath were kids that they were raised as if Pete and Claire were the family's favorite aunt and uncle. And when their parents were killed, Pete and Claire were given custody of the boys and control over their parent's estate. They finished raising the boys as their own. They were always great parents to Shane and Heath, and the love and trust that built through the years only deepened between Shane and Pete.

Pete's office was downtown, near the intersection of Curry and Musser Streets, in a large, old house Pete had remodeled, and now used as both an office and a home. Downstairs, Pete had a lovely turn-of-the-century period office, complete with reception area, conference room with wet bar, two meeting rooms, a small kitchen, and two bathrooms. Upstairs, Pete had three bedrooms, two bathrooms, a living room, a game room (complete with regulation pool table and dartboard), a gourmet kitchen, and most importantly, a hidden walk-in safe. The house was within walking distance of the old downtown area, and its cigar shops, bars, stores, art galleries and trendy restaurants.

The old, downtown residential area was very popular with attorneys, accountants, counselors and other professionals, who restored neighborhood houses to be used for their businesses. The area transitioned from commercial and light industrial businesses along Hwy 395, to a blend of commercial and residential on the streets just one block west, and continued to almost straight residential one to two blocks further west, toward the Governor's Mansion.

Through time, the area had become a maze of streets and alleys, making it easy for Shane to get into and out of Pete's house on foot, without raising any suspicion, or needing to park nearby. There was a great deal of foot and vehicle traffic in this complex maze, and no one noticed much of anything, if it looked like it belonged in the neighborhood.

Pete kept Shane's previous night's external hard drive in his safe during the day. Pete met with Shane when he called at night to drop the primary external hard drive off for copying to a second drive. Sometimes, the meet was at Pete's house, occasionally, at Shane's apartment, but more often, it was at various places in Pete's neighborhood, where the handoff was completed unceremoniously. After Pete returned to synchronize the drives, they would meet again, so Pete could return one of the drives to Shane.

On Friday late afternoons, Shane always retrieved the second external hard drive from Pete, after it was synchronized, and placed it in a safe deposit box at a local bank. The hard drive in the bank would always be up to date, minus any events over the weekend. On Monday, the process would repeat, so there were always two backup hard drives to Shane's computer that contained all the information Shane had amassed during the investigation. Only Shane and Pete knew about the external hard drives. If anything happened to Shane, or his computer, Pete knew how to get a hard drive to Sheriff Roberts, leaving Pete an additional, complete hard drive in his own safe.

Shane suddenly thought about this routine more critically. Every night, there were three hard drives with current information: the external drive that Pete stored, the external drive that Shane updated each day before meeting Pete, and Shane's own internal computer hard drive. Shane placed one external hard drive in the bank safe deposit box every Friday afternoon. Shane was careful to go to the bank in his "old man" disguise. No one could trace that safe deposit box to Shane, or even Daniel Lester Harrington, as the box had been rented in another undercover name Shane had used in the past.

It was unlikely anyone had followed an unremarkable old man, with a different name, to a rented, safe deposit box. Shane figured the hard drive he kept in the bank to be the safest of the three records. It was his ace in the hole. The jogger's card had warned Shane to be careful on Friday, so was the hard drive going to the bank in jeopardy? Or could it be both hard drives, when they were synchronized, or even the computer at his apartment? He decided he might have to change the hard drive backup routine before he moved apartments.

Shane had developed a plan, should anything unusual happen to him. Upon receiving information of his demise or disappearance, he had instructed Pete to copy one hard drive to another external drive, and send the copy, with a letter Shane had already written documenting his assignment, to the U.S. Attorney General.

Pete would then go to Shane's bank, with an authorization affidavit to the bank instructing the bank to release the contents of the safe deposit box to Pete, and retrieve the external drive from the box. Pete would send this hard drive to Shane's friend, FBI agent in Los Angeles, Bryan Holland. If something happened to both Shane and Pete, and Shane made no contact with the bank for one month, the bank president had sealed instructions from the "old man" that would achieve this same result. And Pete's secretary, Tasha McNight, also had sealed instructions, so in Pete's absence, she could accomplish the task at Pete's end.

Shane had roomed with Bryan Holland in college. The two had become fast friends, and maintained a close relationship by calls, letters and vacations through the years. Shane and his dad had stayed with Bryan often, when they would go sport fishing on tuna boats out of San Diego in the old days. When Shane became a police officer, and then worked for DEA, he and Bryan spoke weekly, and eventually worked on a task force together. Bryan was Shane's close confidant when he left law enforcement, and had kept in touch with him at least once a week when Shane went out on his own as an operative. There were few, if any, secrets the close friends hadn't shared.

Bryan knew that Shane was working this assignment as a deep-cover operative for the CCSO. And he knew that the targets were the Magadinno crime family and related cartels. He was prepared to launch an investigation should anything happen to Shane. And he knew he would receive a package describing the investigation in detail, if that event occurred. As far as Shane was concerned, Bryan and Pete were two of the few incorruptible, trustworthy souls he knew. They weren't really back-up, but they were an insurance policy, of sorts...for the truth.

As Shane prepared for Friday, he thought more about the card left on his windshield. Sheriff Roberts had called and told him the crime lab had located no fingerprints, just as Shane expected. The card was blank, business card stock sold at a number of local stores. The printer was an inkjet printer of unknown origin. The font was Times New Roman 14 bold. None of this proved anything, other than the card giver was careful and likely a professional. The jogger had been careful to leave no clues, so the card was a dead end.

Now that Friday approached, the card's warning flashed ever more clearly and frequently in Shane's brain: "BE CAREFUL NEXT FRIDAY."

"Was he supposed to be careful with the Sheriff, the bank, the external hard drive at his apartment, Pete, or the Magadinno surveillance?" Shane wondered.

To date, even after days of phone calls and conversations monitored at the compound, there was still no intelligence about anything unusual on Friday. Shane was frustrated and concerned that, for the first time on this assignment, a problem had surfaced he had not been able to solve. To further complicate matters, Franky and the Alvarez family now suspected a rival cartel had made the hit, knowing it would shake the Magadinnos to the core. That likely meant more unknowns in the equation, *if* their suspicion were accurate.

Shane turned on another video file recently collected from Franky's office. He hit play. Franky and Hector sat together, talking quietly over a glass of wine. Shane lifted weights in his apartment while he watched.

When Hector asked Franky what rationale would explain why a rival cartel would send a warning to their families, Franky responded, "I quote Pete Clemenza."

Shane recalled that Clemenza had been a trusted associate of fictitious mobster, Vito Corleone, in Mario Puzo's "The Godfather" movie.

Franky continued, "These things gotta happen every five years or so. It helps to get rid of the bad blood." Franky laughed.

Hector looked confused. Shane listened intently, momentarily stopping his iron pumping.

"In the movie series, Clemenza was one of the godfather's enforcers, you see. He routinely carried out the dirty work of retaliations, warnings, and murders, against anyone who stood in his boss's way, or anyone who needed a reminder that the family was always in control and dangerous." Franky beamed a wide approving smile.

"The motivation for these random acts of violence was simply…a desire to produce fear and force submission." Franky smiled wider as he searched for words. "You gotta understand Hector, these little individual acts of violence or revenge, by themselves, can't always be rationally explained, you see. Like terrorism at its finest, it just keeps people from feeling secure and becoming brazen. People need to be slapped occasionally, if just to remind them they are nothing. If people are allowed to feel secure they might think they can resist, and once that happens they won't be afraid to rise up and act to protect themselves."

Hector frowned deeply and shook his head. Franky snickered at Hector, as Hector realized for the first time, that even Franky appreciated the thought behind Big John's execution.

"But John and you were close friends for years!" Hector blurted out. "I don't understand how you appreciate someone killing him!"

"Then you miss the point completely, my son-in-law. It isn't the execution I admire. I do mourn my friend. We made so *many* memories together! No, what I admire is that someone else had the balls to play the game, and deliver to me exactly what I would have delivered to them. I respect their planning, their thoughts, their *cojones*, and their methods. They make even people like *us* fear!"

Hector stared at Franky as he continued. "Like Yasser Arafat, the father of modern day terrorism. He was an unrepentant terrorist bastard, plain and simple. He killed and ordered the deaths of thousands of random, nameless souls and eventually brought the Middle East, even the world, to its knees. People feared him you see…but, they also respected him. Hell, the scared sheep of the world even awarded the bastard the Nobel Peace Prize trying to appease him!"

"Don't you understand? Arafat understood fear and the panic that always follows random acts of violence. And he understood that people who are afraid will do anything to make the fear stop. He understood they will even *reward* you for your evil, and give you control. That's what *we* do, my boy. And I respect and appreciate that, even in other people!"

Hector looked bewildered. Franky placed a hand on his shoulder, and said, "But don't misunderstand by thinking that I won't get even. No, my son-in-law...I will find those responsible, take my time torturing them, learn who all were involved, and then kill them and their families, very slowly and painfully, while they beg forgiveness. The debt will be repaid, I assure you!" With that, Franky walked out of the room to smoke a Cuban cigar outside on the rear deck.

Shane thought he noticed Hector shiver a little, as he shook his head. He wondered if even a criminal like Hector didn't like Franky or was afraid of him.

Shane replayed in his mind the events of the days since his visit to the compound, one more time. Hector and Anna had named the newest little addition to the crime family "Frank Alverez Gomez," in honor of Franky. The baby had arrived home, accompanied by his glowing mother and proud father, without a hitch. In the next few days, it seemed the entire Alavarez family had arrived from Mexico. Even with Big John's untimely demise, plans were set, and the families carried on with the celebration, interrupted only briefly by Big John's memorial service. The service lasted less than an hour, and the families were back home, focusing on the celebration of a new life.

All the combined, extended family that had arrived numbered too many people, even for the large compound to hold. Some of the family stayed in the guest rooms in the main house, or in the two guesthouses on the grounds, but the more distant relatives were farmed out to Franky's new hotel-casino, the Silver City Paradise, a now-popular landmark on Hwy 50 East.

Hwy 50 led to the small village of Mound House, and toward the turn-off for the popular old-west tourist town, Virginia City. Hwy 50 also stretched 3,000 miles between West Sacramento, California and the Atlantic coast, in Maryland. Millions of people would travel right by Franky's new casino every year.

The Silver City Paradise casino had the area's largest ballroom, and the fanciest dining room, and soon after completion, became *the* location for the three Magadinno/Alvarez celebration dinners and family re-unions. Unfortunately, Shane couldn't get any listening devices into these rooms. It was just too dangerous and risky.

The Paradise was a very secure facility, with its own overlapping security cameras, listening devices, and well trained security staff. The hotel security, combined with Franky's personal bodyguards and security, and the cartel's unknown security guards, was too large a problem for Shane to overcome on his own, with no back-up. He had no idea what private conversations had taken place at the hotel.

When the clans all got together at the compound, everyone seemed to be having the time of their lives, holding the baby and talking baby talk. Shane thought he had never heard such odd baby talk before, half in Spanish, and the other half an odd blend of Hispanic or Italian-sounding English…and all with different degrees of accents. It couldn't be written in his intel briefs, so Shane referred to baby talk as "MBT" (more baby talk), when it interrupted a documented criminal conversation.

During the last week, Shane had seen Kate each day, but each meeting was not long enough to satisfy Shane, due to his new hectic schedule. The increased intelligence provided by twelve cameras, multiple listening devices, and a cell phone, initially made monitoring each day's activities a virtual nightmare. Eventually, Shane had developed a plan to reduce the workload. He set the computer to record all conversations, photos and calls on all channels, using surveillance software developed by the military and provided to him by the Nevada Division of Investigation, through Sheriff Roberts. And then, at set intervals, he scanned through each channel for important activity, information or photos.

Shane found that, with practice, he could afford to spend just six hours each day scanning data, even though all photo and video channels combined, created more than 40 hours of data in each 24-hour period of normal activity. He still had his other duties and procedures, and he had to eat, sleep, and shower. There just was not enough time in the day. When he was most tired at the end of the day, Shane thought how he hated that this tedious work cut into his time with Kate, and had delayed his opportunity to meet her.

On Thursday night, after the hard drive exchange, Shane met Pete for dinner at the Carson City Nugget. They dropped a few coins in quarter Keno machines as they talked, sitting next to each other at their own machines. Pete could see how tired Shane was, and told him it was obvious he needed a break. They spoke in quiet conversation about the old days, times with Shane's mom and dad, and how both Pete and Shane missed the family gatherings and campouts.

In those days, before Pete moved to Carson City and purchased his law practice, Pete was a fixture in the Beckett family. Pete and Shane's dad had been school friends, worked in the same business, and had moved around to different states together, before Shane's dad met and married his mom. Shane had always called Pete "Uncle Pete." He was 12 years old when he learned that Pete wasn't a blood relative. He still referred to Pete as "Uncle Pete," although now, he was more like a father figure.

But what Pete really meant to Shane was hard to describe. Pete had been Shane's dad's best friend for most of their lives. Pete had helped raise Shane and Heath, even before their parents were killed. More importantly, Pete had been there for Shane and Heath after their parents were killed, as a father, a mentor, and always the closest of friends. Pete was, like Shane's dad, one of the few heroes of his life.

And even now, Pete gave Shane space when he needed it, but always made himself available when Shane needed him. After Shane's parents died, when Pete stepped into the role of being a father without being asked, like it was prearranged, Shane always had the feeling that Pete took care of far more than he knew about. The fit was so good that Shane turned down a better paying assignment in Phoenix, to take this job in Carson City, primarily so he could spend more time with Pete.

Pete was alone now, since Claire, his wife of 29 years, had died of breast cancer last year. He had slowed down in business during his wife's illness, and seemed to have lost some of the fire he had had earlier in life, when he was making his mark on society. As they sat, talked, and dropped quarters, Shane realized once again that the man sitting next to him was possibly the most important part of the small family he had left, and he loved this man very much.

Shane's machine lit up and chimed loudly. He looked up and down and realized he had won a jackpot. He had been playing his mom and dad's birthday numbers, and without realizing it, had hit all six numbers with two quarters in, paying an $800 jackpot. Within a few seconds, the change attendant was at his side, documenting the win. She congratulated Shane as if he had won the Lotto, and paid him his winnings. The girl reset the machine, and told Shane to play off the winnings, which he did, with a single quarter. She again congratulated Shane, and he tipped her a $20 bill, a standard practice in casinos.

Pete slapped Shane on the back, and said, "This is one of the last places around you can really drop coins anymore. Most machines only work on paper currency, and then pay you off with a 'win ticket' when you cash out. I don't find much pleasure in a machine printing me out a ticket that I have to take to the cashier, who then routinely counts out my cash, with no fanfare. I like it this way, with the girl coming up and congratulating you, giving you some real attention, treating you like a winner."

Shane laughed, "Pete, since I don't' suppose there are very many winners in any of these places, I guess it is special to be treated like one." As he spoke, Shane looked at the small, slowly dispersing crowd that had gathered near him to check out his jackpot amount.

"They're all re-motivated to try again now," said Pete. "You've been good for business tonight, Shane. Now most of these folks will stay longer and spend more cash, chasing the dollars you just won. Then they'll wake up in the morning with the gambler regrets that will fade away as soon as they walk through their next set of casino doors. And it starts all over again. You wouldn't believe how many people my office represents in divorce, domestic abuse and bankruptcy cases where the problems all come back to a gaming addiction."

Pete looked sad as he spoke, "But in the end, its just like anything people use, whether its food, drugs, alcohol, gaming, sex, money, whatever…some of us can have fun and use it and not abuse it, and others can't use it without abusing it. It's just too damn bad the addicts don't have the internal fortitude and self-respect to do something about it, when they realize they have a problem. They need to stay away from their own personal nightmare before it takes control of their lives and destroys them and their loved ones. The ones who love the addicts are the ones who pay the biggest price for any addiction."

Shane stood up and laughed, trying to lighten the mood. He knew where the demons lived in Pete's last remark. He said, "Well, Pete, on that positive note, I think I'll call it a night!"

∾

As he turned away from the machine, Shane saw Kate staring at him, and smiling from the other end of the aisle. When their eyes met, Kate smiled even more widely, and clapped her hands quietly three times to congratulate Shane on his win.

Pete couldn't help but notice Shane staring, dumbstruck, at Kate, and said, "And that, my boy, would be *her*!"

Shane never took his eyes off Kate to look at Pete, but said, "Who are you talking about? I never mentioned anything about a woman to you, Pete."

Pete snorted, "You didn't have to say a word. I knew there was something more special than espresso that you rushed off to your café for every morning. And don't even try to B.S. me that it was just work. You should see the look of anticipation on your face every day! Like a schoolboy, Shane!" Pete laughed a kind-hearted encouraging laugh.

When Shane didn't respond or move toward Kate, and Kate stood frozen in time, Pete walked up to Shane and finally asked, "Well, are you going to introduce me, or are we just going to all stand here and stare at one another until security kicks us out for blocking the aisle?"

Shane still didn't look at Pete, but said quietly, "Pete, I can't introduce you. I haven't even met her yet!" Pete looked as if in disbelief at these two star-struck youngsters staring at each other from opposite ends of an aisle, Shane, immobile and mute, and Kate smiling more widely with each passing second. Neither would make a move toward the other, and neither wanted to leave. It was nerve wracking to Pete, a man who always got things done, and who always took charge of any situation.

Finally, Pete couldn't take it anymore. He put his arm around Shane's shoulder, and led him forcibly to Kate. Kate's complexion flushed as they approached, but she didn't move or stop smiling.

Shane thought he tried to resist being led along the aisle, but his resistance, if it existed, was feeble at best, and a few seconds later, he stood, weak-kneed, in front of Kate. Pete squeezed Shane's shoulders a little more tightly, as if to give him strength.

Shane saw Pete extending his hand to Kate, and, as if in a dream, heard Pete say, "Hi, I'm Pete Harrington, and this awestruck, young man is my nephew, Dan." Shane suddenly realized Pete had the presence of mind to use his undercover name, as neither he nor Pete really knew anything about Kate.

Kate said, "I'm Kate O'Leary," never taking her eyes off Shane, as she shook Pete's hand first and then reached for Shane's.

Shane could say nothing. He had never been this close to Kate before, and she was even more beautiful than he had thought. He stared into Kate's crystal clear, emerald green eyes, and extended his right hand. He felt a sudden release of tension when Kate's hand wrapped around his, and he felt the soft warmth of her touch.

It was as if this were a welcome dream, from which Shane never wished to wake. He literally felt as though he had glided down the aisle to meet Kate, unable and unwilling to resist the movement. All he could do now was stare into her captivating eyes, and wish the moment would never end.

The meeting was much better than Shane had expected. He found it exhilarating, familiar, welcome, warm and right. He hoped Kate didn't want to leave too soon. He also hoped Pete would continue talking a little while longer, so he could regain his composure. He found it difficult if not impossible to control his emotions and breathing around Kate.

Shane heard the words as Pete spoke, and realized that Kate's eyes had not left his own, not even for a brief second. Pete was his usual jovial self, going on and on about their family connections, how remarkable Dan was, and how nice it was to have him in town for a visit. It finally dawned on Shane that Pete had been talking for what seemed like hours, and he and Kate were still locked in a frozen handshake, staring at each other intently.

Pete's voice suddenly seemed louder and clearer to Shane, when he said, "Well, I think you two have some celebrating to do, and I do have some work waiting at the office, so I'm going to call it a night. And, Dan, I'm going to walk my dinner off, so have fun, and call me in the morning, OK?"

Surprised, Shane looked at Pete, and said, "Celebrating?" Pete turned to walk away, and laughing, threw back over his shoulder, "Buy your pretty friend, Kate, a drink, and celebrate your winnings before you leave here, so the casino doesn't go broke tonight. Remember, I have to live here. I like this place and don't want to see it go under, just because you showed up and took all their money!" Pete raised his hand and gave the couple a parting wave and a big grin, as he turned a corner and was gone.

After watching Pete leave, Shane turned back to Kate, realized he was holding her hand in both of his hands now, and as he looked down, he saw that she had wrapped her free hand over his as well. They had noticed their hands at the same time, and looked back up at each other. When their eyes met once again, they both smiled widely, and Shane asked, "Would you like a drink, Kate?"

Kate said immediately, "I thought you'd never ask." And then, as if caught in the moment of something they had both dreamed of for a long time, they stood awhile longer, just holding hands, and smiling.

3

"The past is history; the future is a mystery;
the now is a gift, that's why they call it the present."
(Deepak Chopra)

Shane and Kate continued to hold hands as they walked toward the crowded restaurant. The touch of their hands entwined together stirred emotions in both, bringing back memories of school days, notes passed to young loves, and anticipation blotting out all other concerns. But, as they arrived at the reception area, Kate slowed and stopped. She gazed intently at Shane, and asked softly, "Do you really want to be here?" Shane felt butterflies surge in his stomach, as he guessed Kate might be nervous about her quick decision to have a drink with a man she just met.

Unsure of the correct response, Shane said what was in his heart, "I just want to spend time with you, and get to know you, but if this is too fast, I…"

Kate interrupted, "It's just so noisy here, and too impersonal. Will you come with me to my house for a drink? We can talk more freely there, and be more comfortable."

Shane's heart was in his throat. Even though it seemed too easy and out of place, Shane agreed immediately. In less than a minute, they were in the small casino parking lot, headed toward their own cars. With love-sick anticipation he hadn't felt since high school Shane followed Kate's dark green Hummer to Carson City's upper west side.

They drove to a neighborhood between "C" Hill and the Governor's Mansion. Shane had paid to take the tour of the Governor's Mansion with Pete, on a day off when he first arrived. The Nevada State Governor's Mansion was located in one of the oldest neighborhoods in Carson City. The Mansion was built in 1907, with a budget of $22,700, on a large piece of land donated by the wealthy Rickey family, who technically "sold" it to the State for $10. Through the years, the Mansion had been remodeled several times, and outbuildings had been added. It was one of the most impressive Carson City estates Shane had ever seen.

In the years since the Great State of Nevada built the Mansion, neighboring small lots had sold for upward of $150,000 each. The grounds that the Mansion occupied were now worth more than a million dollars. The only estate Shane had seen in the area that could possibly rival the Governor's Mansion, was Franky's compound.

"Funny, that of the best homes in the capital city, one was built with tax dollars, and maintained at the taxpayer's expense, while the other was built on drug money and corruption, and paid for at the taxpayer's expense," Shane thought to himself. He shook his head and laughed aloud, as he drove on toward Kate's home.

Shane turned left on a hill and followed Kate onto the private road leading to an estate several times larger than Franky's, or the Governor's Mansion, and he suddenly felt out of place and confused. Kate's house was a *serious* mansion, larger and more spectacular than the Governor's by at least three times. The electric gate opened for Kate's car and closed immediately behind Shane's, shielding the magnificent grounds from easy entry or escape.

Shane's training kicked in, and he began reading the compound, even as they arrived. He spotted a well-designed system of security cameras, much better placed than Franky's, leaving no holes for someone to slip through. He saw no guards, but he had the distinct feeling he was being watched.

The experienced undercover operative was now abruptly caught between two feelings, passionate excitement, fueled by the hope of being with this extraordinary woman, and the self-preservation panic of being in a bad place, possibly outgunned, in an uncharted compound that may provide no opportunity for escape...or survival.

Shane was filled with excitement, anticipation, intrigue, caution and, once again, adrenaline. He said to himself, "If I fall victim to the wiles of a beautiful woman, I'll be joining a long list of suckers, falling for the world's oldest and most successful con! In that event, I'll have a lot of company to share good stories with anyway!"

Shane parked behind Kate, on a circular drive that faced a six-bay garage. He opened his car door warily, and stepped out, continuing to read the grounds and surroundings, not sure what to expect. Kate walked to Shane, as he completed a 360-degree viewing of the area. She took him by the hand, and said, "Leave your keys in the car, so the staff can park it in the garage. Please come with me. Its okay."

He looked into Kate's eyes, and the warm, genuine caring Shane saw in her, melted away his apprehension. He threw the keys on the seat, left the door open, and walked along, a half step behind his beautiful escort. As he followed Kate, continuing to read the area, she pulled him gently along and up the steps toward the mansion entrance. He took a final deep breath at the door to control his adrenaline.

Shane turned to watch his car being driven into the garage, behind Kate's, by drivers he had not seen before now. He noted that each of the six garage bays appeared to be capable of parking at least three cars in a row. Many other cars were already parked in the lit bays, which had exit bay doors on the opposite side of the building. He saw two guards standing in the garage, waiting for the drivers to park the cars, and, even though he saw no weapons, Shane assumed they were armed. Both guards watched him intently. Shane was once again on high alert, trying to control his breathing and adrenaline.

His mind went into overdrive, trying to figure out who Kate could be, and why she had such a high level of security. He half expected to see a ranking United States Senator waiting inside the house, with a cadre of Secret Service, NSA and CIA agents, eager to interrogate him when he walked through the door.

Shane's stomach was a mixture of butterflies and knots – butterflies in anticipation of being with Kate, the woman dreams were made of, and knots to go with a sense of foreboding of the possibly dangerous and unpleasant evening awaiting him, behind the front door. He mentally prepared for the worst, and began to formulate a 'fight and flight' plan of escape, beginning with vaulting the surrounding fence and escaping into the night on foot. His felt a tinge of pain from his leg injury, and suddenly didn't look forward to vaulting a fence.

As Shane's apprehension continued to rise, he chided himself, "Who am I kidding? I knew this was too good to be true. I'm a little too lonely, after not dating for more than a year, and the first attractive woman who is interested in me, destroys all my defenses with a smile." Shane suddenly felt like he had joined the list of a long line of historic fools, who, collectively, had launched thousands of ships, fought untold battles, lost kingdoms, and squandered immeasurable wealth, all for the love of an elusive, alluring woman. He was disappointed in himself...but not disappointed enough to bail out quite yet.

Kate seemed to sense his apprehension, and said, reassuringly, "I think you will really enjoy the house, and meeting George." She squeezed his hand. He felt somewhat relieved, but not much.

As he and Kate arrived at the nine foot tall front double doors, the entry door opened quickly, but the only person to greet him was an elderly gentleman, whom Shane assumed was a butler. "If anyone still *had* a butler in this day and age," he thought to himself.

The well-dressed man took Shane's coat, with all the formality befitting the lord of a manor, and smiled at Shane, as if they were old friends. He greeted Kate with, "Your cocktails are waiting in the viewing room, Miss Katherine...lemon drop martinis prepared just as you ordered."

Kate smiled, and stopped the old gentleman from leaving her side by tenderly placing a hand on his arm. When he turned toward Kate, she said, "Thank you, George," as she gently kissed him on the cheek.

The old man beamed at Kate, as if he were admiring his own beloved child, and then turned, and slowly walked out to hang their coats on an antique rack in the foyer. Shane stood in quiet amazement, thinking, "Not quite the CIA interrogation team I expected."

George gestured for Shane to follow him to a sitting room off the enormous entry, and he did so, relaxing more with every step he took. A crackling fire in a massive fireplace beckoned him to the cozy room. As he approached, Shane felt the radiant heat from the fire, and his attention was drawn to dozens of photos perched atop a large mantle over the fireplace. He looked back through the doors at Kate, who watched him follow George toward the fireplace. He began gleaning information from the photographs, glancing back and forth from the pictures to Kate, then to George.

Kate didn't follow Shane, but playfully blew him a kiss and winked, as she disappeared up one of two matching spiral staircases on either side of the entry. Shane had entered the room through one of four giant wood and glass French doors. He marveled that the entire room was hardwood, floor to ceiling, resembling the interior of a sailing vessel. He noticed the fine detail and workmanship in the floor, baseboard, walls, crown molding, and ceiling, and then, looking up through the largest glass dome or cupola he had ever seen, discovered stars, shining into the room from above.

Reading his mind, George said, "The viewing room, sir." George spoke properly and proudly, as though he were showing off the finest room in the house. Shane admitted the effect was astonishing, stars shining down through the high ceiling, while firelight flickered and danced off the multi-colored hardwood. There were no other lights on in the room, yet the lighting was perfect, relaxing, warm and inviting. And the soothing effect was immediate. His shoulders relaxed and he felt calm.

Shane continued to study the room closely. His inspection revealed that none of the massively heavy wood contained knots or blemishes. Every board in the room was of the highest quality, and, obviously, hand selected for its place in the room, as if designed and placed by an artist working with a ship designer.

Shane stood in wonder, gazing about at details of the magnificent room, thinking that even the Governor didn't live in a mansion of this quality. When his eyes returned to George, he realized George had been holding out a drink for him.

Shane said, "Oh, thank you, George," as he quickly took the martini, a little embarrassed at the royal treatment he was receiving. He politely sipped the lemon drop martini, smiled at George, and said, "It's really quite good. I don't think I have ever tasted one made this well. Did you make it yourself?"

George did not answer. Instead, he just smiled approvingly, as if Shane's praise made all the difference in the world to him.

Shane said, "Thank you so much, George, for going to this trouble for me," as he glanced down, increasingly embarrassed at the attention he was unaccustomed to receiving.

The old man could contain himself no longer. His face lit up, as he exploded into uncontrolled laughter. "Oh, that Kate, she's a real character!"

The distinguished gentleman held out his hand to Shane, and said, "My *real* name is Walter, Walter O'Leary, and I am Kate's grandfather." Walter O'Leary's words rolled off his tongue, with all the formality and dignity he might use in addressing an audience, and announcing that he was the President of the United States of America.

As a bewildered Shane slowly took his hand, Walter O'Leary continued, "Shane, please don't let on to Kate that you know who I am. She and I like to play this "butler and princess" game when she brings a friend here for the first time. We've been doing this since

Kate was a small child. It's been a very long time since we have had this chance, so we need to get some mileage out of it, if you don't mind." Shane nodded in bewilderment.

With a twinkle in his eye, Walter walked over to the fireplace and stirred the fire, placing another log on top of an already large inferno. As he did, Shane realized Walter knew his real name. He was once again on high alert, with adrenaline surging back into his system. He thought to himself, "Who the hell are these people!? How do they know who I am?! And what do they want with me?"

Shane quickly started talking, trying to get past the knowledge that the old man may have not realized he had slipped up, and given away the secret that he knew Shane's real identity. He was careful, and spoke only about the details in the room, until Kate returned. While talking, Shane ran everything through his brain as fast as he could, trying to figure out the "who, what, where, when, why and how" of it all.

Nothing made sense, and yet, Shane found caution draining away once again, as everything about all of this somehow seemed right, as if he somehow *belonged*. Walter, for his part, answered more questions about the architecture, and continued to put Shane at ease by his very calming and reassuring nature.

Footsteps hurrying down the stairs alerted Shane, and he quickly turned, as he sensed Kate was approaching. Soon, he saw her, smiling that wonderful, coy smile that could light up any room with excitement and expectation. Shane noticed Kate had walked in bare foot, wearing a long, silk robe that outlined a bikini, framing her spectacular curves and toned body. The robe was pulled tight, across Kate's abundant chest, and tied in place with a sash, exposing ample cleavage created by perfect, sumptuous breasts.

Shane thought Kate was the most stunning woman he had ever seen. She carried a folded-up pair of men's swim trunks, which she placed on a coffee table, as she took her martini from the table.

She teased, "George, what have you and Shane been talking about?" George, or Walter, looked at Shane, winked at him as Kate turned to smile at Shane, and said, "Oh, just man stuff, Miss Katherine. I've been showing Mr. Shane the details of the viewing room, and discussing martini recipes. By the way, I turned the temperature up on the Jacuzzi, as you instructed, so it will be a comfortable 102 degrees when you are ready."

Shane realized Kate had called him 'Shane' and a smaller dose of adrenaline surged back. He realized this back and forth between high alert and relaxation was going to wear him out quickly, and he needed some answers. He looked at George/Walter and then at Kate, as if expecting an immediate answer, but received only reassuring smiles in return.

It occurred to him that, if they really knew who he was, then they knew what he was doing here, and they were either allies or deadly enemies. Shane looked from George/Walter to Kate and couldn't see either as an enemy. He decided to play along and not immediately press either for answers. He was sure answers would come along directly, one way or another.

With that, Walter walked to Shane, shook his hand again, and said, "It was a pleasure meeting you, my boy. A word of advice from an old man to a young man." Walter looked at Kate and paused.

He said slowly, "She'll try to tame you quickly with her overwhelming beauty and keen mind. If you're smart, you'll let her. But if you're strong enough and resist just a little, so it takes her some time and maneuvering, you'll be much better off. In the end, Shane, if you are truly a worthy, honorable and loving man, you'll conquer a heart that will surrender to you forever. That heart is more precious than all the wealth of the richest kings on earth. Take very good care of it, my boy."

The old gentleman squeezed Shane's hand tightly and looked up at him as an innocent soul, entrusting his most precious treasure to a man he possibly considered only marginally worthy, and completely untested. He then raised his eyebrows, as if to seal the arrangement, cocked his head, and waited for Shane's response.

"I'll do my best to honor your trust, sir...*and* heed your advice!" Shane assured him, as he squeezed the hand in return. George/Walter's hand felt warm and reassuring, like Kate's, in a peculiar way, as if it were right for Shane to take it...and hold it tightly.

Walter turned to leave and then hesitated, looking back at Shane, and said, "I like your manner, Mr. Shane Beckett, so my prayers for your success are with you." Walter walked to Kate and kissed her gently on the cheek, like she was his favorite person in the world and he might not see her again. "Good night, my precious Katherine," Walter whispered. He left without looking back, closing the double French doors behind him.

Shane felt an odd sadness seeing his new friend leave. "What a delightful, gentle soul. A distinguished, grandfatherly man anyone would wish they had in their life," he said, softly.

Shane stared after the man, and realized how much he missed his own grandfather. "How odd," he thought to himself, "First, this raging beauty of a woman completely disarms me, and now, the unassuming kindness and gentleness of her grandfather finishes me off." Shane decided he might just as well surrender now, and save any pretense of putting up a fight against this family...whoever they were.

Shane was still staring at the closed wood and glass doors, thinking about the advice, warning, and hope Walter had given him, when Kate's laugh brought him back to reality.

"Don't mind Granddad, Shane, he's a character and loves to tease."

Shane smiled as he turned to Kate, "Funny, he said the same thing about you. You two are quite alike, I think."

Kate beamed her approval, and Shane realized that she looked even more radiant, as the firelight danced on her luscious skin. He was once again mesmerized by Kate's sheer beauty. He only wished this were all real and would last forever.

"Am I really standing here with Kate?" Shane thought. He feared he might be dreaming again. He *had* been very tired from all the long hours lately.

Shane heard a faint warning from his subconscious mind, trying to break the moment with a warning from past experiences. He liked planning each move he made, to assure he wouldn't make a serious mistake in life. He liked to know the future as well as could be expected. He rarely lived "in the moment."

Shane's cautious, calculated existence protected him well, but it also insulated him from a normal life and any attempt at happiness. He thought of a quote he had recently read from Indian-American philosopher, Deepak Chopra, "The past is history; the future is a mystery; the now is a gift, that's why they call it the present."

"Tonight," he thought, "I'm going to let go and live in the present, the gift of one moment at a time." Answers to his questions would come with time, but right now, he was willing to take a chance.

Kate took Shane by the hand and led him to a loveseat near the fire, where they both sat and sipped their martinis while they talked. He had never been a martini guy, but this drink was delicious.

He liked whiskey occasionally, but red wine was Shane's drink of choice. If hard liquor was offered, he could drink anything, in mentally measured and noted quantities. Shane had mastered the art of blending into a crowd while drinking, without ever becoming drunk. He had developed phenomenal control with years of practicing this technique of timed and measured alcohol consumption, along with drinking copious quantities of water.

He had only been drunk once in his life, at his cousin's wedding when he was 20 years old. That was a bad experience Shane never planned on repeating. On the morning after the celebration, he had been sick, dizzy and unable to stand. The illness lasted for three days, and he thought he would die. He had even called his father at work and asked his dad to take him to the hospital. Patrick Beckett had just laughed at him, and told Shane he was experiencing the cost of too much fun and too little control.

Shane realized that day, that being drunk came with too high a cost for the few moments of pleasurable buzz he thought he remembered enjoying. Plus, there was the additional cost of the embarrassment he had felt, when he realized he had lost control of his senses and probably made a fool of himself. It was all too much for him, and he promised himself he would never repeat the ordeal. And Shane always kept his promises, even if he just made the promise to himself.

But Walter had told him this lemon drop martini was made with just the right amount of lemon, triple sec, sugar, and *Grey Goose* vodka. The glasses had been chilled, then rimmed with a special lemon-granulated sugar mix. The taste was sweet, tangy and exceptional.

Shane and Kate talked quietly as she stroked his hand gently with her fingers, and he knew he was as safe as he could be, with no reason to guard and maintain total control. He felt he could lower his defenses for the first time in a long time. He melted into the chair, drank in Kate's beauty and sipped his drink without judging a thing. "Live in the moment, accept the gift," he urged himself.

"Listen to the philosopher and to George/Walter, you fool," the little voice in his head encouraged him. But another more distant voice chided, "Beware of a possible trap!"

Soon Shane felt the stress leave his body. Only once in the next several minutes did he read the room and check for any changes. He caught himself and smiled. Kate didn't seem to notice, as she confided to him her interest in formally meeting him. As their conversation developed and grew more intimate, Shane found that he and Kate were totally comfortable with each other, as if their relationship was somehow older, tested and already established. It was like they were meant to be together by some larger design. Although familiar, the feeling was still foreign to him.

Kate sat sideways, on her crossed legs, so she could face Shane as they talked. Suddenly one of the large double wood doors opened and a young lady dressed in an attractive dress and heels, brought two more martinis on a tray, and placed them on the table. Without a word she took the two empty glasses and left, closing the doors behind her. Shane held Kate's hand, stared at the fire, thinking he had died and gone to heaven. He remained quiet...reflective.

After a moment of silence, Kate asked, "Shane, is something wrong?"

Shane looked into Kate's concern-filled eyes, and said, "Kate, nothing could be more right. I just can't believe I'm here with you, after weeks of dreaming about you, trying to find the courage to speak to you. It's almost unbelievable. And to be with you here, in your home, this wonderful room, with the fire…it's so perfect."

Kate found it refreshing that a tough guy like Shane was really so sensitive. He was as she hoped he would be, not overly impressed with himself, but kind, caring, considerate, appreciative, and loving.

Shane smiled and squeezed Kate's hand gently. Kate laughed and said, "So you're not disappointed we left the casino?"

Shane returned the laugh and said, "Kate, I couldn't be happier or in a better place. This is so much more intimate and private. It's a perfect place to get to know you. But I have to ask you…." Shane trailed off.

When he stopped mid-sentence and looked down, Kate asked, "What, Shane?"

Shane looked up and hesitated, as if afraid of the answer. He summoned his courage and asked, "Why me, and why now? I mean, you don't look like a girl who brings a stranger home from a casino to your own Shangri-La, especially on a first date. And how do you know my real name?"

Kate started to reply, but hesitated as though being very cautious. She released Shane's hand, stood and walked to the fireplace. Kate gazed into the fire, as if searching the embers for the right answer. "Shane, I wasn't going to approach you, but I couldn't help it. You see, this isn't really our first date."

Kate glanced at Shane and saw the look of disbelief on his face. "Kate, I'm too young for dementia, and I could never have forgotten meeting you, let alone dating you. I mean it would be impossible for me to forget you. How can that be?" His confusion prompted Kate to continue where she had been afraid to go.

Kate turned toward Shane, with a serious look that he wasn't sure he wanted to see often. But a moment later, she laughed a little playful laugh like she had discovered the way to break the news and save the day. To his surprise, Kate's mood turned in a moment. She now seemed to enjoy her ability to bewilder the man who had everything figured out, or so he had always thought.

"So, you really don't remember me, Shane?" Kate asked, walking to a nearby bureau. "If I show you a picture of us *together*, will that jog your memory?" Kate teased, savoring the moment.

Shane looked stunned, as he racked his memory for an explanation. Kate took her time, allowing him to search his mind, but he clearly made no progress.

Shane finally said, "I guess a picture would have to help me some… maybe." He felt out-maneuvered at every turn, but his curiosity was peaked. He stared at the drawer in anticipation, as Kate strummed her fingers playfully on the bureau top.

Kate opened the drawer and retrieved a small photo album, bound in leather, and sealed closed with rawhide twine wrapped around small brass posts protruding from each cover. She unwound the rawhide slowly, and then almost danced back to her place on the loveseat, teasing Shane coyly all the way. Kate leapt back into the seat next to Shane, while folding her legs under her in one move. Shane was amazed at Kate's agile and athletic body, but tried to focus on the photo album, instead of her beautiful bouncing breasts.

"So, Shane, what do I get if I prove your memory wrong?" He smiled now, completely intrigued and thoroughly enjoying the game for the first time.

"What do you want…that I can *afford?*" He emphasized, looking around the room.

Kate laughed, and thought long and hard as she stared into Shane's eyes. He felt she could see right through him to his very soul. He wanted to look away, afraid she would see something she didn't like, but he was mesmerized.

"Like a cobra powerless to stop gazing at the mongoose long enough to get away," Shane teased.

Kate was obviously pleased with Shane's response, and replied flirtatiously, "I want what I have wanted since I was thirteen years old and first met you, Shane. I want another date." With that Kate opened the album to the exact page and placed the book into his hands.

Shane stared down at a series of photos of his father, himself, one of his father's clients, and an awkward looking brownish-redheaded girl, all smiling happily back at the camera. He realized that the girl was glancing sideways at him in the picture. He looked back and forth in disbelief from the face of the girl who appeared to be about thirteen, to Kate, who raised her eyebrows, cocked her head to the side and nodded, confirming her own identity. He slowly smiled, remembering glimmers of the past.

He finally said, "The girl who wouldn't eat shrimp?"

Kate laughed and admitted, "I don't have that problem anymore, Shane."

Shane stammered, trying to solve the puzzle while speaking the options, "But how did you…did you…all the time, at the café, or when did you..?" They both laughed aloud over the nonsense of his question, as he blushed slightly red.

Shane again looked down, amazed to look into his father's eyes gazing back at him from Kate's album. He finally managed, "But I still don't understand."

Kate snatched the book from his hands and dashed back to the bureau, replacing it in the drawer. "There will be lots of time for more questions later," she said, with a disarming smile.

He began to rise up in protest, but she insisted, "That's just part of what I win, Shane. I get to keep you wondering for a little longer, and we get to go to the Jacuzzi now."

And with that, Kate scooped up the trunks from the coffee table and threw them to Shane in one deft movement. As he caught them and stood up, she pointed to the door of a room he could see just off a set of stairs leading downward. He walked to the door, down the stairs, and into a large bathroom and dressing area. He changed quickly and hung his clothes on hangers he located in a large closet in the bathroom. He placed his Glock in a clothes bag he then folded and set under his shoes. He only briefly considered taking the gun with him, but instantly dismissed the idea.

When he emerged from the bathroom, Shane noticed lights on outside in a sunroom set off and below the bathroom through a hallway. From there four more stairs led down to a sunken all-glass room on the terraced back yard, looking up onto "C" hill and out to the forest to the west. Until tonight, he had not even noticed the stars since he had come to Carson City.

He crossed the room toward the sound of water jets, and saw Kate, sitting in the hot tub, backlit by a row of flickering candles. There were two fresh drinks perched on the tile surrounding the large tub. Shane realized he had already drunk almost two of these martinis, and he felt just a little more relaxed than usual. He had lost track of time. He thought to himself, "The now is a gift, that's why they call it the present."

Shane stepped into the Jacuzzi, and was immediately greeted by stings from the hot, pulsating water. The surges drove electric-like shocks into the exposed nerve ends inside the damaged flesh in his shin.

"Kate *will* see my wound," he thought, as he as he wondered what explanation he would give her.

Fierce stinging, that caused the initial wince of pain, was soon replaced by the feeling of welcome deep-tissue massage, as the hot water ricocheted off Shane's aching muscles. He was still sore from the collision with Franky's tree, and now the combination of martinis and water therapy was a potion he welcomed. He sank deeper into the water and, for the first time in a long time, totally relaxed.

Shane reached for his glass and noticed it was colder to the touch than before. He knew it had been refilled and thought he should slow down a little to keep his composure with Kate. He didn't want to screw up a good thing on the first date. He took a small sip and put the glass down. The drink was ice water with lemon, and he smiled.

Kate asked, "What happened to your leg, Shane?" with a look of genuine concern.

Occasionally, there is an awkward moment in the life of an undercover operative. It's the moment when the operative realizes they must choose to tell the truth, or hide behind the protection of the cover story, which is always a lie. The moment almost always involves answering to a person the operative may care about. In that moment, the operative places everything on the line with their decision. It is an extremely difficult choice.

If they tell the truth, the other person may eventually compromise them in some way, endangering their life or the loved one's life. If they tell the lie, they may be safer, but risk losing the relationship with the person forever. Few relationships recover when it's eventually discovered that the relationship was built on a foundation of lies…even if they seemed essential to survival at the time. Shane knew this was the reason undercover operatives often did not have relationships.

Even as his mind quickly replayed the options, Shane knew he really had no choice. He had waited all the years since the death of his parents to recover to the point he could find the love he desperately needed. He wasn't going to risk compromising a possible relationship with Kate. He would tell her the truth and depend on her to never *ever* betray his trust. He also knew the truth could place her in harm's way. But after all, any relationship with him might place her in harm's way!

Shane began slowly, "Kate, I could never tell you anything other than the whole truth. I hope you will appreciate how difficult it is for me to tell you this, and I need to know I can depend on you to keep my confidence. No one can know what I do for a living, or what I am working on right now."

Kate straightened up in the hot tub, and hit a button that turned down the jets so they could talk more quietly, as she nodded in agreement. "No one can hear us, Shane, and I won't repeat a word of this, *if* you tell me not to," Kate said reassuringly.

Shane read Kate instantly. He recognized truth when he saw it and continued.

"Kate, I work as an undercover operative on special assignments with different law enforcement agencies. I am here in Carson City working an assignment for the local Sheriff's Office. One night recently, I made entry into my target's residence to conduct a close-up surveillance. When I left, I had to jump down into a tree in the yard from an upstairs balcony, and I sliced my shin open on a jagged branch."

Kate's eyes looked down at Shane's leg, and back up at him. Shane shrugged, "Not very graceful, I guess," he said, trying to lighten the moment. "There is a lot more I could probably tell you to convince you I'm not a nut with delusions of grandeur, or trying to give you some romantic line about being a super sleuth, but, it is what it is, and it's really not very romantic or glorious," Shane said, looking down at the swirling water. He added, "My target is the Magadinno crime family and the Mexican drug cartels supporting them." Neither of them said anything for several minutes, as each contemplated how much more they should reveal to the other.

Shane closed his eyes and then felt the water move, as Kate moved closer to him. She took his hand in hers. And as he looked down, Shane watched Kate gently caress his hand and fingers. When he looked up at her, she pressed into him and he felt the soft lips of Kate's tender kiss. He kissed her back, long, slow and soft at first.

The fire of unbridled passion slowly began to rise. Hunger and yearning replaced the tender testing of first touches, and soon their kisses were long and hard. Passion flowed from one to the other, first in spurts and then in streams. Tentative explorations grew to confident caresses and, as each trusted more, they released more into each other until there was no holding back. They reluctantly controlled their mutual desire, checked by the threat of losing the experience by going too far, too fast.

Kate and Shane were locked in an increasingly tight embrace, born of a gentle caress and fueled with the fire of desire. They explored each other's mouths with anxious inquiring tongues. At the end of several minutes, neither wanted to stop, but Shane felt he had to tell Kate a little more about who and what he was, if only to make sure she was sure about what she was doing.

He started to say, "Kate…" But she stopped him cold by pulling him back to her and smothering him with her warm, soft, wet, intimate kisses.

Shane was helpless. He lost any pretense of self-control, and so did Kate. They kissed and caressed each other's nearly nude bodies with hands and tongues, trying to learn and memorize everything about each other. The intensity of this newly discovered obsession spiraled upward at a blinding pace. The heat of the Jacuzzi combined with the heat of lust. After several minutes the two new lovers, chests heaving, not wanting to stop, realized they had to leave the water.

Shane gently pulled Kate upward from the hot tub, realizing there was no way he could hide his erect "package." He drew Kate close to him and kissed her deeply, probing her tongue and mouth with his tongue, and then pulling back, allowing Kate to do the same. He traced the outline of her luscious neck from her shoulders to her ears, and back again with his tongue, until his whole body throbbed with desire. They stood and kissed for several more minutes, pressing their aching bodies closer and closer until it felt as if they were nearly one being.

After a few minutes, Kate took Shane by the hand, leading him back to the bathroom where Shane had changed earlier. She retrieved towels for both of them and they dried off together. She then took Shane's clothes out of the closet, handed him his shoes, and the clothes bag that held his holster and gun, and said, "Shane, if you trust me, come with me now."

Shane looked into the face of the woman he was dying to cover in kisses, and noticed the smile was gone from Kate's lips. It had been replaced by a sexy, serious, yearning expression Shane had recognized immediately, and was not about to argue with. He nodded, and followed Kate out through the sitting room and up the sets of stairs that led to the opposite end of the house.

The room they finally entered was definitely Kate's room. It was located at the end of a long hallway, not unlike Franky's upstairs hallway, with rooms going in both directions from the top of the landing. But that was where the similarity ended. Kate's room was twice as big as Franky's master bedroom, with a larger balcony that looked the same direction as the viewing room and the Jacuzzi below.

Shane guessed the tasteful furniture was probably Amish, made of lightly stained oak. He recognized good furniture. One of his dad's hobbies had been making furniture, in their old wood shop. The matching bed was a four-post design with an uncovered canopy. A huge skylight opened over the bed, presenting the viewer an inspiring glimpse of the night sky, moon and stars.

Oversized windows wrapped around two sides of the room, offering unobstructed views of the tree-covered Sierra's to the north and west. The bed was already turned down on both sides, as if beckoning the new lovers.

"The now is a gift," Shane thought.

As they arrived at the bed, Shane realized he had been reading the room. It was a habit he thought he might have to break when he was with Kate, as he sensed she had noticed his caution.

"We're completely safe here, Shane," Kate said softly. He nodded.

Shane felt secure enough, but knew from experience that no one was ever completely safe. But tonight, he thought, belonged to him and Kate, regardless of what tomorrow may bring.

Kate took Shane by the hand, and pulled him to her. And for the first time in a long time, at that moment, Shane had no security worries. His mind and his body were lost in a growing passionate desire that emerges at the birth of a new love.

In a flash of seconds Shane and Kate were lost in each other again, entangled in each other's bodies, their fiery kisses fueling their desire to make love. Shane made no moves on Kate, content to let her lead. He instantly responded to Kate's every touch and gesture, as she explored and caressed him further.

They were soon united in a reciprocating rhythm, trading touch for touch, as their hands, fingers and tongues travelled to the depths of each other's bodies. Shane felt as if he had known Kate forever, yet each touch was fired by first-time passion. Constrained desire gave way to raw lust. Rapidly building hunger built and surged in waves. Finally, both lovers yielded to the intense craving they felt deep within their bodies, minds and souls.

The sexual fervor grew to the point of confidence that displaced uncertainty, and Kate undressed Shane, slowly and methodically, as if respecting and honoring the body she yearned to claim.

Shane responded by removing Kate's bikini top, and covering her erect nipples and large, perfect breasts with kisses. He relished tasting the luscious skin he had dreamed about, with his tongue, and he lingered over each breast and nipple before returning quickly to the other.

When neither could stand the intensity any longer, and both were nearly overcome in breathless desire, Shane gently removed Kate's bikini bottom. He caressed every inch of her buttocks and pubic area. When Shane moved to her thighs and began to probe Kate with his tongue Kate nearly orgasmed. She quickly pulled him back up to her, and buried her tongue into Shane's mouth, driving the tip deep down his throat.

Kate wanted Shane, and needed him inside her now…yet, she fought the urge to rush, and tried to slow her pace. The lovers mirrored each other's moves, as they felt those intimate places reserved for making love, they were experiencing together for the very first time.

Shane could resist the primal urge no longer, as Kate teased and stroked him sensually, light strokes alternating with firm caresses. He raised himself on to her body, and entered Kate slowly, but firmly… steadily.

When he was completely inside her, Shane kissed Kate as passionately as he could, pressing his throbbing penis deeper and deeper in to her, until there was no deeper to go. It seemed to Shane he had just discovered the tingling, surging rewards of French kisses, paired with accompanying sensations, racing forth from every surface of his body. He felt new heights of passion never known, before Kate.

Each second left both lovers more fueled by pinnacles of fiery desire, a level of passion they had never experienced with anyone else. The two lovers soon moved together in heaves of hot breath, and wet luscious kisses. Hands and fingers were unable to rest. Muscles tensed and retracted, only to tense and retract, and repeat the movements, over, and over again. Toes curled, as eyes opened to see the incredible sight before them, only to close again, as they each relished unimaginable sensations.

Their bodies fit together as if they had been designed for just that purpose, to produce the greatest height of sexual passion and gratification possible. Shane opened his eyes and saw Kate's heaving chest, her sumptuous breasts rising and falling, her red lips parted and gasping, as she strained for another breath. He kissed her even more lustfully, nearly losing control.

Kate opened her eyes without missing a thrust, pulled back to see her lover, and then pulled Shane's mouth back to her, as she gave him a faint smile. Their tongues immediately met, and resumed the dance they had briefly left.

The lovers continued this blissful rhythm until they could barely move, continually urged on by the fuel of love and lust that now filled their minds, hearts and bodies. They began to arrive at the peak of desire, each wanting more, wanting to achieve the ultimate climax, and yet each, …not wanting it to stop.

They craved to feel each other more, to please each other as much, and as long, as possible. Neither wanted to slow the pace, as they were both urged on to seek new levels of sexual expression and release. They both yielded to some previously unknown force inside each of them…a force that demanded they continue, each releasing more to the other.

Both lovers gained strength to continue from the other, feeding off, and taking all they could from their new lover, while giving back even more than they had each dreamed possible. The pace and height of passion continued to race onward, spiraling upward nearly out of control, until there was no stopping the inevitable.

Suddenly Shane felt Kate's orgasm rock from deep inside her, and move quickly toward him, seizing and releasing him in spasms. He feverishly kissed and licked her firm full breasts, as they revealed the telltale reddish spots of climax, nipples fully erect and enlarged. Kate moaned with fits of pleasure as her orgasm intensified. She released uncontrolled, enraptured gasps.

Shane felt the sudden ecstatic rush of release, and filled Kate, over and over, as he thrust deeper and faster in to the depths of her body, urged on by the rush of Kate's blissful, contented convulsions. Her rapturous cries built to a crescendo.

Both Shane and Kate renewed their deep final kisses in the frenzy that the climax of lovemaking brings, ultimately slowing, as the last few thrusts brought Kate a second, shorter, but deeper, orgasm.

Kate smiled the pained smile that signals the blissful end of the pinnacle of sexual passion and romance. Then the two new lovers locked on to each other's eyes, and simultaneously kissed their last deep lingering, romantic kiss, holding on as tightly to each other as they could.

Their tongues finally slowed and said their final goodbyes, and their wet lips finally parted. Shane smothered Kate's neck in rapid tongue flicks and kisses, and then rolled over, bringing Kate with him, allowing her to rest on top of his spent, heaving body. The lovers spoke in hushed tones about the wonder of the night, and how neither wanted it to ever end. Neither could believe what they had just felt. And suddenly, neither lover could picture continuing in life, without the other.

Shane was totally drained of stress. He couldn't remember ever being happier. "If I smoked, I think I'd smoke a pack of cigarettes right now, Kate, because I don't think anything like that could ever be repeated, and I would just want to savor the moment," he teased.

Kate looked down at him and smiled. "You had better repeat that again," she countered quickly. "You can't ruin me for all other men and then just move on, Shane Beckett," she said with a grin.

Shane laughed and said, "I didn't mean we would never try again to reach that magnificent place we just discovered. I just meant that I would never have thought it possible to go there, until I met you," Shane explained tenderly. "In fact, I never knew something so wonderful *could* be possible!"

As they lay in silence, Shane realized that they were both covered in sweat, and he savored the sweet lingering scent of a night of lovemaking. He loved Kate's scent, their scent together, and feeling like he did right now.

Realizing the same thing at the same time, Kate rose slowly off her lover's body, and pulled him up to follow her to the shower. They entered a large tiled shower with a glass surround. The lovers showered silently, grinning at each other, as they carefully washed each other's bodies for the first time. When they were done, they dried each other, and Kate slipped back into her suit and her robe. She threw Shane the trunks he now realized she had known, would fit him perfectly.

She led him back downstairs to the hot tub, stopping along the way at a full bar in a game room to make two more lemon drop martinis and grab a large glass of cold lemon water they could share. Shane followed Kate back into the hot tub without saying a word. He was in awe of the night, but he sensed that Kate wanted to talk and he thought he needed to listen to whatever his new lover wanted to say.

Kate set the jets to a steady motion of water that massaged Shane's wound and kept the noise low. She raised her glass to his and they clinked to celebrate their newfound love. Then Kate just sipped her drink and gazed into Shane's eyes for the longest time, as if trying to build the courage to move on to the topic she wished to discuss.

Shane said nothing, having already decided to accept what was to come, however it played out. He had met the girl he had dreamed about and just had the most exhilarating lovemaking experience of his life. And now, he was in a hot tub with this wonderful woman, sipping a lemon drop martini in her mansion. Whatever was to come, it was okay with him.

"I may even adopt this martini as my signature drink," he thought, grinning to himself.

Kate began, "Shane, you have been totally honest with me and you have waited patiently to hear about our real first date, or dates, to be correct." As Kate spoke, Shane thought he detected a note of sadness in her voice.

"Shane, I need to start by taking you back to why my father met with your father, when we were just kids. My hesitation in telling you this is that I need you to promise to hear me out completely. Some of what I tell you may be painful for you to hear. Some of it you may not believe. But just as you made me promise to keep your secret, I need you to promise to think about what I tell you, and never repeat it to anyone else, not even your employer."

Shane looked at Kate intently. He saw the worry in her eyes and heard the concern in her voice.

"Kate, there is nothing you could tell me that would possibly cause me to doubt you or change my feelings for you. This may sound silly and premature, Kate, but I am falling in love with you. For the first time in my life, I can imagine being with only one person, and that person is *you*. I've been wanting this to happen for months, but never dreamed it could, and now that it has…"

Kate put two fingers over Shane's lips to stop him. "Shane, I feel the same way, but I don't want you to finish that sentence or say anymore until you hear what I have to say. If you still want me when I finish my story, then we will have a lifetime to explore our love together, but first you need to hear the whole truth."

4

Kate's face took on a solemn foreboding look as she spoke. Shane watched her closely, his stomach tied in knots by the anxiety and fear of losing this magical woman he had just found. Shane had been in love maybe once before, so he thought. But after six months of a building relationship he and she lost the spark and drifted apart. He felt relieved when they broke up. Since then he had always believed that something was wrong with him, and that he lacked some essential essence of normality to be able to fall in love. He thought he would always be alone...until now.

But then he had seen Kate, a woman seemingly designed by the Creator just for him. If the truth were known, he had been falling in love with her day by day, as he watched her and listened to her with friends and staff at their favorite café. To finally have all his dreams fulfilled and experience the wonder they had known in such a brief time, was more than he could have hoped for.

Already though, he felt the stinging fear of loss of the greatest love in his life. Kate sounded and looked ominous. It was as if a horrible storm were approaching that could possible destroy everything they had just begun to build together. He felt helpless. But he was committed to fight for what he wanted and needed. He would make it work, whatever the problem.

Kate searched Shane's eyes for the sign that everything would be all right. His return gaze conveyed the reassurance Kate needed, and she began to speak to him softly.

"My hesitation at telling you this is partly based on the belief that I should have told you what I knew many years ago. For reasons you will understand soon, I was prevented from coming to you, and later chose not to tell you all I knew out of a growing concern for you. Some of this you may know, but since I don't know exactly what you *do* know, I'll start at the beginning."

She continued cautiously, "Our fathers were more than business associates, Shane. They developed a close friendship and trust that grew from their business contacts, which spanned many years. My father was part of a construction empire that my grandfather and his brother built in southern California. The brothers, working part-time when they were in college, started a concrete business that eventually became the largest concrete and excavation company in California, and one of the most successful in the country."

"The business was always family owned, but Great-Uncle Charles had no children. When Charles died, my dad took over more and more of the business to help Grandfather. Eventually they began expanding out of the State of California and focused on large government projects.

By then Grandfather had begun additional businesses and was buying land and developing shopping centers. Finally they began working in Nevada. But I'm getting ahead of myself."

As Kate spoke, the words seemed to come easier, and the tension drained from her speech. She continued the story in the melodic tones that Shane was used to hearing; tones that comforted the listener as they conveyed truth and trust.

She went on more confidently. "Your father was more than an attorney representing interests in my family's business. He was also dad's personal attorney and friend. They spent a great deal of time together in meetings about work, but they also travelled a great deal together. Some of what they did together I knew about, but there is much I didn't."

"Eventually your dad was selected by the California Department of Justice to review an investigation completed by a task force that targeted organized crime in California in the construction industries, especially involving state and federal contracts, and focusing on government corruption. The California State Attorney General and your father had gone to law school together, and he held your father in high esteem as an honest, incorruptible and ethical person and attorney."

Kate's words were flowing freely and quickly now. "Your dad specialized in corporate law, specifically in business and corporate contracts and contract fraud. And although the Attorney General had specialists in his own department, he suspected ties to organized crime compromised his department, along with many others in state government. He knew your father was competent, discrete and trustworthy, and he convinced your dad to take on the role of special prosecutor to review an investigation and make recommendations to him for prosecution."

Shane sat wide-eyed as Kate filled in the gaps he had needed, to understand all that had happened to his family.

Kate continued. "As I understand it, when your father was personally selected by the Attorney General himself, there were only a handful of trusted people outside the task force who knew about the investigation and the identity of the special prosecutor."

"The California State Attorney General was a man named Scott Mayfield. He had made quite a name for himself in Orange County, prosecuting organized crime and large fraud cases that took many millions in savings from a large number of innocent trusting people. He was brash, dedicated, outspoken and aggressive, and as such, his list of enemies was as impressive as his reputation as an incorruptible prosecutor. He earned the nickname of "The Little Pit Bull with the Large Bite," from both his size and the power of his successful prosecutions. He sent some wealthy, powerful people to prison, and easily won the next Attorney General election on his spotless reputation."

"Mayfield knew, from his contacts in law enforcement, that contract fraud in California was costing taxpayers hundreds of millions of dollars each year, and he ran on a platform to expose those responsible and save the taxpayers a bundle. My dad used to talk about him for hours during the year before the election. Dad supported Scott vocally and openly to anyone who would listen. He served on Scott's campaign committee and did all he could to help Scott get the support he needed to win."

"Once Scott Mayfield won, he wasted no time organizing the task force and assigning members he believed he could trust. He created a state-wide tip line, targeting government contract corruption. The task force worked on the investigation just short of a year, and already had more people identified for prosecution than a team of prosecutors could charge and bring to trial in twice that time. But the biggest surprise to the team was that the loss due to corruption didn't run in the millions…it was in the billions!"

Shane marveled at the knowledge and eloquence of Kate's speech. She was enthusiastic, knowledgeable and committed, to say the least, but her mannerisms exposed the pain, anger, and contempt for corruption she felt. He was intrigued and enthralled as she continued.

"Of the four people in the original task force, two died in suspicious accidents, leaving an FBI agent named William Conrad, and a California Department of Justice investigator named Craig Robinson. The only other people who knew details of the investigation, and the identity of the special prosecutor, were the Attorney General, my dad and your Uncle Pete."

"My dad, your dad, and your Uncle Pete were the inner circle of family and friends, outside the investigation, that consulted on the details of the investigation and made recommendations to the task force. They also formed their own plans for security and protection of a back-up copy of the files and documentary evidence."

Shane bolted straight up and jumped angrily out of the Jacuzzi. "You mean to tell me that my own Uncle Pete knew about all this and didn't tell me?! I can't understand why…I mean…but we don't have any secrets. He's like a dad to me." Shane was obviously in distress. He flailed his arms about, looking around as if searching for a way to vent his disappointment.

Kate had planned for this moment she knew would come. She was already out of the hot tub, holding Shane's hand and standing at his side. She grabbed two towels, gave one to Shane and then, thinking better of it, started back toward the Jacuzzi, looking back at Shane as she pulled him gently along behind her.

She spoke softly, but with such authority and reassurance that Shane could only listen. "Shane, I told you this would be difficult, and you *promised* that you would listen to the entire explanation before you made any decision about who did what, or how and when you should have been included. Shane, you *promised,* and I won't hold you to anything more than that…your own word! So, do we end all of this, or do we move forward, as agreed?!"

He looked at her sheepishly and nodded his head in agreement. When Kate had begun the account, Shane had relaxed and sunk deeply into the hot soothing water, feeling the welcome deep massaging of his exhausted and sore muscles. He had finished the martini, and almost all of the cold lemon water in the bottle, not realizing how thirsty he was. Now that he was up, he was beginning to feel sore and stiff, and he wanted another drink. But he followed her and got back in the water.

They sat silent for a few seconds as Shane contemplated what he had learned. He picked up the glass of lemon water and as he swallowed the last sip of water, Kate smiled, and stroked his face and lips with her fingers. "Think we could use a little more?" she said coyly. Kate picked up a remote that had been resting on the Jacuzzi surround and asked for two more drinks and a pitcher of lemon water. A woman's pleasant voice answered that they would be delivered shortly.

Out of habit, Shane promptly said, "I really shouldn't…I'll need to drive home." But, immediately after the words had left his mouth, he realized the folly of the statement.

Kate gave him a knowing smile, and countered, "I really don't think so, Mr. Beckett. I have more plans for you." Their eyes connected with the love and joy that lover's eyes convey, as they both laughed together. Kate's eyes also flashed a hint of embarrassment that her cheeks confirmed with a crimson glow. But Shane's face soon returned to a confused and concerned expression.

Kate suggested they shower, and get into white cotton robes waiting in the shower room. She promised to continue the explanation when they met back in the viewing room. She wanted to give Shane a chance to be alone for a moment, and reflect on what she had just told him, before she continued. She knew the next part would be much more difficult for both of them, and she wanted to buy more time.

Shane agreed and showered quickly. He found a pair of slippers, a fresh pair of underwear in his size, and a robe waiting for him in the shower room. He figured he would beat Kate to the viewing room, as he was ready so quickly. He was surprised to see her waiting for him, with drinks, when he got to the top of stairs. As he reached the comfy over-stuffed leather chairs in the viewing room, Kate handed him another lemon drop, and continued with her account.

"The investigation had been long and complicated, involving thousands of documents which were the individual building blocks that put the entire case together. Your dad kept the master case file copy in a secure place known only to him, while he worked from one of two working copies we now know existed."

"The final piece of the puzzle was follow-up investigation provided him by Craig Robinson and William Conrad, who had worked together as a team in Mayfield's task force. Your dad reviewed that piece in a little over a week. We believe that your dad made the recommendation for prosecution about a week before his death, in a document that broke down a synopsis of the case, identifying all the suspects, witnesses, and evidence. It also recommended specific charges for each defendant."

"Your father completed a flow chart showing the suspect companies and corporations, the identity of the suspects who controlled them, a detailed account of how everything interacted, and an explanation of how the government contracts were delivered to the suspect companies. Among those identified as targets for prosecution, were a dozen state legislators, five local officials of large cities, three United States Senators, six United States House of Representatives Congressmen, and dozens of corporate executives...some of whom were known or suspected crime figures. In short, the case had become the largest public corruption case in American history...or so we believe."

"The final typed draft of the completed Investigation and Recommendations for Prosecution was delivered to your father for review, as he ordered, just prior to the date he was scheduled to deliver it to Scott Mayfield. By then, the task force had begun to focus on identifying corrupt law enforcement officers involved on the periphery of the case, and organized crime figures involved in dummy corporations."

"The day after your dad received the final draft report, my dad left for Nevada to work out the final bid rewrites on the Yucca Mountain nuclear waste project." My grandfather elected to stay at home, and work on cleaning up loose ends with the project. He has never really forgiven himself for that decision, allowing his son to make the trip with an assistant."

Shane had been patient and captivated by Kate's story, but couldn't resist knowing the answer to one burning question. He knew part of this story from the intelligence reports he had read when he had taken this case. He was in an undercover role and he now knew he was the only one out of the loop. He could stand it no more.

He almost pleaded with Kate. "Why didn't I know all this, and how and when did you discover it?"

Kate slowly lifted her gaze to meet Shane's, and said reassuringly, "I didn't know either until much later, after your Uncle Pete contacted my grandfather. They came up with a plan to protect us both, as best they could, and give us as normal a life as we could have, until they could learn the details surrounding our families' deaths." Shane frowned and Kate read his mind.

"Patience, my dear, and all will become clear," she said, confidently.

The double doors opened and the young lady delivered more drinks, an iced pitcher of lemon water, and an iced pitcher of martini refills. Turning to greet her, Kate said, "Delores, this is Shane, and we thank you. I know it's very late, and this is all we need tonight. Please get some sleep, and good luck on your test tomorrow."

Delores thanked Kate, said it was nice meeting Shane, and promised Kate she would tell her the results of her test as soon as possible. Delores left the way she had come. As she did, Shane cocked his head for a better view and followed her with his eyes, appreciating that she, too, was very attractive. Maybe Puerto Rican he thought.

Shane glanced at Kate, and realized she had been watching him watch Delores. He was a little embarrassed that he might have looked too hard and too long at this attractive woman. Kate laughed, and said, "Down, boy, remember who you're with tonight, and at least for this evening, you're taken."

Realizing he had been exposed, he smiled meekly, as he made a feeble attempt to change the subject. "Test?" Shane inquired.

Kate refilled Shane's martini glass, and answered. "Good attempt save! Delores takes her real estate associate broker's test tomorrow at noon. She is a family friend's niece, and has worked for our family while she attended college. She decided to go into real estate, and will continue to work for our family, once she is licensed.

"Your family owns a real estate company?" Shane inquired. Kate refilled her own glass, while sending him a stern look, indicating that she wanted get back to the story.

"Yes, we do own and manage a great deal of real estate. My great-uncle, grandfather, and dad became very wealthy through shrewd and honest business dealings, and by keeping their employees happy and loyal. You'll hear more of that later, though. No more interruptions now," Kate said, as she shook a finger at Shane, pretending to scold him.

Shane couldn't resist one more interruption, just to see that pretty, annoyed look once more. He blurted out, "And George/Walter is the wealthy grandfather in the story?"

She returned the appropriate, and expected, cute, yet irritated, look and said, "Stop! You know he is…now no more!" Kate locked on to Shane with a glare that told him to push no further, at least for now, and he yielded, immediately sipping the martini as he shot her a smile.

"Whenever my grandfather, great uncle and dad could, they promoted friends and helped friends along, to strengthen those loyal to our family. They made many people very successful over the years, some very wealthy. We have generations of families that work in our companies. My grandfather knows the names of all his employees, and most of their children. Most of them consider us friends, as well as employers. Delores will be moved into our real estate division, and will have a good life working with us. She's very bright and very nice."

Shane nodded and raised his eyebrows. Kate added, "You'll be invited to her wedding soon. She and I have been friends for a long time. I'm her maid of honor, and you *will* be my escort, right?" Kate cocked her head up at Shane inquiringly, looking for reassurance. He was taking this well for now, but she didn't want to risk losing him.

"I wouldn't miss another date with you for all the money or all the women in the world," Shane said emphatically.

"That's a great relief, Shane. I don't think you could manage what we did tonight with all the women in the world," Kate laughed.

She continued, "You already have enough money, Mr. Beckett, but we are getting ahead of the story there." Kate refilled both water glasses, noting that Shane had already gone through half the pitcher of water. "Save me some water, or you're getting the next refill," she quipped playfully. "Now no more interruptions, please!"

Shane was wondering how Kate knew how much money he had, and how that little bit of cash he did have could be enough, and if it were enough, what was it enough for? He suspected, however, that he would be wise not to interrupt and question her at this point.

Shane leaned in and kissed Kate passionately, broke the kiss off suddenly, and then leaned back, smiling widely. "Okay, Kate, have it your way," he taunted, in a poor attempt at looking hard-to-get.

"I didn't know you were going to be this difficult," Kate said, actually relieved at his playfulness. Her worry about Shane accepting the facts of their lives had all but vanished. She knew he was wondering what she meant about money, which he did *not* have very much of, on his own. But, she pressed on with the rest of the story he would hear this evening…about *the case*.

Kate looked down into her glass, taking on a determined look that Shane found irresistibly attractive, and continued. "My dad was murdered…officially, *disappeared*, while he was in Nevada working on the Yucca Mountain project, preparing the final bid. The bidder against him was Franky Magadinno, the Magadinno crime boss, who remains the obvious suspect in the case." Shane had already put all this together before Kate made the statement, but he wasn't prepared for what came next.

Kate's eyes conveyed the sadness of the facts that followed. "The week after my dad *disappeared*, Attorney General Scott Mayfield died of an apparent heart attack. He was a health nut, jogged at least five miles every day and was in top physical shape. *My* dad was athletic, but Scott beat him at racquetball nearly every game they played."

"His remains were released to a mortuary by the medical examiner before an autopsy could be performed, and *accidentally* ordered cremated. The cremation was stopped by Mayfield's family, but the medical examiner later refused an autopsy. Scott was the only person in his office we know of, who had knowledge of the existence of the task force, the identities of those working in the task force, and the fact that there was a special prosecutor."

"The remaining work of the task force was assigned back to the California Department of Justice by the FBI, and then shut down permanently a month later. The surviving working copies of the case, flow chart, and planned prosecution were removed from the task force office by *unknown persons* and haven't been seen since. We have never been able to find your dad's master copy case file. The last person we know to have had hands on the working file was a California DOJ investigator named Brian Grant, who is now the Carson City Undersheriff."

Shane leaned back in his soft chair, took a long swallow, draining the remnants of the drink, and looked down in thought. Kate paused, allowing Shane time to digest and examine what she had told him. She knew that every detail she gave him led to a hundred questions. She had planned this conversation for a long time, and the anticipation and planning had exacted an emotional toll.

Realizing her mouth was dry from both stress and talking, she took several long refreshing swallows of the lemon water, and then sipped her martini. The liquid replenished her spirit, giving her strength and a renewed spirit to continue. Kate glanced at Shane, who was looking at her intently, and knew he was running through these questions in his mind, looking for answers. She remained silent for more than a minute, allowing him to collect his thoughts. She freshened both their drinks.

Shane continued to watch Kate, as she continued. "When Attorney General Mayfield died, your mother and father rushed you to your Uncle Pete's, and he took you to a friend's mountain cabin in the Sierra Nevada range, near Markleeville, California. The plan was simply to lay low, while your dad planned his next move. You must remember that, because the very next day your mom and dad were killed in a traffic accident." Shane looked down, as tears filled his eyes. He was barely able to nod his head.

Kate continued, as her voice, cracked with emotion. "A week later, Bill Conrad's wife was murdered, and he was found dead next to her, with the murder weapon in his hand. The investigation quickly concluded it was a murder-suicide. By the way, Bill Conrad's family, and his wife's family, never believed the results of the investigation. After trying to get pregnant for years, it turns out the couple had discovered they were pregnant…and with twins. They had only told their families, and they were all so excited about the news, they could hardly wait for the births. They had planned a multi-family reunion around the births."

"Craig Robinson just disappeared, and is still listed as a missing person. His wife and daughters believe, to this day, that he was kidnapped and murdered. But the DOJ continues to refuse to assign any manpower to the case. You see where this is leading…don't you, Shane?"

Shane nodded, continuing to look down. He dried what were left of the tears in his eyes, and suddenly struggled to get back in control. He downed an entire glass of lemon water, and tried to shake off the emotion.

Kate continued. "Pete began his own investigation into these coincidental deaths and disappearances. After several months, he felt all leads pointed to some type of connection between my father's disappearance, the Yucca Mountain project, Franky Magadinno's corporation who won the project bid, and your parent's murders. But Pete could locate no one who would talk or knew anything about the evidence that had been collected by the task force. He only knew your father was working *with* the task force, and hypothetical connections your father had related to him. But he didn't know identities of the task force members. He didn't even know specifics about past murders, disappearances, and suspects. And no one he spoke to wanted to open an investigation."

"A few weeks later, Pete contacted my grandfather. At their first meeting, Pete explained what he knew, and told Grandfather that your parents had called him just before they were killed. They told him they were driving to meet with a United States Department of Justice attorney that your dad knew and trusted. That was the trip they were on when they died in the fiery car crash you know about."

"Everything was lost in the car, which exploded and burst into flames when they collided with a semi hauling a gasoline tanker trailer. No bodies, no evidence, nothing was ever recovered. Everything was lost."

The words, "everything was lost," echoed in Shane's mind. He squeezed his eyes closed as hard as he could to keep the tears from falling again. He and Pete had never spoken of the details of the crash. It was just too difficult for him to think about. His parents were killed, and he became an orphan in an instant. He had thought he and his brother Heath were just on a camping trip with his uncle when it happened. He didn't even learn of his parent's deaths until a week later.

"Pete had then taken Shane and Heath to Alabama for a brief time, to stay with Pete's dad, while the family estate was handled and their home sold. Shane had never thought anything about the house. He didn't want to go back to an empty house full of memories anyway. Now 16 years later, it was as painful as though it were just yesterday, but it all made a lot more sense now. Anger surged in Shane. If he only knew for sure who was responsible, justice would prevail, one way or another, he thought. He and Heath had lost everything, just as Kate had.

Kate sensed the anger growing in Shane and squeezed his hand. She continued the story. "My grandfather used his influence and wealth to investigate my dad's death for more than three months, with little success. Even your dad's law firm had no idea that your dad was working on this case for the Attorney General. Our private investigator met with Pete, and Pete connected the dots from your parents to our family. The meeting with my grandfather and Pete followed. Pete asked to continue the investigation with my grandfather. They have been close personal friends ever since."

"Together, they managed our lives for us, as much as they could, anyway. They agreed to keep us apart for as long as possible, under the assumption that whoever killed our parents knew about their connection, and we may put each other in danger. That's why I never got my next date, with that older boy I had a crush on when I was 12, until now."

Kate paused to test Shane's response, to make sure he was all right for her to continue. He said nothing. She studied him intently. There was no 'Shane smile' that lit up her heart. In the last moments, the man Kate was falling in love with, had lost the self-assured confidence, the little boy charm, and possibly the deep concern he had shown for her. It was all gone from his mind and body, as Shane slipped deeper and deeper into anger and hatred for those responsible for his pain and loss.

Kate's heart began to ache, as she thought she might have said too much, too soon. She wondered if Shane was angry with her. She couldn't bear to believe that he might hate her, for telling him the truth. Then, in an instant, Shane looked up at Kate, with tears in his eyes and said, quietly, "I will *never* allow anyone to hurt you or take you from me. I love you, Kate."

Kate released her own bottled up emotions in quiet sobs, as Shane drew her close and smothered her with tender kisses, first on the cheek, then on her nose, and finally on her lips. They held each other for a long time, as calm finally returned to both aching hearts. Kate stood up slowly and pulled Shane, who followed willingly. They grabbed their towels in silence and went to the dressing room and dressed in their separate bathrooms.

They met and returned to the viewing room long enough to refill their drinks. Kate excused herself to make a phone call, and asked Shane to wait in the loveseat by the fire. Shane did as she asked, amazed that he was suddenly re-energized. He didn't feel tired in the least. He knew he wasn't dreaming, and was both sad and happy at the same time.

He wondered who Kate was calling so late, or early, as it may be. Shane had lost track of time, which he now considered his enemy. He didn't want this night to end, even with the pain he just relived. But he had obligations the next day. He had to change apartments. Details began to race through his mind as his thoughts returned to his job.

Kate returned and leapt into the loveseat, folding her legs beneath her prior to landing, and facing Shane when she landed. He smiled, "You're going to have to teach me that maneuver. I wouldn't have believed it possible, if I hadn't seen it with my own eyes."

Kate laughed, took a sip of her martini, and began again. "I know you have a lot of questions, and I have a few more answers. I hope and pray this is okay with you. I can't go back to just being your friend from afar, pining away for you. I'm not 12 anymore, and we both now have a timeline and a case to rebuild!"

The way Kate phrased the statement shocked Shane, but Kate gave him no time to respond. "Shane, your Uncle Pete not only took on the job of raising you and mentoring you through college, he was the contact for all the security that surrounded you for the first few years after your parents' murders."

Shane looked stunned. "Security, what security?" he snapped. "Patience, Shane Beckett," Kate chided, wagging her finger at him again.

"Our *guardians* were convinced that the people who killed our parents would continue to look for the missing master file and might eventually try to use us to acquire it. My grandfather was determined you and I would survive, so he hired a security team that guarded us both, full time for the next five and half years. By then, I was 18 and attending a private college, with its own high level of security, and you were out of college, and had graduated from the police academy."

"Granddad's private investigators were convinced that there had been no evidence of any attempt to gather intelligence on either of us, or make any move on us, so the security was *greatly reduced*."

Kate's emphasis on the words "greatly reduced" led Shane to begin to inquire, but Kate cut him off with a stern look, and he relented. He found "the look" adorable.

"Your surveillance team only occasionally got involved to assist you…in making sure you were safe…a few times. I mean, once you were off probation, and working alone as a police officer, you rarely needed a hand."

Kate winced as she said the phrase, "a hand." Shane bounced up as if shot from a cannon. "You mean I was followed while I was on duty?" he demanded.

"I swear I didn't know anything about it," Kate pleaded. "They kept most of this from me until four months ago." Once the words "4 months" were out, she knew she couldn't take them back, and her chagrined look gave her away even more.

"Four months ago!" Shane exclaimed. 'Are you telling me that you knew all the time I was looking at you, and you were looking at me in the café… and I didn't know who you were, and you knew who I was…and we were supposed to…and what about Pete? Well, of course, he knew all along…and your grandfather knew, and everyone *else* knew…but me?!"

Totally perplexed, Shane gave a great long sigh, and sat down in a slump of defeat. This knowledge, however, kicked his mind into overdrive.

Kate flew off the loveseat as effortlessly as she had landed, and said, "Drink?" as she refilled the martini glass from the iced pitcher." The irresistible look had returned to her face.

Shane gave her a pretend irritated look as she handed him the glass. "Well, they're small glasses," she replied in defense, successfully changing the subject.

"Does anyone in our families make any moves on their own?" Shane asked as he glared down at the floor. Kate dropped back down on the loveseat, cross-legged, as effortlessly as always, and this time with the martini in her hand. Not a drop was spilled…Shane just looked at her and groaned. He knew he was completely taken by this captivating woman he just couldn't seem to be angry with.

Shane said, "Let me ask this then. Am I the only one in the dark about everything?"

Kate smiled wide. "Why, no, Shane, we haven't told Heath anything! You know a lot more than he does!"

Shane knew Kate was playing with him now to lighten the moment. He said, "Well, that's just fine, since Heath has spent most of his last few years in prison! I suppose it was just way too difficult to bring him up to speed while he was in the pen!!"

Kate leaned close, took Shane's hand in both of hers, and said gently, but playfully, "So, you *are* upset with all of us?" Before he could respond, Kate offered, "Well, you can take it out on those mean old men, when you see them at breakfast. And remember, I had nothing to do with it until four months ago. I was just the girl who wanted another date with her dream-man," Kate smiled.

"So if you're angry with me, I guess we could go back to just being friends…if that's really what you want." Kate didn't even bother looking up at Shane. She knew for sure now where his heart was. She smiled, looking down at the loveseat, with full knowledge that Shane was unable to be angry with her for telling the truth.

Shane couldn't resist Kate's smile, but he couldn't shake the feeling he had always been one step behind. Now he knew he had been one step behind for the last 16 years! He decided he had questions that someone was surely going to answer.

He took a long, slow sip from his martini, put the glass down authoritatively, and began to state his position, when Kate said, "So where was I?" as she slyly eyed the ceiling. Once again, Shane slumped back in the cushions out-maneuvered, as Kate took control...again.

"So you'll want to know how we all got here now. And please remember, I only know what I have learned in the last few months." After a little pause, Kate said, "Well, that's not entirely true, because I did manage to force Grandfather to keep me updated on your whereabouts while I grew up and went to school. I knew you had never married, and I had all the pictures. And I was at some events that involved you and your life." Shane groaned and closed his eyes tightly.

Kate playfully repeated the wince as she waited for the reply.

Shane rolled his eyes at the ceiling as he said, "Oh, I give up." He folded his arms across his chest and waited for the explanation.

"Well, I kept pestering grandfather about you, and asking when I could see you again. He finally told me that your parents had been killed, and I guess he felt sorry for me, and gave me a picture. By the time I was 18 and off to college, I had a room full of pictures and articles, following you through high school sports, going to college, graduating from college, and going to the LAPD police academy."

"My roommates at college teased me about my shrine, dedicated to a secret lover." Kate stopped and looked down, as if remembering something painful. Her voice became softer and almost frail as she continued. "After losing my dad, you and Grandfather became my family. And later, Pete, of course," she added.

Shane unfolded his arms as he looked at the tender sadness in the face of this woman he loved more and more each moment. His heart was bursting, but he tried to remain collected, even as the martinis continued to relax him a little more than usual. He thought he really had lost track of his controlled existence. Looking at Kate, Shane saw an innocent child, who had become a woman, still concealing feelings that had been crushed by a childhood tragedy.

Shane thought how that look of hurt innocence was a chilling reminder of the small child in each of us that sometimes hurts intensely, and desperately needs love and support. Shane thought about his own loss, as words from somewhere deep inside him welled up...his mom and dad telling him they loved him each day.

"What about your mom?" he asked tenderly.

"What?" Kate looked up, as if pulled from the trance of her thoughts by a distant question. "Mom died in childbirth. That's why Dad and Granddad and I were so close, I think. I always wanted a mom, but they more than made up for it, and gave me all the love I needed...until I needed you."

Kate looked into the eyes of the man she knew was now the center of her life. Whatever came, she knew they would face it together. The two lovers stared at each other, with love in their hearts, and growing sad smiles on their faces. They had come to an unusually clear understanding of the importance and depth of their powerful new love in a very short time.

They both realized this love and need would live forever in their hearts. Each had found what they had needed to complete their souls. They could already feel that together they were more loving, more powerful, more sensual, and more complete than they could ever be alone or with someone else. They were in love that special way people were supposed to be in love.

They both leaned in at the same time, as if on cue, for a passionate and sensuous, yet gentle kiss. Kate finally pulled back and placed her free hand over Shane's lips, feeling his warm hot breath. She explained,

"I have to finish my part of the story before breakfast, and we still have to go to bed and get some sleep."

She smiled up teasingly at Shane, as he said, "Part? We have parts? Who else has parts?"

Kate kissed Shane again seductively, and again withdrew, saying matter-of-factly, "Well let's see…there is Grandfather, Pete, and then you'll want to hear from Jim and Doug among others."

Shane couldn't believe his ears. "Who the hell are Jim and Doug?" he demanded.

"They have been your bodyguards off and on for many years, and it's about time you met them and showed some appreciation, mister!" Kate said with a smile. She continued, "Besides, they have to bring you up to speed on your investigation, and what the rest of the team has uncovered."

"*My investigation?*" Shane challenged. "Now, wait just a minute, Kate," Shane said as he stiffened in response. He tried to stand to protest, but was stopped cold by Kate's firm hand on his shoulder, and the fingers from her other hand over his mouth.

"Now, which is it, buddy, are we in love and listening to our partner, or stubbornly refusing to cooperate, over some misplaced sense of macho pride?" she said, only half-teasing.

Shane marveled at how quickly Kate had mastered him. It caused him some concern, but he thought that with time, he might learn to outmaneuver her enough to keep her interested. He thought he should heed her grandfather's earlier cautionary warning. Once again he sank into the cushions.

Kate started again. "So, you became a police officer, then a narcotics detective, and finally, you were assigned to vice and intelligence. But then, you discovered the Chief of Police, and one of his captains (and closest friend) in your department, were both corrupt. You began an investigation on them that looked promising. They were into everything from theft of public money to misappropriation of drugs and evidence. You linked them to a series of high dollar residential burglaries that resulted in the theft of millions of dollars' worth of cash, guns and jewelry."

"You worked the case and turned it over to the California Department of Justice investigator, assigned to finish what you started and prepare it for prosecution. The case went nowhere, because someone in the DOJ was paid off. So you quit and went to DEA, and worked for deep cover in a task force for four years, and we all know how badly that turned out. Corruption and pay-offs once again destroyed the chance at bringing down a lot of bad people."

Shane threw his arms up and asked in dismay, "Who are you really? CIA? NSA? You know everything about my life, and how, I can't even imagine. After all, I just met you again after many years. Kate, this just isn't fair for you to know everything, and me to know nothing!" But the short protest was once again cut off by *the look* from Kate that was disarming, to say the least.

She continued, "You're in too much danger now, and we had to get more involved, Shane. If you can give me a little more time to explain, you'll understand everything."

Shane nodded in resigned agreement. He knew that the assignment had been dangerous. But this additional information already made it considerably more perilous than he could have imagined, at least in his mind. After all, he worked alone, or so he had always believed.

"First, your police career was going to die there with your nemesis, the Chief and his unholy henchmen, still in place, and then things went so badly at DEA...so Grandfather used a contact that needed someone with your talents, to uncover corruption, and you were recruited by Denver PD for that brief assignment."

"Then, there was Huntington Beach PD, where you worked undercover for a year in narcotics, without anyone in the department aware you existed, except for the Chief. After that, you worked the special assignment at Houston PD, and then the *long* assignment in Florida. Then you had the job offer from Phoenix PD and, here we are now, on assignment in Carson City. We may have all continued on the way we were, with me working in Grandfather's company and you doing your work, but then something *unusual* happened."

Shane couldn't resist the barb, "Oh, something *unusual* is going to happen in *this* story?" Kate again gave him *the look* that said it all. Shane called it the "stink eye" when anyone else did it, but Kate's unique "look" was different and conveyed so much more.

She continued, uninterrupted. "For several years, our private investigator firm has been making behind-the-scenes inquiries into the deaths of our parents, slowly building a case through the years. Our law firm, your dad's old firm, has been working with our PI firm."

"The investigation has gained ground on uncovering documents leading to the creation of the task force that AG Mayfield ordered which led to your parents' deaths. Our attorneys say we are getting close to a release of necessary information under the Freedom of Information Act, and other related motions they have filed. They learned the investigation has been closed for years, but some documents do remain."

"The constant investigation and filing of court documents has made some people nervous. There are too many of us involved now to kill or attempt to silence all of us. They can't just 'make it go away.' A few months ago, our private investigator firm received an anonymous tip that an investigation was going to be conducted into the death of California State Attorney General Scott Mayfield, who hired your father."

"Within a week, the PI office received an email, containing an attached PDF, sent by an unknown person using a library computer in Sacramento. The PDF attachment was a copy of the order to exhume Mayfield's body. The order included an affidavit, with the witness's names blacked out, stating there was new evidence that 16 years ago, Scott Mayfield had been murdered by an overdose injection of the experimental drug Cardacan. Two days later, you were offered this job by the Carson City Sheriff's Office."

Shane was filing and calculating information as fast as Kate threw it at him, trying to find the pattern that led to the answers.

She increased the pace of the information with each sentence. "Carson City Undersheriff, Brian Grant, worked at the California Department of Justice when your dad was the working with the task force. He was involved in a suspected bad shooting that resulted in the death of a suspect in another corruption case. The suspect may have been trying to surrender and cooperate with law enforcement, when Grant shot and killed him."

"Grant's father was a wealthy, influential California politician. Grant breezed through a low-key shooting review board, took an early retirement from DOJ, and with his father's help, landed a job as a patrol officer at the Carson City Sheriff's Office. Fifteen years later, he was promoted to Undersheriff, and when Sheriff Roberts hired you, he placed Brian in charge of the administration of the assignment, not knowing who you really are, or the details of the case."

Shane's mind was racing. Kate guzzled some iced lemon water from the pitcher and sipped her martini. She then resumed the story, increasing the pace to a machine-gun-like delivery.

"Pete had purchased the law practice and moved here, as you know. Grandfather and I built the home on lots we bought here about the same time Pete moved. By that time, the investigation our PI firm had completed, led us to believe that Big John Galliano had been involved in your parent's murder. They located a microfiche copy of a traffic citation Galliano received, just four blocks from the scene of your parent's accident, one day before their deaths."

"They located rental agreements, showing he rented a series of vehicles in the week leading up to the deaths of your parents, and one of those vehicles was a semi-truck with a tanker trailer. He had a CDL and was licensed to drive a truck that size. We know no body was ever found in that truck, but the coroner said that the heat of the burning gasoline could have consumed the bones." Shane winced and closed his eyes at the thought of the heat consuming his parents, too.

Kate squeezed his hand, but didn't slow her pace. "The details on the semi-truck and tanker trailer registration disappeared almost immediately from the traffic accident records at the LA County Sheriff's Office. And, sometime later, those from the California Highway Patrol accident investigation went missing also."

"In those days, the Sheriff's Office employed some Records Clerks that have been linked to biker gangs that supplied methamphetamine to Franky Magadinno in the LA area. They did favors for organized crime, as directed by their gangs, like making case files disappear."

"Franky and his father made several trips to the area just after the accident. They even attended a social fund raiser for the then LA County Sheriff, who was running for re-election." As an aside, Kate noted, "The Sheriff has been cleared of any ties to Franky, but two of the Sheriff's Office Records Clerks made sizable deposits to their checking accounts after the accident. Both of *them* died in suspicious accidents within a few months."

Kate again picked up the pace of the recap of events. It was like a sprint to the finish, and Shane wasn't about to stop her. "While you have been here on assignment, Mayfield's body has been exhumed, the autopsy completed, and the Coroner's conclusion is that he died of an overdose of Cardacan."

"Before his death, a relatively new company, known as Delta Pharmaceutical Exchange, worked in a joint venture with Regenisis Developmental Laboratories, to develop Cardacan. This new drug, Cardacan, was never released, due to the severity of common side effects. Our PI firm has just received another email containing records proving that the Cardacan development had already been cancelled by the time it was administered to the Mayfield, so he could *not* have been a test subject or under a doctor's care. In addition, Mayfield's family has released medical records showing that he had no known heart-related disorder."

Kate had become increasingly excited as she got to the guts of the investigation, and Shane was impressed with her command of the facts of the case. He smiled in admiration, as she continued.

"The night you prepared to make entry into the Magadinno compound, your back-up surveillance team, provided by us, observed a car park on the far side of the compound, away from your line of sight. A subject exited the car, wearing all black clothing, a balaclava, and a black hooded sweatshirt. While you were inside the compound… and I was biting my nails, by the way…" Kate stopped to emphasize to Shane in a glare, that she thought the entry was too dangerous.

Shane understood the implied meaning, nodded, and Kate continued. "The unknown subject later jogged to your car and left a note on your windshield. He then jogged off, on foot, out of sight. He knew your car, Shane!" Kate glared again.

Shane was completely fascinated by Kate's performance. He thought this look of pretend anger was even more entertaining than the last one. This expression was also combined with an eye flash that emphasized Kate's deep emerald-green eyes. Shane gazed into Kate's eyes, grinning like a love-struck teen. He thought it possible that the martinis had completely destroyed his inhibitions.

Noticing his silly grin, Kate quipped sharply, "Are you even listening? And by the way, I know you're wondering, the car was a Reno 'reported stolen' with dealer paper plates. The jogger never returned to it so our team made an anonymous call to CCSO the next day. When the responding deputy ran the VIN and learned the vehicle was stolen, CSI responded to process the car. There were no latent fingerprints or any other evidence recovered."

Shane managed to quickly toss in, "Of course not," which had no effect on Kate.

She picked up her narrative again. "That night, fifty minutes after you left, Big John Galliano was murdered by a single gunshot wound to the head. We only had a two-man team left on the house, making sure you weren't followed, and they weren't in position to see the shooter, so we have no knowledge of the suspect's identity or a motive for the hit."

Shane had to know, and said almost mockingly, "Where was the *rest of my team?*"

Kate smiled, "They put you to bed. That's surveillance-talk for 'followed you home' if you didn't know already," she teased.

Shane asked quickly before she could start again, "So you knew that I was injured in the jump off the balcony?"

As fast as lightening, Kate slugged him in the shoulder with a closed fist that rocked him, as she yelled, "No. We only knew you made a trip to Minden Urgent Care. But you walked in and out under your own power. And don't do something that crazy again, now that you have me! Our relationship demands you act responsibly and safely! Jumping off balconies, at night, in the rain, in to trees, is not responsible in my book!" Kate shook her head in disapproval.

She continued in a normal tone, as Shane grinned, "And if you're wondering, your team only waits about thirty minutes at your house once you're home. It seems your home patterns are fairly predictable, and the team never has to follow you out again, once you come home that late. By the way, Mr. Beckett, you can thank your lucky stars you weren't dating anyone and bringing them home." Kate shot Shane *the look* again, and he knew he would never bring anyone else home, wherever home was to be.

Shane shrugged and gave Kate a boyish look. "Never, of course," he smiled sheepishly. He rubbed his shoulder and winced, realizing that Kate's punch had quite a bit of force behind it.

"Shortly after you were hired here in Carson City, Grandfather and Pete realized this was this case you were hired to investigate. It took us a week to get your back-up team assembled, equipped and settled here. Some of them are the guards in the garage you saw when we arrived. The rest I hope you didn't see, or the security isn't quite as good as we think."

Kate waited for Shane's honest assessment. "I'm good, and no one is perfect, but I think these guys are pretty damn good. I knew I was being watched when we arrived here, but I had no idea from where. More importantly, I never knew I was being followed at work, and I use counter surveillance techniques."

Kate reassured Shane. "They used a micro transmitter implanted in your car. You also have one in your belt, thanks to Uncle Pete, so it's not difficult for them to hang back out of sight and never lose you. Plus, we rented a house near the Magadinno compound, so our team wouldn't draw any attention to you. If you're wondering, Lee says you're the best he's ever seen, at what you do."

Shane figured he had to ask, "And Lee is?"

Kate couldn't resist a sly smile. "He is the owner of our Private Investigator Company, and has been in charge of your protection teams for the last 16 years. He was one of dad's friends, and he and Grandfather have become close since our parents' deaths."

Seizing the opportunity at the first observed discrepancy in Kate's story, Shane said, "Sixteen years, I thought it was five and a half years?"

Kate shook her head disapprovingly and teased, "Shane Beckett, you really must pay closer attention. I said that we had *full time* surveillance *teams* for five and a half years. After that, we just had one part-time team each, until four months ago. I'm really surprised you missed that. Maybe you aren't as good as Lee thinks after all!"

Kate stood up and walked to a cabinet in the viewing room. She pressed on the wood panel, released it quickly and it instantly sprung open, revealing a hidden refrigerator. Kate opened the door, reached in and retrieved a cold dish, lavishly covered with peeled cooked shrimp, surrounding a boat of spicy cocktail sauce. She also removed a dish that contained ultra-thin crackers, shredded lobster, and a matching boat laden with gourmet roasted pepper and olive lobster sauce, and assorted cheeses.

"Pete said you liked lobster and I *love* shrimp, so Jesse prepared this especially for you. You'll meet him at breakfast."

"Shane inquired, somewhat hesitantly, "And Jesse is the chef?"

Kate laughed, "Oh, no, he's Lee's surveillance equipment and communication expert, but he's a great frustrated amateur chef, and constantly surprises us with special treats like this."

Shane shrugged, as if the answer was expected, "Of course he does."

Kate returned to the loveseat, knowing that Shane had followed every movement of her body to the refrigerator and back with his eyes. As she smiled and leaned over him, her perfectly formed full breasts stretched the robe to its limit, allowing Shane a glimpse of several inches of gorgeous cleavage.

Kate smiled, and said, "Like something you see?" as she presented him with the plates.

Shane grinned, and answered, "Yes, and the food looks great, too."

Kate loved that Shane couldn't keep his eyes off of her. She appreciated his attention more than he knew, having dreamed and fantasized about him for so many years.

They took a break from the recap of their lives since the tragic murders, and ate and talked about something they really cared more about now, each other. They took turns asking about favorite colors, movies, music, food and hobbies. Then they turned to each other's turn-offs, pet peeves and dislikes. They were really getting to know each other, and they were falling more deeply in love with each passing moment. Each of them was amazed at how well they fit with the other, and how exciting the other was to them.

Shane couldn't help but notice that Kate devoured the shrimp. He thought back to the shy girl with braces who made a fuss about eating shrimp 16 years ago.

Kate seemed already able to read Shane's thoughts, and as he was wondering, she confided, "I've always liked shrimp. I just didn't want you to see me with shrimp parts stuck in my braces. You would have never really noticed me then!" They both laughed.

They shared secrets and dreams for at least an hour, and when the food was all gone and the plates were on the coffee table, Kate walked to the fire and put another log on the embers. She bent over and swiped her hands over the log bin to remove any wood dust. Shane was again instantly transfixed, just watching Kate move. He watched every movement, as if relishing a flowing masterpiece. He began to feel the growing warmth between his legs, as Kate turned to meet his eyes. She stared at this man she now loved, and wondered if he could really be this wonderful.

"You may not realize it, Shane, but while you were pining away over me at the café, I was doing the same for you. I think I always knew that my girlish crush on you had to be explored someday. I secretly hoped and dreamed it would end up this way, with us falling madly in love, and together forever. We share a special bond that began with our parent's friendship, and tied our families together with their murders. I couldn't wait to see you every day in the café. My biggest dilemma was what to wear to keep you watching, waiting and wanting. What was your favorite outfit?"

Shane looked at her and grinned, "You have to ask?"

Kate returned a knowing smile, and said, "I guess I'm going to be in high heel sandals and stockings on a regular basis."

Shane let out a relieved laugh as he felt the red flush of embarrassment that gave him away. "If you don't mind, that would be fine with me!"

Kate said quickly, "Don't ever stop wanting me, Shane. You just remember that I've been fantasizing about you since I was 12 years old. I wore that outfit just for you, hoping it would drive you crazy."

Shane confided, "It worked. I had to leave the café or die for lack of oxygen. When I got home, I had to work out twice and take a cold shower. And then I dreamed about making love to you. But the dream wasn't even close to the real thing."

Kate made her flying, cross-legged entrance onto the loveseat once more, and facing Shane, grabbed him by the back of the head and drew her to him. They kissed and fondled each other until the robe could not conceal Shane's' arousal, and then they departed for Kate's room.

When they arrived at the bed, the new lovers repeated the events of earlier in the evening. They attained new heights of arousal and release they both previously thought impossible. Each secretly feared this great love might be too good to be true, and each committed silently they would do everything in their power to love the other as completely as they could, so they would remain together for the rest of their lives.

They whispered, "I love you" many times. They asked each other new lovers' questions for another hour. Too tired now to take another shower, they fell asleep slowly, still in each other's arms, holding on tight, afraid to let go.

The alarm went off as programmed six hours later, having affording just enough sleep to replenish their bodies, but allowing enough time for them to shower and dress for breakfast. Shane silenced the alarm with a touch allowing Kate to sleep a few more minutes. Shane had awakened still holding Kate in his arms just before the alarm sounded and smiled realizing she was holding on to him just as tight.

He didn't move his body, and soon lost himself in the day dreams of watching his new love sleep. He traced over the parts of her face and neck he could see with his eyes. Once again he drank in Kate's incredible beauty. He gently stroked her dark brownish-red, flowing locks of hair, exposed her ear and kissed her cheek and lips so softly she didn't awaken. Love and commitment swelled inside his soul.

He looked down at the exposed breast he could see, and admired its firm perfectly formed shape. He wondered if God had personally sculpted the details, creating him a full-sized incredibly shaped masterpiece, covered with sumptuous flawless skin. Kate's large nipple was erect and inviting, even as she slept.

Shane resisted the urge to smother it in passionate wet kisses and make love to his beauty in the minutes before they had to rise. In the end, he remained motionless, in awe of how much his life had changed in 24 hours. He thanked God Almighty for these extraordinary events. He said a long silent prayer as he touched Kate's temple, in the ancient way of blessing a loved one, his parents had taught him as a child.

As he finished, the alarm sounded again and Kate opened her eyes. Shane was immediately lost in her smile. He gazed into her sleepy green eyes as they lit up in the golden refracted light the skylight admitted. There was a slight hint of blue in Kate's eyes, courtesy of the streaming sunlight.

Before he knew it, Kate's lips were pressing against his and her tongue was in his mouth, as she greeted him as new lovers do. They kissed for several minutes and reluctantly pulled themselves apart to take their showers and get ready for the scheduled breakfast meeting.

Shane discovered that he had three changes of new clothing already hanging in "his side" of Kate's closet. She explained that, even if they hadn't got together, the plan was for Shane to move from his apartment into the O'Leary house where it was safer, due to all the events of the last four months that culminated in Big John's murder.

Shane finished dressing and anxiously asked Kate if he looked all right. She fixed the back of his shirt collar, enjoying being needed for such a small task, and assured him he was perfect.

As they strolled down the hall, hand-in-hand, Shane suddenly stopped. "What do I tell your grandfather? He'll know I spent the night."

Kate loved the boyish look on Shane's face, and the concern for her grandfather she heard in his voice. "Shane, have you noticed I'm all grown up now?" She playfully placed his hand on her breast and kissed him deeply.

Shane said more assertively, "Kate, what about your grandfather?"

Kate relented. "Grandfather has been one of your biggest fans since he started to know you. We even had a special seat behind your Uncle Pete at your graduations from college and the police academy. He was very impressed that you were co-valedictorian at the academy, by the way."

Shane pleaded, "Kate!"

She assured him, "Do you remember what grandfather's caution and advice was for you last night?" Shane remembered and smiled as they walked downstairs, still holding hands.

When they arrived at the dining room, there were far more people present than Shane had been prepared meet. In addition to Kate's grandfather, Pete, and Lee Sprague (the owner of the security company and PI firm), there were six bodyguards including Jim and Doug, 14 surveillance team members, Delores from last night, an accountant named Spencer Pinetta, and an assortment of staff and grounds keepers.

Walter introduced Shane to everyone, and apologized to him, in his elegant manner, that everyone already knew Shane. After all the pleasantries were completed, seven remained for breakfast. The others had already eaten and were not needed for the meeting that followed.

Walter and Pete took turns explaining that three members of the surveillance team would go to Shane's apartment and clear it out, while two other members would conduct surveillance from the rented house near the Magadinno compound.

Pete finally chuckled, "You won't be going to work today, my boy. We have too much to do here now."

Shane and Kate sat together and held hands through most of breakfast, much to the delight of Kate's grandfather and Pete, neither of whom could stop beaming wide smiles of approval.

After breakfast, the group adjourned to a meeting room complete with audiovisual aids. The meeting began with each remaining surveillance and bodyguard shift supervisor recapping his team's observations and intelligence, gleaned from years of working the death investigation of Kate's dad and Shane's parents. The recap culminated with the information that Shane's "back-up" team had learned while shadowing his movements with the Magadinnos.

Once the entire 16-½ year recap was presented and discussed at length, Lee narrated current photos and surveillance video, until everyone was familiar with all the players and had shared information with Shane, and then invited Shane to bring everyone up to speed on what he had learned. He complied immediately.

"With your permission Shane, this will no longer be a one-man operation," Walter declared.

Shane couldn't help but add, with playful sarcasm, "Not that it ever really *was* a one- man operation." He then added quickly, "And I appreciate it being a *team* effort more than you know! Thank you all." He gave everyone a genuine smile.

Then Lee left with the other members of his team, leaving the families together for an intimate chat. The family afforded Shane a lengthy question and answer period to become comfortable with all that he had learned.

Pete and Walter sat, smiling as if they had swallowed all the canaries that lived in the state, as they glanced back and forth from one another to Shane and Kate. Shane sat quietly, still holding on tight to his lover's hand, eyes fixed on the table cloth, trying to decipher all the details.

Finally Pete said, "Shane, I didn't see any reason to speculate to you on our theories of what happened to your parents, until this last development. I wanted you to live life, not constantly chasing after ghosts or looking over your shoulder for assassins. Walter and I tried to see that happen for both you and Kate. It just didn't end that way. You landed smack in the middle of it all over again. I'm so sorry this happened."

Shane smiled at both his guardians and reassured them, "From what I heard last night, you two probably saved both of our lives." He glanced lovingly at Kate. "I thank you for all you did for both of us. But, if this last development had not happened, I question whether I would ever have really met Kate."

Shane locked eyes with his beloved Kate, and the two stared intently into each other's eyes until Shane recalled they had company. Somewhat embarrassed, he said, "Now I can't imagine my life without knowing Kate."

Pete and Walter laughed almost uncontrollably as they told Shane about the reports they had received from Kate after his daily café meetings. Even Shane had to laugh.

The two Cheshire cats across the room beamed with smiles so wide that finally everyone, looking from one to the other, was laughing.

Walter couldn't resist adding, "I just love it when my prayers are answered. If all goes well, you two should have a long extraordinary life together."

Shane looked at Walter and Pete in earnest, and said, "I would love for exactly that to happen someday, if Kate would. I mean…I can't support Kate in this kind of lifestyle, with the security she needs. I just don't see how it could work. I couldn't ask her to take the chance of a life without the safety you can provide. I have to take these jobs and move around the country, you know."

Kate immediately scolded Shane, saying, "Shane Beckett, you're not getting off the hook that easily. Don't I have something to say about this after all these years of waiting for you to notice me? If we decide to be together, I have some income and savings, too, you know. At least you can relax while we *date* and get to know each other a little, without worrying how to fund the rest of our lives. We don't need to be wealthy, we just need to be happy and in love."

Shane's face took on a serious look, as he continued. "I wouldn't have it any other way. You know I have fallen in love with you. It's just that I want you safe and protected forever, and that takes money, and I don't have it. I didn't mean we couldn't find a way, dear," Shane chided back smiling.

Before Shane could protest any further, Pete said, "Walter, why don't you tell the young man about his money."

Caught completely off-guard, Shane looked at Pete and said, "What money?"

Walter stood up and walked toward Shane. "Well now, Shane, my boy, it seems that your parents left a very sizable life insurance policy for you. In addition to that, Pete eventually sold your family home and entrusted all the money left in the estate to my financial manager, Spencer, here." Walter O'Leary placed a hand on Spencer's shoulder, and continued, while Spencer adopted the Cheshire cat grin.

"You were making your own way in life, and we thought it best that your money be grown to a point to give you real options you may wish to exercise, at some point in life. Your parent's trust named Pete as executor. Your parents also instructed Pete to transfer your investments to you, when he believed you *needed* access to them, and then in the amounts he believed you needed at the time, until you were 45 years old, at which time all the remaining funds would be transferred and placed in your control."

"You never really needed anything your work income couldn't provide. We took care of your security detail. Pete and I have made some modest additions to your investments over the years, but Spencer here has the information you seek. I think this is maybe a good time for Pete and Kate and I to leave you alone with Spencer. We have asked him to bring you up-to-date on your investments.

Pete stood up with Walter to leave the room, but Shane held on tight to Kate's hand and she knew not to move.

"Please wait," Shane asked. "Walter, you and Pete have been there for me when I didn't even realize it. Now I want to be with Kate, and for Kate and me to be there for each other, and for both of you. It seems to me that all the cards need to be laid out on the table. We seem to be the family we all need and want. I'd like you and Pete to stay with Kate and I while we talk to Spencer."

Walter and Pete immediately reclaimed their seats. Walter exclaimed, "Marvelous, even more than I had hoped for, Kate. This truly is the exceptional man we always thought he was." Turning to Kate, Walter added, pretending to be serious, "You'd better not screw this up, my dear, or I may just keep him, rather than you." With that, everyone laughed.

Finally Spencer had the floor, and while they sipped coffee, he went through a list of investments that Shane could barely believe belonged to him. Rounding off the numbers, and with recent estimates of growth not yet recorded for the quarter, Shane had amassed close to $17,000,000 dollars in the 16-½ years since his parents died.

He sat back in shock and disbelief. "And just how *little* did you both add in these *modest* additions over the years?" he said, with a restrained laugh, while looking from Walter to Pete.

They both grinned, and said in unison, "Just a little here and there," bringing laughter from all at the table.

"But, your dad's law firm also added a sizable sum from another insurance policy the firm maintained for its partners. And some investment stocks, that split and doubled ten to fifteen times in those years, also helped immensely, thanks to Spencer" Pete added.

"This is a lot to take in all at once, and I want to thank you, Spencer, for your diligent work," Shane said.

"Now, that's not including the real estate investments," Spencer added.

Shane looked at Spencer in disbelief, and asked, "Real estate investments? I have real estate investments? When did I make real estate investments?"

Kate squeezed Shane's hand and nodded, as he looked from her to Spencer for an explanation.

Spencer explained how the family believed that, due to the circumstances of both family murders, all real estate holdings should be held in the names of both the O'Leary's, Shane and Pete, as equal partners in LLC's. The thought being, that this would discourage any attempts on their lives for profit or revenge, while shielding the knowledge of their wealth from the general public.

Spencer added that once the families became intertwined, Walter demanded this procedure for all his future investments. Through the years, the families had grown so close, they considered themselves one family, and there were no other heirs to consider. Eventually Walter and Pete instructed family attorneys that all real estate holdings, corporate holdings, and LLCs be reconfigured or transferred to the four partners, being Shane, Pete, Walter and Kate.

"Your dad had a partnership in a house his firm owned at the beach. We purchased that house in the name of the first LLC that was set up to leave everything to you and Kate, and the idea just grew from there," explained Pete.

Spencer interrupted, "The total worth of just *your* share of real estate, alone, last year was estimated at a little more than $58,000,000, but that's likely increased significantly in the past six months." Shane was speechless. He looked at Kate, who nodded in agreement.

"By the way, I love staying as a guest at your Harbor Island home. It is *truly* private and spectacular. You should visit it sometime," Spencer added, with the Cheshire cat grin.

With that, Spencer stood up, and said, "I'll be leaving now to go back to the grind. Tough bosses to work for, you know," he said, pointing to Walter and Pete. "Pete, please let me know if you want Shane to start signing the deeds, and how we want to handle the taxes in future years. Nice to finally meet you in person, Shane."

Shane stood up. Spencer shook Pete's hand, long and hard, before he left.

Shane sat down in a trance. After a lengthy silence, Shane looked at Kate and they both smiled.

"No money excuses, now, Mr. Beckett," Kate taunted.

Shane grinned, and confided, "All my life, after my parents' deaths, I thought I was surrounded by acquaintances, with few family and friends to lean on. It was always just me, Pete, and for a time, Claire and Heath. I was so wrong."

Walter walked over and took Shane by the hand, saying, "Acquaintances are always there when they need you. Friends are always there when you need them. *My* friend, Lee Cunningham, told me that many years ago, and I have found it always so true. Our family tried to do what *family* should always do, be your best friend when you needed us. And now, my boy, we are complete, family and friends for life."

With that, Walter gave Shane a hug, and asked, "Is there anything else we can do for you right now, Shane?"

Without hesitation, Shane asked, slyly, "Just one thing. From now on, can I know what my family's plans are, so I can be prepared to be a part of them?" They all broke out in laughter.

Walter and Pete filled their coffee cups, and left in a serious discussion about some plan they were working on, and Kate and Shane stood there in wonderment, fingers interlaced, and their minds racing about future possibilities.

5

*"The success or failure of fairness and justice in any society
is dependent on the goals and ambitions of those in charge."*
(Lee Parley Cunningham)

Lee Sprague popped his head back in the door. "Your team is at your apartment, Shane. They'll recover all your belongings, and clean out the apartment. The plan is to move your work tools to a desk we set up for you at our office here, if that's ok. Lana will attend to your personal effects and clothing. Anything special we need to retrieve?"

Shane thought for a moment as he considered Lee's request, and said, "The only hidden items are two waterproof USB memory sticks taped to the top of the ceiling fan in the living room."

Shane looked at Lee and smiled, "You can't have too many back-ups, you know."

Lee returned the grin. "Good place." He closed the door.

Kate walked Shane to a huge picture window, overlooking a space that would be a spectacular garden in the late spring or summer. She gazed hard at the cold landscape, as if trying to draw strength from its stark April beauty.

"Shane, I want this to be right for both of us. I want you to be safe, so we can have a chance at a real future together. I don't want to pressure you." She stopped, her eyes troubled and searching.

Shane placed his fingertips on Kate's cheeks, and ran the back of two fingers down to her voluptuous lips. "What is it, Kate?"

Kate released a sigh. "I don't want it to appear to you that I, or we, have taken over your life. We've made some plans to help insure your safety. I made some plans, because I …I'm falling in love with you. And then, there is tomorrow, it's going to be Friday. We must prepare for that, whatever *that* is. Everyone is concerned that you know *you* still run your investigation, even if the *team* is involved to assist."

Shane sighed, "I appreciate the concern, Kate, but it seems there has been a *team* involved in both of our lives for a long time. That won't be an issue. I hated the apartment anyway. It's *very lonely* there," Shane emphasized, as he encouraged a smile from Kate.

"And I believed, almost from the start, that this assignment should be run as a task force. I welcome having other professionals to work with, watching my back, and thinking of things I missed. I need other people's perspectives. This is a complex situation. It's no longer just an investigation into drugs, murders, corruption and missing people. It's about our families' murders *and* our future safety. And to be totally honest, this case is way too big and complex for one man…maybe even for one task force."

The look of concern had not left Kate's face. "That's not what's worrying you, is it Kate? I trust you," Shane encouraged. "What is it?" Kate looked down. "Please, talk to me," Shane pleaded.

Kate continued looking down as Shane's tension grew. The knot of anxious uncertainty that new lovers feel made its presence known in his gut. As much as he loved the newness, he already looked forward to the confidence in a relationship that only time builds.

Kate looked directly into Shane's warm golden brown eyes. She had always thought they were wonderful eyes, enticing, and warm. Her own eyes began to glisten, as she held back tears of fear. Kate's eyes were riveted to Shane's. She was unable to look away, or break the lock she had begun on them.

She finally found strength, compassion and love in the eyes staring back at her. She swallowed hard.

"It's only been one day, Shane, and yet I know I have loved you for so long. Will you move in with me, to *our* room? I'll understand if you think it's too soon. Most people would…think it's too soon, I mean. I just need you, and want you, but I also want it to be your decision, too. Not something I force. I want you to need this too, as much as I do."

Shane smiled, as he once again touched the luscious troubled lips he longed to kiss. "Kate, I don't think I could even sleep without you anymore. I don't want to leave the room you're in or even stop holding your hand. I can't imagine not seeing you in the bedroom I walk into, or not knowing where you are 24 hours a day. I want to be side-by-side with you always."

Kate didn't look convinced. Shane said, "Before, when I hesitated, I was just worried about your grandfather's reaction, and how it would look to everyone else. There are so many people here. They don't all *really* know me. But they all do know and love you and your grandfather. I want it to look right for them, too."

Kate pressed herself into Shane, and held on to him tightly. "Everyone will be thrilled we're together. But even if they're not, it's the right thing for us, and the right time…and that's what's important." Shane nodded in agreement.

When the moment broke, Kate took Shane on a tour of the rest of the house, guesthouses and the grounds. She introduced Shane to staff members he had not yet met, and made sure he was familiar with everyone who should be on the property.

Two hours later Lana returned with Shane's belongings and clothes, checked with Kate and Shane, and then took everything to Kate's room. The surveillance team placed Shane's work tools, lap top, and back-up drives at his desk in the main house game room. The entire area had been converted into a meeting room and open-bay desk space. The teams agreed to have a 3:30 briefing.

Technicians took over the task of monitoring the cameras, microphones and cell phone Shane had placed at the Magadinno compound. They also made another back-up copy of the intelligence Shane had acquired, and began merging it with their own intelligence. They searched for any discrepancies, and began the work of producing a combined master file.

Shane marveled at the speed, organization and dedication with which the team worked. He felt a great burden begin to lift from his shoulders. This was a good change for the investigation, especially after Big John's murder.

Shane was left with Kate for some time off, as the rest of the team got everything ready. It was his first real day off in more than a week, and his body and mind needed the "R-and-R." For the first time, the job stress seemed to leave him, and he and Kate settled into easy low-key conversation in a family room. They stroked each other's hands, and interlocked their fingers as they talked. They soon found they were more comfortable, and more at ease in their own skins, when they were together, than when they were apart.

Shane also discovered he was incredibly hungry. "I should have eaten more breakfast, Kate, but I didn't want to let go of your hand," he confided with a grin.

Kate laughed as she admitted she was hungry too, for the same reason. They walked to the kitchen hand-in-hand. Everyone they passed seemed to already know they were 'together,' and everyone seemed pleased. Only approving faces greeted them. Shane couldn't stop thinking how much his life had changed for the better with Kate. Even this soon he knew he would never want to go back to a life without her. They walked into a busy kitchen.

"Ready for another masterpiece?" Jesse asked, as he stood proudly over another of his creations.

Jesse had layered shredded smoked salmon onto thin slices of his freshly baked bread, riddled with baked-in nuts and seeds, and lathered with wasabi mayo. To this he added generous shavings of avocado, which he garnished with sprouts and a hint of diced red onion. Next he sprinkled on a layer of chopped roasted pine nuts. Finally, he covered this half with lettuce, added his secret seasoning, dotted the pile with thinly sliced cherry tomatoes, and married the two halves to create a sandwich phenomenon that begged for consumption.

There were several platters of the sandwiches, and he promptly gave a plate with two to Kate and Shane, before he wheeled the remainder out on a stainless steel cart toward the task force room.

"Enjoy! We're having my slow-smoked mesquite prime rib, salad, and twice baked potatoes tonight at 7:30, if you can make it," Jesse called over his shoulder, with a wave. "And you won't want to miss dessert!"

Shane and Kate sat and ate in the kitchen at a small table normally occupied by staff, as others prepped side dishes for the night's dinner. Kate produced a cold, Eastern Oregon brewery IPA from one of the refrigerators. They inhaled the sandwiches, which they washed down with the beer. The flavors of the rich homemade bread, nuts, salmon, tomatoes, mayo and spices combined to create an incredible dining experience for Shane, who rarely made more than a tuna fish sandwich for himself during a workday.

Kate explained, "The IPA is from Terminal Gravity in Enterprise, Oregon. We have a ranch in Wallowa County, and we always bring cases of the locally brewed beer home after we visit. The county is one of my favorite places in the late spring, summer and early fall. I hope we get to spend a lot of time there together."

Kate began filling Shane in on the family ranch, Wallowa Lake, the artist community of Joseph, and the layout of the rest of the rugged, picturesque area. She spoke with shining, excited eyes of the bald and golden eagles, elk and deer you could see while hiking or driving in the rural country. She regaled him with tales of the times she had spent on horseback at the ranch. She described elk herds in the hundreds, huge mule and whitetail deer populations, and sunsets crowning the Eagle Cap Wilderness Area's snow-capped peaks.

The slightly bitter IPA complemented the sandwiches perfectly, and they both had a second microbrew as Kate talked. Shane appreciated a woman who was comfortable enough to eat in front of him and thoroughly enjoy her food and drink.

Shane watched Kate as they ate, and was surprised that he found even the way she ate to be sexy. He liked everything about Kate. A weight of loss, grief and loneliness had been lifted from his body, mind and soul. He was happy that each minute he was falling more deeply in love with this wonderful, exciting, intelligent woman.

Shane stared at Kate. Kate's long, red fingernails beckoned to Shane to be nibbled on, even while holding a sandwich. Shane stood up quickly to redirect his passionate thoughts. The sight of Kate doing the simplest act boiled his blood with sexual desire.

As if reading his mind, Kate said, flirtatiously, "We need a few fuel breaks to keep our strength up." She smiled up at Shane, her velvety skin taking on a soft blush. The lovers were immediately lost in love-talk once again, as they dreamed about moments of love and passion the future promised…and the time, precious time, they would have to explore life together.

The 3:30 briefing came all too soon, and the "war room" (as Walter called it) was packed. Jesse outlined details from Shane's computer file his techs had managed to retrieve, compile and compare against their own intelligence. Jesse's team had also completed an augmented photo array of the Magadinno crime family and known associates, with Franky at the top of his pyramid, and known associates split off into their own crime family or cartel pyramids. By the time the team had added vehicle and compound photos, and merged their intelligence with Shane's, the array took up an entire wall in the massive workroom. Shane was more than impressed.

Shane's cell phone vibrated as a call came in. He made excuses to Sheriff Roberts to change the meet to the following Friday. He told him he had no new information, and needed to rest his leg, which he said had become infected. The change in plans seemed to surprise Roberts, and he insisted Shane make contact with the doctor who had seen him, to treat any infection, and report to him quickly. Shane promised he would do so. When he hung up, Shane gave Jesse the physician's card, and Jesse began a background check on pretty, young Dr. Leslie Graham.

The team then began discussions about the unknown subject who placed the note on Shane's car. No one had an acceptable theory about what any Friday would bring, and no one had found a clue to the subject's identity. The consensus was that Shane should lay low on Fridays, until they discovered something, and the team would immediately increase security at the O'Leary estate, and surveillance from the house near the Magadinno compound. Lee also requested that Shane, Kate, Walter and Pete not leave the estate on Fridays for now. They would wait to see what was going to happen this first Friday, if anything, and then modify the plan going forward.

Lee then ordered round-the clock" counter surveillance in a 1-mile radius around the estate, and handed out shift assignments. Shane suggested Lee also maintain a rolling surveillance on all Magadinno personnel who left the compound on Fridays.

Walter and Pete requested a new surveillance team be added to track Undersheriff Brian Grant, and Shane quickly agreed. The newly discovered information on Grant had been deeply troubling him. Lee made additional surveillance assignments to handle the tasks. The team was now stretched very thin.

When the meeting ended, Lee began planning all the next day operational details for the teams, and Shane spent an hour getting to know his back-up team and his bodyguards. Kate left with Walter, Pete, and their own team, to go to Pete's house and retrieve some things Pete would need for his stay at the estate, starting tonight. They decided to retrieve Pete's computer files of the investigation that were locked in his safe. It was only Thursday, but everyone was nervous, and no one wanted any mistakes.

Shane felt conspicuously out of place in the house, without Kate. He walked to the garage and talked with some guards in the attached guardhouse, making himself familiar with their equipment and tasks. He retraced an earlier tour of the grounds, and then walked through the large house once again to make sure he had every door and window down in his mind. He then found himself back down in the garage before Kate had returned.

Next he surveyed all the cars in the structure, finding two classic Jaguar XKE's and a very nicely restored 1960 Ford pickup. But the car that brought back memories was a candy-apple red, 1965 Ford Thunderbird convertible. The car was also a classic, but it brought back visions of very special times to Shane. He couldn't resist the urge to sit in it, and reminisce being with his dad in *his* old T-Bird convertible.

Shane ran his hand over the upholstery, caressed the steering wheel, and pressed himself into the seat, trying to remember driving with his dad in a similar car many years ago. The car seemed strangely familiar. He opened the glove box. To his surprise he found an old bible that looked like his old family bible. He removed the book and slowly opened the faded cover. Then he saw it. The bible was a gift from his grandmother to his own father. Shane read, "Patrick Shane Beckett."

Shane read the name again aloud, and added, "This can't be." He turned the page and saw his family tree with each name filled in by his mother, the way families of that era had done for generations. Shane grabbed for documents resting beneath the bible, and found a current Minnesota State vehicle registration in his own name.

He sprang out of the vehicle and checked the license plates. They matched the registration. Shane read the older registrations, placed in the plastic sleeve behind the most current one, and found his father's name. This really was his dad's old car. Shane could only stare at the car, and wonder how and when all this happened, and what more secrets about his family he would eventually discover.

"And why Minnesota?" Shane said aloud, to himself.

∽

Pete's voice came from the doorway to his right. "Because it's a hell of a long way from California and Nevada…and the Magadinno crime family."

Shane turned to find Pete grinning at him. "Amazing isn't it? It's just the way you remember it, only better. Everything we could find and collect, we bought and saved to put together with the old car, so it would be as original and personal for you as possible."

"Your dad left instructions to give it to you when the time was right. I thought you would like to have it to share with your own family someday and relive some of the good memories with your *own* kids. I remember, so many times, watching you and your dad take off, just to drive anywhere in this old car."

"You both loved this car so much, and you loved your time riding in it together. I told Walter about the car, as he was learning about our family and I was learning about his. He tracked down a specialist in T-Bird restoration, and we had it completely restored. I hope you don't spoil the surprise. He plans on us making a presentation of it to you when the time is right."

Shane looked at Pete in disbelief. "But where has it been all this time?"

"Well, that's a simple question, with a complex answer. Your dad had given me some instructions in case of both his and your mother's deaths. He knew they were both in grave danger. He asked that I move the car to my storage unit in Encino, California. It was a full garage-size unit where I stored some *sensitive* and older case files I didn't want in my office."

"Walter eventually had the car shipped to the restoration company in Wisconsin. That process took almost nine months. When it was done, we didn't want to ship it back and title it in California or Nevada, where your name, on your dad's old car, could be easily discovered by some biker bitch working in DMV on Franky's payroll."

Pete's frankness shocked Shane briefly, as he had rarely heard Pete, the consummate gentleman, use any vulgarity or colorful language.

Pete continued. "Walter had a home and guesthouse near Leech Lake in Minnesota, with a private airstrip on some acreage. Walter and I spent a lot of time there, just fishing and talking, when we first started getting close, and you were in college. Do you remember calling me back east when you were in school?"

Shane answered, laughing, "I do. And I always wondered who was keeping you back east so much."

Pete continued, "Claire loved it on the lakes in the summer. She would spend hours each day reading, while Walter and I fished, travelling to some of the lakes nearby. There are more than 4500 lakes in the State, you know. She had well-deserved vacations, while Walter and I became inseparable in those days."

"That's where Walter came up with the plan to create the LLCs with himself, Claire and I, as full partners that would eventually transfer ownership of businesses and property to you kids. Once he seized on the idea, there was no stopping him. Walter is a business *machine* when he wants to be, and he isn't used to taking 'no' or 'you can't' for an answer."

"After the car was restored, we had it moved to the home in Minnesota, where it was stored in the garage. Walter and I had it shipped here for you a few weeks ago, after it was registered to you in Minnesota."

Shane understood Pete's words, but needed more information in order to be comfortable with this turn in his life. "Why would a total stranger do all this for us? It's hard to believe, Pete."

Pete laughed. "Total stranger! For you, this is all an overnight development, so he is a total stranger. For Walter and me, this relationship was born more than 12 years ago, and developed slowly, aging like a fine wine. You only see the end product, not the life the product led to get here now. And, there is one other important detail you need to think about, Shane." Pete's face turned serious.

"Walter lost his only son, Kate's father, just as you lost both your parents. You need to realize that when he came to me, and we started the idea of tracking down our families' killers, we spent more than just a great deal of time together. We became obsessed with our two families, and keeping them safe. The bonds grew incredibly strong between all of us. You just didn't see what had happened, even though it involved you."

"Walter is, perhaps, the most unassuming, genuine soul I have ever met. He thinks of you as a grandson. He thinks of me as a son. His life for the last 12 years has been devoted to our two families, which have become *one* in his mind."

"The money, the protection, the planning is all great, but his only true love is the people he cares for. That's pretty much wrapped up in you and me and Kate, now that Claire is gone. We are all he lives for. The money from the businesses and investments just makes it all work."

"And one other thing, Shane, you need to know that I feel the same love for Walter and Kate. They *are* my family, just as you *are* my *son*." Pete looked deadly serious and Shane knew to not question any of this family's motives any further.

"What about Heath? How does he fit in?" Shane's eyes searched for an answer, but Pete, uncharacteristically, dodged both the answer and Shane's gaze.

Pete avoided the question, saying, "Maybe another time we can travel down that road, but not now. There is too much at stake right now, to complicate it more with Heath. And we need to go now...but first, I have something for you." Pete reached into his coat pocket and retrieved an envelope. He handed it to Shane, ceremoniously, and said, "Now remember, you don't know about the car."

Pete placed a hand on Shane's shoulder and led him out of the garage. Shane knew that he had just been *handled*, and he wanted answers about Heath, but he allowed the maneuver to work for now. His suspicious mind knew something was wrong, and he wasn't used to leaving problems unresolved. Shane knew he must confront Pete quickly about his brother Heath, so he had no distractions while he worked. Otherwise, he feared the problem would continue to grow out of control in his own mind.

Once back in the house, Kate rushed up to Shane and took him by the arm. "I'm glad I found you. We have some time. How about a dip in the pool? We just have to change in our room and go down."

Shane smiled, as they walked to their room together. He liked the sound of *our room*, when Kate said it. When he looked back at Pete, the smile on Pete's face told him that Pete liked it, too.

Once in the room, Shane walked to a chair by the bay window, where he sat down to open the envelope. It held a letter from his dad written just a week before his dad had been murdered. Shane froze on reading the first words aloud, "Dear Shane," his eyes afraid to move any further.

Kate came to him immediately, and asked, "What is it Shane?"

Her voice was filled with the concern that Shane had come to appreciate and love. He needed her caring for him, now more than ever. He choked out, "It's a letter from my dad, written just before he was murdered." He read the letter slowly aloud, as Kate knelt by the chair, her hand on his knee.

"Dear Shane, I hope you know, and will always remember, how much your mom and I love both you and Heath. Any father wants to love his children equally, but you and I had a very special bond, that was just ours. I had plans to watch you grow into a wonderful man, and looked forward with your mother to seeing you complete all of life's challenges. I wanted to see you graduate from college, pursue a career, maybe even with me, in our own law practice, and then, marry and raise a family of little Becketts your mom and I could spoil. I often dreamed about the future we would all share together."

Shane's expression softened, as his dad's dreams sprang to life in his own mind.

He continued, "If you are reading this letter, then my fears have come to pass, and your mom and I aren't with you anymore. If Pete is still alive, and has managed to take you boys to safety, he will finish the job of parenting your mom and I could not. Pete is much more than a good man, Shane. He's the best man I have ever met. He won't let you down. But he also won't let you know about the details of our deaths for a long time. I have given him very specific instructions on how to raise you boys, what to tell you and when."

"My request to Pete is far more to ask of another man than any father has a right to, but Pete has always been there for me, your mom, and you boys, and he has consented to our wishes and happily agreed to take on the responsibility. And Pete will have had a far greater responsibility than you may fully appreciate, by the time you read this or discover the details of our deaths."

"Pete's number one priority has been, and is still, keeping you and Heath safe, and giving you both help, *but* only when you need it, and in the manner he sees fit to provide the help. He is the executor of our estate, and has a timeline of instructions about money we have left for both of you boys. He can deviate from our wishes *only* if he thinks it is in *your* best interests."

"You will find that our estate is not divided equally between you and Heath. There are reasons for this that you may never understand or agree with, but this is both your mom's wish and my wish, and Pete *cannot* deviate from these instructions. He also cannot tell you the details of our deaths until he knows you are ready to digest everything and react appropriately. And, the decision about when you will be ready is left up to him. We want you to have a normal life, Shane. To us, that wish is more important than any feeling you might have now, about when *you* think you were ready to learn everything."

"Remember that, as much as I love you, I know you even better. I believe I know you and understand you, even better than you know and understand yourself. If your mom and I have been murdered, and if you knew the details of our deaths at an early age, I am sure you would spend a lifetime seeking revenge."

"If you do ever go up against the people who killed your mom and me, you have to win both the battle, *and* the long-term war. I couldn't bear you losing. And to win, you have to be *the best*, far stronger and smarter than the people you will be fighting and maneuvering against. You must have total focus, with no distractions, and you must be fully prepared. You can't afford to have a myopic mind, forged by grief and revenge. You can't allow revenge's power to twist or consume you. Remember this, you can *never* make up for the loss of your parents."

"Pete will know when the time is right, and he will tell you what you need to know *then*. Don't give him a hard time. Don't judge him. He probably will have gone through quite an ordeal, especially with Heath, by the time you are reading this."

"Remember Shane, Heath isn't as strong as you are, and he doesn't have your good character. Heath doesn't have your pure heart...at least not yet. Maybe someday, once he has gone through the trials I fear he will face, then and only then, will he be able to develop into a man who possesses the kind of character I wanted for him."

"Everything has always come too hard for Heath, with him fouling the situation, and suffering the consequences, before the tough lessons made sense to him, and he changed for the better. Heath will take much more time to come around, if he ever does. Remember that, Shane...and remember, there will come a time when even *you* can no longer bail your brother out of trouble."

"And most of all, remember this one most important rule: *Always, and I do mean always, trust Pete.* He has become your father more than your uncle by now. And, to care for you and Heath the way I know he will, he has invested his life, not in his own dreams, but in our family and in you two boys. You are *his* family now. Always take Pete's advice very seriously. I *always* did, and it *always* served me well."

"Now, this is *my* advice. Have a good life, with the right girl when she comes along. You'll know who the right girl is by her character. Don't settle for anyone less than the perfect one for you. She must love you for who you are, support you in all that you do, and be willing to give her life for you. And you must do the same for her, as your mom and I taught you, and showed you with our lives. Marry the right one, and make babies for your mom and I to enjoy from heaven. We *will* be watching."

"Remember, Shane, you are my very special boy. Your mom and I are so proud of you. We could never have asked for a more perfect son for us. We both love you, son."

"Remember, also, that *trust is earned by doing the right thing when nobody is watching.* You have always shown us we could trust you. And we *believe* in you. Demonstrate your love of truth and fairness in life. Don't worry about us. You worry about *your* life, and the lives of your family. Pete and Heath are family. You will extend that family to your wife, her family, your few closest friends, and hopefully, your own children. You worry about all of them, and nothing else."

Both Kate's and Shane's eyes had filled with tears. He looked at Kate, kneeling on the floor in front of him. He reached over and gently wiped the streaming tears from her cheeks. A lump in his throat prevented him from speaking as he struggled to form words.

Shane's voice cracked with anguish, as he finally said, "It's signed, "Love always, Dad.""

Shane could not hold back the tears. He let them flow. Kate came into his arms and he held her tightly, as her tears fell in huge, grief-filled droplets onto his chest. It went on for a long time, as neither could stop crying, try as they might. Years of anguish and pain, once released, flowed freely, no longer inhibited by practiced composure.

When the tears slowed, and they once again controlled their breathing, Shane and Kate stood up together, supporting each other as they rose. They leaned together, drawing strength from one another, drained by emotion. Shane kissed the final tears from Kate's soft cheeks. He wanted to take away all her pain, momentarily forgetting his own sorrow, but there was nothing to do now, but hold on…to each other, and their future together.

Shane tried to redirect their thoughts, saying they should get ready for the pool. He began to fold the letter to place it back in the envelope, when he noticed more writing. On the back of the second page were these words, in his dad's hand: "P.S. Enjoy our car. Remember to care for it as I always did, and do the maintenance the way I taught you. Trust me on this. It's very, very important to do the maintenance *exactly* as I did, when the time is right. If you do this, it will serve us both well. The car will care for you and protect you in return. Remember the lessons. Remember well. Love always, Dad."

As they dressed and walked to the poolroom, Shane turned his dad's words over and over in his mind. He finally had to stop thinking about them, and return to the here and now. The past held immense sorrow for him. He needed to focus now on Kate, Pete, Walter, Heath, and this assignment, and get up to speed on his own destiny. He needed to be there for his family, extended family, and friends, exactly as his dad had directed. He knew it was imperative for him to make good decisions, as his dad had advised.

As Shane and Kate walked toward the pool, he watched her walk ahead of him, descending the stairs. He tried to focus on Kate, and take his mind off his dad's letter and post script. But he kept feeling there was more to his dad's final words than a reminder about scheduled maintenance on the old car. His mind kept drifting back to the car, and his dad, as he tried to remember.

Kate moved like a dancer, her tight muscular body bouncing in all the right places. But as mesmerizing as the view of Kate was to him,

Shane's mind struggled to be free of his dad's caution. He fought to focus on the incredible sight before him, and reminded himself of his anticipation he had felt just to see her at the café each morning. He knew he could never take the gift he had been given, this wonderful new love, for granted. Still…his dad's words returned time and time again.

As they arrived at the ground floor, Shane again stared at Kate's long and shapely legs. He feasted his eyes on her dream butt, a small, tight and muscular masterpiece, perfectly curved, and now framed in a hot red bikini that matched Kate's lips, toenails and long fingernails.

Michelangelo couldn't have created a waist as perfect as Kate's, or the magnificent breasts and shoulders of a diva that led to her inviting neck. And then there was Kate's beautiful face and long, flowing dark brown hair, with red highlights that shimmered in the sunlight. Even though Shane was behind her, he could still picture and taste her full red sweet lips, and drink in the deep pools of her eyes, as if she were facing him.

Shane suddenly realized he was having a hard time keeping his eyes off Kate, and her bikini. He quickly glanced around the area to make sure no one else was watching, embarrassed by his now growing lust. He also realized that, once again, he was hard as a rock, and he immediately slowed down as Kate moved into the viewing room. Shane stopped on one side of the overstuffed chairs and sat down, embarrassed to continue on in his current condition. He thought to himself, "I should have just focused on dad's message…there *is* a clue there!" He smiled to himself.

Kate was a few feet ahead before she realized that Shane wasn't behind her. She looked back, saw him sitting in the chair, and made her way back to him. "Shane, we don't have to do this now, if you don't want to. We can go back to the room and just take some time."

Shane blushed, his manhood throbbing like he was still in high school and had spent the night slow-dancing with his girlfriend. "It's not that, honey…I just can't stop appreciating your beauty. You have this unusual effect on me, something I've never felt before. I can't control it. At the most inappropriate times, the sight of *your* body just takes over *my* body, and seduces my thoughts."

Shane smiled sheepishly, as he glanced up at Kate standing over him. Kate sat next to him and looked down, smiling, as she understood his dilemma. Imitating the old movie star, Mae West, she said with a smile, "Don't ever stop that, if you know what's good for you, big boy." They both laughed as Kate put her arm around Shane.

Once it was safe for him to walk, they strolled to the pool, side by side, talking about inconsequential things, taking no chances with stray amorous thoughts. They spent an hour swimming in the indoor pool and chatting, before they left to change for dinner. Kate marveled at Shane's well-defined, muscular body. He was obviously in great shape, but his proportions were perfect in her mind.

She wondered where his "flaw" was hidden, as she believed everyone had some flaw, some part of their body they secretly wished could be better. Like the conformation of the horses she loved to ride, Kate found room for improvement in everyone's physique, including her own. She thought her own breasts were too large, a full double-D size, and wished them a cup size smaller. But try as she might, she could not find the flaw in Shane.

After swimming they returned to their room. Shane was more pensive than Kate had ever seen him. They changed for dinner in silence. Once downstairs, they ate quietly with the team in the workroom, while Pete, Walter and Spencer ate in the dining room and discussed the acquisition of a shopping center in Orange County, California.

Shane didn't want to think about anything other than this assignment, solving the death of his parents and Kate's father, and his future with Kate. He was getting comfortable with the team, and especially liked Lee, Jim, and Jesse. He felt he had to get to know everybody very well, and as soon as possible.

As wonderful as everything had become, Shane knew something was seriously wrong between Heath and Pete. He knew he also had to find out what it was, and quickly. A big piece was missing from the stories he had been told by both Heath and Pete. Shane decided he didn't want any unresolved distractions. He was going to take his dad's advice and not be too demanding, but he needed to push Pete now for an answer. He also knew this was one subject about which he could not trust himself to be objective, and he knew what he needed to do to evaluate Pete's response.

After dinner, Shane picked up his cell phone and called Pete. He put a finger to his lips and Kate remained quiet. Shane was on the hunt for the truth. "Pete, can you meet me in the sitting room in half an hour. We have to talk." Pete agreed, although somewhat reluctantly.

When Shane ended the call, he turned to Kate, "Pete and I have some unfinished business you need to hear. I need you to know this, without Pete knowing you are listening, so he won't hold back. I may be too emotionally involved to be objective or understanding, and I need your read on the conversation. For better or for worse, right?" Kate nodded her understanding and agreement, although she hated that what she felt could be viewed as deceptive.

The meeting had been arranged for privacy in the sitting room. Kate left before the meeting to go to the women's shower room, where she knew that a vent in a connecting storage room would allow her to hear the conversation in the sitting room above, without being obvious. Still she felt she was not being honest with Pete. Worse, she felt like a spy. But she wanted to support Shane at a time he seemed to need her opinion.

Pete walked into the room to find Shane waiting, standing next to the loveseat. Pete studied Shane, and said, "I recognize that look on you, Shane. You always wear your feelings on your shirt sleeve when it comes to family."

Pete's remark brought no response from Shane, as he tried to control his emotions. Pete said, "What can I tell you, other than what has already been discussed? You are obviously upset at me for something. Knowing you, you would have wanted me to tell you what was going on during every step of the way through your life. I'm sorry. I thought there were too many things you didn't need to know. I was following your parents' specific instructions."

Shane tried unsuccessfully to recall all his dad's advice, when dealing with Pete. But his emotions had overcome him. "And when was I going to be ready, old enough, or wise enough for you to share the details of the death of my parents, Pete?" Shane challenged.

Shane's fair complexion reddened, as blood rushed to his skin, pushed by adrenaline, released by anger. "We had no secrets, you and I, Pete. It was just us after your own wife, Claire, passed away. Maybe even before then, we went over the death of my parents a hundred times, and all I ever got was lies…lies, or *I don't knows,* from you!? You and Heath were all I had left. I needed the truth!"

Pete sat in the loveseat, relaxed his body into the depths of the cushions, and let loose a deep sigh. "I can't pretend I always knew what was right, or did what was right when I did know it. I didn't really know *anything* for sure about their murders for more than a year after the *accident.* I had suspicions it was a murder. But not until Walter and I got together to compare notes, and he shared information the PI firm had uncovered, did the details begin to take some form and start to make sense. And that didn't come right away. Everything took so much time, and time just began to slip away."

Pete continued. "Over time, Walter and I became very close. He took a keen interest in assuring your safety, and I got to know and love Kate as a father would love a daughter. Walter had the idea and the resources to offer you and Heath protection. You were in college and I had my hands full with Heath. And still, the meaty facts in the cases came out slowly over the years."

"We eventually had a better understanding of why and how it happened...and even had some proof, that your parents, and Kate's father and his assistant, had been murdered. But it never seemed the right time to tell you kids. Plus, I thought I had to wait for Heath to grow up and become a man. And that never happened. So I put it off. It became the easiest thing to do...always searching for more and more evidence, always waiting for a better 'right' time, and always trying to keep your lives *normal.*"

Shane's complexion turned a deeper red, as his neck veins bounced with the surging blood from his quickened heartbeat. "Speaking of Heath, where does he fit into all of this now? Is he protected, and what about his wife and kids?"

Shane's expression demanded an explanation that Pete clearly didn't want to give. Shane continued his relentless stare until Pete knew there was no more waiting. He knew now was the time to come clean about Heath.

Pete sank further down in the cushions, as if a beating had pummeled him into submission. He began slowly. "Heath was protected and guarded, just like you and Kate, until a year before he went to prison. There was nothing we could do for him then…really, even long before that…he would never listen to me! With Heath in prison, it was quickly determined there was no threat to Heath's wife and kids. She moved on with her life and nearly lost contact with Heath."

"I placed the assets from your parents' life insurance policies and the sale of their house in a trust, per your dad's instructions. I split the assets of that trust as directed by your father. Spencer now also manages Heath's investments, but Heath is not part of our LLCs, and he has not been included in the family's financial plans for the future."

Pete struggled to speak. "He was a drug addict…*is* a drug addict. He's seemingly doing great now, but he placed himself far from the family a long time ago. He and I had it out hundreds of times when he was using drugs. He stole from Claire and me, from you, and from anyone else he could steal from, to feed his habit. He and I said our goodbyes after he broke a thousand promises to Claire and me, and I had no more hope, respect, or compassion left for him."

Shane walked to the loveseat and sank into the deep cushions next to Pete. Years of training and practice enabled him to shrug off the adrenaline quickly, and regain control over his emotions, at least on the exterior. The blood drained from his face and the bulging arteries in his neck receded.

Shane admitted in a clear, calm voice, "That explains a lot. Heath never would talk to me much about you after he got out of prison. He just said you could never forgive him."

Shane studied Pete's eyes, searching for an explanation. "Forgive him for what, Pete? What did he do that was so unforgivable? We were family and we didn't have anyone, but each other. Stolen things can be replaced."

Pete buried his hands in his face, fighting back the tears. After a moment he sat straight up, nearly rigid, as his body stiffened. Burning anger, once buried, again surfaced from a place deep within his soul, where it had been temporarily confined.

Pete's gaze returned to Shane. He angrily blurted out, "Heath stole from Claire. She caught him and forgave him…and she didn't tell me. Not once, but over and over and over again. By the time I found out about the thefts, Heath had stolen most of the jewelry I had given Claire over our whole life together. He even stole her wedding rings. He pawned everything for drug money to feed his habit, and the habits of his low-life friends. When there was no more jewelry to steal, he stole her cancer and pain medications to sell on the black market…for months before her death."

Pete was sobbing in anger and frustration now, as he recalled all the pain as if it were yesterday. "My Claire was an angel, and she loved you boys, like you were her own sons. Heath betrayed the love of that sweet woman, and stole the medicine that could have saved her, or at least prolonged her life. She was afraid to tell the doctor or me until it was too late, and she was dying, fading quickly. She wanted to protect Heath, so she pushed on, in incredible pain that the drugs could have diminished."

"Heath took her last chance, and wasted it getting high with his buddies. He threw away our Claire's life. And he didn't have the right to do that, Shane. He didn't have the right to kill my Claire." With a face formed in anguish, Pete sobbed into his hands, as if his wife had just died. All the pain and agony returned in huge waves, as if stored up for years behind some dam, waiting for this one-time quick release. It gushed forth relentlessly.

Shane couldn't bear to go any further and inflict more pain on his beloved Uncle Pete. He felt ashamed he had been angry with a man who obviously had too much on his plate to be held accountable for any of his or Heath's mistakes, or provide them with soothing explanations.

Already Shane realized he should have listened more clearly to his dad's message. His father's words flooded back to him now as his own anger faded, replaced by love and compassion. He placed a hand softly on Pete's shoulder, and whispered, "I'm so sorry, Pete. I didn't know any of this. I am so, so sorry. I loved Claire like my own mother. I just didn't know. I am so sorry."

Pete stood up, and Shane moved in front of him and took Pete's pained red face in his hands. He kissed Pete gently on his cheek. They hugged, and when Shane said, "I love you so much, Pete, and I have been so blessed to have you," Pete cried even harder.

The knowledge Shane had demanded now brought him more grief, as he finally understood why Claire lost her fight against cancer so quickly. He soon fell into sobbing, along with Pete. All he could say was, "I'm so sorry, so sorry. Please forgive me."

Once Pete and Shane regained some composure, they talked softly, reminiscing about Claire and how they had loved her, recalling special times together. Shane reassured Pete, and emphasized how much he appreciated all that he and Claire had done for him and his brother, Heath.

Shane had really loved Claire, and couldn't bear to think that one of his family had been used to the point of death. And, as much as he loved Heath, Shane knew that things were going to be different between them now. The whole family relationship was painfully clear to Shane. He hugged Pete one last time, long and hard, and again told him how much he loved him.

Pete said his goodnight at last and left for his room, while Kate returned and rejoined Shane in the sitting room. They walked to their bedroom in silence. Once inside, Kate spoke softly. "Shane, you couldn't have known. I never heard any of this either. I don't know that Pete ever told anyone."

Shane looked defeated. "I don't think even your grandfather could have fixed this. I know I can't. And I don't think I can cry anymore tonight, either. These two sessions today have taken it all out of me."

∾

Shane and Kate undressed and lay in bed together without talking. They looked up through the skylight to the clear night heavens that bathed them in starlight, the beams somehow comforting their sorrows and caressing their spirits.

As they held each other, Kate's head on Shane's chest and her hand on his shoulder, she asked, "Do you believe in God, Shane?"

Shane smiled and kissed Kate's sweet head, and said, "I do, more and more each day. Why do you ask?"

"I do, too" Kate explained. "I want you to know that, since I was a little girl, I have always known that God is real, and that He is with us always. My dad used to say that the sad people who have no hope blame God for everything bad in the world. But it's not true...not His fault, you know. God wants the best for all of us, but He gives us free will to deal with life as it comes."

Kate looked up at Shane. "Some people choose to do bad things to each other and God can't always intervene, or we would all be puppets and free will wouldn't exist. I think our parents are with God. We need to live good lives and make them proud, and eventually, we can be sure to join them."

Shane's heart softened at the revealed inner beauty shining from the women he cherished. He said, without thinking, as if it were somehow automatic, "I love you, Kate. I can't begin to tell you what you mean to me. I've been looking for you and praying to God to find you all my life. I formed you in my thoughts, hopes and dreams, and then one day, there you were, even more beautiful and wonderful than I had imagined."

He kissed her softly, and said, "*You* are my living proof that God is real and is alive. He answered my prayers by placing you in my life. I don't ever want to lose you, Kate. Besides, my parents have plans for us, remember? Dad said!"

They both smiled and held each other tighter, filled with hope, each one finding tenderness and answers to desires and prayers in the other. They clung together as new lovers do, each holding on, not just to a person, but to all their hopes and dreams for the future.

Kate fell asleep quickly. Shane's mind raced through the day's events. He listened to Kate's breathing, felt the rise and fall of her chest on his, and softly stroked her head and hair.

He had gone over and over his dad's letter in his mind a dozen times, until he knew exactly what he had to do. Just before he drifted off to sleep, he again blessed Kate in the ancient way, and kissed her head tenderly, one last kiss for the night.

As he drifted into a deep sleep, Patrick Beckett began to take shape and beckoned to Shane from the recesses of old memories mingled with a fresh dream. Patrick drove down the sunny, coastal highway in the T-Bird, as his young son questioned him about life, and the absence of fairness and justice in the world. Patrick smiled at Shane and said, "Son, the success or failure of fairness and justice in *any* society, is dependent on the goals and ambitions of those in charge."

As Shane was drifting further in to a deep sleep, another man, a few miles away, lay in a motel bed going over his plan for the next day's events. And he, too, knew exactly what he had to do.

6

"Coffee in England always tastes like a chemistry experiment."
(Agatha Christie)

Shane saw the glow of a campfire far off in the distance, as he made his way down the last mile of trail, from the mountain pass to the "valley of the river." The annual trek to this fishing spot had become a summer tradition for Heath, Shane, their dad, Uncle Pete, and a few close friends. It was the last full week in August, before school started. The fishing was good, the nights cool, and the last summer days hot, and perfect for swimming in the deepest holes of the small river. Cool water bathed hot bodies in refreshing waves of outdoor heaven, after a long day of hiking and fishing in the alpine sun. The annual trip was a summer highlight for everyone.

Shane's dad, Patrick Beckett, always remarked on the trip, "After a long, hot day, a cold swim in a clear mountain pool rejuvenates the soul." He made this same declaration each year, as the familiar group of family and friends sat around the campfire after the evening swim, just before dark. This was one of many valued traditions born over the years, on this most special trip that began when Shane was a small child.

At the nightly campfire, his dad's close friend Kent Murray, a DEA agent, always sat to his dad's right, and Pete always sat on the left, making it difficult for Shane to sit and talk to his dad. Having just arrived at camp from fishing, Shane thought he would wait until one of them got up, and he could take their place to sit next to his own father. After all, it should be his special place, sitting next to the man he idolized.

Shane waited patiently, standing silently behind his dad. Kent suddenly stood up and walked to a camp table where the scotch and glasses were waiting. Shane had carried two bottles of the scotch up in his back pack, as that was his trusted assignment each year. He did so proudly, and always received appreciated praise from the fellow campers as the scotch was unpacked. After all, the liquid in glass was heavy, and it proved he was both trusted and strong, he thought.

Shane was just about to sit down by the fire next to his dad, to ask him the question that had been bothering him, when he heard, "Shane, we need to get up, honey."

The scene began to fade quickly. Shane still needed to ask the important question, so he tried to hold on to the scene. But, try as he might to embrace one more second and glimpse of his father, the voice was persistent. "Shane, honey, are you awake?"

Shane opened his eyes to see Kate, and for a split second was sad to see her instead of his father. He didn't have the chance to speak to him in the dream, and he urgently wanted to talk to his father. Shane missed his dad, and knew he was the one person who could fill in the blanks, and help him right the wrongs in the lives of these two united families.

"Two families merged into one by a terrible set of murders that destroyed lives and changed a normal history," Shane thought out loud. "I still need to ask the question!"

"Shane?" Kate shook him by the shoulder in an attempt to make sure he was awake.

Shane looked at Kate and smiled. "Just a dream, but I seem to be having more of them lately."

Kate gave him a look of concern. "How long have you been having these dreams?" Shane looked down at the sheets, as if searching for the answer hidden in the thread count.

"It doesn't matter," he said, without emotion, throwing up a flimsy temporary barrier he immediately realized Kate saw through.

"Shane, that won't work for us, if there is to be a lasting *us*. We need to grow through everything together, and become stronger everyday. I can't have the relationship I need with you, if you don't trust me enough to let me inside your pain and concerns, as well as your joy."

Shane let out a sigh of humiliation. "I know you're right. I *really do* know you're right," he persisted when she cocked her head at him. "It's a learning experience for me. I haven't had this close of a relationship since my mom and dad, except for Heath, Pete and Claire. Three of them are dead, one went off the deep end and ended up in prison, and Pete and I drifted apart a little when I began working in police work. I have spent so much time alone. I hope you can forgive me. You deserve so much more than that. I'll try harder."

Kate flashed a smile that lit up Shane's heart. Then with a quick, but soft, rap on his shoulder with her fist, she said, "Then let's try it again, mister, the right way…our way." She leaned in and kissed Shane softly, tenderly, passionately. When she pulled back slowly, and waited for an answer, Shane continued.

"I started dreaming about mom and dad about a year after they died. In the next few years, the dreams became more vivid, more alarming, really. There were nights when I spent hours just running, trying to prevent their inevitable deaths. Other nights, I was fighting with shadowy figures that kept coming at us, over and over again, regardless of how hard or long I fought. I would wake up in sheets soaked with sweat."

"I began speaking in a foreign language. Claire and Pete would come in and sit in the room, listening, trying to figure out what I was saying, hoping to learn how to help. Sometimes they would ask me a question, and instead of answering, I would repeat the statement I had just made, in a strange language they could never identify. The more they asked, the more I became irritated, until finally, they would remain silent or wake me. If they did wake me, I was even more irritated, and tried to go back to sleep and back to the fight."

"When I would wake up after an all-night ordeal, with sweat-soaked sheets, I would be so exhausted, Claire would change the sheets and let me go back to sleep to get some rest. After a few years, they were half convinced I was battling some evil demonic force. Claire and Pete were *so* concerned that they sought a physician's advice. He advised them to let me continue on my own and work through the dreams. The dreams lasted for a few years, but, during that time, became less frequent and of shorter duration and intensity."

Shane looked up at Kate, who was expressing wide-eyed concern. "Sounds kind of spooky, I know, but it was so real. Sometimes I could remember the dreams for days, but never clearly enough to give me a clue as to what forces I was really fighting. I never won, but I never lost…I just kept on fighting…running and fighting…never winning or losing!"

"Heath could sleep like a baby every night, but not me. Its just part of the curse of being me, I guess. The funny thing is, the dreams had subsided until recently. I was only having them every few months or so. With all the rapid changes in my life, I guess they have accelerated again."

"And now, a lot of them are not about fighting. It's more like I'm just trying to make contact with my dad to ask for advice. Yet, I know as well as I know I love you, I know that there *is* something, some clue in these dreams that I just keep missing." Shane looked into the eyes that calmed him, reassured him, and gave him hope.

Kate picked up Shane's hand in her two hands and studied it, as if she were reading his palm. She closed her eyes and spoke remotely, as though to someone else. "I love this man, and I pray that he will find peace, with me, and with our future. I have never wanted anything more than this. I tell you this because you have known my prayers and dreams all my life, and you know this to be true."

Kate softly kissed Shane's hand, caressing the calluses grown from lifting weights, vaulting fences and jumping into trees at night. Kate kissed each of the small scars born from the wounds of countless days of training and missions past. Then she kissed the partially healed small wound the strong right hand had suffered during this assignment, as if her kisses had special healing powers.

Shane sat mesmerized, looking at the cut on his hand when she pulled away, almost expecting it to be completely healed. She then took the injured hand and placed it against her soft cheek, pressing it tightly into her face, as she again closed her eyes. She rubbed it slowly against her face, as though she could take any pain and roughness away, leaving just tender, unwounded skin in its place.

Shane had learned that Kate was sensitive to his needs, independent when she needed to be, understanding of his emotions, desiring him and only him. Most importantly, she was not self-absorbed, like so many women he had known. Having this relationship with him was more important to Kate than anything she could attain alone. She thought like he did, had values like he did, and loved like he did. Yet she maintained an independent and strong nature, not at odds with him, not striving to be in front or behind in life, but rather, to be a true partner, side by side.

"What a rare find in a sea of people, and what a gift," he marveled.

For her part, Kate was ready to sacrifice anything necessary to protect family, and now that included Shane. And, while it seemed to Shane that God Himself, had taken time from His busy schedule to design the perfect woman specifically for him, to Kate it seemed that God had placed Shane in her life at the right time, in answer to her prayers.

In truth, the right set of circumstances had come together, under many different pressures, to allow the new lovers to grow their relationship and lean on each other for what they both expected would come…a long and protracted battle against evil. And now, the time was right, and they were ready for each other's love.

Both Kate and Shane knew that, at this point in their lives, they were ready enough and experienced enough to not waste their one chance at true love. Shane leaned down and gently kissed the top of Kate's gorgeous head, drawing her to him tightly with his free hand. They held each other until there was a fast knock on the door.

"Shane…Kate! Sorry for the interruption, but I need to speak to you. It's important." It was Pete's voice coming from the other side of the door.

"I haven't heard that much concern in Pete's voice since Claire was sick," Shane whispered to Kate. "We'll be right there, Pete," Shane called, as he and Kate threw on robes. Shane half ran to the door.

But when he opened the bedroom door, Shane was greeted by Pete, Lee and Walter. They rushed through the doorway, in unison, seemingly pulled in by some invisible force. Lee slammed the door behind them.

Pete placed his finger to his lips to indicate no talking, as he said loudly, "So do you know whose birthday you forgot?" Without waiting for an answer, Pete said, "No… I didn't think you'd remember." Kate and Shane stood, confused, searching the three new faces in their room, waiting for some explanation, as both complied with the request for silence.

Pete launched into a bogus story about a fictitious distant relative who was having her 80th birthday today, and who would be crushed if Shane didn't call her. While Walter stood with his finger over his lips to reinforce the request for silence, Lee scurried about with a "bug finder." Lee swept every nook and cranny in the bedroom suite and bathroom, including the closets and all the clothing, and finally Kate and Shane themselves.

Then, with Pete droning on about the fictitious person's life (she had become Shane's great-aunt by now), Lee re-swept the room, with another electronic device retrieved from a case he had brought into the room. Kate and Shane stood watching, honoring the silence, until Lee gave the all-clear sign with a thumb's-up.

Lee spun around quickly, and said to Shane and Kate, "We have a problem."

"This family? A problem? No!" Shane said sarcastically, with a wry smile.

Lee continued, "You had a delivery today at your old apartment. The surveillance team picked it up directly from the UPS driver, who was going to leave the package at the manager's apartment. The team took the box to a field near the apartments where Jesse met them and used his sweepers to check for explosives. He x-rayed the package with his portable unit, and found an electronic device inside. When he placed his audio enhancer on the package, he heard a ticking. The software discerned that the ticking was a digitally-created sound. Further inspection revealed there was no bomb."

Kate and Shane relaxed, releasing a little tension.

"I gave the go-ahead to Jesse to open the package as soon as I arrived. Once I was at the field, I made sure I was the only other person in the area with Jesse at the time…no sense in too many people being injured, if we were wrong," Lee smiled.

Shane returned the smile, recognizing and appreciating swift, decisive, unselfish action and leadership. He was beginning to admire Lee.

Lee continued, "The device is a 10-inch computer, containing two files on the hard drive. One is a dossier on Undersheriff Brian Grant, and the other is a timer, with the audible digital ticking, set to count down to 2:00 PM today. Jesse is digesting the entire file on Grant right now, but it doesn't look good. So far, we have discovered that, according to the file, Grant is working for someone connected to the Magadinnos, and we have a mole here in *my* unit reporting to Grant."

"I cleared the house of my staff. They are all out doing counter surveillance, or grounds and exterior building sweeps, with Jesse's staff. They have not been told about the computer. For now, we have to assume that the Magadinnos know everything we know."

Lee suddenly sat down on the bed like he had lost his strength. Then, realizing he was sitting on someone else's bed while they were dressed only in robes, he stood up quickly, and said, "Sorry, I'm a little preoccupied. The best thing is for you to replace me immediately, with another security company. I can give you some excellent references, and you can have new men here in 24-48 hours. The mole will have to go when I go."

Pete and Walter nodded in agreement. Kate walked slowly to a window, and stared out in thought.

"No, no, no...this is perfect," Shane said quickly. "What a blessing in disguise."

Walter and Pete looked at each other in disbelief. Lee searched Shane's face for an answer, not knowing what to expect. Shane continued, pacing slowly in a circular motion around the room, as the plan formulated in his head.

"We have a way to communicate directly to the Magadinno's contact, and maybe the Magadinnos themselves, without them knowing they are receiving the information we *want* them to have. As long as they think their spy is intact, we can feed them disinformation they will automatically believe. And then, *we* will have someone working on the inside of both the Magadinnos and our own forces, feeding them misinformation. We can use this setup to protect ourselves!"

"All we need to do is keep a few of us, who are beyond suspicion, in the loop with all the correct information, and let some disinformation go out to our entire force, bit by bit, knowing it will find its way to Brian Grant and his contacts. While we slow everything down, we'll focus on identifying our mole, by changing the information we share with each person. We can also work on discovering the identity of our friend on the outside. If we can keep everything in place long enough, we'll have a double advantage over the people who now believe they have the upper hand over us."

A slow smile formed and then broadened on Lee Sprague's face, while Shane explained his plan. He was no longer the dejected man who believed he had failed an important client and friend.

Lee now joined Shane's excitement. "Shane's right! We can feed selective facts to segments of our own forces until we find the mole when the specific fact comes back to us from the other side. We'll have to start with a list of our own people who are above suspicion. Each day, we'll pick a handful of the others and release the key information. Then we monitor whether it goes to Grant or the Magadinnos, so we can narrow the field until we have our man."

"We have another important twist to consider," Shane said. "Obviously, the Magadinnos aren't receiving all the information. They are still talking business in Franky's house, where my bugs and cameras are planted, and Hector is still using the phone I provided, for business. We have confirmed their plans with surveillance, so they must not know we are watching and listening."

"Just yesterday, we monitored Hector overseeing a meth shipment our surveillance team video taped. The mole and Brian Grant aren't giving all the information to the Magadinnos, so who are the mole and Brian really working for? What game is someone playing, and who are all the players?"

Kate was still gazing out the window at the Sierra Nevada mountain range, as she often did when in deep thought. Her excitement had built with Lee's and Shane's, but no one had noticed. When she could contain herself no more, she turned back to the room, excitedly.

"This *is* even more perfect than we thought! If the mole is working for Brian Grant, then the information is going to Brian and someone else. If the Magadinnos knew that Grant was holding out on them, then Grant would be dead…and could be dead in the future, *if* they were to find out."

Now Kate walked slowly toward Shane, her thoughts unfolding as she spoke. "If Brian is a bad guy, working against us for someone else, then the Magadinnos will eventually find out, and he will be taken care of the hard way. But you have to wonder what his end game is, and who he is working for…or, more importantly, what he is working *toward* to take such risk with these killers. Maybe he and the mole are holding all the information between them, until the time is right for them to use it for some other personal gain."

She continued. "Why would you be connected to the Magadinnos and holding out on them, at the risk of death?"

Before anyone else could respond, Kate answered her own hypothetical question. "Because you're trying to use the information to take the Magadinnos down, so you could control them, or you need to put someone else in place. It's the only logical motive."

She spoke quickly, "Brian Grant must want to destroy the Magadinnos, or change the rank structure, and it's not with Hector, since he didn't warn Hector about using his phone. How many cartels and syndicates are working with the Magadinnos? And do the others like being number two or three in the pecking order? No, of course not. The key is going to be finding out where the information goes from Brian, and that means surveillance, with a tail, bugs and cameras on him."

Pete and Walter had been following the conversation, rapidly bouncing from Shane to Lee to Kate, like they were watching a doubles tennis match, excitement and fear building in both of them.

Walter blurted out, "Who are you!?! And what have you done with my sweet, innocent granddaughter?!" as he grinned at Kate.

Pete smiled cautiously, and added, "We have a lot of work to do, and no place we can do it, where we're certain we will be safe from being monitored by the mole."

"We can work here in our room," Kate offered, as she pointed to the desk in the corner. We know it's safe and free of listening devices and cameras, and it will have to do for now."

Shane gave her a look she understood, as they would lose their privacy temporarily. "For now, Shane, just until we can discover and monitor the mole. It's the only place that has been swept and we can lock and easily monitor, and its one of the rooms the mole probably can't risk getting into easily."

Shane knew she was right, smiled in agreement, and gave Kate a hug. "Beautiful and smart," he bragged, as the others nodded their approval and agreement.

Lee's phone rang, startling everyone. When he answered it, he straightened up with such excitement, he almost jumped in the air. He whispered into the phone, "Come up to Kate and Shane's room immediately, with the file, and make sure you aren't followed…and bring Tom Bradshaw."

Lee wheeled, a Cheshire cat grin splitting his face, for all to see. His eyes stared off a thousand yards away.

Walter couldn't stand the suspense, and fired off anxiously, "Well, what is it man? Don't keep us in the dark like mushrooms!"

Lee's mind was going a hundred miles a minute, yet he spoke slowly, while looking down. "The mole is Wesley Wilkinson. We have a very knowledgeable anonymous friend."

He looked up at Shane, and then glanced at the other faces in the room. "I'm so sorry this happened. I'm still embarrassed that I have let you all down."

Lee smiled, "But, the beauty of this is, that Wesley joined us just recently for his first in-house briefing, and so far, has only been assigned to outside surveillance. He doesn't have all the facts of the case or know the meat of the investigation. He doesn't even know Shane's identity."

Shane walked to Lee, took him by the hand, and said, "Don't beat yourself up, Lee. Most people can be bought, my friend. All it takes is money on one side and self-centered greed on the other. You can't be in all your people's heads at once to be assured they remain loyal. You know, Lee, we have even been betrayed by our own family." Shane shot a glance at Walter and Pete. and they nodded in agreement. "I trust you, and I'm sure the other people in this room do, also."

Lee looked around as all the heads nodded reassuringly.

"You are all great people, and have become some of my closest friends," Lee said with a note of pride in his voice. "Now, about Wesley..."

Before Lee could finish his thought, a knock came at the door, and Lee nearly ran to it, opening it quickly, allowing Jesse and Tom Bradshaw a fast entrance before the door closed behind them. "Tom, put this briefcase camera on the bench outside the door in the hallway, and come back in quickly."

Bradshaw was a tall, good-looking, black man who spoke few words to anyone but Lee. He was one of the few people Shane hadn't gotten to know in his time at the estate. Normally, Tom could be found at Lee's side. He seemed to operate as Lee's right hand, providing soft-spoken insight, and a second mind that checked and double-checked all the plans Lee made. Tom spoke quietly, and often only directly into Lee's ear. Shane couldn't recall ever hearing much of what Tom said to Lee.

Bradshaw was out of the room in a flash, gone for less than 5 seconds, and back inside so quickly and quietly that everyone marveled at the big man's agility and the softness of his step. How a large, muscular man like Tom Bradshaw could move about so fast, without making so much as a sound, surprised Shane. He thought he would have to speak to Tom more directly in the future, and get to know this man much better.

Lee set up a laptop from his bag, and selected an icon that brought up the camera screen showing the hallway outside Kate and Shane's room. "We need to make sure this is private," Lee explained. "OK, first some things you should know about Tom Bradshaw. He's my brother, and I trust him with my life. I trust him with my kids, and my wife, all of whom he has taken on vacation without me, when I couldn't go."

All eyes bounced back and forth between Lee and Tom, trying to see a resemblance through the difference in skin color.

Lee smiled. "Tom and I had different fathers, but the same mother. I'm older, and when my father died in a traffic accident, my mom raised me alone, until she met and married Tom's father. He is my half-brother, and his father became my dad and raised me from the time I was three years old. Tom and I are family, and he is the partner in my business. He is completely trustworthy, and one of the most honorable men I have ever known." A barely perceptible smile crept onto Tom's lips.

Lee continued rapidly, "I tell you this, so that you may know and trust, that if the dossier is wrong, and Wesley Wilkinson is not the mole, you may rest assured that Tom is not. By the way, I kept my biological father's name, Sprague, only to honor his memory. I think of myself as a Bradshaw." Tom smiled wider now, as he turned toward Shane, his light brown skin turning a little darker with the prideful embarrassment that flushed his face.

"Secondly, Jesse and I were in Iraq together. We served in the same unit, fought side-by-side, and survived together, protecting each other's ass. Jesse is my kids' godfather. If it weren't for him, I wouldn't be here. He took two rounds in the backside from an AK-47, pushing me out of the way to save my life. He has been with me in the business from the start. He is the other person I have always trusted with all that's important to me. I have bet my life on Jesse, and lived, but more importantly, I would bet my brother's life on Jesse. He isn't the mole either."

Walter interrupted, "Lee, you don't have to do this..."

Lee interrupted, "Yes, I do, Walter, for all of you and for me. You need to know where we're starting from in this game of life and death we seem to be caught in the middle of...you need to know who you can trust." Everyone slowly nodded in unison and thoughtful agreement.

Shane added, "So, we start with this group. We know we're safe with the people in this room. Anyone else we should add?" Shane looked around the room.

Jesse offered, "My techs, Mike and Pete Panos, are brothers I have worked with for years. Both go back to college days with me. We were all roommates. Mike had the opportunity to show a vengeful side when I ended up with his girlfriend, who became my wife. He was one of the ushers at my wedding. I was the best man at his wedding, when he married my wife's sister. Pete is his twin brother. Where Mike and I were, there was Pete. I trust them both implicitly."

"I'm comfortable adding Delores to the list of the trusted," Kate added. "She and I have been friends for a long time. She wants for nothing while working in our company, and knows she has an even brighter future with our group. I introduced her to a suitor of mine, who became her fiancé." Kate cast a teasing smile at Shane.

"Howard, in the garage, is one I have to add," offered Walter. "He has been with me for 40 years. I helped him grieve the loss of his wife, and gave him a position and place in our home and business. He later married another of our employees, who eventually became ill with Lupus. We still pay her salary and medical insurance, though she can't work anymore. Howard has been a friend for a long time."

Pete raised a hand, when there was a moment of silence. "Tasha McKnight, my secretary, has been with me for many years, and helped me, more than I can explain, getting through the death of my wife, Claire. I know that Tasha is in love with me, and I have been too stubborn to act on the mutual attraction yet. But we both know it's only a matter of time. She's completely trustworthy." Pete looked at Shane, who was beaming and nodding. "I was going to tell you when the time was right, Shane." They both just grinned.

"Anyone else on the outside?" Lee asked, as he looked around the room at the gathered faces.

"Bryan K. Holland, FBI agent, extraordinaire," Shane said proudly. "He's a special agent-in-charge out of the LA office, knows what I do for a living, and would risk his life to save me. He's already risked his career to help me a number of times. He is our ace in the hole. Whatever he does for us is as untraceable as it gets."

After a period of silence, Lee announced, "Then, we start with that group, as a precaution. Now, Jesse can bring us up-to-speed on the dossier delivered by our unknown informant." Lee exuded the renewed confidence of a redeemed man, as he once again sat on the bed.

Kate and Shane smiled at each other, and sat on either side of him. Shane put his arm around Lee's shoulder, and said, "I think we need to have some chairs brought in." The room erupted in sorely-needed laughter.

Jesse sat on the floor in front of the group. "Alright then, the dossier obtained from the laptop, which is void of identifiers and fingerprints, by the way, is completely devoted to Brian Grant, and links him very convincingly to organized crime, dating back to the days when he served as an agent with California's Department of Justice. The file contains attachments, documents retrieved by someone with a high degree of clearance, from DOJ files."

"Those files indicate that Grant was the subject of an internal investigation involving the death of Shane's father, when he *retired*. More importantly, the file contains credible information linking Grant to Franky Magadinno, and even more directly, to Big John Galliano."

"One document contains photocopies of a cashier's check withdrawal from Grant's account of $1,283.95 four days before Shane's parents' murders. Two days after the murders, Grant deposits $26,283.95. This is damning evidence. The vehicles used in the murders of Shane's parents, rented by Big John Galliano cost $1,283.95, and we have a photocopy of the rental receipt to prove that. Grant paid the fee to reserve the vehicles for Galliano, *before* Franky and Big John got to town, and then was reimbursed the fee, plus $25,000, for his troubles. He was stupid enough to deposit a check from one of Franky's business accounts into his own bank account."

"Or arrogant enough to deposit it," Shane said angrily. Shane's skin burned hot with rage, but he controlled his breathing. He slowly looked to see that both Pete and Kate were studying him carefully. He gave them both a wink, indicating he was okay. Then he noticed

Jesse, too, was watching for a safe sign to continue. Shane smiled and nodded.

Jesse continued. "So it seems that Big John has been busy killing people for Franky, and with Franky." Jesse hesitated, eyed both Walter and Kate, and continued. "The informant has provided us with hand written notes and plans, from Franky Magadinno and Big John Galliano, for…Harold O'Leary's murder." Jesse stopped and looked at Lee.

"Go on, Jesse. Kate and Walter have waited a long time for these answers, and they can't be any more prepared for it," Lee assured. Jesse looked at both Walter and Kate. He got the assurance he needed to continue.

Jesse proceeded, hesitantly. "The plans called for Harold and his assistant to be kidnapped, and then…*buried alive*… at the site of the first building to be built at the Yucca Mountain facility."

He looked up for reassurance and, when no one said anything, he continued. "There is a copy of a letter of congratulations from Big John to Franky, sent from Las Vegas. The letter says that the 'problem' is buried under the first layer of concrete in the basement storage room, encased in its own *special* block of cement. The informant says that Franky keeps the original letter in a scrapbook in his house wall safe…along with a Polaroid of Howard and his assistant being covered in concrete."

Walter had walked to Kate and sat down beside her on the bed. They looked at each other, but there were no tears. Kate asked Jesse, "please continue."

"At this point, we haven't had time to verify all the information in the dossier on Grant, but he was allegedly involved in Harold's kidnapping, posing as an agent assigned to protect Harold. The informant provided a local Nevada bank account that has allegedly had a deposit of $50,000 made to it, by one of Franky's LLCs, every year, on the anniversary of Harold O'Leary's death. It's Grant's bank account, and the deposits should be easy to verify. I'm so sorry to bring this news to you both," Jesse said to Walter and Kate.

Walter assured Jesse that he and Kate were fine, and urged him to continue. The room was silent for a moment. Shane had moved, and given Walter and Kate their own space. He knew they were dying on the inside, as they processed this awful news of the brutal destruction of their loved one. He knew the anger a person could feel, when they begin to deal with such loss. He vowed silently to himself to make Harold's death personal for him, also. Franky and his minions would pay a horrible price for these senseless murders, spawned of greed, he thought.

Excitement crept into Jesse's cautious voice, as he continued. "Now, here is the kicker! Our friendly informant has his *own* informant, inside the Magadinno crime syndicate. That informant is none other than Grant's primary contact, which explains why the Magadinnos aren't being fed *all* the "intel" about Shane and his operation. The end of Grant's file explains this, but doesn't identify the second informant."

Pete broke in. "How do we know that Wesley is the mole?"

Jesse looked up at him, as the other faces nodded. Everyone's minds were racing to find answers, and they all had different questions, but each person respected the group, and struggled to proceed with organization and clarity.

Jesse looked back at the file for a moment. "Our informant says that his contact in the Magadinno family has met with Grant and Wesley on two occasions. One occasion was in a coffee shop in Reno. Wesley told them he is English and lived in London for most of his youth. He used to order a Peruvian coffee popular in his local English coffee house. The coffee is called *Cecovasa*. And the informant said, at the meeting, Wesley quoted his favorite novelist, Agatha Christie."

Jesse continued to read. "Christie once said, *'Coffee in England always tastes like a chemistry experiment.'* Our informant offered this as proof that his information is good. I quietly checked with the kitchen to see what type of coffee we have on hand. They advised me that we use a coffee from a small local coffee roaster, but that Wesley provides them Peruvian Cecovasa, Wesley has kitchen staff make him a small pot of the Cecovasa every morning. He has his mother ship it to him. One of the staff said he often refers to this same quote with his first sip of coffee."

Jesse reflected out loud, a final concern. "We need to make everything appear as normal as possible. We need a way to communicate quickly to meet to exchange information in our *safe* room. Can we agree on a group text to initiate a meeting with our trusted group, designated by the numbers 911, and the time of the meet in military time? 911 1530, for example, would request a meeting for all of us here at 3:30 P.M." Everyone nodded in agreement.

"One final request. We should notify the others we trust so we have more sets of eyes on the same page with our group," Jesse asked.

Jesse called Mike and Pete Panos to the room. Kate called Delores, while Walter called Howard. Pete made a phone call to have Tasha meet him at the O'Leary estate, with her clothing and personal items, and said he would fill her in with details she needed to know once she arrived. The cadre of trusted comrades discussed what Tasha would need to know, so they would all agree. As they proceeded with final plans, Mike and Pete arrived at the room, followed by Howard. Although the bedroom suite was large, it suddenly seemed very crowded as people maneuvered for comfort.

Mike, Pete, Delores and Howard were brought up-to-speed. There was a brief discussion about what could possibly happen at 2:00 P.M. (1400 military time, Jesse had chided), but no one had a plausible theory. Questions were raised about Carson City Sheriff Mark Roberts, who had hired Shane, but all information re-affirmed the Sheriff's credibility.

A communication text group was added to everyone's cell phone. Jesse made a final suggestion that Lee and Tom meet with everyone, except Wesley, and let them know Wesley was leaking information to the Magadinnos, and they were to treat him normally, but not share information with him, at any time, unless it was approved.

Jesse had finished the dossier review, and, finally, had nothing else of importance to add. Lee suggested that the group leave one at a time, with Kate and Shane leaving last. Everyone would filter into the meeting room or kitchen, and make an appearance at breakfast, so there was no suspicion of anything being out of the ordinary.

When they were alone, Kate and Shane walked to the bathroom together and grabbed towels for a quick shower. Shane stood in the shower, allowing the hot water to cleanse his body and refresh his mind. As his head cleared, he noticed the details of the tile in the master suite bath. Each tile had the appearance of being handmade, with faint, almost imperceptible, differences in the various subtle horse design patterns.

The over-sized shower featured two shower heads, one each on opposing walls. The tiles were an off-white color, with a sandy appearance, placed in a pattern with sporadic, but tasteful matching tiles featuring horse drawings, spaced every six tiles. The horse designs resembled four different breeds: quarter horse, thoroughbred, Icelandic horse and Lipizzaner. Each horse was distinctive, and easily recognizable to Shane, who had ridden and studied horses for years. Yet each repeated tile was slightly different from the next matching tile, displaying a beautiful variety. "Definitely hand-painted," Shane thought to himself.

Shane placed his hand on a horse tile and felt its texture, as his hand slid downward. The tiles were glazed and smooth to the touch and yet, appeared to have a 3-D effect. The horse drawings were light and muted, yet well-defined and full of character. Shane was still marveling at the designs when his eyes finally met Kate's.

She explained, "I love theses tiles. They were handmade by an artist we met at one of the bronze foundries in Joseph, Oregon, on a trip to our ranch. He *is* an incredible artist and sculptor. Specialty tiles are his hobby."

Shane seemed pleased, and she continued. "My tiles are horses, and Granddad's are cars. He loves old pick-up trucks, like the one he had restored in the garage. It was one of his first pick-up trucks. It took him quite a while to relocate it, buy it back, and restore it to what he remembered."

"He likes to take me for rides in it, and when I don't go, he takes Howard. Some days they cruise down to Genoa and have lunch, or they drive all the way up to Markleeville to their favorite bar. It's an eclectic place…kind of a yuppie-biker bar. It has bras and panties hanging from the ceiling, so I'm told. I don't get to go there," Kate said, with a smile.

Shane couldn't resist the opportunity and re-assured her. "That's all right. I'd be disappointed if I walked in and saw your bra on the ceiling," he laughed. "Who offers up their bras and panties to a bar anyway? I have to believe there's alcohol involved."

As she turned off her shower head, Kate taunted, "Well, you don't get to just bring them in and hang them up. You have to wear them

in and take them off, in the bar, to earn the right to hang them up…
or so I'm told." She shot a quick sideways glance to Shane and said,
"So Delores tells me." They both enjoyed their teasing and bantering
sessions. The effect was good for both their spirits.

Shane dressed quickly and left first for breakfast. He was down
the stairs in a flash and realized, as he arrived at the kitchen, he was
hungry, with a taste for bacon. Smells from the kitchen assaulted his
nose on entry and made him crave a good coffee. Shane had been
used to drinking a good espresso each morning, either a cappuccino
or latte, depending on the day and his mood.

He had often been on his second cup by the time Kate walked
into the café to order her drink. He had liked to get there first and be
ready for her "appearance." He thought to himself, as he walked to the
kitchen today, that he would miss the anticipation of Kate arriving at
the shop. He made his mind up to continue their rendezvous when
things settled down.

With the events of the last day, he had come to realize that Kate
was also there to see him. She had been occasionally accompanied by
Delores, or Delores and another of the O'Leary staff. Looking back on
the Kate-coffee-shop-saga, Shane marveled at how he had noticed her,
become attracted and then obsessed with seeing her. And now, he was
with her. And all the while, she was doing the same with him. He couldn't
resist a smile while deep in thought. A voice broke his concentration.

"Want to try a cup of my special coffee?" Wesley Wilkinson
offered. Shane turned around to see Wesley standing behind him.
He responded quickly, trained and practiced to look normal, as his
heart raced. "What is it?" Shane asked politely.

Wesley's response was measured. "It's a Peruvian single roast, not a
blend. Some folks think it can be a little strong or bitter. My mother

sends it to me. It reminds me of home in England, where coffee always tastes like a chemistry experiment." Shane smiled.

Wesley continued, "England has tea, tea and more tea. Teas of every variety and blend, from every country in the world that exports tea...it all finds its way to England. Coffee is the American way, you know...after Boston. England hasn't seemed to get coffee quite right yet, but I still like it."

Shane smiled, "I wouldn't know. I've never been to England, although I have done some reading, and think it would be a great trip someday." Wesley seemed to like the response.

Now, standing next to one of the kitchen staff at the expresso machine, Shane turned to Wesley and said, "I'll take a rain check on trying it, if that's OK. I'm having a latte today. Maybe tomorrow? What's the 'special' for breakfast today? I seem to be more hungry than thirsty, anyway."

Wesley pointed to his plate resting on a nearby table. "Crab omelet, hickory-smoked bacon, poached pears and yogurt. Jesse *is* a culinary genius, and the staff love learning his creations. If I didn't work out every day, I'd gain 40 pounds eating Jesse's chefs-d'oeuvre," he laughed. Wesley picked up his plate and coffee, and walked out as Kate walked in, smiling at him as she passed. There were no tell-tale looks and Wesley could have read nothing in the brief contacts.

Once Wesley was out of sight, Shane whispered to Kate, "We're having latte's today, if that's okay...I made an excuse not to drink Wesley's coffee when he offered it up. Could be poison, you know," he kidded. "Wesley used the quote on me, but didn't get a rise with it. I can't quite figure him yet. He seems like such a nice guy. I'd love to know who he's working for."

With their breakfast plates and lattes in hand, Kate and Shane sat at their corner table. Kate explained that the pork came from a local rancher in Wallowa County, where their ranch was located. The bacon was then smoked at a shop in Elgin, Oregon, about an hour from the ranch. They had just received a shipment, and the bacon was Kate's favorite, thick sliced, slow smoked and cured perfectly. It melted in Shane's mouth, surprisingly complemented by the crab omelet, made with farm fresh eggs, spices and parmesan cheese.

As Kate continued on about the ranch and some of the local food, Shane sat relaxed and comfortable, with day dreams about a getaway to the Oregon ranch, where Kate could show him all that she loved about that corner of the state. He sank into the rhythm of her voice, and pictured the places and things she described so eloquently. Shane could tell that this place was special to Kate, and he was anxious to become part of it. After all, Kate probably didn't even know he could ride horses. Shane longed for the time when he could show her.

Shane's phone suddenly went off, with a programmed ring that drew him back to the reality of the present.

It was Undersheriff Brian Grant. Sheriff Mark Roberts had given Shane Grant's number, and had advised Shane that he and Grant could contact each other *only* if something happened to Roberts, or he was unavailable in an emergency. The number was programmed into Shane's cell phone.

Shane answered, "Hello?"

"Dan, this is Brian Grant, Mark's Undersheriff."

"Yes?" Shane said hesitantly. He looked around for Wesley, who had left, taking his coffee and plate to the garage. Tom flashed Shane a thumbs up, all clear.

"We have an emergency. I need you to meet with me today, at a new location, at exactly 1400 hours."

"That's very unusual, sir. Is Sheriff Roberts aware of this?"

"I can't go into this on the phone, but there has been an emergency and Roberts is completely unavailable. I'm following his instructions, and I'm afraid I must insist you do, as well."

Shane remained silent, forcing Grant to continue.

"Please be ready. This is a life or death situation. I will text you the location 40 minutes before the meeting. You will have plenty of time to make it there."

Shane said nothing, and Grant ended the phone call before he could object. Shane looked at Kate in silence.

7

"There is nothing more deceptive than an obvious fact"
(Arthur Conan Doyle)

Shane glanced at his watch, and noted the time, 0923. Kate watched him intently, acting like nothing important had happened. She knew the explanation would come when Shane was ready, and they could talk safely. Shane continued eating. Kate couldn't resist watching the staff as she glanced around the kitchen, checking to see if anyone was paying extra attention, or anything seemed out of the ordinary. She could detect nothing. She was self-committed to double check the staff, in case there was more than one mole.

Kate continued small talk about Wallowa County, the towns of Joseph, Imnaha, Wallowa, Lostine, Enterprise, and, of course, Wallowa Lake, the crown jewel of the valley. Kate told Shane tales of her experiences with the animals that lived in the area, fishing and hunting...and especially, of the ranch.

When they finished, Kate took their plates to the sink, where Juanita greeted her with a cheerful smile. Juanita took the plates and offered Kate refills on their lattes. Juanita was a gentle, quiet woman, 50ish and attractive, who had always been kind to Kate and her grandfather. She had been with them for longer than Kate could recall. Juanita was a master with the espresso machine, and a great cook in her own right. Kate had special memories and deep feelings for Juanita.

As she watched Juanita grind and tamp the coffee, and then work the espresso machine, Kate recalled so many times that Juanita had made her hot chocolate when she was a child…handmade hot chocolate with small marshmallows floating on top, concealed just below a circular cone-shaped layer of whipped cream.

Juanita loved to see the white moustache that always ended up on Kate's upper lip, as she tried to slurp up a marshmallow through the whipped cream. They would both laugh, and Juanita would give her a gentle hug. Kate missed those hugs now that she was grown. Juanita had become very important to her over the years, a part of Kate's extended family.

When Juanita handed Kate the lattes, Kate immediately took them, then set them down on the counter. She gave Juanita a big hug and thanked her, explaining that she missed the old days and her white moustache. Juanita's smile conveyed that she missed those days too, and her eyes brightened. Kate turned in time to see Shane talking to Lee and beckoning to her to make a trip upstairs. As she left the kitchen, Kate looked back to see Juanita waving and smiling after her.

Arriving back in their room, Shane described Grant's phone call to Kate and Lee in detail. They discussed options. Wesley was now an integral part of the estate counter surveillance team, and the decision was made to leave him with the team guarding the estate garage. The original thought had been for Pete, Walter, Shane and Kate to remain at the estate today, due to the warning about Friday. Shane seemed to have no option to stay now, and none of them could think of a plausible excuse to cancel the meeting, especially with Grant's statement about his safety being at risk.

Somebody had planned something that Shane had been warned about by their friendly informant. But everyone agreed they had no clue what might happen, and they needed to formulate a plan to ensure Shane's safety, as best they could.

A long conversation seemed to go nowhere productive, and Lee finally summed it up as, "How do we plan for an unknown event at an unknown place involving unknown people?" No one spoke, as their collective thoughts arrived at the same dead-end conclusion.

Lee called Tom, Jesse, Walter and Pete to the room. After a great deal more discussion, a plan began to take form. Two counter surveillance details would leave 15 minutes ahead of Shane, and would maintain a safe distance in front of him, once they knew where the meet was to be held. Shane would communicate to the team by handheld 2-way encrypted radios, so no one could monitor the conversation. Only the inner circle of trusted souls would know the plan or have access to programmed radios.

Once Shane received information about the location of the meet with Undersheriff Grant, he would leave the estate, but slow down the drive long enough to give his team a chance to arrive first and scan the area for threats. The team would advise Shane accordingly, and offer him some measure of protection.

Nobody was totally comfortable with the plan, but it was the best they had at the moment. Jesse left to program the radios being used, and make team assignments that would include himself, Mike Panos, Pete Panos, and Tom Bradshaw. Using these four of the trusted cadre, would also remove them from the estate, making everyone remaining potentially more vulnerable, and everyone knew it. But once again, there seemed to be no good alternatives.

Tom and Pete were excellent marksmen, and each had training and experience as a member of a sniper team. Once in place for the meet, they would use their skills to provide protection for Shane. Everyone's stress levels were rising, as they all knew that the 15-20 minute window ahead of Shane's arrival, wouldn't give them much time.

Kate left to get another latte for Shane, and arriving at the kitchen, asked Juanita to make her a third, also, breaking her own rule of no more than two in a morning. Juanita gave her a look of concern, which Kate shrugged off unconvincingly. Kate was obviously preoccupied and that worried Juanita, but she understood she needed to conceal her concern for Kate.

Mike and Pete Panos swept the SUVs to be used in Shane's surveillance and protection detail, scanning for bugs and tracking devices. Tom secured his sniper rifle, and a spotting scope for Pete. Howard was charged with keeping watch on the four vehicles to be used, once they were outfitted with all relevant equipment. He would also keep tabs on Wesley, when Wesley was assigned to the garage, after the teams departed.

The small teams of trusted investigators worked on the details of the surveillance and protection, while Shane, Walter, Pete and Lee brainstormed what-ifs until they ran out of ideas. Kate sipped her latte, watching and listening, trying to think of something everyone had missed. They all became increasingly frustrated, as time invested produced no improved results.

Shane looked at his watch. It was noon, and the time when people would be filtering into the kitchen for lunch. The group left in the room decided that some of them should put in appearances, to avoid raising any suspicions. But soon after they all began to filter down to lunch, suddenly, everyone's phones lit up as Jesse initiated a "911 1205" text to the inner circle. Within a few minutes, the inner circle, minus Howard, was assembled back in Kate and Shane's room, each person seated in their own chair. All eyes were on Jesse.

Jesse held up the computer the informant had provided. He explained, "At 1200, a hidden file was activated by a timer within the computer. The file displays a map of Grant's proposed meeting place at Genoa, Nevada. Near the center of town is a Genoa landmark, the old bar."

Shane interrupted, "I know that place, built in 1853, and supposed to be the oldest bar in Nevada. Fun place. I played tourist in the town, and had a drink at the bar. Lots of history in the old town and the area." Pete and Walter cast anxious glances at Shane, and he deferred to Jesse.

Jesse continued, "Just past the bar, about a half-mile south on Main Street, is a dirt road that takes off to the right, heading up toward the mountain. About a quarter-mile up that road is a dirt parking lot that looks like it leads to a trailhead. The parking lot is marked on the map as the meeting place for today. I don't like this at all. It seems our friendly informant knows where the meet will take place, and is giving us a head's up, but he isn't telling us why, or what is going to happen."

Lee spoke quickly, "Maybe he doesn't *know* what is going to happen. Like us, he may have part of the story, but not the whole story. The good thing about this situation is we know where and when, and we have been warned to be careful. At least that's something of an advance warning." Walter and Pete nodded in agreement.

Shane stood up and walked slowly to the bay window. "I wish we had one more trusted soul here in the inner circle. Tom and Pete could leave now, and get there enough ahead of time to recon the area and set up a position of advantage. They would be in place in time to surveil the area before anyone arrives."

He continued, half thinking out loud. "They could give me a heads-up by radio on where to park to afford me the most protection. And, they could choose both a foot and vehicle escape route for me, should something go wrong." Shane glanced at Kate and saw she was watching him intently. He knew what she was thinking, but there was no way she could be there with him. It was killing them both on the inside.

Shane continued, "But we need three vehicles, minimum, in the rolling surveillance, with two ahead of me checking the route for bogies, and one behind to make sure I'm not followed. I'll use Jack's Valley Road off Hwy 395 to drive to Genoa. That will make it easy for the surveillance team to leap-frog ahead and tail me in the surveillance. But, we are a person short for that plan." He looked from Jesse to Lee, hoping for a solution.

Lee said he could suggest Lana, as efforts to clear all staff of suspicion had cleared her first, but he explained that she had already been detailed to partner with Wesley, and monitor his actions during the days ahead. Lee looked to Jesse, and Jesse shrugged his shoulders.

He said, "I am 90% sure about most of the staff, but 90% isn't good enough to join this cadre. There is just too much at stake."

Walter surprised everyone, when he said, "Take Howard Martin. He's ex-special forces and has served as my bodyguard many times in years past. In the military, he worked as an undercover operative during the 'war on drugs' in both Mexico and Columbia."

Everyone looked surprised. Walter continued, "Howard is not exactly as he appears...he's much more than he seems. He keeps his skills honed and ...let's say, I wouldn't want to test him." Walter chuckled.

Lee nodded, saying, "Lana will be enough to keep tabs on Wesley." He called Howard, advising him that Mike Panos would relieve him at the vehicles, so he could attend the meeting and be briefed.

After Howard arrived, and a final briefing plan was created, assignments were double checked, and everyone left, one at a time, to go down to lunch. Tom and Pete grabbed a sandwich and a few bottles of water, and left to travel to the meet location. Shane and Kate delayed in their room the longest, before going down to lunch. Neither of them was hungry, and both wanted more time together before Shane left. There was nothing about the upcoming meeting left to talk about, until they received the text from Undersheriff Grant.

While they were waiting and trying to de-stress, Kate seized the opportunity, now that they were alone, to ask Shane a question from their time at their espresso café.

"Shane, who was the older man you often talked to at the espresso café? I noticed you almost always sat with the gentleman, and when you weren't looking at me, you seemed to be talking...mostly listening, intently to your friend. There must be a story there, and I'm dying to know it."

Shane said, "I'm surprised you noticed him, or paid any attention to him at all."

"Well, you do recall that, even though it was the best espresso I've found in the city, other than Juanita's, I actually went there to see you, right? Since I was there to see you, I didn't miss anything you were doing."

Shane smiled, still getting used to events of the last few days, and his new partnership with Kate. Now, his comment seemed foolish.

Shane looked out their bay window at the distant hills, as he pictured the man. A smile came to his lips, as he explained, "When I arrived at the espresso café my first day here, I walked in and placed my order, then looked for a place to sit. The place was packed, as always. This old gentleman was sitting at a table by himself, and motioned for me to come over and share his table. He had been reading a newspaper, and asked me if I wanted to share a section."

"We introduced ourselves. He said his name was Jimmy O'Brien. He told me he was recently retired. We chatted about nothing really, just easy talk getting to know each other. Before I left that first day, Jimmy said he came in nearly every day, and he would save a seat for me. It became part of my routine."

Shane looked up at Kate and grinned, "Every day I came and sat with him, and couldn't take my eyes off you. Eventually, Jimmy started teasing me about you. I'd walk in and order while scanning the place for you, and if you weren't there, Jimmy would call out, 'She's not here yet, Romeo,' while laughing out loud from behind his newspaper."

"I told him he was blowing my cover, and he would just laugh at me and tease me more. He kept prodding me to go up to you and introduce myself. On the rare occasions he wasn't there in the morning, I really missed his prodding and conversation. Jimmy is quite a character."

The smile drained from Shane's face, as he continued. "He's had some sad turns in his life, though. His only son was killed in a traffic accident, while driving Jimmy's grandson and daughter-in-law to a soccer practice in Sacramento, where Jimmy and his wife lived. Jimmy ran a produce business there, with his longtime best friend and business partner. His daughter-in-law and grandson died of complications months later."

"About a year after the accident, Jimmy and his business partner sold their company to a large corporation, and then, Jimmy's wife left him and took off with his business partner. The tragic events of that year broke his heart."

"Jimmy's whole life had been his family. He was still in love with his wife, who had worked in the business with him for 20 years, as the purchasing agent. He and his wife had planned for their son to take over Jimmy's part of the business, when Jimmy retired. Their daughter-in-law worked as the bookkeeper and billing agent for the business. Jimmy was so proud of his son and his family."

"Jimmy brags that he brought his son up the right way, teaching him everything about the produce business, from the ground up. The kid started out sweeping floors and loading trucks with produce, using a forklift, on weekends. Eventually he graduated to driving a delivery truck. Then they taught him the purchasing side of the business, and finally, he started securing new accounts."

"Jimmy said his son was a whiz at business. He also said he was the best son he could have asked for. Jimmy loved his son's wife like a daughter, and he doted on his grandson. To make matters worse, as a result of the autopsy after the accident, Jimmy learned that his daughter-in-law had been pregnant with a little girl when she died. The whole thing was a family tragedy, and he and his wife never fully recovered."

"Jimmy told me he just lost interest in the business, and when he convinced his partner to sell to the corporation that had been after them for years, the last thing he expected was to lose his wife in the deal, too!"

Shane took the opportunity to tease Kate with a grin, saying, "You know you just can't trust women." Kate's jab to his ribs came with the speed of a summer-time rattlesnake strike, catching him completely off guard. He held up his hand in submission, "Just a joke, a joke, a bad joke, a *really* bad joke...okay?"

Kate eyed him suspiciously. "Are you making this up?" she demanded. "Because if you made this whole story up and I was sad enough to cry at Jimmy's loss, the next jab is really going to hurt, buddy!" Once again Kate drew back a hand like a coiled rattlesnake, preparing for the strike, casting a sly smile at Shane.

Shane threw his hands up in submission and assured her. "It's all true, I swear! Jimmy said he couldn't bear to go to his favorite places anymore. He and his family used to go through the shops in Placerville on weekends, or in Nevada City during the winter festival. He and his wife got away for special weekends to their favorite Bed and Breakfast there. Jimmy told me about family vacations to the Oregon Coast, and the beach house he rented at Cannon Beach, near Haystack Rock. The family had a great life that suddenly came to a screeching halt."

"His family was his life, and, in the space of a year, he lost it all. After Jimmy sold the Sacramento house, he moved to Carson City just to get away from the bad memories. That was nine months ago. He said he'd started over and made a few friends here, mostly fishing at Topaz Lake, hiking and playing golf in the valley and up at Lake Tahoe. Still, when he talks about the loss of his family, you can see the enormous sadness in the man...even through his well-developed sense of humor."

Kate pressed Shane for more. "Well, what happened to his wife and his *best* friend? And why did he come here? And does he date anyone? Because Delores' mom is single, and maybe we could introduce them, you know...I, I mean we could bring her to coffee. I think he might like her because she is very nice and pretty, and she loves hiking... and she's a golfer!"

Shane threw his hand up again, "Whoa, whoa, whoa, you have him dating already and you haven't even met him? I mean, slow down, girl...let's start with him meeting you first. You can't plan his life like you all did mine...well, and yours. I mean, he is his own man. But he is very lonely...and maybe it wouldn't be such a bad idea..."

As Shane realized Jimmy didn't know yet that he had finally met Kate, he started to like the idea. He pictured walking into the café with Kate, and he suddenly wanted to see the startled look on Jimmy's face. He said quickly, "Okay, after this all calms down, we'll set it up. Seeing the look on his face when I walk in holding hands with you will be priceless!"

Somewhat surprised by the quick turnaround, Kate placed a hand on Shane's knee, giving him a conspiratorial smile, as she started to make plans, wondering what Delores and she could come up with as a special outfit for Delores' mother to wear. Her mind was racing.

She said, "We can do better than that. I can go in first and sit down. Then you walk in and wave at him, and come up to me and give me a big passionate kiss. That will surprise him!" They both laughed.

Shane continued, "Jimmy is a smart guy. We spent hours in conversations about everything from women to politics...not that the topics are much different."

Shane immediately jumped up to avoid the jab. Kate's mental plans for the blind date had distracted her and slowed her response.

She missed him with a delayed strike. Shane chuckled triumphantly and sat right back down, quickly grabbing the jabbing hand playfully, to hold and caress, and prevent a second strike.

Shane really liked Jimmy, and continued to describe him to Kate. "He really is a character, though. One day we were talking about political debates, and Jimmy recalled the days when people were courteous to each other, even in disagreement. He said people used to talk to each other and listen, rather than yelling at and talking over each other. Jimmy said he missed the days when you weren't demonized or accused of being some type of misogynist or 'phobic' just because you had a different opinion than someone else."

"Jimmy is disgusted at how people twist and spin facts now, just to make their point. He said the media take sides, reporting *facts* with such bias that they cut *out* all the facts and information that doesn't prove their case or further their agenda. Jimmy said that nowadays, the media leaves us with no clue as to what is true or false. They just spew out enraged opinions that foster more hatred and division. He often quotes a guy named Arthur Conan Doyle, who said, *"There is nothing more deceptive than an obvious fact."* He hates what the world is becoming."

Shane suddenly thought aloud, "I can't believe I remember Doyle's name. I guess I've heard it enough times now, so it left an impression. Anyway, Jimmy explains very eloquently what we all really know… facts can belie, or give a false impression, when they are forced to stand alone, having been surgically removed from the rest of the story. He says the proof is in the video that edits out the reason the police officer made an arrest, using force. Or the picture of the guy holding the gun that killed someone…after he took it away from the real killer. Jimmy hates the way society is manipulated by an angry media he says is working, not to report the truth, but rather, to deceive the public and promote its own agenda."

"Jimmy always says he was born 50 years too late. He longs for the good old days of honor and integrity. He wishes we could all go back to a time when all people, who were capable of working, did work for a living, and didn't expect handouts from the government. A time when you could look back on a lifetime of achievements, and be proud of what you built, on your own. A time of loyalty and honesty…and most of all, commitment."

"You know, I don't know why you brought him up right now, but I just realized I miss the old guy. Just talking about him makes me feel good." Kate smiled.

Kate was visibly touched by Jimmy's story and his obviously good heart. Tears welled in her eyes as she thought how much Jimmy longed for the same things she and Walter had always wanted. Knowing Delores' mother as well as she did, Kate couldn't help but think that she and Jimmy would be perfect for each other. Nor could she imagine why they would want to continue on alone, both yearning for a companion and the right match.

Kate sat up straight and pledged confidently, knowingly, "We're definitely getting them together." Shane realized, maybe for the first time, how utterly lonely Jimmy was, and he knew Kate was right. They looked at each other, smiling and nodding in agreement. The plan was forged.

Shane checked his watch, drawing him and Kate both back to matters at hand. It was 1240. Back in their room, he walked to the closet to change clothes, donning his level IIIA body armor vest, which he placed over a T-shirt and under a long sleeve shirt that was one size too large for him. The extra size concealed the vest nicely, but gave the appearance of adding 15 pounds to his trim, muscular frame.

He then pulled out his duty bag and selected two handguns. He placed his *Glock 17* into a shoulder holster on his left side. The smaller *Glock 19*, he placed in a flat holster, strapped by his belt to the small of his back. It was a left-hand holster, so when he reached behind, with his right hand, the gun would be in the correct position to retrieve. Both handguns were 9 MM caliber semi-autos. Extra magazines, each holding 17 additional rounds, made for the larger weapon, could be used interchangeably in both weapons. Shane placed the two extra magazines on his right side, in the magazine pouches provided by the shoulder holster.

Next, he strapped a *Kimber Micro* .380 caliber semi-auto handgun, in an ankle holster, on his left leg. The *Kimber* was small and easily concealable, and he was going to be prepared for a gun fight, if it came to that. As a final touch, Shane strapped a tactical knife in a sheath to his right calf. The knife had a 5-½ inch blade, and a smaller handle than a typical military knife. It was balanced, easy to conceal, and retrievable with his right hand, in case of any emergency.

He jumped up and down to check that everything was secure. He immediately winced in pain, having forgotten about the shin injury. He hoped he didn't have to run anywhere.

As he turned to meet Kate's eyes watching him, Shane grinned and said, "You know it just occurred to me, that Pete was the one that recommended the espresso café the first day I arrived. Coincidence you think?"

Kate smiled and cast a sideways glance his way, saying, "As a general rule, I don't believe in coincidence, my love." She took his hand in hers, and they walked out of their room, down to the kitchen for water and a snack.

Shane was still thinking about Jimmy and how much he really liked and cared for the man. Jimmy had been the only person, other than Pete and Kate, he had looked forward to seeing in the last few months. At the top of the stairs, Shane looked at Kate and asked, "What's her name, anyway? I only know her as Delores' mother. What does she do?"

Kate's voice brightened, as she said, "Delores' mother is a wonderful woman. Her husband, Delores' dad, died of cancer at a rather young age, a few years back. Her name is Angela, and she is a complete and unbridled riot. She loves to laugh and have a good time, and is always teasing someone or instigating some type of innocent misadventure. She likes to be called "Angie" by her friends, and brags that she is no angel. But she really is…an angel, I mean."

"The woman doesn't have a malicious bone in her body, and she would give you the shirt off her back, if you needed it. Angie won't rest until everyone is comfortable and has everything they need at a get-together. And then she's the life of the party, but not trying to be the center of attention. She's more like the force that drives the good times, encouraging everyone to participate, until the ball is rolling and she can back out and let it happen. Do you know what I mean?" Shane nodded his understanding.

"She's a good golfer. Angie, and her late husband, travelled and golfed, sometimes camping along the way in their travel trailer. They brought Delores up golfing. She's pretty good too." Shane cast a doubting look at Kate.

Kate countered, "Good enough to get a golf scholarship to a four-year college! Delores was too focused on school, though, to make golf her life, but she might have been able to make it to the LPGA, if she had been so motivated. That's what her coach said, anyway. But Delores has always wanted to come back to work for our family, in a more important role for us and for her. She has always been very focused on making a good life for herself...something that lasts a lifetime, and limits the need for constant travel away from home."

As they reached the kitchen, the aroma of homemade tamales filled their senses. The place was bustling with people filling plates and talking loudly, as they filtered in and out. A large bowl at the end of the line offered a sweet-looking rice pudding affair. Juanita handed first Kate, then Shane, plates she had personally prepared for them. Today was her turn to be the chef at the second crew lunch, and she had made two of Kate's favorites, to complement her infamous pork tamales. Shane was intrigued. He loved good authentic Mexican food.

Juanita explained, "The small bowl on the plate is filled with arroz con leche, my grandmother's recipe for rice pudding. The larger bowl is champurrado, a special drink, also from my grandmother. The little pretzel-shaped pastries are churros, from my mother's recipe. Kate can show you how to dip them in the champurrado, which doesn't have any alcohol in it today," Juanita added with a smile, as she left.

Kate was obviously pleased with the surprise, and beamed with pride, as if Juanita were family. As they sat at their usual table, Shane marveled at the meal. The combined aromas tantalized his taste buds, and he realized he was very hungry. Diving into his first bite of tamale, authentic flavors burst through Shane, forcing him to wonder about the roots of the dish.

"These tamales aren't like any I ever ate before," he exclaimed. "They're wonderful!"

"Thank you," Juanita said, as she returned to them with water. "The original recipes go all the way back to my family's Aztec and Mayan roots."

Shane tried to imagine the Aztec and Mayan civilizations that created the original recipes which had been handed down through generations of time. Juanita explained that these root dishes had been modified by the influence of the conquering Spanish. This special plate prepared for him today, by a distant decedent of that culture, had been passed down through countless numbers of grandmothers to mothers to daughters to their children, all over again, for hundreds of years.

Kate said, "I like to take the churro, and dip it into the champurrado for a few seconds, letting it absorb some of the juice, before I take a bite. I do that after every bite of tamale, but Grandfather thinks it's weird. He eats the tamales first, followed by the champurrado and churro, and finally the arroz con leche. Definitely not as fun!"

Juanita laughed.

"I think your way will be my way," Shane said, having followed Kate's advice. "Very tasty! And I have to think we are so spoiled to eat like this. I know I'll need to work out more often."

Kate looked stunned for a second. "Work out. Damn! I forgot to show you the basement. We have a gym there, with a steam room. That's where I take my karate lessons every Friday afternoon. Shit! I need to call Jack and cancel today."

Kate grabbed her cell phone and hit a speed dial number, explaining to Jack that she would have to cancel today, due to a family emergency, but that she would plan on next week for sure. Turning to Shane after the call she said, "Delores, Lana and I take a lesson together every Friday."

Shane just smiled and shook his head, saying, "When do the surprises ever end? No wonder the jab was so fast! How long have you been training, anyway? Should I be worried about you abusing me? I mean, I do bruise easily, as you have seen," he teased. "And you said 'shit' by the way." He smiled as he ate.

Kate's look became serious. "Grandfather started me on lessons about 6 months after my dad was…murdered. I understand better now why. He said it was a good way to blow off steam and develop both a skill and self-control. But then there were the trap and skeet lessons, archery lessons, marksmanship classes, hunting, fishing and survival classes. I see the big picture much more clearly now. It all seemed so fun at the time, but it was also part of a long-term survival plan."

Shane sat back in amazement. He said playfully to lighten the mood, "Damned if you just aren't the perfect woman! We could live on a desert island, and I could drink Pina Coladas all day, while you hunted, fished, gathered and cooked. I *would* build the fire for you, not that I'd *have* to, you know." He smiled, but realized the attempt to cheer her had failed. Kate's look was focused and determined.

Kate stared ahead, without reacting. They ate in silence for a while before she said, "Shane, we have both been protected all our lives as we were being prepared for the worst, and I feel that the worst is coming. Maybe today the worst will come, or maybe not, but it *will* come. It's just part of who we are, all because of other people's greed. It's not right and it's not fair, but it is our lives and we do need to win…to survive, for each other and our family."

As she looked at Shane, Kate answered his previous question as clearly as she could. "I will never use violence for anything, other than to protect those I love, to protect my family and friends, or someone innocent. But I am a second degree black belt, and a trained marksman. I have been trained with fighting knives and archery, and I can hunt, fish and survive in the wild. That's who I am…and it is also part of what I do best."

"What I can't do is stand idly by and let anyone I love be hurt, by anything or anyone. What I'm not, is someone who will wait patiently at home, and worry that I should be doing *something* to make sure my loved ones come home safely. I'm sorry, but I'm going with you today!"

Shane immediately began to object, but Kate was ahead of him. Her phone was out, and she dialed 911 1300. She stood up and gave Shane *the look* which, he had already come to realize, meant any argument would be futile.

She took him by the hand, saying, "Come on, I have a last minute modification to add to the plan. No one will even know I'm there. This is the way it's going to be. And by the way, just so you know, I'm a much better shot than Tom Bradshaw, at least out past 400 yards."

All Shane could do right now was follow her back to their room. As his mind raced for ways to dissuade her, he couldn't help but think about his sweet Kate shooting a target at more than 400 yards. She may really be the perfect woman after all, he thought.

8

*"How ridiculous and how strange to be surprised
at anything which happens in life"*
(Marcus Aurelius, Meditations)

When they arrived at their room, Kate and Shane found Walter and Pete waiting nervously. As she walked in, Kate flashed them both *the look* that seemed to possess a power of communication beyond speech, and yet, at the same time, transcend all understanding. Shane watched the event and thought this was a unique force of nature that most women, but no man, seemed to possess. *The look* commanded silence from the others in the room, while it also conveyed a demand for no interference, as clearly as a flashing neon sign.

Walter was most experienced with Kate's force. And while Shane watched, Walter sat down on a chair, appearing already defeated before he was even sure of what was to come. He cradled his forehead in his hands, and muttered, "Oh, boy, I know *that* look."

Pete sat silently beside him. Having been married to a woman for decades, who had also possessed this strange magical power, Pete was much too intelligent and experienced to enter the unwinnable fight that brewed.

Unfortunately, Shane, who had the least experience in these matters, began to say something flippant, but Kate shot up a hand, as she tossed another *look* quickly his way. She reinforced the message defiantly with, "Wait until everyone else is here. My mind is made up, and I will not be dismissed like a child!"

Kate paced slowly back and forth from the bay window to the bed as the others filed into the room. Shane sat on the bed and finally, lay back on a stack of pillows, putting his hands over his eyes, as if afraid to watch. He began to understand the way this meeting would go, and how little power he would have to impact the outcome. Everyone coming into the room could feel the tension and somehow clairvoyantly respected the silence.

Once the team was present, minus Howard, Kate said, "There is an addition to the team…and for good reason. We need to buy some time, and we need more bodies. We have been focusing only on Undersheriff Grant, who we now know is dirty, and the Magadinnos. The more serious problem is that we have three additional variables: one, being whoever the Undersheriff is working for or with; two, being our friendly informant; and three, being the informant's plant inside the Magadinno syndicate. We are sending Shane out with very few people to support him, outnumbered by the relevant threats from five different sources. It's a recipe for disaster."

"We have one sniper team. We need a minimum of two teams to cover both sides of any perceived threat at the meet location. And before anyone offers an alternative, I *have* hiked that trail to the waterfall, and I know that one team can't cover the area."

Shane shot Kate a questioning look, but she responded, "I know this to be true. I've also studied the topo map. Teams will have to be set up at both the north and south sides of the canyon, and west of the parking lot, where the trail leads from the parking lot up the canyon. There are houses down toward the road heading to town, and Grant won't likely try anything too close to them or the road. It's likely he will want to leave the parking lot and travel up the canyon trail for privacy. And that's a likely place for a sniper to be lying in wait. That's the only thing that makes sense."

Kate was on a roll and accelerated the pace of her presentation. "Our sniper teams will have to be far enough off and above the trail to ensure cover and concealment. If it comes to one of our team taking out a threat to Shane, the shot could be 500 to 750 yards from either side. I know that Tom and Mike can make that shot from one side. Who else is here that can make that shot from the other side?"

Walter moaned, and Pete looked down at the floor. Both knew what was coming. Silence filled the room.

Shane broke the silence, saying, "You all know I can, or, at least, if you know as much about me as I think you do, then you know I can."

But even as the powerless words landed on the dead air in the room, Shane knew the statement made no sense. He couldn't be his own sniper team. He instantly regretted trying to change the subject, and a third glance from Kate conveyed her displeasure at the attempt. He figured that was probably his allotment of "looks," and he laid back on the pillows again, and listened as she continued.

Kate continued, undaunted, "You all know I am the only other person in the room, and at the estate, who can make that shot. Let's not beat around the bush. I need to be part of the second sniper team, and I need to leave soon, if not now."

Walter and Pete leapt to their feet, in unison. Walter shouted, "You can't go by yourself," as Lee said, "You don't even have an observer."

Pete added, somewhat feebly, "It's out of the question!"

But Jesse chimed in, "She has an excellent point. If the first team sets up on the wrong side of the trail, they could never effectively take out a target on the other side of the trail head, due to the elevation problems with the meet location. But it's a moot point. We don't have another body to act as Kate's observer." Lee and Walter sat down as Jesse spoke.

Kate spun around from the window, where she had been patiently waiting for the objections to stop. "Yes, we do," she said calmly. "Lisa Martin got back from California 20 minutes ago. She texted me from the espresso café and asked me to meet her there as soon as I could."

Lee was on his feet again. "When was anyone going to tell me, Lisa was back!?"

Jesse offered, "Should I program another pair of radios?" As a practical man, he believed the decision had just been made, as required by necessity and common sense.

Pete and Walter looked at each other and smiled, as Shane asked, "Who the hell is Lisa Martin?"

Lee and Jesse began making plans for another surveillance and sniper unit, as Walter and Pete explained to Shane that Lisa Martin was Mike Panos' girlfriend, and a longtime member of Lee and Tom's PI Company.

Walter added, "In fact, Lisa is a certified firearms instructor and range master, who served two tours in Afghanistan as part of a special operations sniper team, before it was publicized that women were serving in covert special forces. And, by the way, we had a company picnic last summer. And, at our rifle competition, Kate won, competing against Tom, Mike, Pete and Lisa. Lisa came in second past 500 yards."

Shane groaned a submissive, "Of course she did." But, as Kate smiled a victorious smile from where she stood by the window, Shane lodged his final objection. "It's too late to get everything together for them to be a second sniper team. We just don't have the time, and Lisa hasn't even been briefed. Grant should be calling any second."

Pete and Lee said, simultaneously, "We'll have the equipment ready."

Kate added, "I have a plan to delay the meet for the time we need to get Lisa on board and up-to-speed."

Shane realized he was outnumbered and looked to Walter and Pete for support. When they both shrugged in resignation, he realized it was a lost cause. Kate gave a final explanation that she would text Lisa a location to meet her, outside the compound, and would leave to meet with her, as soon as her vehicle, rifle, spotting scope and radios were ready. She asked Walter to retrieve her *Bergara Custom Heavy* tactical .308 caliber rifle, outfitted with a *Burris Eliminator* scope, along with the *Vortex Razor HD* spotting scope they used for the summer competition and general shooting practice.

Walter hurried out, as if on a mission, leaving Shane without his last hope of support for talking Kate out of the idea. Pete slapped Shane on the shoulder and said, "This *is* the wisest decision, you know."

He then followed Walter out, while Shane wondered how he had become the lone objector. He turned to Kate to plead his case but found only *the look* to greet him and immediately conceded defeat. He *was* learning, although it seemed very slowly to Kate.

Shane had only two questions left for Kate as her plan unfolded, and everyone left to equip the final surveillance vehicle. He asked,

Lee Cunningham

"So, what is your plan to give you enough time to get there and delay the meet, and how do you and Lisa hook up, to avoid taking up more time?"

"I already texted Lisa to meet me at a parking lot at South Carson and Stewart Streets. She may be waiting there for me already. When Undersheriff Grant calls, you are going to say that you are being delayed, getting last minute intel from your surveillance. Tell him to give you another hour, and that you'll have something extremely important for him that's just coming together."

Shane was intrigued. "And what do I tell him when we meet, and I have no information that just came together?" he asked.

Kate said firmly, "But you will have information. One of our surveillance technicians downstairs, Sam, texted me an update that an unusually large meth shipment is arriving at Lake Tahoe tonight, and that Vick and Bobby are going with Hector to pick it up. Per agreement with the seller, they will be carrying more than two million dollars in cash and gold coins as payment."

Kate continued, obviously now in charge of the last-minute plans. "And, before you get all upset that you weren't in the loop, know that I told Sam to text me with any update because you were busy. I'm sure Sam can be trusted and the information has only gone to me, and now it has gone to you. So, if there are no more objections or concerns, I need to leave to pick up Lisa, and you need to give me a kiss goodbye…and then another kiss for luck!"

With that, Kate walked over to Shane, and he gave her kisses as instructed. She wished him the best of luck and started to walk out the door.

She spun around, and added, "You might want to think about how we can use the information about two million in cash and gold to prod

224

Undersheriff Grant into doing something stupid. We need to get total control over that clown. And I know you know this, but don't give him any details as to who is involved, or where the deal is to take place."

Kate gave Shane a last confident smile and walked out, leaving Shane wondering *what* exactly *he* had control over anymore. He was alone in the room, feeling totally outmaneuvered, but totally and comfortably supported.

Shane walked to his duty bag, removed a few items he wouldn't need, and added a good wide- field-of-vision set of 12 X 50 binoculars. He threw in his old *Remington Wingmaster Model 870*, 12-gauge pistol-grip pump shotgun, loaded with 00 buckshot, that sported an extended tube holding a total of 8 rounds, with one in the chamber.

Shane knew he had plenty of long distance fire support. If he were to be involved in a fire fight, his responsibility would be to handle close-up threats. He knew he needed the additional firepower. He took a black jacket and set of ultra-thin leather gloves to wear. His duty bag contained a warm camo jacket, camo hat and set of thin camo gloves, just in case he needed to hit the brush on foot for an escape route, while he evaded a sniper.

On the way to his SUV, Shane stopped and met with Sam in the tech room. Wesley was nowhere in sight. Sam gave Shane additional information gleaned from the surveillance videos. As a unique twist to the Tahoe dope deal, a regional outlaw motorcycle gang was going to be making the delivery at the Tahoe meet. Sam advised Shane there had been a lot of chatter in the Magadinno compound about the Mexican cartels being cut out of this deal, due to the new clandestine alliance with a biker gang that could deliver cheaper meth.

Shane laughed, as he thought it funny that there was no honor among criminals. Franky and Hector were playing a dangerous game, trying to force a price war amongst the cartels, using a biker gang. Someone was likely going to get hurt, and probably very soon. Shane knew that the uneasy peace among the cartels wouldn't last, with a biker gang moving into their already crowded market.

But something else was obviously wrong, Shane thought. No one does a two-million-dollar dope deal on the first exchange. Deals of *that* size are built on trust resulting from dozens of deals, starting with small amounts that increase in size slowly, over time. And in the months he had been conducting surveillance on the Magadinnos, he had never heard anyone in the compound mention a biker gang, even though they were obviously already doing business with them. This was a new twist, and maybe a clue to some of the unknown players in this game.

Shane threw his bag in the SUV, as Howard gave him a nod. The teams were ready to go. Kate was already gone, and he pictured her meeting with Lisa and briefing her on the plans. A smile came to his lips. Shane would be the last to leave.

He made a final check of his equipment and radios. Everything was ready. He already had dry mouth and heartburn, side effects of the stress. He grabbed two bottles of water from the back seat and threw down three of the antacids he kept in the center console.

Shane's phone sounded, and he saw "Grant" on the screen. He delayed until four rings had played, and answered like he had hurried to the phone from some distance. "This is Dan." Shane always used his undercover name, in case someone on the other end of the line had been compromised, or their phone had been stolen...and, after all, Grant didn't know his true identity.

The voice at the other end sounded rushed and irritated. "It's Grant. We need to meet now. There's an old bar in the town of Genoa about 25 minutes south of Carson City. Take US Hwy 395 south to the turnoff to Genoa…that's State Route 206, to the right. When you get to Main Street in Genoa, turn left. As you pass the Genoa Bar and Saloon, start watching for a dirt road that turns off, up toward Tahoe. It's about a half-mile south of the bar."

Grant continued, "Go up the dirt road for a quarter mile or so, winding past a couple of homes, and you'll see a dirt parking lot on a bluff, with a hiking trail that runs up a canyon. Park on the far side of the parking lot, to the south. Here are the GPS coordinates, 38°59'44.61"N, and 119°50'52.27" W. I'll be there in 25 minutes. Any problems or questions?"

Shane replied quickly, "Hold on a sec…just finishing writing the coordinates." After a couple of seconds, he continued, "Perfect timing. Something really big has come up I need to inform your boss about. It's a special, unforeseen deal involving much more money and product than we've ever talked about. I'm just finishing up gathering the details from my equipment. But I need to review the audio at real time speed. It looks like I'll probably need another hour to get there."

Grant sounded even more irritated. "Give me a god-damned good reason we need to postpone for an hour!" he demanded, angrily.

But Shane continued, undaunted, in a half-code speech, in case the phone call was scanned. "I could give you more than two million good reasons. But, if we follow the golden rule, then you'll be even more than interested in who's coming to dinner tonight. If I leave too soon and don't get all the info for you, you'll be upset, because I won't have time to come all the way back and figure it out in time for us to travel to dinner…that is, if you or I, or your boss want to attend the party."

Grant was intrigued by the reference to an amount of money and the mention of gold. He pressed for more information. "So, the dinner party is out of town…how far?"

Shane knew to keep the details vague, for security and control sake, and said only, "Yes, at least an hour away. More like two, if we want to arrive early to get a good seat at the table."

In the end, Grant conceded, motivated by the thought of that much money. He quickly consented to the delay. He said, "Fine, but this better be good info. Call me as soon as you leave, so I'll know you're on your way!"

Shane knew his apartment had been under surveillance by Lee's team ever since he left and thought it a plus that Grant hadn't figured out he was no longer staying there. He also knew that he was going to leave Carson City and *then* call Grant, to delay whoever had plans to set up early on them for the meet in Genoa. But if they were already waiting at the location, he needed to *move* them now.

He said, "We need to pick an alternate location, closer, in case this intel takes a little longer than I think it will to extract. I need to monitor a phone call that is going to be placed in about twenty minutes. Can we choose a second location, about fifteen minutes closer, say, at the first turnout up Clear Creek Road, in the canyon west of Hwy 395? You know the area? There's a trail that goes back north from the turnout to an old logging shack."

Grant grunted disapprovingly but consented. "Damn it…okay, but no more changes!" He hung up. Shane smiled. He knew if an ambush had already been set up in Genoa, it would have to be pulled back to Carson City, in case the meet happened there. It would give his teams more time to set up in Genoa, where he would keep the meet.

Shane had an extra hour and knew exactly what he needed to do with the time. Almost everyone on Lee's teams were gone from the estate, on various assignments. He walked into the tech work room and asked Sam to keep a watch on the garage cameras and call him by radio should anyone come toward the garage. He checked to make sure Wesley was off-shift. They agreed to communicate on one of the surveillance frequencies not being used by any of the teams, and both switched their handheld radios to that frequency. Sam knew not to ask why they were doing this.

∽

Shane returned to the garage maintenance room and located a tool box. Taking it to the T-Bird, Shane pulled on some extra-large mechanics coveralls, that he had seen earlier on his tour, hanging in the maintenance room closet. He removed the rear spare tire mount and cover from the vehicle. He needed to perform the only maintenance his dad had ever taught him on this vehicle (spare tire pressure) and see why his dad had left that clue in the letter he had written Shane. Hopefully, the tire would be intact the way his dad had left it. He removed the tire. It appeared unused, with only slight age-cracking on the rubber sidewalls.

Shane examined the tire carefully and checked the air pressure with a gauge he had found in the tool box. It was correct, 32 psi. Taped to the tire was a plastic bag that read, "Instructions for Changing Tire." Shane opened the package, and found it contained a photo-copied schematic of step-by-step instructions for changing a tire. Inside the bag, concealed in the folded instructions, he located another, smaller bag, containing a single photograph. Pictured were Shane's mother and father, Pete and Shane.

Shane studied the photograph carefully. The only notable feature was that his dad was holding his hiking stick. Shane recalled that, after his dad broke his ankle hiking with friends in rough country, he had always hiked with a hiking stick, supporting the weak ankle, which had never been 100% after the injury. His dad always left the stick in the trunk of the car where he had installed a pair of clip holders to keep it out of the way.

Shane stuffed the photo into his shirt pocket and re-read the instruction for changing a tire. He saw no clues there. He opened the trunk. The hiking stick was still there, held in place for all these years by its clips. Shane removed the hiking stick. He studied it carefully for the first time.

It was a custom stick his dad had asked an old friend to handmake for him. The stick had an oversized metal grip that allowed the user to press down with a great deal of force, to push himself up, or hold himself from going down too quickly. The grip had been machined with grooves to afford his dad's large hands more surface area, to prevent slipping, even if wet.

Attached to one side of the grip covering the top of the stick, was a strap that could be adjusted for length, allowing the user to tighten the strap against his hand for added stability. The strap was secured to the top of the handle by a quick-release pressure pin pressed in to an indented drill hole. The strap continued down over the top of the metal grip and attached to another point several inches lower with a similar quick release pin.

Shane shook the stick and felt the balance, looking for some clue. He placed his own large hand through the strap and adjusted it to his grip.

He then closed the trunk and replaced the tire in its mount as he had found it. He walked to the maintenance closet with the stick and tool box. He removed the coveralls and replaced them and the tool box as he had found them. Still in the closet, he depressed the walking stick strap's blue release button on each pin and pulled them both out, one at a time, using the chrome ring attached to the release side of each pin. He removed the strap and placed the pins and strap on a shelf.

Shane then pulled up on the grip, but it remained firmly in place. He twisted the grip counter-clockwise against the stick, but it didn't budge. He tried twisting clockwise, and the entire grip and cap assembly began to unscrew. Shane removed the one-piece grip assembly, and found the stick had a hollow metal tube located beneath the brass grip assembly. The sheath appeared to be made of thick aluminum, maybe aircraft aluminum, he thought. It was very strong, and light weight.

Shane removed his pen Maglite from one of the cargo pockets on his *5.11 Tactical* pants. He turned the light on and pointed it down the hollow shaft, immediately seeing a baggie resting at the bottom of the metal housing, just a couple of inches down. Using some needle-nosed pliers he found in the tool chest, Shane recovered the package. He replaced the grip and strap assembly, returned the pliers to the tool chest, and unrolled the baggie.

The baggie contained two identical flash drives, each vacuum packed separately in thick plastic. The drives appeared to be of heavy duty military or industrial grade, and waterproof, being further encased in thick rubber. Shane recalled seeing USB flash drives like this shortly after they became commercially available the year his mom and dad were murdered. His dad told him they were the way of the future, since they were much handier, smaller and faster than the old floppy drives or even CDs or DVDs. Plus, they were immune to electromagnetic interference and scratches.

The technology was much different back then than it was now, and Shane knew he needed to have Lee's team retrieve whatever the drives contained. He was unsure of the storage capacity of these old flash drives. But knowing his dad was a tech geek, whatever he had, even then, was probably the best money could buy, or a prototype obtained from a Silicon Valley or military friend.

Shane placed the walking stick back in to the trunk. He called Sam and said, "Sam, I'm done here, so you can terminate the surveillance. Can you meet me here in the garage maintenance room?"

Sam arrived in less than a minute. Shane explained the significance of the old T-Bird, his dad's letter with the clue, the walking stick and the flash drives, including their probable age.

Sam looked at the drives intently, slowly saying with a growing smile, "I've seen this type of drive...military grade, waterproof USB flash drive, vintage of the time you're describing. If there's anything on these, we should be able to retrieve it."

Shane grabbed Sam by the wrist, then met his eyes. "Sam, you know what these may contain. If the information on them is what we think it is, they could be as lethal as lethal comes. Many important and powerful people would pay anything to get this information, or do anything to conceal or destroy it."

"Knowing my father, these drives are most likely two copies of the same information, placed in one safe place, just in case something happened to him. He would want to ensure that if one got damaged, the other was still intact. Each is vacuum packed in its own layer of thick plastic, then wrapped in a baggy, and finally placed in what appears to be a water-tight hidden chamber in his walking stick. He took a lot of precautions to conceal and preserve these, and now, so must we. We must also ensure that one of us can survive to get the information out of them."

Shane continued. "I'm going to keep one of these and find my own safe place for it. I'll share the location with Kate, Walter and

Pete. You take the other, and find a safe place to work on it, and make copies of the information as quickly as you can. You give copies to Tom, Jesse and Lee, and make additional copies for me, Walter, Pete and Kate...just in case the information is different on the drives. When that's done, we'll switch and repeat the process."

"We'll all meet later, after the meeting with Grant is over, and agree on a plan to move forward. No one will ever be able to find all of our collective safe spots, and the information will survive. It will also ensure we will all survive, once it's split up and duplicated in so many places."

Sam agreed, saying, "I sure like the way you think!" They left the maintenance room, Sam to work on the flash drive, and Shane to drive to the meeting with Grant.

∽

After re-entering the SUV, Shane tuned the 2-way radio to monitor the radio traffic from the surveillance and counter surveillance teams. All members of the team were trained to only use the radios when necessary. Too much radio traffic flooded frequencies, making it difficult for someone to get necessary traffic out. Too much blabber also had the effect of lowering attention to radio traffic, making it likely that someone could miss something important.

Flipping through the channels, the only conversation he heard was from the Magadinno surveillance team. There was a great deal of activity at the compound, with several new vehicles arriving in the last 30 minutes, and additional guards stationed outside the residence on the grounds.

Lee's teams were highly trained and experienced. Shane admired their diligence and commitment. He switched to his surveillance frequency, advising the group he was leaving and would make the phone call in 15 minutes. He received "10-4" acknowledgements from each of the units in his detail.

Shane guessed the one voice he didn't recognize belonged to Lisa Martin, meaning that Kate was driving. He should have guessed that, as Kate told him she always liked to drive. She explained her insistence on driving had been a problem with potential boyfriends, but he assured her it wouldn't be a problem for him. He had told her, however, that he wanted details on past boyfriends. And he had quickly received a jab in the ribs for his chiding.

He smiled as he remembered the conversation when he told Kate, teasingly, that he had been trained as an Emergency Vehicle Operations Course (EVOC) instructor and, although he was likely a much better driver than she was, he felt he could use the rest when they travelled. He had quickly received Kate's rattlesnake strike to the ribs for that one, too, but the look on her face was priceless, making it worth the pain.

He loved the coy "hurt" look Kate shot him when they bantered back and forth and he teased her. "Man, oh man, she can be stubborn though!" he laughed to himself.

Reaching US 395, Shane turned right to travel south toward Douglas County. The highway was always packed during the day. He drove through the bustling traffic, and watched the restaurants, car dealerships, auto body shops and shopping centers go by, one by one. The air smelled of diesel from a passing GMC pick-up as the driver hit the accelerator to cut off a car in the next lane. Black diesel smoke poured from the exhaust.

He passed the angry pick-up driver, now stopped in traffic. The young man was still waving his middle finger at the Asian driver of the small sedan, who he felt had somehow offended him. A Carson City Sheriff's Office unit raced up several vehicles behind him and, when it caught up to traffic, the deputy activated lights and siren. Traffic behind Shane began to pull to the right. All the traffic yielded, except for one dummy, who just kept driving...the angry young man in the pick-up.

Traffic ahead of the pick-up had yielded and finally boxed the angry driver in, so he too was forced to yield. The frustrated deputy was on the loud speaker now, ordering the pick-up to stop. Shane pulled left into the fast lane to allow the marked unit to get directly behind the pick-up. As Shane passed the pick-up, he observed the passenger apparently stuffing something under the seat, while the driver's eyes were glued to the rear-view mirror. The deputy switched the siren from wail to yelp. The unyielding driver began to pull over slowly behind Shane.

Shane resisted the urge to back up the deputy. He knew that the passenger could have stashed anything from a gun to dope, or even an open container of alcohol, but Shane couldn't delay getting to where he needed to be, or jeopardize his assignment. The deputy would figure it out...they almost always did. But to make sure, Shane dialed the Sheriff's Office from his cold phone, where the caller ID was blocked, and let the dispatcher know that the passenger had stuffed something under the seat. He hung up.

Shane flipped channels to monitor the Sheriff's Office frequency, and heard them notify the deputy making the stop of the phone call, after they dispatched a second marked unit to his location as back-up. Shane couldn't help, but smile.

Shane watched in the rear-view mirror. Traffic began to move around the car stop very slowly, as looky-loos had to slow down to see what was happening, even in the left-hand lane. Shane was reminded of the constant frustrations patrol officers face. It's always the same B.S. and lame excuses. People just don't ever seem to get better at some of these routine things in life, he thought.

He shook his head as he thought about people shopping at the super market, who block the entire aisle with their cart, while standing on one side of it so no one can move past them, and when confronted, act like it's their first-time shopping, and they had never thought of being courteous.

"Lamos," Shane thought to himself. "It's just one more reason I'm more comfortable with dogs than some people," he said quietly under his breath. "I have to stop talking to myself," he said out loud, as he laughed at his own comment.

Shane notified his team by radio that he was approaching the "border," referring to the county line. The team responded with acknowledgments. Both sniper teams were in place, and the surveillance vehicles were already waiting for him, all in different locations along the route. Shane turned off on Jacks Valley Road, just before Indian Hills.

He picked up his phone and called Grant. Grant answered on the first ring.

"Where are you?" Grant demanded.

"Just leaving my place...in the city. Headed to the first meet location."

"Where are you?" Shane countered.

"That doesn't matter. I'll see you in a half an hour." Grant sounded irritated and immediately hung up.

Shane knew that Grant was likely making a quick phone call to send someone back to the first meeting place...where his own teams would be waiting. He smiled once again, as he whispered, "Asshole!"

As he travelled south, the road got closer and closer to the Sierra Nevada Mountains that rise up from the Carson Valley to the Lake Tahoe basin. As he drew nearer, the trees that dotted the foothills began to come into focus, and Shane appreciated the stark, cold beauty of the majestic mountain range.

The Tahoe area is just a small piece of the Toiyabe National Forest, which contains more than 6.3 million acres or 6,828 square miles of land. About one-third of the famous Lake is located in Nevada, with the remainder residing in California. The entire area was beautiful, and Shane had always loved to hunt, hike and camp in the area with Heath, Pete and his dad. These mountains held many good memories for Shane. He relaxed as he drove onward in familiar country.

Shane looked up at a corner of the expanse, and mused, "No one could see it all in a lifetime." It was the largest and possibly most diverse national forest in the lower 48 states, and Shane had a sudden urge to be camping and hiking with Kate there…and with Pete, Heath and his mom and dad.

These random thoughts and daydreams kept Shane from getting "amped up" before a stressful event. They had become part of his routine. As he drove on further south, he picked up one of his team's counter-surveillance SUVs waiting at the turn-off to Hobo Hot Springs. It was Howard Martin, who fell in a respectable half-mile behind him. The other units would be ahead of him. The two sniper teams would already be hunkered down, scanning, in place.

Shane felt confident, not wanting any more surprises. This was a good plan. His phone rang and it was Grant.

Shane answered, "Hello?"

Grant said, "It's me. I'll be there in 25 minutes." Grant immediately hung up. Shane felt more uncomfortable again. He knew he had to control his adrenaline.

Shane's thoughts drifted back to hiking and camping with his dad and the rest of the group at the annual trek to the "Valley of the River," as they all fondly referred to that favorite camping place. One of the traditions for the trip had been to stop at the last restaurant, which they had nicknamed "The End of Civilization as We Know It."

The large group always sat at the same table, having called a week ahead to reserve it. The table was the only one in the place that could hold 12-15 people. It sat up on a pedestal of sorts, about a step higher than the main floor of the dining room, and seemed almost like a separate room. It was their formal meeting place, as they embarked on a trip filled with anticipation and excitement for men and boys alike.

Those were great days, Shane thought. He and Heath would sit scrunched up on one end of the table. Shane would always order *two* plates of Huevos Rancheros, a traditional Mexican dish known as rancher's eggs. Two fried eggs sat atop a pile of cheese, guacamole, lettuce, refried beans, and sour cream, covered with enchilada sauce, and resting on a large homemade flour tortilla.

The same Mexican family had owned the restaurant the entire time Shane and his family and friends had been going there. They always stopped there twice…once, for breakfast, going into the back country, and again, on their way out, for lunch.

Shane suddenly remembered the owner's daughter, *Catalina*. He had developed a crush on pretty Catalina when he was in his early teens. The affection was mutual, and apparently obvious, as both Shane's and Catalina's fathers had teased them in a friendly way in front of the entire group…every year.

Shane recalled, with a growing smile, how Catalina had walked outside with him when he was leaving the restaurant for the camp-out the last year he made the trip. She had held his hand and made him promise he would come back and date her, now that she was old enough to date. She told him she planned to marry him someday, and then she kissed him. He had flushed red and his heart had raced so fast, he thought it might beat right out of his chest. Even now, he recalled how much he had enjoyed that kiss.

Catalina was all he could seem to think about during that outing. He and Catalina had a similar meeting after lunch on the way out, and he promised he would return as soon as he got his own car. They exchanged phone numbers and addresses. They began writing letters and making calls, each conversation more committed than the last.

But the group of family and friends never made the trip again. Before the date of the next annual trip, Shane's parents were murdered, and he never returned. His whole life had changed…altered by outside forces beyond his understanding and control. He just now realized how, in the years that followed, he had forgotten about Catalina, until now. He wondered how his life would have turned out if not for his parents' murders. He was suddenly melancholy.

Shane began to think hard, trying to remember why he and Catalina had broken off their talks.

"The albatross has landed." It was Lisa Martin's voice over the radio. Grant was already there! He had lied to Shane, telling him he would be there in 25 minutes! This turn of events even surprised Shane, who thought, sometimes, he could no longer be surprised.

He thought to himself how ridiculous it is to be surprised at anything that happens in life. But he was disappointed in himself for not suspecting this possibility.

He had just arrived at Genoa, and now he had to stop and *lose* some time, or Grant would know Shane had called him long after he left Carson City. He informed his team by radio of the planned delay.

Howard radioed that he would take up a position in the parking lot of the Mormon Station State Park, across the street and on the other side of the main intersection in town. Shane parked out of sight and walked into the old bar.

Shane ordered an "old-time root beer," a favorite soft drink at the bar. He drank it slowly, checking his watch, as he watched the light traffic on Main Street out the front window. Eleven minutes passed. Shane got back into his SUV, and drove on to the meet.

State Route 206, coming west from US 395 to Genoa, is also called Genoa Lane. At the center of town, it turns left and becomes Foothill Road, as Main Street has ended. "Road names are one of Nevada's unique mysteries," Shane thought to himself, remaining calm and in control as his anticipation of danger increased.

His eyes had been scanning forward, left and right, up and down, and checking the side and rear-view mirrors for threats, just as he had been trained, and had further trained himself. He turned off Foothill Road, well aware that this was the route Grant had told him to take. He drove up the dirt road slowly, now allowing some adrenaline to flow, as he focused on the task of meet and survival at hand.

Shane saw Grant's 4-door Jeep Wrangler parked near the south end of the dirt parking lot. He continued to scan the area as he slowed his approach. The sniper teams would report nothing, unless they observed a threat. The radio was silent.

As Shane drove on slowly, he angle-parked beyond Grant's Jeep in order to turn and face the vehicle head on, while heading out slightly for a possible fast exit. He wanted to be able to quickly drive around

Grant, back to the highway. Shane slowed, almost to a crawl, before he stopped his vehicle and waited to get out. He knew he would exit on the sniper team side of his vehicle, with part of it between Grant and himself. Grant would have to exit on the highway side of his vehicle, also with some cover afforded by his Jeep.

Shane opened the door, his shotgun's pistol grip firmly in his right hand and concealed by the door, while the barrel rested on the driver's seat. With one foot still in the SUV, Shane waited for Grant to exit, but Grant remained seated. Shane's adrenaline surged. He controlled his breathing, but felt his heart pounding and the telltale throbbing of blood in his ears. He struggled to expand his focus, from Grant and his vehicle, to include his surroundings, while the adrenaline struggled against him to narrow his focus.

"Creak!" came a sound. Shane's narrowed vision immediately zeroed in on the source of the sound. Grant's door was partially open.

Lisa immediately called out, "Bogey!" on the radio. Instantaneously, a single rifle shot rang out.

Grant slammed his door and started his engine, but Shane was ahead of him, having not turned the engine off. Shane accelerated past Grant's vehicle. The radio was silent.

As Shane reached the highway, both teams reported that they had not fired at the target, but the bogey was down.

Shane's phone rang, and he answered instantly. It was Grant.

"What the fuck just happened?" Shane demanded, adrenaline now fully surging through his system.

There was a deafening silence on the phone, as Grant replied feebly, "I don't know. I can't figure out…what happened!"

As the silence again lingered, Shane keyed his radio mic, with his phone on speaker, so the team could hear the phone conversation.

He demanded, "You and I are going to meet at the old bar, inside, and I'm going in first! I'll see you there in five minutes." Grant sheepishly agreed.

Shane was inside the bar within a minute. He ordered another root beer and waited for Grant. He knew his team would be investigating and reporting what had happened later. Howard had taken up his former position to watch traffic. Shane was in control of his adrenaline by the time Grant walked in, but he was seething inside.

As Grant sat down at the table Shane had selected, farthest from the only other patron in the bar, Shane unloaded on him in a controlled, but firm, manner. "What the fuck, Grant? Who else knew we were meeting today?" Shane said the words softly enough so no one else could hear, but conveying all the anger the situation demanded. His eyes burned holes through Grant, who couldn't even look at him.

Grant offered pathetically obvious lies and excuses, but Shane was having none of it. He watched as Grant looked down and to the left when he answered Shane's questions. Combined with Grant's other body language, Shane recognized all the outward signs of a liar.

Grant squirmed in his chair, as he tried to convince Shane of his innocence and complete lack of involvement. He jerked his head around, avoided looking directly at Shane, and stared, without blinking, when he did look at Shane. He pointed his fingers frequently, covered his mouth when he spoke, repeated Shane's questions giving himself more time to formulate a lie, and accelerated his breathing… again, all classic signs of a liar.

Shane got up to leave, and told Grant, "I'm leaving first. You wait five minutes. You call me *after* you have some information on the shooting."

Grant began to object, "This isn't even my county, and we don't know that there is anything to investigate!"

Shane was ahead of Grant. "What you're going to do is get on your phone and call the Douglas County Sheriff's Office and report shots fired. You have them meet you at the Mormon Station parking lot down the street. You take them back to the area. Have them search it and see what they find. When you get some information, call me, and I'll pick the place for a meet."

Grant posed one last objection. "But, what do I say I was even *doing* here in the middle of the day? They'll want to know why I was up on the hill to begin with."

Shane asked, "Weren't you just telling Sheriff Roberts that your wife wanted to move to a larger house?"

Grant nodded a confused look, wondering how Shane knew this fact he had brought up only recently in conversation with his boss.

"Well then, we passed two real estate signs advertising lots for sale, on our way to the parking lot…acre parcels I believe. You tell them you were taking a break to check out the lots as possible building sites. You have time before they get here to look the lots up on your smart phone. Now, wait until I drive away before you make the call. And rest assured I'll be calling Sheriff Roberts to inquire about this meeting and the alleged emergency."

With that, and no more objections, Shane got up to leave, watching Grant as he stared down at his phone.

Shane left the way he had come, driving back to the estate on the same route. Halfway there, Tom announced that the entire team needed to meet and debrief as soon as they arrived back at the estate. Nothing else was said on the radio. Shane's mind raced on the drive back. He thought only of Kate and the rest of the team, and wondered who fired what shot, and at who.

By the time Shane arrived back at the garage, parked his vehicle and stepped out on to the concrete, he realized his injured leg was still sore. He had banged it against the door frame, diving into the unit when the shot rang out. He looked down and saw that a small area on his khaki pants was soaked with blood. The old wound had opened up.

Shane didn't go up immediately to his room. He stopped at the kitchen and asked Juanita to point him in the direction of a bottle of Scotch. He wanted a stiff drink. She expressed no surprise, and said she would bring a bottle to his room, asking him to give her a few minutes. Although he thought it was a little odd, Shane walked slowly up to his room, knowing the rest of the team would be there within a few minutes.

He walked into the room, and saw Kate's red sweater lying on a chair by the window. He sat on the bed and stared at the sweater, longing for the girl that had been inside it. She had been wearing that sweater just before she left to go to secure the meet location ahead of him, to protect him. Kate had done her job. Shane hadn't even noticed she had taken the sweater off, but now remembered she had changed into a tan tactical jacket before she kissed him goodbye.

"Shit, my girlfriend has a tactical jacket!" he thought to himself. Focusing on what he now remembered of the jacket, he added, "And it's even nicer and more functional than mine!"

He walked to meet the footsteps that approached the door, and opened it immediately after the knock came from the other side. Juanita entered with a sterling silver tray that supported a bottle of single malt scotch, 6 crystal glasses, 4 bottles of water, and a sterling silver bucket, which Shane surmised must contain ice. She had a large red bag tucked under her free arm.

She set the tray down on the antique bureau, and turned to Shane, with the bag in her hand. "Please take your pants off," she announced."

Disbelieving what he had just heard, Shane sputtered, "What?"

Juanita pointed to the growing blood spot on his leg and asked, firmly, like she was his mother, "Do you want Kate to walk in and notice that? Now, hurry up, we probably don't have much time."

Shane took off his pants, not sure what Juanita was going to do, but trusting her, none the less. He sat back down on the bed, as she began her work. She unzipped the red medical bag which he realized now was the type of bag a paramedic would carry.

Juanita unzipped the medical "Go Bag," put on a pair of surgical gloves and began cleansing the wound. She injected some local anesthetic around the rupture in the wound, and after waiting just a minute, began re-stitching the wound, as if she were a nurse. Feeling Shane's eyes on her, and without looking up, Juanita said, "I'm not just another pretty face. I'm an advanced EMT…part of my job requirement here." Juanita smiled up at Shane.

"Of course, you are," Shane offered in return. "I have come to expect nothing but surprises from everyone in this group."

With that, they both burst out in laughter, Shane occasionally wincing as an additional stitch was pulled tight. Juanita finished and packed everything up in her medical kit, while Shane put on a clean pair of pants.

Juanita was headed for the door when Shane asked her if he, too, could give her a hug. She gave him the same look she had earlier given Kate, and blushed slightly as he thanked her and hugged her, kissing her softly on her cheek. Juanita retrieved the stained pants, saying she would get the blood out, and she was out the door, glancing back at Shane with a smile, as she closed the door behind her.

Shane walked to the drink tray, his leg feeling better from the anesthetic. He poured a stiff, three-fingered drink from the bottle, while checking the label, which read, "*Laphroaig* 18." It was an 18-year old single malt scotch he had never heard of, but after only one sip, he was convinced he would be drinking it again, probably soon.

The door opened, and Shane's eyes met an anxious Kate. "You've changed your pants. Why?" she asked instantly.

Shane laughed, "Well, it's nice to see you, too, dear!"

Kate pressed on, "It's nice to see you in one piece, but why did you rush back to change your pants?"

Shane attempted one more evasion, asking, "Have you been talking to Juanita?"

Kate stopped her approach, just short of Shane, as he reached for her, and said, "Juanita? Where were you injured? The sniper died before he ever fired a shot!"

Shane's eyes widened with the news, but, before he could ask another question, Kate quickly shot *the look* his way, and he promptly conceded.

"Okay, I'll go first. On the jump back into the SUV, when the shot was fired, I smashed my old wound on the edge of the door. Juanita noticed some blood on my pants when I walked into the kitchen to ask for some scotch. She came up with the scotch and a first aid kit and fixed me right up."

He added playfully, "She's an advanced EMT, you know, all part of the job description of espresso expert, chef and medical technician." His humor got no reaction from Kate.

As a pretty, young woman in her thirties walked into the room, Kate replied, dryly, "I *know exactly* who Juanita is. Now take off your pants!"

Shane ignored the request, held out his hand in the direction of the approaching beauty, and said, "Hi, I'm Shane Beckett, aka Dan Harrington, and you must be Lisa. Hope you don't mind, but I have to take off my pants now…all part of the job, you know!"

With that, Shane shook Lisa's hand as she laughed nervously, and said, "Anything for the good of the mission. Please continue!"

Kate watched with growing concern as Shane removed his pants. She slowly unraveled the fresh bandage and checked the wound, while Shane turned red, and Lisa tried to hide her smile, pretending to look away. The door opened again and Tom walked, in followed directly by Lee, Walter, Pete, Mike, Howard and Sam. Shane just smiled and sipped his scotch.

Sam closed the door as Pete said, with a chuckle, "Well, I see you're giving Lisa a full introduction!" The entire room burst out in laughter.

9

"I may not have gone where I intended to go,
but I think I have ended up where I needed to be."
(Douglas Adams, The Long Dark Tea-Time of the Soul)

After Kate quickly inspected his wound, Shane pulled his pants up, while fielding a few more humorous jabs from the crowd as they poured their own drinks. But then the mood quickly changed, and everyone was seated and all business. The meet was debriefed quickly, as there was not much to tell.

Kate nodded to Lisa to begin. She said, "Both sniper teams had been in place for about 40 minutes when we saw a backpacker hiking down the trail, coming to a stop on a bluff overlooking the parking lot, about 500 yards out. Kate and I watched as he sat down on a rock, pulled out a sandwich and ate it, while drinking a can of soda. After about 20 minutes, he moved down on our side of the bluff, out of sight from the other team. Kate and I took responsibility for his surveillance, as the other team couldn't see him once he was on our side of the small ridge and bluff."

She continued, "After another ten minutes, the man appeared to lie down and, although part of his backpack was still visible, he was temporarily out of sight. Kate and I continued to monitor the area where he was last seen, along with our quadrant, and his backpack."

She paused and looked about, nervously. "But then, just as Grant's Jeep door cracked open, the backpacker popped up from a new position, previously out of sight, and immediately assumed the prone position with a rifle and scope resting on a tripod. I notified Kate as the backpacker took aim in the direction of Shane and Grant. Suddenly a shot rang out, before Kate acquired him as a target. She never fired, and he never fired. He just slumped down over his weapon. There was blood visible on his head and neck."

"Once you left, and Grant drove off, Tom ran down to check the man, since he was closest, even though his view had been blocked by the small bluff between the sniper and his team's location." She looked at Tom and he nodded.

Tom said, "The backpacker/sniper was equipped with a high-grade military style sniper rifle and high powered scope. Both had the serial numbers obliterated by filing. He had no wallet or identification on him. The only other items the man had in his possession were two photos, one of Grant and one of Shane. I retrieved the photos, took my own pics of him and the scene, pressed the dead man's fingerprints onto a plastic card, and obtained a hair sample for DNA testing, if needed. I don't recognize him from any of the surveillance photos or intelligence we have obtained. I left him as I had found him, minus the two photos we will process for fingerprints."

Tom continued. "Both sniper teams hoofed it to the next canyon to the south, where we had parked our vehicles. We continued to surveil the area behind us and, just prior to arriving at our vehicles, we observed an athletic man with a tall backpack, approximately one and a half miles up hill, walking fast in the opposite direction. We surmise this is the man who shot our backpacker/sniper, as his backpack was long enough to conceal a rifle, and I believe the shot came from his general location. At his pace, he would have reached State Route 207, the Kingsbury Grade, or one of the cul-de-sacs north of the grade, before our team could intercept him."

Tom continued in a measured, confident manner. "The two sniper teams made the decision not to attempt to find and identify the man, and drove back to the estate. Due to the distance, as they observed him through the spotting scope and binoculars, the only description the teams could collectively provide of the man was that he tall and slender, with great athletic ability, dressed in desert camouflage from head to toe, matching his backpack."

"I calculated the approximate location of the position he fired from, by his pace and the distance he would have needed to remain concealed from our two teams, as perhaps 800 yards from his target. That makes him a very good shot, and very dangerous as an unknown entity. The only additional point I have to add is that we plan on returning to search his route for evidence and tracks, once the police have finished their scene examination, since they won't likely search that area, not knowing where the shot would have originated." Tom glanced over to Lee.

Lee said, "Sam, can you bring us up to speed on developments you've uncovered while we were all at the meet?"

Sam reported, "The Magadinnos have already left for Tahoe, and Hector has not used his phone since they departed the compound. We have two surveillance vehicles following the Magadinno caravan, which consists of four vehicles and nine men. We monitored radio traffic on the Douglas County Sheriff's Office frequency, and they were responding several units to the scene of the shooting, where they are meeting with Grant."

"The first unit has already arrived and requested a canine search team, along with additional units. The on-duty responding patrol sergeant requested their mounted unit be assembled and staged at the Mormon Station parking lot, to assist in a search of the canyons, due to the mountainous terrain. Once the area is secured, the teams will only have a brief time to search the surroundings before sunset. They should be able to find the dead sniper, but the *friendly* shooter would be long gone. We will continue to monitor their progress, and determine when they abandon the scene."

A long discussion ensued about who the dead man's intended target was...Grant, Shane, or both of them. Making no progress with *this* dilemma, neither could the next riddle be solved, that being *who* the *friendly* shooter was protecting. An hour-long barrage of speculations, hypothesis and outright conjecture, proved no help in solving the mystery. All possibilities came to the same dead end, with no facts to back up any proposed explanation. Lisa left the meeting to check on Wesley and the counter surveillance teams. Silence filled the room.

Finally, Shane spoke. He filled the group in about the flash drives, first apologizing to Walter for spoiling the surprise about his dad's T-Bird. With the explanation, Walter assured Shane he fully understood, and said that he still planned a formal presentation and party when things calmed down.

Shane explained he had requested Sam copy and protect one of the drives, and that he had hidden the second drive prior to leaving for the meet. Upon his return to the estate, Shane gave Sam the second drive to copy and compare to the first drive. He looked at Sam, and said, "Sam, can you bring us up to date with any discoveries you have made?"

Sam was obviously excited. "Bearing in mind I just started looking at the drives, I can tell you, with some degree of certainty, that they *appear* to contain the same information, 2,986 pages of information and documentation. After a very brief scanning, the *report* appears to be Shane's father's synopsis of the entire corruption investigation, along with some supporting investigation, documents and attachments. What is daunting is that there is so much detail that it will take a team weeks to read and map out the web of suspects and events, in order to fully understand the totality of the case."

Sam continued. "You must understand that the case involves *decades* of corruption and conspiracy, with multiple crimes and murders, intertwined for some overall purpose that won't be clear until we understand, in detail, what the Attorney General's investigators took more than a year to discover and document…and Shane's dad months to collate and synopsize."

"It's a momentous challenge, and we need an experienced team to start on this ASAP, if we hope to use the information anytime soon. And to complicate the matter, the information is very highly encrypted, with what appears to have been state-of-the-art military encryption for that time. That alone will slow the process considerably until we have the correct cypher…*the Beckett Cypher*, as it were"

Walter asked, "Lee, Sam, how do you propose we proceed?"

Lee had been pacing back and forth, as he was known to do when he was thinking. He sighed a heavy long sigh, and sat in his chair. "Can I have a drink of that scotch, Shane?"

Shane replied, "Straight up…with ice…or water?" as he got up and walked to the bottle.

Lee replied, "Straight up. I wouldn't want to contaminate a great scotch with city water." He smiled, but the mood was still very serious.

Shane poured the drink, and asked, "Anyone else?"

Kate, Walter, Pete and Lee all held up hands. Only Walter and Pete requested ice. Tom and Mike got up and each grabbed a bottle of water, while Shane prepared the drinks. All six glasses had been used, and the bottle of scotch was now half empty.

A knock came to the door, and Juanita entered quietly. She carried another tray with more water, fresh ice, six more glasses, and another bottle of scotch. No one said a word.

When she left, Shane asked, "How did she know there would be six of us drinking...and how does she know we may need more scotch?!"

Kate smiled and said, "The rest of us in this room are non-drinkers!" Shane began to challenge the statement, with an objection about the probability of Juanita guessing correctly who would be in the room drinking scotch, but Kate saved him the frustration of trying to figure it out. "Juanita knows her job *very* well. It's just part of the job description you know!"

Shane smiled, while the rest of the room toasted each other, with drinks held over their heads.

Lee continued. "We're stretched very thin right now with the number of people working on the Magadinno mobile and compound surveillance, the intel coming from the cameras and bugs in the estate, Shane's old apartment surveillance, Grant's surveillance, and now this. Plus, we are still double checking all of our own people to make sure Wesley is the only mole. Now, we've added two sniper teams, counter surveillance, and are preparing to digest a year's investigative work and a lengthy synopsis into a couple of weeks. Our people are already working 14-hour shifts, seven days a week."

Lee took a long drink from his glass, sighed, and continued. "This investigation has seen two people killed in less than a week. Even though they were both bad guys…*very* bad guys, we don't know who pulled the trigger, or why. We need to reduce our responsibilities or increase staff. We need to slow down, to be able to check and double check what we're doing, before one of *us* gets hurt. I'll just throw this out as a suggestion…in the end, the decision belongs to Shane, who's taking the biggest risk, and Walter, who's footing the bill. We need to add more staff, if we don't feel comfortable going to the Feds yet…and another thing…" Lee stopped and looked around the room. No one said a word.

The room was filled with anticipation. Lee took another hefty swallow, and the glass was empty. "I suggest Shane meet with Sheriff Mark Roberts, after Douglas County discovers their dead sniper. Shane can explain to Roberts what we know about Undersheriff Grant. We know we can trust Roberts. He has a special motivation, just like this family does. Hopefully, Roberts will suspend Grant, pending the shooting investigation. He will likely lay low for a couple of weeks, while the investigation gets under way."

Lee continued. "We can leave a four-man surveillance team on Grant, and place a four-man team on the Magadinno compound in our safe house. The Magadinno team can handle documenting the intel coming from Hector's phone, and monitoring the cameras and bugs in the compound." Lee stopped and looked at his glass, not to imply his drink was empty, but to collect and organize racing thoughts. Shane poured Lee another drink, while Lee stared at the glass.

Lee continued with a smile. "Let's abandon Shane's old apartment. There's no longer a reason to keep a detail on it. If our friend on the outside knows as much as I think he does, he won't be delivering any more packages to us, once our surveillance team is gone. Let's leave a skeleton crew here at the estate that will include Wesley. That team will also monitor Wesley's activities. Let's take support staff, our cadre, which should now include Lisa and Sam, to a safe out-of-state location. If we are being surveilled, even our random patterns could have been discovered by now."

Lee continued, picking up speed as his thoughts began to take shape in his mind. "Let's commit the next two or three weeks to deciphering these new files, so we can cut to the chase, and figure out who the hell we are dealing with. It will be much more productive in the end…and a lot safer for all of us. The other added benefit will be, we won't need to bring in additional people not familiar with our operation…and, Walter, you'll save some money!"

Lee looked at Walter, and Walter instinctively smiled, but everyone in the room knew that money wasn't the thing that was on his mind.

Lee stood up and walked to the bay window, as he said, "I have one more suggestion. Out of the group we have left, two of my team need to leave to go to a family event. Ron and Patty Simon, the married surveillance team from your apartment, Shane…their son is getting married in two days." Shane nodded and said, "They seem like nice people, and very thorough."

Lee added, "They're both military trained intelligence operatives, and among the best surveillance and counter surveillance professionals we have. If you agree to this plan, I'll fly them home and back to meet us after their event. We need them on our protection detail, with a select few others. I can rotate five people out of our group, to go on much needed days off. They can come back and relieve others in the group, and so on. We can also give everyone left here a break, while we're gone. I'd like to leave Lana in charge, while we're away. She is more than trustworthy, and a good supervisor."

Lee sighed and sat down. He said, "That's all I've got."

Everyone had been listening intently and mulling the ideas over in their minds, but no one said anything, waiting for Walter or Shane to respond.

Walter spoke first. "Where do you suggest we go, Lee?"

Lee offered only, "Someplace remote, somewhat isolated or nearly inaccessible and easily protected. A place we can immerse ourselves in our work, not be disturbed and plow through all this stuff. Then we'll all know as much of the story as had previously been discovered."

He looked up and said, "We'll actually know and understand the events that led us to this point in time."

Walter said, "Both the Newport Beach house and the Wallowa County ranch are easily protected, but only the ranch is remote. We could rent a place, if you have one in mind."

Lee shook his head, not offering another choice.

Walter said, "Well, then, the ranch it is! Once we're packed and ready we can drive there in about 11 hours, more or less. If we take the King Air, we can be there in two hours. It can haul the pilot, 11 passengers, plus their baggage, and quite a bit of cargo. The final decision is yours, Shane."

Shane looked up at Kate and she nodded, in agreement with the plan. He said, "I like it, Lee. It's all very well thought out and planned. Plus…this will buy us much needed time catch up in this game. I feel like we're playing against unknown opponents, who keep changing the rules. We need to get on a level playing field to have a fighting chance. When should we be ready to leave?"

Lee said, "For us, my team can be ready by tomorrow, when we change shifts at 1000."

Walter added, "Pete and I can figure out the support staff to take. We'll likely have a few things to do in the morning, before we're ready to leave, but we should be able to make it by 1000."

Pete nodded in agreement, saying, "I'll be ready. But, with your permission, Walter, it's time to include my secretary, Tasha, on this trip. No one reads and collates legal documents faster, and she needs to be brought up to speed on what being involved with this family really means, to give her a chance to consider opting out."

Walter smiled at Pete, and laughed, "Fat chance she'll not choose *you*, my friend."

Pete seemed pleased with the response, as the grin on his face broadened and his cheeks flushed pink.

Shane marveled at how close Pete and Walter had become. He noted they worked together, by choice, as a team, often on the same projects. And, just like Lee and Tom, they fed off one another, each seeming to grow stronger and more creative with input from the other. Their confidence grew exponentially when they were together.

Shane understood now, more and more with each passing day, what Pete and Walter really meant to each other. He thought how neither of them had ever intended to end up here in life, but both were exactly where they needed to be. The same was likely true for him now. And, as Shane watched them talking, he felt a growing sense of pride and commitment to his extended "family."

Kate said, "I need to call Jack to cancel karate instruction for a few weeks."

Shane said, "I'll call Roberts and have the meet set ASAP, before Grant is free from the shooting site."

The team agreed to meet at 2000 hours, for a last-minute check list, and to be ready to pack. They all agreed they would figure out who was flying, and who was driving, once they met back in the evening and confirmed the teams and responsibilities. Walter requested they have the cadre meet in the dining room, and discuss it over dinner. Jesse would be freed up to barbeque some baby back ribs he had been dying to serve, while Wesley would be assigned to the parking garage.

∾

Kate was out the door before Shane could even talk to her. As soon as he was alone in the room, he called Sheriff Roberts, who answered on the first ring.

Roberts said, "Dan, what can you tell me? Grant told me he would explain later, and asked me not to come to the scene of the shooting. I only found out about it when the Douglas County Sheriff gave me a courtesy call about fifteen minutes ago, as I was leaving a meeting with the DA and Mayor. I had to call Grant myself... he didn't even call me!" Roberts was obviously more than irritated. He was downright pissed, and not one who appreciated being left in the dark.

Shane asked, "Can you meet me at the end of Oxoby Loop in Mills Park in 15 minutes? I'll explain everything then in person, not over the phone. If Grant calls, don't mention anything about the meet. This likely relates to the two cold cases we talked about. The cobra's nest has been exposed. Grant's one of the king *snakes*."

Roberts immediately agreed to the meeting, recognizing the codes "cobra's nest" and "cold cases," he and Shane had agreed on, either of which would require a face-to-face meeting between them, alone.

Shane started downstairs, wincing in pain with each step, from the recent re-injury. He was going to be sore tonight. He met Pete and Lee talking at the bottom of the stairs, and advised them he was on his way to meet with Sheriff Roberts.

Pete told him he was leaving to pick up Tasha. She was packing and would be spending the night at the estate. He said Lee was meeting with Jesse to go over scheduling, while Tom saw to it that the King Air was fueled and ready.

Shane started to leave and asked, as an afterthought, "By the way, what do we know about the pilot?"

Lee and Pete laughed out loud.

Pete answered with a grin, "Walter, Lana, Kate, Tom and I are all pilots and checked out in the plane, but I'll be flying this time. Walter and I flew a lot together when we travelled back and forth from Minnesota. He's a damn good pilot and a certified flight instructor… his hobby. Getting my certification was his first gift to me. By now, I have a little over 400 hours logged in the ship. Great airplane. You'll enjoy the ride," he called over his shoulder to Shane.

Shane walked out, thinking to himself, "Everyone here has to be a jack-of-many-trades to be a part of this group. I'd better expand my knowledge base before they kick me to the door!" He passed Juanita at the door, and wondered what additional skills *she* had that he hadn't already learned about.

Kate was in the garage when Shane arrived to pick up his SUV. He quickly briefed her on the plan with Roberts.

"Are you staying at the park for the meeting, or driving somewhere else?" she inquired.

Shane saw *the look* and knew what was coming. He stressed, "Please, we'll stay at the park, unless there's a reason we can't talk there."

Kate immediately fired back, "Is your radio in the charger? And what is the back-up meeting location?"

Shane nodded his head, saying, "It's in the charger, and I don't have a back-up meeting location." Kate pulled out her phone and texted Lisa to meet her in the garage.

Shane objected saying, "This is Roberts, the Sheriff of Carson City, who hired me. We already established we can trust him. No one else knows about the meet. I don't need back-up!"

Kate remained calm and collected. She lowered her chin and cocked her head, as she looked into Shane's eyes. After admiring the eyes of the man she loved for a second too long, she collected her thoughts, and said, "So, are you telling me that you're willing to bet your life on a man you didn't know until a few months ago, that you *think* is a good guy?"

As she continued, the pace of her verbal assault increased. "And this is the same good guy who kept the old, corrupt Undersheriff from the last administration…that same Undersheriff who happens to be working for a crime cartel, and other unknown persons, who are willing to murder people? And it's okay for you to go it alone, even though we have a mole in our unit, and there is an assassin on the loose outside, who killed two people in the last week, and we have no idea who that person is…not to mention, he seems to know every move we make, before we make it?"

Her glare intensified. "And, have you ever considered that these murderers may be using the same readily available software the National Security Agency has been using for years to listen in on anyone's phone calls…including ours? Are you really telling me this is all okay, and you don't need any back-up, and you'll *somehow* just be fine?"

But before he could respond, Lisa arrived, and Kate said, "Just get in your ride and give us a two-minute head start. We'll set up in the parking lot, where you'll have to pass us to meet Roberts. And one other thing…don't play these silly games with me again!" She didn't bother to give him a loving glance. In fact, she didn't look at Shane at all, as she climbed into her SUV and drove away with Lisa.

Lamenting there was no kiss or hug, and not even a smile this time, Shane realized he had screwed up, and made a note to himself, quietly whispering, "You are *not* a sole operative anymore…check with team before planning a lone wolf move of any kind. And P.S.: Think twice before speaking when Kate is in the room."

He repeated the phrase over and over, as he sat in the car, checking his watch after Kate and Lisa drove off. He thought he'd claim that the anesthetic Juanita used on his leg had affected his judgment, when he saw Kate again.

Exactly two minutes later, Shane drove out of the garage and passed the gate, thinking, "She won't buy the anesthetic story. I'd better just leave well enough alone and move on."

He flipped on the handheld radio, and advised Lisa he was leaving. He received a polite, but impersonal, "10-4," acknowledgment. He had already reached Carson Street when his phone rang. The call came over the inside vehicle speaker, and he activated his radio mic, so Kate and Lisa could hear the conversation.

Shane said, "This is Dan."

Roberts replied, "Grant just called me. He asked me where I was, and told me he needed to see me before I met with anyone else. He said all of our lives were in danger, but wouldn't tell me anything else, until I met with him."

Shane queried quickly, "Did you tell him anything? Does he know where you are or where you're going?"

Roberts replied calmly, "No, I told him nothing, after what you told me, but he knows something's up. I'll need to come up with a plan to handle him, and soon."

Shane advised Roberts, "If there is anyone in your department you trust implicitly, *I mean with your life*, call them and ask them to meet you tonight, as soon as you and I finish our meet. Can you suspend Grant, and tell him it's just routine, until the shooting investigation is finished?"

Roberts replied quickly, "Yes and yes. My Assistant Sheriff over Detectives, Bill Rodgers. He and I go way back, and I was already planning an administrative suspension leave for Grant, when I vented about the shooting investigation in *Douglas County* he was involved in today."

"Good," Shane replied. "Then that's the plan. You and Rodgers can handle the suspension together, leaving Grant no way of getting you alone. You'll have back-up and a witness. Make sure you aren't followed. I'll see you there in a few."

Shane ended the call and un-keyed the mic. He received a quick, "copy," from Lisa, ensuring him that she and Kate had heard the conversation.

Shane turned right onto E. William Street, also known as Hwy 50 East. "A road with multiple names…another Nevada thing," he thought to himself. He then turned right onto Oxtoby Loop. He passed Kate and Lisa's SUV, which was blacked out and stopped in the angled parking, facing south. He continued on to the end of the loop and stopped, leaving Roberts enough room to park north of him, where Kate and Lisa could monitor them both easily, from their position.

There was no need to say anything on the air. Silence was golden. He, Lisa and Kate all knew what they had to do. Lisa would be in the back seat by now, where she could check all foot and vehicle traffic, unrestricted, using binoculars. Kate would have her rifle and back-up hand gun ready, and also be checking Roberts's vehicle with binoculars, as soon as he arrived.

Roberts turned right off E. William, within a few minutes of Shane's arrival. Shane watched him with binoculars as he approached. He didn't appear to be having a "hands free" conversation with anyone, like Shane suspected Grant had done, when he arrived at the last meet.

Roberts pulled up next to Shane's vehicle, and parked. Shane immediately exited his vehicle, and walked to the rear of Robert's Jeep, checking the luggage area and back seats, while pretending to give the parking area and grounds a "once over." Shane quickly entered the rear passenger side of Robert's vehicle, and leaned over into the front seat. Roberts had to turn around to talk to Shane, leaving Shane in a position of advantage, should something be amiss.

Roberts' phone rang. He quickly explained he had left a message for Rodgers, and it was Rodgers returning the call. Shane nodded, and Roberts played the call over the "hands free" vehicle speaker.

Roberts answered, "Bill, thanks for calling back…are you busy?"

Rodgers replied, "No, what's up boss?"

Roberts said cryptically, "Bill, I need to see you in person and enlist your help with a touchy matter. And, I need you to avoid talking to Grant, if he attempts to contact you for any reason. That's crucial, Bill, understand?"

Rodgers answered quickly, "Yes, sir. Where and when?" Roberts looked at Shane. Shane flashed all ten fingers twice.

Roberts answered, "Bill, let's make it in 20 minutes at the Old Globe Saloon. It'll be too loud there, on a Friday night, for anyone to hear our conversation. We'll sit as far toward the back as possible. I want to be somewhere very visible."

Rodgers answer was now more of a friend talking to a friend, than employer to employee. He answered, "Okay, Mark, you have my interest peaked. Just like old times!" They both laughed and ended the call.

Roberts turned around, and said, "Okay, Shane, it's your show."

Shane gave Roberts as capsulized a version of the events of the last few months as he could, focusing especially on the last week's developments. As Shane delivered the rapid-fire briefing, Roberts sat silent, first looking at Shane, and then looking down, as if trying to focus and process all the information.

Shane left nothing out, covering the highlights of the intel he had obtained from the cameras and bugs inside the Magadinno compound, his injury the night of Big John's murder, the note he had found on his car when he left the area, conversations he had with Grant appraising him of the cartels deals with Hector and Franky, and the charts outlining alliances between the cartels and Franky's syndicate.

Roberts listened intently, as if hearing the information for the first time, even though Shane had already given him some of the info. Shane went on to cover the warning and files he had received when the computer was delivered to his apartment. He then brought up Grant's phone call in detail, claiming Roberts was unavailable due to some emergency…and the meet Grant had arranged, that ended up in a hit man being killed by an unknown assailant.

Finally, Shane told Roberts that he had brought other trusted people into the investigation, as it had expanded beyond his ability to control it safely, but he did not identify his team.

Roberts interrupted. "Shane, I don't *need* or *want* to know any more about your team, at this time…for their safety and for your safety. Plus, if needed, then I could pass a polygraph or withstand a forced interrogation, if it comes to that, without giving up any information."

Shane nodded, and then told Roberts about his dad's files. He assured him the files had been copied and delivered to multiple sources, in case anything happened to him. After planting the seed of information, he observed closely to measure Roberts' reaction. There was none. Roberts finally nodded approvingly.

Shane continued, explaining that Grant appeared to delay exiting his vehicle on today's meet, and may have been communicating with the hit man, who mysteriously appeared just as Shane exited to talk to Grant.

He watched Roberts' reaction as he fed him different facts in the story. By the time he was finished, Roberts' complexion had turned from pale to a bright red. He was visibly angry.

He turned and met Shane's eyes, and nearly shouted, "That son of a bitch! That lying bastard. That worthless, corrupt prick is going to be more than suspended, when I get through with his sorry ass. I'll have the District Attorney convene a grand jury and indict the little fucker. He can spend his last days on earth in a prison, hanging with his bros!"

Roberts slammed his fist down on the dash, so hard, Shane thought it might crack. Roberts remained furious.

Shane said calmly, "Sir, we need him for a little while longer. He's our ace-in-the-hole."

Roberts looked at Shane in disbelief. "Explain to me why we need that lying little rat bastard for anything, other than to anchor a boat, offshore, in deep water. Shane, he not only jeopardized this entire case, working for those murderous, drug dealing cartels…he almost got you killed!"

Shane laughed, and explained, "And I do take that very seriously, sir. But Grant is now supplying the Magadinnos, and whoever else he really works for, information he gets from me, through a mole in our group. I can feed Grant *misinformation* through our mole, they will all believe. In addition to that, once we get the files my dad put together completely collated, read and understood, we can use that information, to figure out a plan, that will lead to discovering who the *Grant rat bastard* works for. Then we can use Grant to identify and help us capture all the other rats. So, right now, sir, we need to think of Grant as the *key* rat bastard!"

With that explanation on board and understood, Roberts' mood changed, and he released a smile to his lips. "Shane, you don't know how much pleasure I'm going to get placing the cuffs on our *key rat bastard* someday!"

With that, the mood was lightened, and they both laughed.

Roberts said, suddenly, "Shane, I don't want to know any of the details on the people you are working with, or where you go, or what you do, until you are ready…for your own safety, keep it close to the vest. Just keep me briefed in face-to-face meetings from now on. You can fill me in with the results of the investigation, and feed our *rat* just what you want him to chew on…the dirty, little prick!"

"The one thing I do need to know, from time to time, is that you're safe. No more than that, until you're ready to give me the whole case.

And even then, if this thing is as big as we both think it is, we need to bring in more people to present it to, when we're ready. Agreed?"

Shane nodded and agreed. "I left the apartment when we learned it was compromised. I'll be gone for some days or weeks, while we work this all out. I'll try to contact you at least once each week, to let you know we're making progress, and I'm okay. If I don't contact you for more than ten days, assume something happened to me. If *that* happens, you'll receive a case file at your home, by special delivery of some type."

Roberts sighed. "Okay, then you'll go dark for a while."

"What more can I do right now, boss?" Shane reached over the seat and touched Roberts' shoulder.

Roberts looked back intently at Shane. "They've killed so many people, Shane...my wife didn't leave of her own accord. There's no knowing what happened to her. But *I* want to know someday, to have some closure on it. Your mom and dad, my wife, and so many more people...all for money, power and greed. Just get the evidence on all the other rat bastards, Shane. Please solve this! And please be careful! I got you into this, and I don't want you, or your friends, on my conscience!"

Roberts turned all the way around and extended his hand over the seat. Shane grabbed it firmly and nodded as they shook hands.

As Roberts drove away to meet his Assistant Sheriff, and Shane re-entered his SUV, both men realized they had been right all along about the magnitude of the corruption in this case. And both men were filled with more resolve than ever, to put an end to it, once and for all.

∾

Shane drove past Kate and Lisa, and, after waiting a minute, they followed, bringing up the rear. They tailed him back to the estate. He wasn't followed. At the garage, Shane waited for his tail.

As Kate and Lisa met him, he said smiling his boyish grin, "See? No worries."

Lisa then gave him *the look*. He pleaded, "Oh, god, no…not you, too."

Kate grabbed Shane by the hand and spun him around. "Shane, Roberts was followed. We had another surveillance team behind us. A vehicle drove slowly down E. William behind Roberts as he arrived, and then sped off, turning south on North Roop and east on East Robinson. The other team followed him."

"What!?" Shane leaned back against his SUV, and slumped his shoulders, in thought.

"A few minutes later, they radioed us, as the subject began approaching you both on foot. He came in fast and quietly, dressed in black, half running up Mills Park Lane, from the area of Palo Verde Drive. He was only watching with binoculars, from cover provided by a tree. It looked like he had the same backpack as our friendly shooter today. If he would have taken his rifle out, we would have had to take *him* out."

Shane looked down, as he said, "Sorry, I was just trying to lighten the mood for a moment. Who the hell is this guy?"

Lisa said, "I don't know, but I shot video of him through our spotting scope. We can look at it later. Right now, I need to go get cleaned up. We have our meeting in 40 minutes."

Shane looked over toward Lisa and realized she was covered in mud from the waist down. He didn't ask why. He looked at his watch, realized how late it was, and took Kate by the hand. They walked toward the house. On the way he asked, "Do you think it would be possible to get another lemon drop martini? Or a pitcher?"

Kate smiled, and they walked hand in hand to the kitchen. Juanita was sitting, finishing her dinner at a table. Jesse was coming in with racks of ribs, from the outside barbeque. They were handed off to one of the staff, who was covering mounds of ribs with tin foil, and placing them in a warming oven. The aromas were wonderful.

Kate asked Juanita if, when she was finished with her dinner, she could make them a pitcher of lemon drop martinis, and bring it, and three salt and sugar rimmed glasses, to their room. She said, "Please join us, I have a favor to ask of you." Juanita smiled and nodded.

As soon as they arrived at their room, Kate kissed Shane passionately, and then pulled away. She pushed him toward the shower, and said, "Honey, please relax and take a hot shower. Get dressed for dinner. When you're done, I'll take mine. I have some things to ask of Juanita."

Shane nodded, kissed Kate again, and held her tightly for a moment. He walked toward the shower, lost in thought about the mystery sniper he would never have known about, if not for Kate and Lisa, and the second team. He had just undressed and turned on the water, when he heard a knock at the door and Juanita's voice. He turned the shower volume up, and closed the bathroom door, to give the ladies more privacy.

Juanita walked in with the tray, as requested. She poured two glasses, took one, and handed one to Kate. She sat in an overstuffed chair in the large room, while Kate sat in a matching chair that faced her across the small antique table. Kate thanked Juanita for the drinks and toasted her by clinking glasses.

Kate asked, "Juanita, you have worked for my grandfather since before I can remember. How did that come to happen?"

Juanita looked at Kate fondly, as if granting approval to a daughter. She said, "I came to work for your grandparents when your grandmother was sick. I had been with your family for about a year, mostly cooking and shopping. I had never married, and my family was scattered around the country. It was a good opportunity for me. It gave me a home and a happy purpose."

"When your grandmother died, your grandfather still needed help, and I just stayed on. He was always so good to me. He sent me to a culinary school one summer, while you were away at camp. Walter encouraged me to take some college classes, and, over the years, I got my degree in business, but my heart was always in culinary arts. He sent me to the *Marco* Barista School and bought all the equipment I needed. He encouraged me to pursue whatever I was interested in accomplishing. Walter is such a sweet man...a true gentleman. I love him dearly."

Juanita suddenly stopped and blushed slightly, realizing her thoughts had taken her a little too far.

Kate seized the opportunity. "Exactly my point," Kate said. She smiled, as she leaned across the little table, and took one of Juanita's hands in her own hand. I've watched you two for years. Walter dotes on you and follows you with his eyes, like Shane does me. The man is in love with you, and I know you have the same feelings for him. He's just a few years older...so what?"

Juanita added, "He's seventeen years older, to be exact, not that it matters to me. But I don't think he feels what I feel, exactly. He's just nice to me, like a trusted old friend."

Kate stood up, releasing Juanita's hand, and smiled knowingly at her. "Funny you should say that, because he used almost exactly those same words, a few weeks ago, when I asked him about you...

and he admitted he was in love with you." Juanita's eyes widened, as a brilliant smile crept over her lips.

"I just want you to know, that I waited and pined away for Shane, from the time I was a teenager, until now. I could have acted on it, and insisted I be allowed to get to know him, years ago, but I just went along with life as it was. Finally, we got to meet and be together, and I have never been so happy. So, how long has it been since my grandmother died?"

Juanita sighed. "19 years and 7 months…and thirteen days," she said thoughtfully. "She was a nice lady. I could never take her place, even if Walter wanted me to." Juanita blushed, as the smile fled her face.

"Exactly my point again," Kate said firmly. "You don't need to take *her* place. You need to take *your* place…your *real* place in our family. I could have lost Shane today to a sniper's bullet. We came close. None of us have time to waste…and you and Walter have waited almost twenty years to act on your feelings. Maybe this is the time to go all in! It's already gone on too long. No one is in mourning anymore."

Juanita's facing was glowing, with a blend of excitement and embarrassment, at Kate's suggestion. She managed to ask, "What is the favor you want to ask of me?"

Kate said, "We are getting ready to leave for the ranch tomorrow. I would like you to come with us, and not just for the espresso and churros! We'll likely be at the ranch for a few weeks. I only ask that you think about our conversation, and talk to Walter…tell him how you feel. Carpe Diem, like you used to tell me, remember? Seize the day!"

Juanita looked down at the drink she cradled in both hands, and smiled. She looked up at Kate, her eyes shining, and said, "I'll go, and I'll try to get up the courage to do what you ask."

Kate looked at her doubtfully, but Juanita insisted. "I promise!"

Shane came out in a fresh change of clothes. Kate rose to walk to the shower, and Juanita stood up to go.

Shane asked, "Hey, what about me? Can't you stay and have a drink with me, too?"

Kate waved a hand behind her, and said, "You two kids have fun!" as she closed the bathroom door behind her.

Juanita poured Shane a drink and sat back down in the chair. She said, "You know I really do like these!" She raised her glass and smiled. Shane didn't think he'd seen her look so relaxed and happy, before this moment.

He said, "I'm not surprised, so do I! But then, I'm not surprised by anything much that happens in life anymore…especially around all of you!"

Juanita smiled, and added, "After today, neither am I. You know, Shane, I may not have gone where I intended to go in life, but I think I ended up where I needed to be."

Shane smiled and raised his glass. "Amen to that, Juanita, the same goes for me! I guess we're both pretty damned lucky!!"

As they sat and talked, getting to know each other, each thought how much they really appreciated and liked the other. They toasted with another drink, before Kate came out of the bathroom, dressed and ready to go to dinner.

Kate and Juanita became involved in an intense conversation about a past business deal Walter had made, ten or so years ago. Juanita recalled he had taken her out to lunch and dinner every day for nearly two weeks, while he bounced ideas off her, just to get her reaction. In the end, the deal was completed, and Walter thanked Juanita profusely for putting up with him, and calming his nerves, during the negotiations. At that time, it was the largest and most important deal he had ever put together, and involved Pete as a full partner. Walter said he had depended on Juanita to keep him focused. It was one of the highlights of his career, he had told her.

Juanita explained that it became a routine after that, whenever there was a serious negotiation, Walter would spend more time with Juanita, and ask her opinions. He used several of her ideas over the years. He said it was his secret weapon against the competition...two good minds, rather than one.

Kate had been standing quietly, listening while she finished her drink. "Imagine that," she said coyly. Juanita smiled.

They all walked down to the dining room together. Shane later remarked that there seemed to be a special spring in Juanita's step. She seemed to float down the stairs.

Dinner conversation was a more serious and organized matter, with each person making final suggestions for the upcoming trip. There were sixteen people at the table. Kate had asked Juanita to stay, and led her to sit next to Walter, which seemed to please him immensely. Shane thought he perked up and looked ten years younger than he normally did. At times, he bubbled with enthusiasm.

Pete sat next to Tasha. Lee, Jesse, and Tom sat around one end of the table. Jesse, Mike, Pete and Lisa sat along one side. Delores and Lana sat together and chatted. Kate and Shane brought up the other side, next to Howard. Sam was still working on documenting conversations at the Magadinno compound, and keeping Wesley occupied and monitored with his own team.

The decision was made that Walter, Pete, Tasha, Kate, Shane, Jesse, Lisa and Mike would take the King Air from the Minden airport to the ranch. The remainder of the group would drive up together, in three of the larger, fully equipped SUVs. Ron and Patty Simon's son's wedding in Denver was on Sunday. They would fly commercially from Denver to Lewiston, Idaho, on Tuesday. Sam would pick them up at the small airport and drive them to the ranch, about two and a half hours away. The various groups would pack up all the gear in the morning.

Wesley was going off shift tonight, and was going to be sent to Sacramento on a ruse, to meet with an old California DOJ acquaintance, and request assistance in locating arrest records on criminals involved in a now-defunct organized crime syndicate from the '90s. Everyone knew it was a waste of time, but it was a good way to put Wesley on ice. They wouldn't have to deal with him or detail a surveillance group to monitor his activates. His vehicle would be outfitted with a tracker.

A contact Lee had in Sacramento would verify Wesley was there, as soon as he arrived. The staff remaining at the estate would all have assignments, and were told that the group would be back in a few weeks. No one, outside the cadre that was leaving, knew where they would be, nor did they ask, or want to know. Everyone in the cadre team had been cleared and was considered beyond suspicion.

The highlight of the meeting were Jesse's smoked ribs, which had been rubbed with lemon pepper, seasoned salt and garlic, and slowly smoked on low heat for six hours. The ribs had then been seared on the hot barbeque for ten minutes a side. The meat literally fell off the bones in wonderfully flavored, soft chunks, that were a little crisp on the outside.

A simple salad of three types of lettuce, cherry tomatoes, roasted sunflower seeds, and dried sweetened cranberries, topped with blue cheese crumbles, and a mixture of blue cheese and balsamic dressing, was a perfect complement to the ribs.

Finally, a 2013 J. *Lohr Mourvedre* wine from Paso Robles, was served, as the crown jewel of the feast. Shane nominated the wine for the best supporting role award, and with a unanimous vote from the attendees, the wine was guaranteed to win. Everyone, except Juanita, had started the feast hungry, but no one could eat another bite when the last one stopped. Juanita and Walter were the first to leave dinner, and were in deep conversation as they walked out.

As the expanded cadre adjourned for the evening, Shane apologized to Kate as they walked upstairs. He said he was tired and sore, and too full to do anything, but sleep, although he had been dying to talk to her all day.

Kate smiled, "That's all right, honey…I'll talk you to sleep tonight." They fell asleep in each other's arms, with Kate detailing what to expect at the ranch. As she drifted off to sleep, Kate smiled a hopeful smile. Getting away from all the stress and danger would be a good thing. They needed to slow down for a while. After all, they were just falling in love.

10

*"The explanation requiring the fewest assumptions
is most likely to be correct."*
(William of Ockham)

Heath Beckett was running as fast as he could, down a trail from a mountain ridge, toward a river. He was pursued by someone who was gaining with every stride. There seemed to be no escape. Heath started laughing, and jumped off the trail onto a large boulder, dropping him like a rock to a place six feet below. The landing was softer than Heath had expected. He seemed to be able to land, as if on a trampoline, and spring off down the slope, to the next large rock. He was keeping just ahead of the pursuer.

As Heath ran faster and faster, he leaped further and further down the slope to the next landing site, until the inevitable crash came. He grabbed his left leg in pain, and called out to Shane. Shane and Heath had always had a special bond, Heath deferring to Shane's judgment, looking up to Shane, and always counting on Shane to bail him out of any jam. They had called this game "aerospace tower leaping," but their father had warned them against it, saying someone was eventually going to get hurt.

But they were young, athletic and bullet proof, or, so they thought. They had done this for years, when the agility and lighter weight of youth had been their friend. Through the years, as their bodies had grown, the leaps had become further and more dangerous. But this time, the small boulder had moved on Heath's landing, his momentum causing his ankle to roll over. He felt pain like he had never felt before.

Shane was with him in an instant, checking his injury, and assuring him that he would take the blame. He immediately helped his younger brother turn over onto his back, as he elevated Heath's left leg and stabilized it, as best he could. Then Shane ran all the way down to the river below, to soak his shirt in the ice cold water.

Shane managed to get back up the hill, and wrap the swelling ankle in his wet cold shirt, in less than ten minutes. He ran to a nearby willow tree and cut a branch with his survival knife. He quickly fashioned a homemade splint, which he formed and tied to Heath's ankle with his web belt. He then lifted Heath, and positioned him at his right side, so he could take the weight off his brother's left side.

Within just a few minutes, they were on their way down to the *valley of the river*, where their father, Patrick, would be waiting. They would be the last ones back to camp, as always. Shane would not lie if they were to be in trouble, but he would protect Heath, as always.

As they got close enough to see the men at the camp down below, Shane felt a sense of failure. Somewhere, he had missed recognizing the delicate balance between allowing Heath to do what Heath wanted, and restraining his brother, to the point that he could be safe and still have fun. He must do better next time, he thought to himself.

Shane knew he could make all those jumps, as he had many times, even dropping as much as six or seven feet, but Heath could not. He had to scale back his own abilities when they played and encourage Heath to do the same. He must find the correct balance in life to protect his brother.

When Shane and Heath got to camp, their father was in the tent changing after his evening swim. Shane got a bucket of cold water and sat Heath at a table, placing his brother's foot and ankle in the bucket to reduce the swelling. Shane went to a place by the fire to wait for his dad. Pete was seated by the fire already, watching him. Pete smiled at Shane. He knew something was up.

Kent Murray, their dad's other very close friend, was also at the fire. Kent worked for the Drug Enforcement Administration, and had come on this annual event each year, bringing his own boy, Hunter. Kent made his way to the camp fire to warm his hands, and was ready to move back and sit to Pete's right, leaving a space between him and Pete for Shane's dad. But Shane needed to ask his dad a question that had been bothering him for a long time. He needed to position himself at the fire. He wanted to take Kent's seat.

Just then, Heath called out to him in pain, and Shane half ran to his brother, taking him the acetaminophen and ibuprofen *cocktail* their mother had taught them to use when they needed to reduce swelling and pain. But by the time Shane gave Heath the four pills and returned, his father was already seated between Pete and Kent, and he had lost his opportunity. He'd have to be faster next time if the riddle was ever to be solved.

Shane heard a now familiar voice, calling again and again. But he ignored it, knowing he must find an opportunity to somehow ask his father the important question. He fought to keep his dad's face in focus as it began to fade from view. Pete was watching Shane, and seemed to understand how hard Shane was trying to stay with the scene…but, suddenly, it was gone, again. He never could hold on to it long enough to ask this one question.

Shane called out in frustration, "Damn it…damn it all to hell!" Shane's shoulder was rolling, as he fought to stay in what little was left of the picture, but the light was coming in as consciousness won the battle.

"Shane!" Kate called as she shook him… "Shane, are you awake? Honey, your phone is ringing." Shane opened his eyes. The dream scene was gone again, having yielded to the reality of the penetrating morning light. With a throbbing head, Shane now struggled hard to be fully awake and sharp, just as he had struggled against it a moment before. He took the cell phone, and answered it, saying, "Hello?"

It was Grant. "Dan, where the hell are you?"

Shane was instantly awake, and on guard. With a throbbing headache, he replied, "I was still asleep, with a girl I met at a bar last night, why?"

Grant was upset and demanded, "What were you doing at a bar? I'm in deep trouble, and you need to stay focused!"

Shane seized the opportunity for an offensive assault. "Damn it, Grant, you could have gotten one or both of us injured, even killed yesterday. I'm taking a few days off. And what are you talking about, anyway?" Shane forced Grant to tell him what was going, reversing Grant's assault.

Grant whined, "I need to see you, and I don't want to talk over the phone. I've been placed on administrative leave!"

Shane smiled, realizing the plan he and Roberts had made, was in play. He said defiantly, "Look, Brian, if you're on admin leave, you know I can't have any contact with you until you're reinstated. And I'm not sure I was ever supposed the meet with you to begin with! How soon will you be reinstated, so we can both meet with Roberts, and see what's really going on here?"

Grant replied sheepishly, "Maybe a week or two, whenever the shooting review is complete, and the review board makes its decision. Roberts said I'll be fine in the shooting, since I never fired a shot. But I know he's pissed that I was there, and he won't talk about you at all."

Shane said, "Then, to keep us both from being fired, I'll talk to you then. We both need to keep a low profile and not call any attention to ourselves. Whoever knew we were going to both be there, can know again if we meet. And I'm not sure who tipped them off. I'm out of the picture until this cools off. Tell Roberts to call me when the board makes its decision. I'll be on vacation until then, and not talking to anyone, but him."

Shane hung up as Grant began to object. When Grant called back almost instantly, Shane didn't answer. Kate didn't need to ask about the call. She had been lying next to Shane as he talked to Grant.

She did, however, need to know what Shane was fighting in his sleep. "Shane, another bad dream?" she asked with a look of genuine concern.

He nodded his head, briskly rubbing his face with his hands. He released a deep sigh, saying, "I get right to the point where I'm going to ask my dad an important question, and then it leaves me. I can't figure out what clue I'm missing. But there is something there, locked away down deep in my memory, being pushed to the surface in these dreams."

He looked at Kate, and explained, "It may just have to do with Heath injuring his leg in the jump, but I don't think so." Kate looked puzzled.

Shane said, "He tore some ligaments and a muscle in a jump off a boulder, when we were playing a game we shouldn't have been playing at our annual camping trip. He eventually recovered, but afterward, he always had a unique way of running that favored his left leg." Shane was silent, deep in thought, wondering.

Kate wondered what he could be thinking about so seriously. She probed, "What is it, honey?"

Shane looked up at her, as if coming out of a day dream. He said, thoughtfully, "If I didn't know better…but it couldn't be…I need to make a phone call…to Heath…to see how he's doing."

With that, Shane threw back the remaining covers, and walked to the cell phone Walter and Kate had provided him. It was still lying on top of the chest of drawers, connected to its charger. He had been talking on his department issued phone, and wanted his *cold* phone for this call.

As he walked away from her, naked, Kate admired Shane's muscular body and near perfect butt. She had always admired a good butt, but Shane's was the nicest she had ever seen. "It's not as if I've seen a lot of naked men's butts," she thought to herself, with a smile. She had been to the beaches at Newport, Laguna and Huntington, and had seen thousands of scantily clothed men in her summer days in sunny southern California. And there had been a couple of boyfriends in college…short unsatisfying relationships.

Kate was sure Shane had the nicest she had ever seen, though, and she felt herself begin to warm and tingle deep inside. Familiar butterflies were churning above the tingle. She thought she should look away to quiet those feelings, as they didn't have any extra time this morning to act on them. She blushed slightly, as she stared at the indentation between the top of Shane's butt cheeks, and fantasized about running her finger down there, as she pulled him deeper inside her.

Shane turned around and saw her staring, just before she looked away. A smile coming to his lips, he turned back to his new phone. He made the call, and waited for Heath to answer, turning again to face Kate. He would tease her a little more, he thought.

Kate was slightly embarrassed at her obvious desire, but couldn't help, but take a long hard look. She thought, "The front view is outstanding, too!"

She was glad they both liked to sleep naked. Clothes were great, but just not in bed, unless she wore something sexy and silky. Shane waited for Heath to answer, as Kate continued her gaze.

Shane got back into bed when Heath answered, and Kate escaped her embarrassment, saying she needed to take a shower.

"This is Heath. Who's this?" Heath asked, not recognizing the new phone number.

Shane snapped, "It's your brother. You know, the brother who's a little taller, more buff, and a tad better looking than you. Ring a bell?"

Heath quickly shot back, "You must have the wrong number. My *only* brother is taller…that's true. But he's *also* slightly overweight and not exactly *aging* well. It's really rather sad. I try to encourage him to work out, and hold on to what little looks and fleeting youth he has left, but it's a lost cause!"

"In your dreams, my brother!" Shane countered, laughing. "Seriously little bro, how are you doing? How's the landscape business?"

Heath answered quickly, "I'm great, and the business is booming. I've hired two new guys…*illegals*, but, before you lecture me, I'm trying to help them get their work visas. I'm trying to do it all right this time."

Shane listened for the telltale signs of a lie, but, unfortunately, had lost his ability to read his little brother when Heath had become such an excellent liar, during his druggy days. Without body language to read, Shane just couldn't tell.

They chatted until Kate was out of the shower and nearly dressed, and Shane knew he was pressed for time, although he wasn't really sure what time it was.

He said, "I have to go, my brother, but I'll be in touch, and when I get done with this assignment, I want to spend some time with you. Can we plan on that?"

Heath said, "When do you think that will be?"

Shane hesitated, unable to give any reasonable answer. He said, "It could be weeks or a few more months. I'm not sure. But it should be good weather then. I'm thinking a Mexico trip, maybe Cozumel or Cabo. What do you think?"

Heath answered with a huff, "Hell, it's going to be 100 degrees in Mexico in a few months. I'm thinking north, not south. You know I can't take extreme heat!"

Shane smiled and said, "You got it buddy! I keep forgetting how delicate you are. Keep it straight and narrow until then, and we'll have a good time…my treat."

Heath assured Shane he was "doing the right thing," as Shane had pleaded with him to do for years. Before he said his goodbye, Heath said, "I don't know exactly what you're working on, but knowing you, it will probably be dangerous. Just stay safe so we can make that trip together, okay? You're all I have left."

Shane promised Heath he would be safe, and ended the call. He turned to Kate, who had been listening intently to the end of the call. "You know, that's the first time he ever asked me to be safe. He always just assumed everything would be alright. Maybe he's finally getting it…god, I hope so."

Then, with a frown, Shane mused, "Or maybe he knows something he shouldn't..."

Kate smiled, and said, "You shower. I'll get coffee. Any special requests?"

Shane moved toward the bathroom. "Surprise me, you know what I like."

Kate waved behind her as she left the room, pleased to oversee even some of Shane's little decisions.

Shane was thinking the same thing, as he turned on the shower. Kate had made some big decisions so far in the case. And they had all been the right decisions. The fact that Kate cared about the small decisions in his life, now warmed him on the inside as effectively as the hot shower did on the outside. He liked this feeling, caring about another human being to the point that you looked forward to pleasing them and being with them, doing anything or simply nothing. He thought how much he loved this woman...and he was going to remind her as soon as she returned!

In the kitchen, Kate found Jesse at the espresso machine. "Where's Juanita?" she asked.

Jesse turned and said cheerfully, "No worries, I'm your barista man today. Juanita and Walter had breakfast this morning early. I don't know what's going on with those two, but Walter told me he and Juanita are riding in their own SUV with the convoy to the ranch. He said he wanted an extra rig on the road, and available in Oregon. They left to transfer her luggage for the trip to a fourth SUV. Looks like we will be taking an extra 250 pounds of gear in the King Air, which makes my unit happy. We'll have all the equipment completely set up before the convoy arrives."

Kate's smile told Jesse something special was up with Walter and Juanita, but he elected not to press the issue. "What's your pleasure this morning?" he asked.

Kate thought for a second and asked, "How's your caffé latte today...maybe caramel?"

Jesse loved doing something different, but the traditional drinks were his favorites. He was a purist at heart. "Two, I assume?" He looked somewhat disappointed.

Kate nodded.

"Coming right up!" Jesse grinned.

Kate was back upstairs before Shane was out of the shower. He loved a long hot shower, and the bathroom filled with steam held the proof. She walked in and placed the drinks on the granite counter near the shower. She admired Shane's form through the steamy glass shower door and sides. But, as good as the view was to her, she knew they would be pressed for time and she was hungry.

She urged, "Come on, water boy! We need to get a move on. It's almost 0830. Your flight leaves in an hour and a half, with or without you!"

Shane turned the shower off, mimicking the whine of a scolded child, "OK, OK...I'm coming, mom." He opened the shower door and was immediately hit in the face with a rolled bath sheet. He grinned at Kate, "Jeez, a guy can't even take a shower anymore! Is it really almost 0830? If it is, I'm glad we packed last night. I need to eat...and I'm starved! Hard to believe after all the ribs I ate last night, but I am!"

Kate laughed, "It's a good thing you have some money, buddy, or the food bill would kill us!"

Shane thought about having money, and said, "Yeah, having some money is something I'll need to get used to...for the first time.

Hopefully, you have someone in mind to help me manage it!" He dried off quickly, still thinking about having some real money. He knew it was a blessing, but also an additional responsibility.

Kate knew what he meant, but teased, "Oh, of course. You'll want to spend a lot of time with our accountant, Spencer Pinetta."

Shane wrapped the bath sheet around himself, and grabbed Kate quickly, in a bear hug. "You know exactly what I mean, young lady!"

He kissed her deeply, and when he pulled back and looked her in the eyes, he said tenderly, "I love you, Kate...I mean I *really* love you. I'm hoping we can make a lot of our decisions together."

Kate melted into his arms, and kissed him back, softly at first, and then passionately. She pulled away slowly, and said, "I love you *too*, Shane Beckett." She turned to lead Shane back to their room, and then broke away running, as she added, "But my financial advice comes at a price. I'm not that easy!"

She ran to the far side of their room, laughing, with Shane several steps behind her. He caught her, lifted her up and threw her on the bed gently, pretending to playfully attack her.

Shane tickled and kissed Kate and rolled her around the bed lovingly. Finally, the kisses became serious, and passion revealed the desire that quickly rose between them. They kissed and fondled each other, until the intensity built to a point of no return. They both knew there was no time for making love. They should already be downstairs, having breakfast, and hurrying to meet with the group scheduled to drive to the Minden airport and fly out.

One long, last passionate kiss between them delighted their imaginations as their tongues rolled and flicked a goodbye in each other's mouth. Both were sufficiently primed for love making, and they had to allow the feelings to slip away, the stimulation and preparation wasted…for now.

Shane asked, "Will there be a room for us at the "outpost" ranch?"

Kate replied, using her best western accent, "Nope, you'll be sleepin' with the boys in the bunk house, pard. We'll give y'all a bedroll, though, pilgrim!"

Seeing the look of disappointment, Kate quickly assured Shane they would have their own room, but added that there really was a bunk house, if he would rather sleep there with the boys.

Shane held up his hand in submission, "My single bunk days are over! Besides, I want a bed *role* with you."

Kate smiled in agreement. They held each other for a moment, and sealed the bargain with one last passionate kiss. Shane jumped up and dressed in less than a minute. Their luggage was already downstairs. He finished his latte on the way to the kitchen, and found Jesse who made them both another.

"Where's Juanita?" Shane asked, looking around, "She's usually here this time in the morning."

Kate said, "It seems she is riding with *Walter* in one of the SUVs. I'll explain on the way to the airport," she said, with a grin.

Jesse had made sure the breakfast was a good one, having thought about the long trip ahead. He had poached pears in orange juice, with brown sugar, cloves and cinnamon, and served them face-up, filled with the reduced sauce, on a bed of Greek vanilla yogurt.

The main dish was Jesse's crispy hash brown potatoes, made with two different kinds of cheese blended in with the potatoes, topped with a dollop of sour cream, crowned with a pair of fried eggs and flavored with a drizzle of Mexican mild Chile Verde sauce.

Kate's favorite thick-sliced smoked bacon was available in abundance. The meal went down smoothly and quickly, and both Kate and Shane ate until they were slightly uncomfortable.

∽

At the garage, Kate and Shane met Walter and Juanita, and Pete and Tasha. Both couples were holding hands. Walking toward them, Shane whispered to Kate, "What the hell happened here?"

Kate said only, "A good story for the ride to the airport."

Shane probed further, saying, "I think you probably played some major role in all of this."

Kate countered, "Like you *didn't* with Pete?"

Everyone greeted each other with hugs all around. Kate assured both Walter and Juanita that she couldn't be happier for them, while Shane did the same for Pete and Tasha.

Walter, blushed slightly as he teased Kate, "So your old butler has your approval, I see?" An answering blush from Juanita was met with hugs again for both of them.

Shane held one each of Tasha and Pete's hands, saying, "Tasha, this guy is my most favorite and cherished man in the world, and I couldn't be happier for both of you. But I have to warn you, this rapidly growing family is one crazy bunch!"

Tasha hugged Shane again and kissed him on the cheek, saying only, "Thank you. It means so much to hear that from you! Pete could never do anything to hurt you. He loves you as a son."

Shane assured her, "I know that, now more than ever, and he means the world to me. He really always has... and now he always will be...my father."

Tears had welled up in Pete's eyes, as he leaned over and kissed Shane on the check, still holding his hand. "I love you my boy," was all he could muster with a shaky voice.

"Well," said Walter, giving everyone a moment to regroup, "We should all be off now, going in different directions to the same place. Everyone be safe." With that, Walter and Juanita climbed into their SUV and drove out with the convoy, while Shane, Kate, Pete and Tasha got into an SUV with one of the support staff, who drove them, with another convoy, to the airport in Minden.

The ride seemed to be over quickly once they left the traffic in Carson City. As it was Saturday, the traffic was lighter, once you passed the turnoff for *Costco*. The airport was located in Douglas County, between Jacks Valley and the town of Minden, not far from Carson City. The airport was famous for its excellent soaring, due to thermals that rose from the high desert basin, located between the Sierra Nevada Mountain range to the west, and the Pine Nut range to the east. The airport was used by many soaring enthusiasts, and by competitive teams, as a training site. For years it had also been home to borate bombers, called to assist firefighters in the west.

The airport provided an asphalt runway more than 7,000 feet long, and sat at just under 5,000 feet in elevation. It was the perfect place for the Super King Air 350 to pick up this group. It was an easy facility to get in and out of quickly, and was conveniently located near the estate. Shane now recalled passing it, on the way to the clinic where the pretty young doctor worked.

On arrival, once they unloaded and got to the airplane, Shane was duly impressed with the twin engine Beechcraft. He had seen one or two of the Super King Air 350s during his flying years with DEA, but he had never flown one. This plane featured state-of-the-art technology sporting all the latest avionics. It had a range of more than 1,800 miles, and was powered by twin turboprop engines that could push it at more than 350 miles per hour. The max climb rate was over 2,700 feet per minute, and, the airplane had another advantage…it could take off and land on relatively short runways.

Stepping inside, Shane found the interior immaculate, appointed with heated leather passenger seats, drink ports, pull-out tables, power outlets, electric shade windows and WIFI, to name just a few of the amenities. The plane was fast, powerful and practical for someone needing to take off and land at altitude, or on shorter than typical runways, with as many as 11 passengers, baggage and cargo.

Pete had the bird off the ground and climbing at a rapid rate within a few minutes. Once he reached cruising altitude, the ride was smooth. There were no storms in the forecast and the day appeared to be perfect for flying.

Shane realized how much he missed flying airplanes, although everything he had piloted was much smaller than this ship. He wondered if he would get to fly this plane, at some point in the future. As if reading his mind, Tasha walked back to Shane's seat and asked if they could switch for a while. She had been sitting in the copilot seat next to Pete. Pete wanted Shane to join him in the cockpit.

Shane jumped at the chance, and soon was sitting next to Pete, buckled in the seat, with the headset in place. The avionics were impressive, to say the least. Money had not been spared with this airplane. To start, there were three large touch screen displays. He had never even seen some of the features that were standard on this plane.

Pete began to explain things like synthetic vision, integrated charts and maps, and graphical flight planning. There was an automated flight guidance system, and terrain awareness warning system. Shane thought he *could* learn to fly this bird, but he knew it would take time and commitment. Shane didn't have time right now, but the tour was great. He felt the juices flowing, like the days he had flown Cessna 210s and 310s.

After about 15 minutes, Pete said, "Okay, that's enough of the tour for now. Take the stick. I have to go to the men's room."

Shane laughed and said, "Yeah, right Pete!" But Pete stood up and turned to go.

Pete said, "It's no different, really, than the 310 you flew to places like Colombia and Panama. It's a twin-engine airplane, for God's sake. You've flown turboprops before."

Shane began to object, but the stick felt good in his hand, and the rudders on his feet felt right. He felt at home.

Pete said, "Think of it like driving a car. You've handled a muscle car, and can race it around the track without crashing. Now you're driving an Indy sports car that goes twice as fast and costs 50 times more than your old muscle car. If you get nervous, just slow down a little, and stick with the basics. It works the same. Don't be a pussy!" Pete added as a tease.

A few seconds later, Pete was chatting with Kate and Tasha, as he worked his way back to the bathroom. Shane found himself flying an airplane that must have cost more than four million dollars, when it was purchased new in 2009. He was learning not to be surprised at the changes in his life, but, to say the least, he was amazed, sometimes multiple times daily. As he studied the avionics, with hundreds of lights and indicators, he felt a presence behind him and suddenly, Kate slid into the pilot's seat to his left. He felt he shouldn't let her get too comfortable, with Pete coming back soon.

Shane said, apologetically, "I do love to fly. Pete's just letting me handle her a bit before he comes back. He should be here any minute."

Kate thought how cute he looked, just like a little boy with his new impressive toy.

She said confidently, "Oh, Pete won't be back for a while. He's spending some needed time with Tasha, filling her in on what to expect at the ranch, and maybe, for the rest of her life. I'd give them an hour or so. They seem to be in love." She smiled brightly, as Shane frowned.

He straightened in his seat, as Kate buckled herself into the primary pilot's seat, and placed the headset on, as if she knew what she was doing.

Objecting, he said, "But Kate, I don't know the route or..."

She interrupted with, "That's all right, dear. I know it's your first time with her, but I'm here to help. I'll make sure she's gentle with you."

With that, Kate took the stick, and said, "Give me control, I want to show you something on the way."

Shane reluctantly released the stick, and said, "You really do know how to fly? And you know how to fly *this* plane?! But, I just assumed..." His voice trailed off and stopped.

Kate gave Shane a somewhat disappointed look, shaking her head, and said, "Shane Beckett, you really can be a slow learner, can't you?" With that, Kate made a course correction to the right, and said, "Look out the window, down there to your right. Do you see all the flashing neon signs just this side of I-80?"

Shane checked the navigational chart, and looked down. He nodded, and said, "Okay, I have them."

Kate asked, "Do you know what they are?" Shane shrugged and said, "No clue." Kate replied smugly, "Good, let's keep it that way."

The lights and freeway passed quickly by, and were soon out of sight, without an explanation. Shane finally pressed Kate for an answer, saying, "Well, Kate, come on, tell me, what were they?"

Kate sighed and said, smugly, "Brothels, my dear…places you never *will* get to know!" With that she laughed a hearty "gotcha" laugh, until a call came through the headset.

It was Walter, asking for their location. Kate responded, telling him they were in the air, and already passed I-80. Walter advised her that the convoy was ahead of them, but would soon be hours behind.

Shane sulked, thinking how he always seemed to be the last to know anything in this family. He was becoming the butt of too many jokes, but he did love the change, having family to tease him.

Kate seemed to sense Shane's mood, and said, "Okay, it's yours again. I want to talk to you, anyway, while you fly her."

Shane grabbed the stick and began to focus on the flight, as Kate explained more about the route, and showed him how it was programmed into the equipment. Kate was actually a very good instructor, Shane thought. He finally asked, "So, when did you learn to fly?"

Kate replied, "I soloed when I was eighteen, but Walter and Pete had already taught me to fly, long before then. I got my Aircraft Single Engine Land, followed by Multi Engine Land Certification, when I was nineteen. Once Walter bought this plane, they insisted I learn to fly it, in case one of them were involved in some type of emergency…I never asked about what they thought might happen, I wanted to learn anyway. They didn't want to hire a pilot. They wanted us all to be trained. Once this is over, they'll want you to be checked out on the ship also. Then you and I will be *sharing* stick time. And I do mean *sharing*, buddy! We'll both have to fight Pete off as it is. There's no hogging the stick here." Kate teased.

"I'm starting to get it, really!" Shane said.

Kate said, "Yes, you're doing a great job. You'll pick it up quickly."

Shane frowned. "Not the flying. I know how to fly. It's you and this family. Everyone has struggled to better themselves, and overcome obstacles. Everyone is multi-talented, even the people you hire. I mean, I should have guessed you would know how to fly, with your grandfather owning an airplane."

Kate smiled at Shane, as she turned to receive a bottle of water from Lisa. She took another for Shane. She turned to hand the water to Shane, and said, "You still have a great deal to learn about us, my love. It's not Walter's plane. It belongs to all of us through our real estate LLC. So, as far as I figure it, you're flying your half of the cockpit right now. By the way, I hope you brought your credit card, because we always split the gas…4 ways!"

Kate laughed saying, "I know I tease you a lot, but I'm afraid it just won't last very long, so I'm getting all the mileage out of it I can now!"

Shane countered, "What won't last long. Are you afraid that since you showed me where the brothels are, you won't be able to hold me?" he laughed.

But, as soon as the last words left his lips, he knew it had been the wrong thing to say. He flinched just in time to receive the rattlesnake strike to the ribs. He winced in pain, and jerked the wheel to the right away from the jab. The plane veered toward a right turn, and Shane quickly recovered.

Pete called out from his seat, "Kate! Is the rookie having some trouble?!"

Kate called back to Pete, "Nothing that I can't handle, Pete. I'll bring him along."

Pete called back, "Well, see that you do. He almost spilled my coffee!"

Shane smiled and refocused on the task at hand.

Kate focused on him, and said, "I was talking about not being able to tease you too much longer about our family. I thought you would be spending so much time with us, you'd learn all our secrets quickly. But, if you want your other options, you can always take one of the SUVs back," she teased.

Shane said cautiously, "No, after I pay my part of the fuel bill for this flight, I won't have enough gas money to *drive* back, let alone pay for anything else!"

Shane had switched on the autopilot. And this time, he quickly grabbed both of Kate's hands in his, so by the time his remark registered in her ears, he was able to foil the jab. He playfully forced a kiss, saying, "Besides, *no one* could kiss like you can."

The flight route took them east of US 395, over high plains, rugged mountains, and desert. They flew over Burns and the Malheur National Forest on their way north east to La Grande, Oregon. They marveled at the landscape, changing from the pine and spruce forests to the west, to the pinion pines and sagebrush lying to the east. As they continued north, the landscape changed again, from sage to rolling hills, to pinion pines scorched by the wildland fires of 2014 and 2015, back to sage, and finally, to pine forests along the mountains to the west. They were quickly closing in on the rugged wilderness areas lying ahead, to the northwest.

They followed Oregon State Route 82 from La Grande, so Kate could point out the small towns of Imbler and Elgin, and then the

Minam River area, famous for steelhead fishing and white-water rafting. From there, the highway turned south east, as it wrapped around the north side of the Eagle Cap Wilderness Area. Shane marveled at the snowcapped peaks. He thought how the area looked like the pictures he had seen of the Swiss and German Alps.

The mountains became even more spectacular, the closer they approached. Snow-covered alpine peaks, deep, rocky treed valleys and meadows, rivers, creeks, lakes and ponds unfolded along the route. Shane saw frequent dots of shining blue, as higher altitude lakes and ponds flickered sunlight back at him. Using binoculars, while Kate flew, he was mesmerized by the number of bodies of water in the mountains. As they approached one valley, dark spots on the snow-covered ground began to move, and he counted more than 100 elk.

As he watched the land below float by, his mind fantasized how he, his father, Heath and Pete could have hiked to some of these remote areas, when they were all together in the past. Shane hoped he would get the chance to make these trips with Kate and Pete, and, maybe someday, Heath. He continued in his daydream, and wondered …maybe even with Kate, and their own children. A little girl child, he thought, who looked just like Kate, and maybe a boy or two, so he wouldn't be outnumbered! Shane chuckled to himself and thought, "If we have all girls, I'll have to get a couple of boy dogs!" He laughed out loud.

Kate called back to Pete, breaking Shane's day dream. "Pete, are you ready?"

Pete said happily, "Coming!" He walked up behind Kate and Shane. "How can I help?"

Kate asked Pete, "Narrate the tour or fly?"

Pete thought a moment, and said, "I think I landed here the last time. Your turn. I'll narrate."

Shane waited, saying nothing flippant. He was learning, albeit slowly. Both Pete and Kate seemed to be pleased with Pete's choice, and Shane's progress. Kate flew over the area, slowing the airspeed, so Pete could narrate and teach Shane the area he would need to know and understand in days to come. Pete pointed out the towns of Wallowa, Lostine, Enterprise and Joseph, all accessed by travelling Oregon Hwy 82.

The first two towns were very small. Pete explained that Enterprise had a population of less than 3,000 people, although it was the largest town in the county, and the county seat. Joseph was less than 5 miles south east of Enterprise, and was known as the artist colony of the area.

Continuing southeast on Hwy 82 from Joseph, it was less than two miles to Wallowa Lake. The small town of Wallowa Lake Village began to come into view at the far end of the four-mile long lake. Hwy 82, now designated Hwy 351, or the Wallowa Lake Hwy, dead-ended into a mountain, about 1-½ miles past the lake. Pete said the area was a favorite jumping off point for hikers, backpackers and horseback riders.

Kate swung the plane around over Mount Howard, and Pete pointed out the tramway a person could ride from the Lake Village area to a restaurant, perched on top of the mountain. Pete said it was the steepest ascent tram ride in the entire U.S.

Within a minute, they were over a road, designated Hwy 350, that left Joseph, running east for a few miles. Once the road ran further east over a ridge, it dropped down to a river canyon, to the Wallowa Mountain Road, designated the "39 Road," by locals.

Pete continued. "There is no access to the county by highway from this side of Joseph in the winter. The road that goes around the wilderness area to Halfway, accessed from the "39 Road," is closed in the winter, and used as a snowmobile recreation road. Other than Hwy 82 from La Grande, the only way to enter the county is from Washington State, coming south into the county on Hwy 3, through Enterprise, or the more secluded and difficult Upper Imnaha River Road, over Pine Creek."

"This county is secluded, with only two viable ways in or out in the winter. That's why we're here. We want to do a fly-over of the ranch now, so you can see the layout."

Within a few minutes Kate had the plane circling, from a position east of Hwy 82, around to the mountains lying just to the west. Between Joseph and Enterprise, they flew over a tract of land that appeared to have nothing on it, save a large pond.

Pete handed Shane the binoculars, and said, "Take a close look at the end of the pond." Tucked away in the forest and partially concealed by a hill, Shane could make out one flat, snow-covered roof line, and then another, appearing to be lower than the first, and concealed by a large rock outcropping.

Pete said, "One way in and one way out, on this road just below us to the right. See the field there with the herd of elk?" Shane nodded. "That's a square mile, with a year-round creek going through it. It sits as a buffer, between the home site and anyone approaching from the highway side. We have a clean line of sight from a crow's nest in the observatory, through that field, all the way across the neighbor's places, to the highway. You'll like it. You'll like it a lot!"

With that, Kate turned the plane toward the Joseph airport, located just west of town. Within two minutes, she was turning onto her final approach. Shane watched intently, as Kate slipped off some excess altitude and landed the twin engine, perfectly, stopping with much of the mile-long runway remaining ahead. He was more than impressed with this talented woman.

Pete had placed a call earlier, and as they arrived, a man drove up in an old, refurbished school bus. He was waiting for them when Kate rolled the plane to a stop near a hanger.

Everyone exited after the relatively short flight, anxious to get out and stretch, and look at new scenery. Pete opened one of the hangers, and disconnected a battery charger from a full size F350 4-door pick-up. He drove the truck out. Gear and luggage was loaded into the truck within a few minutes.

Pete, Tasha, Kate and Shane headed toward the pick-up. Kate offered to drive, and Shane just smiled...and said nothing. Pete and Tasha seemed pleased too, scarcely able to release each other's hands long enough to load themselves into the back seat. With the airplane unloaded of all necessary equipment, it was wheeled in, and safely stored in the locked hanger. The rest of the crew that had flown with them got on the bus and headed off to the ranch. Pete explained that a neighborhood friend often picked up their group, in his old refurbished school bus, when they arrived in town.

Kate drove to Joseph and then turned right, to play tour guide for Shane and Tasha. Pete had seen it all before, on several occasions, and had eaten in some of the restaurants and tipped a few drinks at the local bars and pubs, but he enjoyed watching Tasha and Shane being tourists. The day was still young, and both Kate and Pete wanted to take advantage of the time. Pete didn't seem to mind, relaxing and holding fast to Tasha's hand.

As they drove, Kate pointed out places she wanted Shane to remember, that they might frequent or need something from, during their stay. She mentioned 1917 Lumber, Mt. Joseph Family Foods, the Embers Brew House, Joseph Hardware and the Stubborn Mule, giving a quick synopsis of each, while telling a story about a time they were there, or something funny happened. Within five minutes, Wallowa Lake was coming into view, as they continued to the dead-end of the lake highway.

Shane and Tasha were awestruck by the sheer beauty of the area. Pete said the alpine lake was more than 300 feet deep and more than four miles long. It had been cut out of bedrock by a Pleistocene glacier during the last ice ages. The last glacier had finished moving the earth and rock up on both sides of the lake, and had formed glacial moraines more than 900 feet high during its trek. The surrounding mountains, with their jagged snow-covered peaks and faces, were all riddled with forests of western larch, pines, spruces and varieties of deciduous trees, most pushing high up past the snow. Areas that appeared to be void of vegetation, had been cleared by avalanches running down the steep slopes.

They passed the boat launch area and beach at the foot of the lake, and within another few minutes, passed the head of the lake. Wallowa Lake was fed by a river delivering ice cold water through a spider web of canyons, where unseen creeks combined their flow to build a spring torrent of rushing water. Pete explained that some creeks only lasted through mid-summer, depending on the snowpack. But others, he smiled, contained year-round flows that supported native species of golden and brook trout.

They drove by the Wallowa Lake Lodge, the Wallowa Lake Tramway, a small village with scores of cabins, chalets, shops and a couple of RV Parks.

Within another mile, they made the U-turn at the end of the road. Kate pointed out the trail she liked to ride horses up, that ran from the big trailhead at the end of the road to Aneroid Lake. That lake, she said, was another six miles and 3,000 feet above their current location, accessed only by the winding mountain trail than meandered through the dense forest.

They turned around and headed back through town, and finally, toward the ranch. Both Shane and Tasha talked excitedly on the way, about seeing the area and spending time in the county, while learning the local history. Shane hoped this might be the vacation he had sorely needed for too long. It would also give him some time alone with Kate.

Tasha dreamed of finally being away from the stress of the busy law firm, with Pete. She had fallen in love with him, as she worked side by side with him for many years. She had never allowed herself to believe Pete would actually love her back. She daydreamed about the many times she had wanted to tell him how she felt. She thought he might feel that way also, but she could never get up the courage to express her true feelings.

Tasha was still unsure what had happened to motivate Pete to make the decision to act on his feelings now, but she wasn't going to question anything. She was truly happy for the first time in years, and she was all in, playing for keeps, with nothing stopping her now.

About a mile past Joseph, they drove by a small highway sign pointing to a Bed and Breakfast, a nicely appointed large 2-story home perched on a rim-rock outcropping, about a quarter mile off the highway, toward the Eagle Cap Wilderness Area. Kate told Shane she would introduce him to her friend, Mary, who operated the bed and breakfast.

Kate explained she had met Mary on an ATV ride on Jayne's Ridge, three years ago. Both had been enjoying a nice spring day on their ATVs, collecting morel mushrooms, which sprang up after the snow melted each year.

A heavy thunderstorm that lasted for two days had washed away the last of the snow, and caused the mushrooms to sprout up virtually everywhere that season. A week after the storm, she and Mary happened on each other along a trail on the ridge. Mary had stopped to drink a beer and eat a sandwich, and had shared her lunch with Kate, after they talked for a little while. They spent the rest of the day collecting mushrooms together, riding and talking. Mary showed Kate her first calf's brain mushroom. They had forged the foundation of a lasting friendship.

Kate turned west off the highway and wound through a few short paved roads, that led to a smooth gravel road. A few miles west, they arrived at a narrower road that ran along the edge of a mile-long field with a creek running through it. After two more turns, they were soon engulfed by large old growth trees, some appearing to be more than 100 feet high. They had they entered the forested portion of the property.

Within another minute, they neared a small barn, and then passed a huge garage and shop. They finally stopped below a massive three-story log home, with a wraparound deck. As soon as the vehicle came to rest, the crew that had flown up with them was outside, to help unload the gear from the truck. The job took less than ten minutes with so many hands working. Jesse said he was anxious to set up all the equipment, and relax. He took off inside with the gear and several of his team.

Everyone buzzed with growing excitement, which seemed to be contagious. The entire team wanted some rest and recovery time, and this country promised to provide the fix. May was just around the corner, and a warming trend was forecast, along with some morning showers. The possibilities seemed endless. Shane was anxious to explore the grounds, but felt the immediate need to settle in as soon as possible.

Night came quickly. Equipment was set up, tested and certified as working well. Everyone had been directed to their rooms, and each person seemed to unpack in a hurry, anxious to explore the site, as soon as they were no longer needed. Pete and Tasha drove the truck to the Terminal Gravity Brewery and Pub on a beer run, and then stopped at the Enterprise Liquor Store to stock up on essentials. Kate gave Shane a tour of the well-stocked wine cellar in the basement. It seemed to Shane that Walla Walla, Napa, Sonoma and Mendocino vineyards were all equally represented.

By 8:00 P.M., Jesse and two of the staff had prepared and served steak dinner, featuring locally raised beef. On each plate, the steak was flanked by a simple, but tasty, baked potato and steamed asparagus with "Sauce de Jesse," which tasted like a garlic, parmesan and hollandaise blend. As the meal was served late, by the time they ate, everyone was hungry. As usual, the meal was exceptional.

Kate and Shane took showers and sat in their room, talking and enjoying a fine cabernet from a Walla Walla vineyard. Both were tired, but too excited to sleep, and both seemed to need to talk, although about different subjects. As they spoke through the second glass of wine, they worked their way down to the grand fireplace in the main living room, and sat in a loveseat, where they finished their conversation.

Kate was intent on getting through this safely, and showing Shane the rest of the O'Leary life and world, hoping that he would embrace it all, and find a place for himself where he would be happy. She was afraid to tell him, just yet, that this dangerous life style he pursued, was too risky for the two of them, and their future…at least the future she hoped to plan.

Shane was intent on finding the secret in his dream, and solving the riddle of their parents' murder. He dreamed of seeing that justice was served to those who deserved the full force of the law. And then there was Heath. He needed to figure out how to solve the problems between his brother and Pete. Maybe there could be some mending of the damage between them. He just didn't know how, but he knew he had to try.

Finally, they finished the last of the bottle and worked their way back up the stair case toward their room, and bed. Holding on to each other, in a king-sized bed that Shane felt was far too large for them, they only occupied half the bed.

Shane said, "Kate, I keep playing this over and over in my mind. I keep making all the basic assumptions, using all the known facts, trying to figure out what the answer is in my dream. I just can't quite get it…it's so frustrating."

Kate had drifted almost off to sleep, but struggled, just a little, to answer Shane through the fog of her consciousness. She said in a soft, sleepy voice, "My dad used to say that the explanation requiring the fewest assumptions is most likely to be correct. Try that, honey." And then she was asleep.

Shane drifted off to sleep a short while later, thinking how lucky he was to have Kate. She was smart, beautiful, kind, caring and skilled… so very skilled in many different things. He vowed he would never let her go. He also promised himself to do everything he could to be the *best* for her, to make her happy.

Just before sleep took over completely, he saw his beautiful Kate, talking to her father about a problem. Her dad was saying, "The explanation requiring the fewest assumptions is most likely to be correct. Try that, honey."

11

Heath woke up early, as usual, unable to get a good night's sleep. He stayed in his motel bed thinking, wondering if he should pull the sheets up over his head, like he had done as a child. Maybe the bad dreams would stop then, and maybe then, he could really sleep, really rest. He couldn't recall having a good night's sleep since he had become addicted to meth, many years ago.

Meth had started out as his friend, it seemed. But over the years, he depended on meth more and more, first to party, then to feel higher, faster, and stronger. Then, suddenly, it seemed he needed the meth to feel something, then to avoid feeling pain, and finally…he just needed the habit. He never knew why. It teased, manipulated, and deserted him, laughing at his weakness, destroying his life. And meth continued to laugh, while his real life slipped away, out of his grasp forever.

Meth had snuck up on him, ambushing him from behind at first, and finally taunting and tormenting him head on, every day. How had it come to this, he had wondered so many times? It all started as a seemingly harmless social outlet, a way to meet people and party. The young girls he thought he wanted to know seemed obsessed with drugs in those days…and obsessed with sex, which was even more important back then than the meth.

The meth made the sex better, he had believed. But that too turned out to be a lie. He wondered, trying to remember when he knew that the high was a lie, too. But he couldn't recall much now.

Heath had struggled, over the last few years, trying to remember all that had really happened during those years. But as hard as he tried, he just couldn't seem to clearly focus well enough to see his past life. True, the meth had become his reason for living a long time ago…so long ago, but when? Had it really happened as slowly as it now seemed, the meth becoming his reason for living?

Over time, meth had taken the first and foremost position of priority in his life, even over his children and his wife. Shit! It had *become* his life…before it totally replaced his wife, his children, and his career.

Heath had met his *real* wife at a party, and they had done meth on their first "date." But he was partying hard by then, and she was not. She eventually wanted a home and a family. She stopped using, and wanted him alone, without the meth. She wanted a clean, sober him…a real partner in life.

He had been sure he could do both, so he lied to her. He loved her, he thought. And then the kids came along. They were married after the birth…twin girls. His wife wanted things that cost money, but he made a lot of money, so it was all good…for a while.

But the partying cost too much money. He had friends he supplied with meth, but they wouldn't come around when he was out, so he couldn't be out. They were his friends. He needed friends to fill the hole in his soul that seemed to be insatiable. He couldn't remember why he had been so miserable. He was so happy before the meth took him, mind, body, and soul.

Heath had his landscape business for show, but eventually he had to make ends meet by selling meth. There was so much more money in selling meth, than cutting grass and designing landscapes, even running five crews in his own business. And he needed more money, always more money, to keep it all going. There was never enough. Everyone always wanted more from him…always more.

At first, he only sold to friends, his closest friends. But in the end, he sold to his friend's closest friends, and their friends, and their acquaintances, and strangers. They all looked up to him. He had more *friends*, finally, than he knew what to do with. He couldn't even remember all their names. But he thought he had needed them, and he liked all the attention he got.

And then, there were the young women. Gorgeous young women, with magnificent bodies, all craving their first taste of meth, and partying with him anytime he wanted them. He wanted them a lot at first, but not so much, later. But *they* all wanted *him* all the time. He had the meth. He was the man, the big shot. He had helped them out, he thought. It seemed in the end, he worked all the time to keep it going…the partying, the sex, the good times.

But finally, he sold to a friend of a friend, who quickly accelerated the frequency of his purchases, and increased the weight. This guy wanted heavier weight, and more often…always more. Everyone wanted more, and more often. He tried to slow the guy down by jacking up the price, but this guy didn't care.

Heath was making great money, he thought, phenomenally more than in the landscape business. In the end, he decided he didn't even really need the landscape business. It was slowing him down anyway. He let it slip away. His wife wasn't happy about his decision, but he knew best. He paid all the bills, after all. She just took care of the kids.

Then there were the kids. Doctors, and soccer, and dancing, and gymnastics, and homework, and projects, and scouting, and a new SUV to drive them around in...it was all overwhelming. Heath's wife and kids were dragging him down, interfering with his real life, he had thought. *He* was the man. His friends needed him to keep it all going...and he had needed his friends.

He couldn't even remember when he had taken time to go to a school play, or one of the kid's games. He had thought, they were getting older anyway, and wanted to be with their own friends, on overnight stays. His kids had their mom and their friends now. And his wife had her gym, and *her* friends she went with to yoga, and shopping, where she spent even more money. Heath recalled that one day, his wife told him she was singing in a church choir. Now, his wife had her kids, her church, and her God.

Heath didn't even go to church. Why would he, he had wondered? What could God offer him that he didn't already have? He didn't need more friends, or another girl on the side, or a faster car, or more money. What was left that he really, really needed?

But then came the knock on the door, and the guns and the police...with a SWAT team. And he was arrested, in front of his wife and kids, for sales of methamphetamine, on multiple felony counts, they said. The guy he had sold heavier weight to more often, had been arrested and turned informant. Heath remembered being pissed off at the guy. He was trying to do this guy a favor to meet his needs, and the guy turned out to be a rat, he had thought.

But, Heath found a good lawyer who said he could get him off. He needed to pay the attorney 50 large. He could handle that. He needed to sell more meth, but he couldn't. His attorney said they would be watching him. He needed to stop selling, but he knew he couldn't stop using. And he needed money for the attorney, and money for his meth.

Pete was there, and Pete had helped him so many times. He'd call Pete, and Pete would drive him home, when Heath was too drunk or drugged out to drive. Pete had sobered him up and made promises to Heath's wife to help him straighten up for good. And Pete's wife, Claire, had always been there for him, too. They would loan him the money he needed, he thought. And they did loan him money, at first. A lot of money.

Heath tried to remember it all now, through the fog in his mind. He had gone to Pete and Claire repeatedly, so many times. He needed more money for the attorney, his wife and kids, the bills and the meth he was using...still using. He couldn't stop using. The meth was insatiable...it wouldn't leave him alone. It demanded more.

Pete finally said he wouldn't help him anymore. They had fought about it, too many times. They had said ugly words to each other... words that hurt all the way down to the bone. Some things Heath had said, he knew even now, he could *never* take back. He and Pete were done. He thought Pete was the loser in the deal. After all, it was Heath that was the *real* man.

And Heath still had friends, lots of them. They would help him out now, when he was down, he had thought. He called them all...

one at a time, until he ran out of phone numbers. Not one of them said they could help him. None of the girls could do anything for him. They all said the same thing, one by one. They were all done with him. He couldn't offer them anything they wanted, now.

"Those bitches," he recalled thinking. He had done everything for them. The weed, the booze, the parties, the hotel rooms, the food, and, most of all, the *meth* he had wasted on those ungrateful bitches and their friends. Now, they wouldn't even return his calls. They wouldn't even share what little meth they had, after all he had given them!

But Claire had a soft spot for Heath, ever since his parents had been killed in the car crash. She had wanted children. He and Shane had become *her* kids. Shane didn't need Claire now that he was off playing cop, but Heath *did* need her. And Claire needed to *feel* needed, like a mom. Claire started giving Heath money...money Pete didn't even know about it. When that wasn't enough, she gave him her old jewelry to sell. But that soon ran out, too. The meth demanded more, always more.

When Claire was too sick to realize what he was doing, he just *took* her jewelry. She probably would have let him have it anyway, he told himself. But then, after a few months, she was sicker, and the jewelry wasn't enough. He had already stolen everything she had... even her wedding set she couldn't wear...her fingers too thin now, from the cancer. She didn't have any good jewelry left for him to steal.

Heath stole other things from her and Pete, too. There was the art work, and a silver service her grandmother had given her. But she didn't need those things anymore. She probably wasn't going to survive the cancer anyway, he thought. He didn't think what he was doing was so bad, and if it was, he didn't really care. *Somebody* owed him *something*! After all, he had been the *man*, and he had given so much away to so many people!

As her cancer progressed, Claire needed more pain meds, and one day, he found her OxyContin. Heath knew he could trade "oxy" for meth. "Oh, happy days!" he remembered thinking. Heath knew he needed the meth more than she needed the oxy. She was old, and she was stronger than he was anyway, he rationalized. But soon, the oxy she had just wasn't enough.

But then, there were Clair's other drugs. One of Heath's suppliers was an illegal alien. The wetback's mom had cancer, too, and needed the same drugs Claire was taking. This guy said he would trade him big amounts of meth for those drugs, to keep his mom alive.

This guy's mom was having a hard time getting the drugs from Mexico, and she wasn't strong enough to leave the house anymore. They wanted to avoid the cops and immigration. This guy's whole family was illegal, and Heath leveraged them. He thought Claire wouldn't miss a few pills. But soon, he was taking them all, all for the meth. Everything, by then, was always for the meth. Claire knew it was happening, and yet, she never said a word.

As Heath lay in bed thinking, trying to recall, he remembered one of the last days he had seen Claire. She had called him and asked that he come over and see her. She kissed him goodbye and said she wouldn't be taking anymore pills. She was crying. She said she didn't have any more jewelry. She said there was nothing left for Heath to take. *And* she said Pete had finally discovered what had been happening. She told him Pete was furious. She begged Heath to stop the meth… one more time she pleaded. It was to be her last time.

Heath remembered how he had yelled at her, telling her she was selfish "bitch." It was bad timing for him! Didn't she realize that? He tried to guilt her into giving him more…more of anything. But she just cried and cried. She said she didn't have any more of anything to give him now. He had taken all she had to give. And now she was dying. He left, thinking that even her dying was selfish. She had let herself off the hook with him. She must not even care about him, he had thought.

And then, before he knew it, he was being sentenced to prison, just a week after he had left her crying alone in her bed. He had been found guilty. It had turned out that even his lawyer was a scammer, and just wanted more from him. Now Heath remembered all that money he had wasted on his attorney. The attorney was just like everyone else. Everyone wanted all that he had to give. All, because of the meth. The meth had made him weak, powerless, defenseless.

And then, abruptly, it was all gone. He lost the cars and the house…and now even his wife was going to leave him. She said he wouldn't be seeing his kids. He couldn't even recall the last time he had seen them. They had lost their place in his life to the meth, like everyone and everything else.

Now he remembered that *both* his wife and Claire had cried, as he had walked away, distancing himself from them and their pathetic sobbing. They were useless to him. He didn't need them and their feelings. He had needed the meth…only the meth…or so he had thought.

Heath recalled how, back then, he felt totally abandoned by everyone, even Shane, who was always gone working some new case. And when Shane was around, he wanted them to go hiking and camping, or spend a day at the beach, or have dinner and go to a movie. Heath was pissed at the world back then. He hadn't needed a *fucking movie* with his brother. He *had* only needed the METH!

But he went to prison…and all at once, no more meth came to relieve the pain. He went through withdrawals that made him cramp and sweat, and ache all over, like he had the worst case of flu imaginable. Then it got worse, while his cold, sterile cell offered him no comfort.

He had tremors and shook with alternating chills and fever. He vomited, and when he wasn't vomiting, he was so nauseous he couldn't eat. His heart pounded almost out of this chest, and he couldn't breathe normally. He thought he was going to die.

And then, when he felt the worst, he had to leave the little security his cell provided, to walk outside into the general population, and interact with guards and inmates. He didn't know any of them. And none of them seemed to care about Heath in the least.

But through it all, the only thing he could really think about was the craving…the incessant craving for the METH! He prayed the pain and craving would stop…but it held on tight to his mind, his body, and his soul.

In prison, the guards didn't care about his whining. No one cared. He was all alone. He didn't fit in with the tweakers, or the bikers, or the black gangs, or the Mexican gangs, or the white supremacists. He was all alone and being alone wasn't good in prison. Heath remembered learning that you had to be connected in the joint, just to survive.

But he didn't want to survive, until the withdrawals diminished, and Shane came to see him for the first time. Shane promised to help him once he was released. Heath remembered sitting in prison and wishing he had listened to Shane's pleading for him to stop abusing drugs, long before all the trouble began. Over time he began to hope for a future, away from the pain the drugs had brought to his pathetic life.

He eventually wished he could do it all over. He wanted his old life back. His wife and kids meant the world to him, now that he didn't have them. He could even make it up to Claire and Pete when he got out. He could pay them back. He had thought, "I *will* pay them back, if it takes the rest of my life," he had committed to himself. He would show the world he had changed, and he vowed to be good, responsible and happy, once more. And most of all, he would be at peace, focusing only on the people in the world who were important…his family and true friends, if he had any left that still wanted him.

And then Shane came to see him in prison, to tell him the news about Claire. She had died a horrible and painful death. Pete was devastated, and Shane said he didn't know what he could do to help Pete. Shane had cried, reminiscing about all Claire and Pete had meant to him and Heath, and how Claire had taken the place of a mother in their lives. She had been a saint to the boys, and now she was gone.

Shane had asked Heath to call Pete and tell him how sorry he was that Claire had died. But Heath knew that Shane didn't understand why Claire had died so soon, and why she had been in so much pain. Claire hadn't taken the medicine she had needed for months. Heath understood, even as he had tried to forget.

He couldn't forget, though, and sat in prison day after day, for years, thinking about his failures, his life, the troubles and pain he had caused his family. He knew he had killed Claire. He never called Pete. He just couldn't. And Shane didn't understand why he couldn't call, or why Pete refused to talk about Heath.

Heath remembered the final realization he had while sitting in prison one day, alone in his cell. He knew then he could never make anything up to Pete and Claire. His time had come and gone for that.

There were no more chances, not for him. That ship had sailed. There was no hope for him to be a part of his family again.

Even Heath's wife had remarried, and Heath had allowed the new "dad" to adopt his kids, at her urging. He had also given up visitation, and any future custodial rights. It had seemed the right thing to do, when he had last seen his wife, on a prison visitation. She didn't even want to look at Heath, or have their children see him, especially in prison.

The *new* guy she spoke of was someone she had met in *church*, of all places. The kids would be better off without Heath after all, he had thought. At least this new guy was normal, a stock broker, he had heard. Heath's beautiful twin daughters would forget him. And maybe someday, he, too, could forget…he hoped.

Heath desperately wanted to forget the pain he had caused, and the hole that was left in his soul, by all that meth had taken from him. He wondered if he could ever find some semblance, or at least, some hope of peace.

If he did make it out of prison alive, Heath had planned on dropping out of the life he had known, and starting over, in a different state. He thought he might go to Alaska and become a fisherman, or maybe a gold miner. It didn't really matter, if he had no more reminders, and could free himself from the guilt and the pain…the incredible pain. He couldn't handle the never ending guilt and pain in his mind, always reminding him of who he had become, and what he had done. And, he didn't want to see any of his old druggy *friends*, the pieces of shit that had helped him along the path to his destruction.

Shane had continued to visit him in prison, especially nearing the end of his term. And visiting, Shane brought reminders of all the pain.

But, Shane's visits, letters and phone calls also brought love and hope, even though Heath always reminded *himself* of the regret and shame.

Shane had not given up on Heath, it seemed, so Heath had allowed himself to hope for the future, for a life. Shane told him he could either feed the regret and pain of the past, or feed the hope and promise of the future. Shane said, that the one he fed the most, would survive and devour the other. It was his choice. Heath knew then that he had a choice.

But as always after the visit, Shane would leave the prison, and Heath would be alone, fighting for survival, alone once again. Heath thought how it hadn't seemed fair, back then. Shane still had Pete, and his job, and hope, while he didn't have anything that his brother didn't provide for him. Heath finally realized he was no longer *the man*. He understood he would *never* be the man again. But he still had the craving for one thing the meth had provided...the feeling of being someone important. Maybe he could make it happen again. Sometimes he wondered.

To make matters worse, he almost got "shanked" in prison by some low life biker who wanted Heath to be his "boy," his "punk." When Heath kept refusing, he made enemies with the biker. An "illegal," also in prison for sales of meth, had stopped the biker dude by beating him senseless. He broke the shank off in the biker's hand, sending him to the infirmary and out of Heath's life for a while. The gang that backed his new friend were the cartel "muscle" for a heavy weight dealer. They had saved Heath, but now Heath owed them, big time.

He started out hanging out with them, lifting weights in the gym. He began running and training again, using the track at the prison. These guys took care of Heath, and promised him they would set him up in business when he got out. They were going to pull him up again. He thought he was going to be *the man* again. One more time. He vowed he would be more careful, this time.

Heath now lay in bed in the motel room, thinking back to how he had planned and trained every day in the joint. There wasn't anything else to do. His crew was impressed by how fast he bulked up. He had always been athletic. He could run for an hour, without stopping, and still have plenty of reserve. His chest became massive and his biceps were huge. He was in the best shape of his life. With no meth to screw him up, even the craving had stopped. The crew, *his* crew, got him extra food, and he ate like a horse.

And then finally, the long years in prison were over, and Shane picked Heath up at "the wall," where released prisoners from this hell hole were handed over to loved ones, or a taxi, on their last day. Heath recalled praying that Shane would be there. He didn't want to face that first day on the outside alone. He just couldn't.

And Shane *never* disappointed Heath. He had always been there for Heath, and Pete and Claire, and everyone. And, as much as he was elated to see Shane waiting for him when he walked out the gate, he was angry that Shane *was* there, waiting to pick him up, once again. Shane, the *good* son, rescuing Heath, the *bad* son, the prodigal son, the failure, once again.

Heath had gone to work immediately for Shane's friend, who owned a landscape business. It was a good business in California, and Heath knew landscaping architecture. He could make this work, he thought. But he would always be in debt to Shane, never free. And, there was the nightly craving, the insatiable desire to be high. It had returned. It had been hiding, while he was locked up in the joint, and working out. Now the *meth* told him he was *free,* and could do anything he wanted. It left him alone when he worked during the day. But then came the lonely nights, and the meth tormented him all night, sometimes even in his sleep.

Meth said *it* could make him the big man once again, much easier than working himself up through the landscape business, starting from the bottom, with a boss to answer to all the time. After all, life was *easy* sitting in an apartment, watching TV all day, collecting food stamps, and living in federally subsidized housing, like his new neighbor…when you made a few thousand a week selling meth. But life was hard, when you went to work and busted sod all day, and then came home too tired to even *watch* TV. "What kind of choice was that?" meth taunted.

Now meth reminded Heath he had the contacts from prison, the prison "bro" that was connected, and could intro him to a "family" that would give him a new start, in the business he really knew, the *meth* business. His prison bro had told Heath he could even arrange for Heath to own a landscape business, if Heath wanted. His friend, Bobby, said it would be the perfect cover.

And meth reminded Heath that he still had his old drug contacts, and Heath would love to see them sweat out their embarrassment, seeing him on the top, again. They would come crawling to *him* for drugs. Then, *he* would be the one not returning *their* phone calls. What sweet revenge!

A daily conflict began to rage in Heath as he struggled with these most difficult choices. He could be somebody again, in the world that had destroyed his life, or he could go straight. He had talked a big game in prison, to get close to some muscle that would protect him then. Now, he thought he must, at least, give the crew his old contacts to pay back his debt. It was quid pro quo. He had to repay, one way or another.

But he was clean now, and knew he really hated the world of meth, full of its tweakers and phony friends, all looking to get high on someone else's dime. He didn't want to go back to that world of insanity. He wanted to pay his debts through the landscape business, and, with enough employees to run, maybe he could make these powerful new prison friends rich. Maybe that would be enough to repay his debts.

But Heath feared they wouldn't be interested in that kind of arrangement. After all they were gang members, drug dealers and cartel associates, not venture capitalists. And so, Heath feared the phone call that may come one day. He hoped and prayed it would not come, and suppressed the cravings. Once again, he turned to working out in the gym, and running.

Heath had done well working for Shane's friend, all the while planning and saving, waiting for an opportunity to take over the business. He was exceptionally good at this business. He had been on top before as a landscape architect, and found it to be a true work love.

He had been an exceptionally good employee, and had endeared himself to the owner quickly. To his surprise, the opportunity presented itself, and he bought the business, agreeing to share profits with the owner for two years, while he purchased the business and equipment, using his share of the profit. In less than 3 months Heath had doubled the profit, and increased the crews dramatically.

In less than two years, Heath had quadrupled the business, paid off his remaining debt with the owner, increased his employee's wages, and set up a profit sharing plan for his workers. He had assisted eleven illegal aliens with obtaining a work visa. Once the business was his, everyone there asked to stay on and work for him. One of his leads, Manuel, said Heath was, "the man." Soon, Heath received phone calls every week from people seeking employment, and a fresh start, with a good job. He was trying to do it all correctly, this time…for himself, and for his family.

But today, Heath rolled over in bed, at his motel. He pulled the comforter over his head. Maybe, he hoped, he could go back to sleep to forget, a little while longer. But he just kept thinking back to the past, remembering.

∾

Heath had occasionally kept in touch with his prison buddies, especially Bobby, the one that had promised to someday intro him into the "family" with all the connections. Finally, just as he feared, the call came, and Heath knew he had to explain to Bobby that he couldn't go back. He had chosen to give up the easy-money drug world for the hope of a real life with his own business, in landscaping.

Heath explained to Bobby that he had worked hard and purchased the company, and now could repay his prison debt with cash. He even offered to help some of Bobby's crew who wanted a good life, when they were released. Bobby had just laughed at Heath and explained that the only career Heath would have was one in *METH*. And Bobby insisted. Bobby reminded Heath how well he knew the drug business, and had loved it. He said even now Heath *must* know he couldn't resist it.

Bobby had even threatened Heath, reminding him of the huge debt that was still unpaid…*and* that Bobby's crew knew where Heath's daughters lived. Bobby said it was all there waiting for him, calling to him, luring him once again, one *last* time. And in an instant, Heath knew he had to return to the drug world, for all the wrong reasons.

So, he planned and compromised what he had fought to resist, hoping to do both for a little while, and then get out of meth once, and for all. He could leave the business to be run by a couple of the more trustworthy and sharp illegals he had hired. Manuel could run the business as well as he could. Two of his foremen were maybe as good, or even better, than Heath at supervising the crews. He could negotiate, purchase and arrange delivery of product by phone, whenever he had to be involved. He thought he could pull this off, just maybe, and be the good man once again, doing it the right way. If he could only get enough money, maybe he could even pay Pete back, he had thought.

Finally, the day of the meet and "intro" came, and Heath had driven to Sacramento to meet his buddy from prison, Bobby Saldana. It was an Indian summer hot day in late October, the year before Shane had taken the job in Carson City. He and Bobby sat talking at a pizza restaurant, located off I-80, on the outskirts of Citrus Heights, sharing a beer like two old friends. Bobby had asked Heath to bring a list of dealers he knew in the Sacramento area. These were the "safe" dealers Heath had bought from, or sold to, in the old days. These guys were all good experienced dealers, careful who they dealt with, *and* they all only dealt serious weight. Heath knew most of them very well.

Bobby had been impressed, and quickly arranged for a second meeting, with his bosses, to be held a few days later. But that first night, Bobby took Heath out to dinner at a nice restaurant in downtown Sacramento. Bobby paid for everything, including an $80 steak and lobster dinner, and a bottle of wine, that cost twice that much. Heath said he didn't want to do any drugs. Bobby explained he and his boss were all about the money, not partying.

And Bobby warned that if Heath "came in" with the family, there was *no using*. Being a druggy wouldn't be tolerated. It was literally a death sentence. His boss was just about *the money*, lots of money, with no distractions. Bobby assured Heath that if he worked out, there would be no end to the money. Bobby said Heath could finally have everything he ever wanted.

Over the next few days, Heath called all his old dealers, this time offering not to purchase, but to intro them to a big-time mover, one who could *supply them* with all the cheap meth they could sell. Heath arranged twenty-two meetings where he intro'd Bobby to his old suppliers, one at a time. Bobby provided sample "8 balls" to every one of them. Bobby explained the 1/8-ounce sample of meth was a *gift*, with no strings attached. A simple goodwill gesture, with more to follow, was all that Bobby wanted from each meeting. Each dealer weighed and tested the product, and found that it was indeed, 3.5 grams of nearly pure methamphetamine.

Bobby explained that the gesture accomplished two purposes. It proved Bobby wasn't a cop or a "CI" (confidential informant), and it allowed the dealers to sample the quality of the meth. Bobby promised it would be both higher quality than what they were currently buying…and 1/3 cheaper than the price they were currently paying to any of the cartels. Bobby offered each person who dealt with his group *only*, a guaranteed lower price and "protection," from both the law and the cartels. He provided each dealer with enough information to convince them that his deal was for real, and he could deliver what he promised.

By the end of the week, all twenty-two dealers agreed to purchase, solely from Bobby and his group. Bobby arranged for one more meeting at the end of the week. At the same pizza store on the way out of town, Bobby introduced Heath to his boss, Hector Alvarez. Hector had already received purchase orders from Bobby for nearly 500 pounds of meth from these new dealers.

Once the first trial deals were made, all twenty-two dealers agreed they could move between 15 and 100 pounds per month, each. These dealers had been paying $13,000 per pound to one of the cartels for their supply. Bobby's group was charging $10,000, and providing additional benefits. Everyone stood to make a killing, and spread more meth on the street than ever before. All the dealers could grow, in both size and wealth. It looked like a win-win for everyone. And they all had Heath to thank.

Hector had given Heath a hug and a kiss on the cheek, and handed him a large, heavy zippered bag. He welcomed him into the family, and said they would be in touch with additional instructions. Heath could take it easy for a few days, and take care of his landscape business. Hector promised they would talk more about the business in the future, and agreed to consider helping Heath expand the landscape business, which he could still run, apart from the world of drugs.

At that first meeting with Hector he instructed Heath to go celebrate and to buy a nice, used, half-ton pick-up. Hector wanted him to drive something more reliable, but not too flashy. Hector told him to call Bobby after he made the purchase, to advise Bobby what type and color truck he was driving. He told Heath to buy a matching camper shell in the same color as the pick-up, and to make sure that both the tailgate and the camper shell were lockable.

Hector said the money for the truck and Heath's first payday, were both in the bag. And with that, the meeting was adjourned, and Bobby gave Heath a hug, and a kiss on the cheek. Heath recalled thinking it would take time to get used to the kissing thing.

Heath left the meeting, and sat in his old "beater" pick-up. He unzipped the bag. There were two bundles of money in the bag. One bundle counted out at $50,000, and had a typed note that read, "Welcome to the family. Your first months' pay. Keep up the good work!" The second bundle counted out at $40,000, and had a typed note attached that read, "Buy a nice one, not too flashy, with a matching and lockable camper shell. Do it tomorrow. Relax tonight. H."

Heath remembered how he had sat, looking at the bundles of money sitting in his lap. He had been paid $50,000, and got a new pick-up, for less than one week's work. He had never made that much in a month selling meth before, and he hadn't even had to handle any drugs…and yet it terrified him, and he hated it.

What he *had* been able to do this time, was to arrange for Sacramento area dealers to commit to selling nearly $1,000,000,000 in street value drugs, for their new cartel, in the first year of business. The change would allow the cartel to take over the area market and eventually control most illicit drugs in central California. The cartels projected yearly take, as the market expanded, and competition diminished, would grow exponentially. Heath really was "the man" again, and he feared things would be different this time, even worse than before.

He had picked up the zippered bag to throw it on the rear seat. He noticed the bag was still heavy. He looked inside. There was a box in the bag, covered by a shop rag. He took it out and opened it. It contained a .45 caliber semi-auto handgun with extra magazines and ammunition.

The attached typed note read, "For your protection. Practice and get good with it. We'll be in touch. H."

Heath recalled how he suddenly realized, that there must be some additional risk he would need to take in the future, if he needed a gun. A bolt of fear coursed through him like a lightning strike. His hair stood on end. He knew at that moment, whatever he had gotten into…regardless of what they asked him to do, he just couldn't go back to prison. Not again. At that very instant, he wondered if he had already blown his chance at a normal, happy life.

He had been both excited and scared. He stuffed the gun back in the box and placed it, and the cash, back in the zippered bag, with the cash on top. He remembered thinking about what he should do at that exact moment. He was an ex-felon in possession of a handgun… but he was in the People's Socialist Republic of California, as the convicts nicknamed the state. They didn't even deport *illegal* felons with *multiple* convictions, in possession of firearms. They wouldn't do anything with him if the cops found the gun, anyway. He figured he might go to jail, but he would just bail out the next day.

He had decided quickly, and drove to the closest car dealer he could find in the area. A short two hours later, he had agreed to trade his "beater" pick-up for a two-year old, half-ton pick-up, with less than 5,000 miles on it, paying the $33,000 difference in cash. The prior owner had purchased a matching and lockable camper shell, and had just traded the whole outfit in on a new truck an hour earlier. Heath would pick the truck up the next day, once it was checked by the dealer. He had settled into his new role, and successfully passed the first test, he thought. He had immediately called Bobby, and reported his purchase.

Heath also remembered not knowing what to do next, and how he had driven around in his new ride the following morning, getting to know it, and feeling somewhat better about the whole affair. Eventually, he decided to go to his bank, and put $6,000 in his checking account. He had then opened his safe deposit box. He placed the $50,000 in the box, with a note to Shane directing that should anything happened to him, the money would go to Pete.

He would leave Shane directions to the bank later, with a letter of authorization for the bank to allow him access to the box. He had already placed Shane on the paperwork at the bank, giving Shane access and control of his accounts and the safe deposit box. He was planning redemption, using ill-gotten gains. He knew he wasn't quite "healed" yet, but he felt a little better.

But now, several months later, on *this* day, Heath was still lying in bed, having gone over these same thoughts a thousand times before. He pulled the covers over his head and tried to go back to sleep one last time. But he knew the phone would be ringing, and he knew he was going to have to go soon. He just lay there afraid, not knowing how there would ever be a way out.

He reflected, over and over, how dangerous the game he had been playing had recently become. Any mistake on his part would result in him…or someone else, being killed. These were ruthless people he had come to know. They were his new "family," he thought mockingly, and he didn't like them much, except for Hector.

The phone rang, next to his bed. It was Bobby, notifying Heath of a meeting at the usual place. Heath would meet Bobby at a mom and pop liquor store in the center of town. The store had a large supply of adult magazines, and Bobby liked to look at the pictures, while he talked quietly with Heath, and drank his 18 oz. "*Oly Gold*" beer.

The store was old and run down, just like the owners. But the owners looked the other way, if you bought a beer or a pint of whiskey, and you drank while you looked at their magazines. They didn't really care, even though it was illegal. But then, they looked like they didn't care much about much of anything. They had found their "niche" in life long ago, and they just wanted the money, and to look the other way. No worries and no hassles. And often they even received small tips, left on the counter by their eclectic group of oddball clients.

A person could walk through the store on any given afternoon, and see a handful of people from all walks of life, from construction workers to truck drivers to district court judges, all stashing their drink of choice on a shelf, and sipping it occasionally, while they looked at provocative pictures in their chosen porn magazine. Some people would spend their entire lunch break in the store, and then pay for the open container on their way out, leaving it on the shelf they had used to conceal it.

Heath thought it so odd that the customers almost always left the "empty" on the shelf. He had never seen anything like it before. But Bobby told him it was one of the best kept secrets in Carson City, and on Heath's first day there, Bobby pointed out a local judge, who often came in around noon on his workdays. Heath had since seen the judge in the store many times, while meeting with Bobby. The man made him nervous. After all, he thought, he *is* a judge, even if he isn't a very honorable one.

But Heath dreaded these meetings with Bobby now, so he slowly got out of bed, showered and took his time dressing, and driving to the meet. He wanted to give Bobby time to look at his "magazine girls," and drink his beer, so hopefully the meeting could be short. He didn't even want to be here in Carson City, but found himself committed. Now, he had to be here. He had no choice…he was trapped.

Heath took a shower, dressed, and sat in his pick-up. He marveled at how he had thought he was free, but now found that the meth world had imprisoned him, once again. He was bought and paid for…in far too deep to leave now, especially now, with everything that had recently happened. He drove on to the liquor store and parked. There were several cars in the little parking lot, and one of them Heath recognized as belonging to the district court judge.

"Nothing like adding a little irony to the meeting," Heath thought. "Ex-cons, drug dealers and judges, hiding their drinking, while getting excited over the girly magazines together. One big, dysfunctional family." He laughed to himself.

Heath found Bobby in the usual spot, with his 18-oz. beer tucked away on a shelf, just out of sight. Bobby was chuckling while holding a magazine sideways, looking at the unfolded center feature. Bobby grinned and showed the centerfold to Heath.

"This issue is all short, Asian girls with big tits!" he beamed. "Do you know how much money we could have made on this *one* magazine, when we were in the joint?" He chuckled wildly, "We could have rented it out by the hour, and made major bank!" Bobby laughed.

Heath said, somewhat disapprovingly, "I couldn't have touched it after the first day. Can *you* imagine what condition it would have been in after some of those 'pervs' handled it? You wouldn't have been able to pull the sticky pages apart!" Heath shuddered, shaking his entire body, and closing his eyes in disgust.

Bobby just laughed and teased him more. He then nodded in the direction of the judge, saying, "He's into tall, black chicks with shaved boxes, today."

Heath shook his head in disbelief, and offered only, "Why?"

Bobby kept taunting Heath and finally said, "You're just too much of a prude, man. Lighten up and take a gander. You might enjoy it."

Bobby gestured toward the magazine section, featuring women with grotesquely large breasts, involved in "XXX Action." These features were further separated into various ethnic groups, ending with a lesbian section.

He said, "Man, this is *the one place* where there's absolutely no racism. You could be a one-legged, purple-skinned, bald, midget, lesbian, biker-bitch covered in tattoos, but as long as you got tits and a pussy, someone's buying your photos, and appreciating you for exactly who you are." He laughed heartily and watched for a response, waiting for a reply from Heath.

Heath finally said, "*If* I were so inclined to read one of these, it would be in the privacy of my own bedroom. This place gives me the creeps." Heath gestured at a dorky looking, skinny, unkempt, middle-aged man searching through the section titled, "Young and Firm." The man scanned the magazines briefly, rubbing his long fingers over the titles on each one, before he settled on one from a selection that read, "Young Taboo!" The girls on the cover appeared to be aged in the single digits.

Heath shuddered again, saying, "I wouldn't even want to imagine what turns that 'perv' on, or what he does when he leaves here."

Bobby laughed hard, tears streaming down his cheeks. People began to look their way. Even the judge looked at them, and then left his beer on the rack and walked to the cash register to pay and leave. He seemed nervous that someone was laughing, instead of "enjoying" the unusual ambiance, quietly and secretly.

"I'm just not a kindred spirit," Heath thought aloud, as he stared back at the scowling judge. "His Honor is completely without honor." The judge seemed to have read his lips and walked faster, his nose in the air.

When Bobby was done teasing Heath, and finished drinking his beer, he paid at the register and tipped the old lady at the counter a $5 bill, which she pocketed without even looking up at him.

Heath noted the woman appeared to be 65 or 70, but looked much older...and hardened. She was thin and sickly looking, with not just a little too much beer gut, flanked by doll-thin arms and legs. She wore flip flops that smacked the linoleum as she shuffled her feet about. She likely hadn't washed the faded print dress she wore, for quite some time.

Heath recalled seeing her in the same outfit every time he had been in the store. And each time he had seen it, the frock displayed the same tomato sauce stain, perched proudly atop her left breast, that screamed, "Look at me! You have to *look at me*...again!" He shuddered once more, as he walked past the woman. A grotesque combination of grease, stale cigarettes, beer, and perfume wafted after him as he walked by.

Bobby walked out ahead of him, and said, "My kind of place! They don't even want to look you in the eye on the way out. They just don't care what you do! Definitely, my kind of place!! Why, you could even jack off in there, and no one would care. Some of the clientele might even enjoy the show!!"

When they got to Bobby's car, they got in and sat in the parking lot. Bobby immediately began talking business. Heath listened, while he watched the street traffic on the busy main street to their right. The traffic seemed never ending. There were soccer moms in vans toting loads of kids, truckers from every company, salesmen, delivery vehicles, and all the folks from the rest of the world, whirling by at breakneck speed. Heath thought it odd that they didn't even realize what kind of a place they were driving by each day.

A sheriff's unit suddenly sped by with wailing siren, trying to stop a speeding motorcycle. Heath watched these vehicles and imagined that the normal people driving by, would cringe at knowing what evil lurked in the shadows of buildings, like this old, dirty, perverted liquor store. But if they realized that some of the nice *houses* in their neighborhoods lodged the store's perverted customers, they would likely sell out and move.

But then, as Heath reflected on the thought, he knew that evil was present in some form everywhere. He was experienced enough to recognize evil when he saw it. He had lived in its depths for years, as a druggy. Most people were blind to evil, not recognizing it, even when they saw it up close. And most refused to look for it.

Heath recalled one of his dad's favorite quotes: "The only thing necessary for the triumph of evil is for good men to do nothing."

He thought that the author should have added, "Good men have to be watchful and aware, to recognize evil, so they *can* do something about it."

After all, they had just been in a liquor and porn shop, where the owners allowed open containers to be consumed, by perverts, in violation of a host of alcohol laws. And a certain district court judge was not doing something about it…he was participating in it, and adding to the problem! Afterward he would go back to his court room, continue fantasizing over naked amazon women with shaved boxes, feeling a little tipsy from the two large beers he consumed on his lunch break, and give some poor slob a sentence for committing some *crime*.

And all the while, the honor-less judge had been standing next to an obvious pedophile, and two guys involved in major narcotics trafficking. To make matters worse, this was the Nevada state capitol! Heath shuddered again, in disgust, as Bobby droned on.

Heath thought, that if it weren't for the trained and dedicated cops, and a handful of good solid citizens, who took all the risks to ferret out crime and stop it, there would be no society at all, and criminals would eventually take over everything, including government. Heath considered what a world run by criminals would be like, and then realized it might be the world he was living in already! He laughed out loud, without thinking. Bobby stopped talking, and asked, "Did I say something funny?"

Heath said, "No. I just had some funny thoughts."

Bobby frowned, and said, "I was talking about Big John's murder, and how pissed Hector and Franky are that we haven't found any information about who did it, and why! What's funny about that?!" Bobby was obviously irritated, and Heath had to recover fast.

He held up his hands, and said, "Hey, you put the thoughts in my mind! I can't stop thinking about what a one-legged, purple-skinned, bald, midget, lesbian biker-bitch, covered in tattoos, might look like. Does she have big tits, too?" He smiled at Bobby.

Bobby busted up laughing, and said, "She must have big tits. Her tits are *so* big, she can barely stand up! We got a shelf to put our beers on!" They both laughed, Heath pretending it was funny, but, genuinely relieved he had dodged a bullet.

Bobby began talking about Big John's murder again, and asked Heath to contact all the Sacramento dealers and press them hard to see if anyone had any information. Something this big was bound to be spread around. Sacramento was a big part of the business now. Franky said someone there *had* to know something. Heath promised Bobby he would make the calls and get back to him. He knew it would be useless though, because no one would know anything.

Before the meeting ended, Bobby said, "I know we pulled you in a couple of weeks ago to run some outside counter surveillance for us, and you haven't had a night off in more than two weeks. Hector and Franky want you to keep it up for another couple of days before we shut it down, just to make sure everything is quiet. We rented the doctor's house next door for another two days. Last week, Hector gave him and his girlfriend an extra ten days on us at the resort, so keep using the house. And keep coming over the rear yard fence, so no one sees you on the street. That's working out well. None of our guys even know you're there!"

Bobby continued, "Isn't it funny that we brought you in to make sure there were no problems with any of the cartels, after our takeover in Sacramento, just because Franky was afraid that something might happen to Hector and Anna's baby. We put you *so* close, right next door, and nothing happens to the baby, but Big John gets murdered."

"We put you close enough to watch over the house and the baby's room, but not far enough away to see someone setting up down the street, so you could prevent one of our own guys from being taken out by a hitman with a sniper rifle. Fuck!"

"And then, the kicker is, we hire a guy to shoot this fucking cop and Undersheriff, and *that* guy gets killed. It *has to be* one of the rival cartels. Franky and Hector are so pissed! This will be a full-scale war, when we find out who's behind this shit! It's like I told you in prison, you never know where the threat's coming from, so you always gotta watch your back."

Heath nodded in agreement, and started to get out of the car. Bobby grabbed him by the arm, and said, "Hector wants you to have this. You've earned it, buddy!" Bobby grinned, and handed him a manila envelope.

Heath took it and said, "Thanks, man." He knew what would be inside, even before it was opened. They shook hands, thumbs up, and then bumped each other's knuckles. Heath walked to his pick-up, as Bobby drove past him, making a motion with his hand

and tongue like he was sucking a penis. Bobby burst out laughing, as Heath shook his head in disgust. He shuddered again. Bobby gave him the creeps, too.

∽

Heath opened the envelope in the safety of his truck. There was a bundle of money in typical hundred-dollar bills. A typed note indicated, "$40K bonus. Thanks. Keep it up! H." Heath realized, for the first time, that the money that purchased the meth he had arranged for Hector to sell, from Mexico, to Nevada, to Sacramento, had come all the way back to him, from Sacramento, to Carson City, as payment for his services here. It was dirty, diseased, drug money, and it was all his. He didn't even want to touch it…but he did.

"Pretty ironic," he thought. Bobby and Hector had brought Heath in to help, after Big John had discovered that someone had been feeding their guard dogs. As the guards made their rounds one night, they discovered the dogs eating by the fence, with some of the food still on the lawn. The guards had just missed whoever it was, and Big John was concerned, especially due to the expected birth of Hector's first born, little Franky.

Bobby and Hector had phoned, and asked Heath to come in from Sacramento immediately. He was there the next day. They had set him up for counter surveillance, using the doctor's house next door. They hadn't even told their own people at the compound about Heath, fearing that one of their own might be involved. They had always expected retaliation from a rival cartel, as they took over more and more business, expanding their territory, muscling out the competition. And they feared one of their own might defect, to move up the ladder with the new cartel.

So far, the only thing Heath had discovered was that his own brother, Shane, was conducting surveillance on Bobby, Hector and Franky. He had seen Shane drive by the house, on occasion, and had watched him sitting in his car, night after night, watching the compound. Bobby had told Heath they knew about a planned cop surveillance, and that the undercover cop's name was Dan Harrington, according to their paid informant at the Sheriff's office.

Heath knew, from listening to Shane over the years, that Shane would never use his real name when he worked undercover. Bobby said Hector planned on killing the cop, and stashing his body in an abandoned mine shaft in the desert, after they tortured him for information. Bobby had told him they had used the same mine shaft, several times before. Heath recalled, again, how he had secretly panicked, not knowing what to do.

He knew he needed to protect his brother. He knew Big John's reputation from all the stories Bobby had told him in prison, even before he knew Big John's name. And now that Heath had become one of the family, Bobby had told him more of Big John's exploits. Big John terrified him. The man was a sadist and sociopath...a psychopath on steroids. Heath knew, well enough, exactly what would happen to Shane, if he were captured.

Big John would shoot Shane in both kneecaps, and then, further torture him, using pliers to rip Shane's fingers off, one by one, until Shane spilled his guts about everything. Bobby had told Heath how Big John laughed, as he twisted and pulled the joints off people's fingers, while they screamed and pleaded in agony. And once the digit finally broke and separated, Bobby said the skin was the last to hold anything together. Big John would laugh uncontrollably, as he pulled and stretched the skin to its point of rupture. When that gave way, blood spurted out everywhere. He said Big John was fascinated by the spurting blood, wiping it on his victim's face, using the victim's severed finger, he held in his own hand.

Heath had known he really didn't have a choice. He couldn't tell Shane he was here, in Carson City, working for Hector, Franky and Bobby. And he couldn't tell Shane he was involved in meth trafficking in Sacramento for them. Nor could he allow Big John to capture, torture and kill his brother. He was stuck, knowing he had to protect Shane at all costs, and knowing he had to figure a way out of this for himself. Once again, he had screwed up, but this time he was going to make it right.

Then one night, a week ago, Heath had watched from the doctor's house, while Shane walked into the doctor's yard. He had watched helplessly, as Shane fed the dogs, vaulted the fence into the compound, climbed up a tree, and entered the house. After quite a while, Shane still hadn't come out. Heath seized the opportunity. He had already typed out a note to warn Shane, using a blank business card he had previously prepared on the motel's old typewriter.

He had known that, eventually Shane would leave his car, and he would have a chance to place the card. He ran to Shane's car to leave the note on the windshield. It had been raining lightly, but the card would hold up. Then, he had run down the block, away from the compound, and jumped back yard fences to get back to the doctor's house undiscovered.

Heath had turned to look back at the compound, just in time to see Shane jump off the balcony and into the tree. He watched as Shane vaulted the fence into the neighbor's yard, and walked toward his car. He had seen Shane limping. He had watched Shane take the note off the car windshield. He hoped the warning would keep

Shane from coming back into the compound, or making the meeting that would be scheduled the following Friday, for the sole purpose of killing Shane.

But after Shane drove off, the guards did their patrol rounds, and Big John discovered the dogs had been drugged. He was furious, and vowed loudly to, "kill the son-of-a-bitch responsible." Heath heard Big John say he would only kill the guy *after* he made him wish he had never been born. Big John had yelled at two of the guards in the house, and ordered them to post more guards outside each night to wait for the intruder, so they could capture him.

Heath had no way of knowing Shane would likely not enter the compound again, as he didn't know Shane had planted cameras and bugs in the compound. An hour later, Big John came out to check a noise that Heath had made with a clicker. And Heath was waiting for him. He had placed a bullet from his 22-250 into Big John's fat head, using the same scoped and silenced rifle he had practiced with for years. It had been a gift from his own father, and the one and only thing he had never sold, or pawned, for meth. Now he knew why.

Heath had made extremely accurate shots at various distances, and had been practicing in the desert, not far from Carson City. He had also practiced night shooting, to make sure he didn't miss if he had to shoot someone. Not that he would miss, he thought to himself. After all, he was an excellent marksman. Rifle shooting was one of his few passions. It was one thing he was as good at as Shane…maybe even better. And Bobby and Hector had wanted him to practice, so practice he did.

Heath drove home from his meeting with Bobby, thinking about the irony. He had been paid $40,000 to help protect his crime "family" from an intruder, who turned out to be his own big brother. And now, he was being paid to conduct counter surveillance for Big John's murderer, who was still on the loose…and *he* was the shooter! He laughed nervously to himself at the weird incongruity of his situation.

Yet he knew that if the Magadinnos ever found out, they would torture *him*, before they killed him. He knew if that happened, he would feel pain like he had never felt it before. He also knew he wouldn't do well with a great deal of pain. He wasn't as tough as Shane. But he was in too deeply now to quit. He had been needed *by* his big brother, maybe for the first time. And it was a life and death situation, possibly for both of them…and for Heath's daughters.

He recalled that after he shot Big John, Bobby had confided in Heath that the family had planned on killing the cop for some time. They had never seen him, but their informant told them he was out there, conducting the investigation. They planned to wait until they had received all the information about the investigation, and the cop's real identity, from their informant before they kidnapped and killed him. Now, because Big John was dead, and the information had not yet been received, the family felt that time was running out, and they had no choice. They had to do damage control.

Franky had pressured their "pocket politician," the Undersheriff, to set Shane up for the kill. Bobby said the family had brought in a specialist, a trained sniper, an ex-Bosnian military assassin, to kill the cop *and* the Undersheriff. The hitman would then plant some guns and make it look like a shootout between the victims. They thought it would be the perfect cover.

The Undersheriff was a dirty cop, anyway, Bobby had laughed, and he was holding back on information. Franky and Hector didn't know why he wouldn't tell them everything, and that made them both nervous. Bobby told Heath when and where the hit was planned, and told Heath not to go *sightseeing* in the area that day.

But again, Heath couldn't let his brother die. Shane had always been there for him. Heath really did love his family. So, he got to the meet location at daybreak, hours early, and waited for the sniper to show up. Once he watched the hitman get into position, it had taken Heath two more hours to crawl, undetected, to the exact location needed for him to make the shot. But then the hitman laid down, out of sight. Heath had been forced to wait for the meet to take place and the sniper to get up into shooting position again. And, he had to accomplish this without being seen by the other surveillance teams he had watched move in to place, that he knew had to be with Shane.

Heath had chosen an exit path to get back to his truck before anyone else could detect him. He knew no one could beat him to his truck, once he made the shot. It was parked on another highway, up on the mountain overlooking the little valley he had used on entry. He figured Shane would bring some backup, but he didn't expect *two* rifle teams. Heath had to reposition himself slightly to be out of their visual range, so they couldn't recognize him or photograph him after he shot, and before he turned to run away. And he had to watch these teams to make sure they were *with* Shane. Even with all his precautions, it screwed his plan up enough that he couldn't prevent being seen as he escaped.

Heath had made the shot just in time, when the hitman popped up, but before he acquired his target…and at a distance of almost 775 yards. Heath immediately took off running uphill, and escaped, as planned, without being stopped. He knew the two rifle teams had seen him as he ran, but he also knew he posed no threat to anyone, and that they were busy tracking Shane, the Undersheriff and the downed sniper. He doubted they would shoot him for saving Shane.

Heath had now spoiled Hector and Franky's plans twice. He knew he couldn't keep this up for long, without being discovered. He just wanted to leave now, and go back to Sacramento. But now he couldn't leave. He had to stay, watch, and listen, and *protect* his brother. Shane had not heeded his warning, and had kept the meeting. So, Heath knew he would be out there again tonight, and the next night, sitting in the doctor's house, watching and waiting, and hoping it would all be over soon.

He just didn't know how to end it. He still couldn't tell Shane anything, especially now that he had killed two men. But he also knew he couldn't stop, not until Shane left the assignment and was safely gone from this mess. He had to think of a plan to end it, and soon.

Heath arrived back at his motel, glad the meeting with Bobby was over. He hadn't slept much, and he was so tired he felt drugged. He crawled back into bed. Maybe he could get some sleep before nightfall…he hoped. Maybe he could figure out a way to get out of this alive. But now he had killed two people…two murderers.

Oddly, Heath felt the world was a better, safer place without either of these killers alive. Maybe he *was* doing the right thing for a change. Maybe he really could be "the man" someday, the *good* man, like his brother. He felt a strange peace come over him. He wondered if it was the same peace someone would have felt had they killed Adolf Hitler, before he started a war, killing millions of soldiers, and then exterminated millions of innocent civilians.

Under the covers, Heath finally started to get drowsy. He pulled the covers all the way over his head, feeling his own breath bounce off the sheet and back into his face. The breath was warm, and, in a strange way, he was comforted, just like he had been when he was a kid.

When Heath was young, Shane always tucked him in at night, and if Heath was scared, his big brother would tell him to pull the covers up over his head, and feel his own breath. Shane said that way, nothing bad could see him, and in the morning, everything would be okay. Heath had fallen asleep then…and he fell asleep now. As he drifted into a hazy fog, his dad said, "The only thing necessary for the triumph of evil is for good men to do nothing."

"What should I do now, dad?" Heath pleaded, obviously distressed.

"Do the right thing, son. You'll always know in your heart what the right thing to do is…always." His father placed a hand on his shoulder and smiled at him. He smiled back. Heath loved his dad. He closed his eyes tighter and drifted into a deeper sleep. He would do the right thing. He was strong enough now.

12

Shane was excited, as he ran down the trail from the lake toward the valley of the river. Somehow, he knew, this time, he had to get to camp earlier than he had before, during the first days of the trip. There would be no aerospace tower leaping today. Heath was following him at a respectable distance, and *much* slower pace. They would take no unnecessary risks now.

His mom's anti-swelling and pain relief cocktail, combined with Shane's all-night care of Heath's ankle, had worked. The swelling and pain had been diminished. Shane had wrapped Heath's ankle a dozen times, in a towel he soaked in ice cold river water. Heath was feeling much better, although he still complained that he was stiff. The left ankle appeared normal, save a slight bruising around the ankle ball.

Shane had worked with Heath, after breakfast, stretching his ankle. And he made sure the supportive wrap he had fashioned from an old T-shirt, was firmly in place. While the two brothers worked on Heath's ankle, their dad got the fishing gear ready for the hike. The group always fished at the same lake on the first Thursday of each annual trek. It was a two-hour hike to the lake, perched high up in a mountain valley, well above the valley of the river camp.

Patrick Beckett had watched his sons carefully during the trip. He marveled at how Shane took care of Heath, and, even as a father, he rarely interfered, allowing the bond between the brothers to build. He knew that someday Heath would need Shane, and he wanted both of his sons to know they could depend on each other. Patrick hoped and prayed that Heath would return the love and commitment to Shane, but he worried about Heath's character. He never stopped hoping, and he prayed that his fears about Heath, were misplaced.

Heath was young, and Patrick, and his wife, Annie, routinely prayed together each night for both boys to be safe, and to always be there for each other. For Patrick and Annie, family meant everything. They believed that family is forever, and family grows with time, as close friends become family, and are referred to as such. And they believed that no family member should ever be forgotten, used or abused.

They taught their sons that those close to you should be cared for, nurtured and loved. It was the Beckett way, and Patrick could see it in Shane every single day. Sometimes, he felt there was a glimmer of hope for Heath, too. So, he raised his boys as best he could, and he hoped, and he prayed.

When the group reached the lake, they had fished in the mid to late morning hours, and then swam in the cold lake water, as the summer sun began to get hot and high, before noon. Then they had eaten their lunch, and relaxed…napping, hiking or fishing again. By 4:00 in the afternoon, the group was on their way back down to camp, with their fish cleaned and ready to be cooked over an open fire. Everyone anticipated the coming dinner of fresh trout, fire roasted potatoes, baked beans and canned fruit.

All the adults were looking forward to an early meal, a game of cards under campfire and star light, and a "bump" of the scotch Shane had carried to camp in his backpack. Everyone had left to hike back at the same time, except Heath, Hunter and Shane. Heath and Hunter had wanted to swim longer, so Shane remained at the lake to take care of the younger boys. But today, he only delayed an extra half hour for the swim, because *today*, he was making sure he got a seat next to his dad at the campfire.

Shane had overheard a conversation between his dad and Hunter's dad, Kent Murray, while they had all fished at the lake. Shane had been just out of site, sitting behind a boulder on the lake shore. Kent said he was working a case that had begun with information received from a mutual friend of theirs in law enforcement, who was working with a confidential informant, a high-ranking government official.

The case involved corruption, government contracts, and narcotics trafficking, with a strange twist. Kent had a theory that people in key government positions had set themselves up to take over narcotics trafficking, and cut out the cartels, for two important reasons. He believed the money they made would not only make them rich, but would eventually give them enough control to accomplish their goal… something they referred to as a "primary objective."

Shane hadn't heard the whole conversation, and he didn't understand it all. Normally, a conversation like this wouldn't have been a big deal to him. But, Kent had warned Patrick, that the Attorney

General's task force he was overseeing was focusing on many of the same people as the DEA investigation, and there was bound to be some "blowback."

Shane remembered that word, "blowback." He needed to know what the word meant, because Kent told his father that no one was safe from the people involved. Kent had said these people were capable of murder. He said the DEA had recently been ordered to stand down from the investigation. The order had come from the very top of their command structure. Kent said he now feared for Patrick and his family. So today, Shane was going to get his seat at the fire, and make sure his dad told him what it all meant, who these people were, and what he could do to help protect his family.

The hike back down the trail was faster than the hike up. Still, Shane, Hunter and Heath wouldn't arrive back until 6:00, and, by then, the view of the sun would be blocked from the valley by the high mountains that surrounded and protected it. A hot, crackling fire would be burning in the large fire pit, and people would already be positioning for seats, depending on the direction of the smoke from the campfire.

Shane wanted to get there in plenty of time to ask his questions today, so he pressed Heath and Hunter to move faster, as he turned frequently to check their progress, and call back to them. Hunter was right next to Heath, and would help him if his ankle bothered him too much going over some rough terrain. Heath was a tough, wiry, kid.

Shane knew if Heath worked at it, he could do anything, but he lacked the motivation, the will, *and* the drive. Hunter didn't lack any of these things, and he shared a common interest with Shane... he was always to be there to help Heath. And Hunter enjoyed Heath as a friend.

Almost every day Shane tried to motivate Heath, using stories, history or a life lesson, that demonstrated how much people could accomplish, if they just had the will and commitment…*and* conversely, how they would likely fail, if they lacked *either* will, or commitment. Depending on the situation, Heath might lack one or the other, but often pushed himself to please Shane. Today was one of those days. Shane was sure they were going to make it in time.

By 5:45, the trio had made it to the rock outcropping overlooking the valley of the river. They looked down through the forest into a winding river canyon, guarded by steep, hard-rock walls, that seemed to confine the rushing river, as it continuously pushed back and struggled to be free. In some places, the river was narrow and deep, it's water rushing fast to get through the small opening. In other spots, the river slowed as the canyon widened, making it possible to walk through it, from side to side, and even float and swim in its lazy, cool pools.

The camp was set up at the largest and widest pool, a spectacular spot with a large, permanent fire pit. The accompanying tables and chairs, made from logs and planks, had been cut and pieced together by campers from seasons gone by. Each year when they arrived, their group discovered a new addition, left by people they had never met. Unknowingly, all the campers from all the seasons past, had worked collectively, through decades of past springs, summers and falls, to add amenities to a campsite they might never see again. It had become an unwritten tradition to improve the site, and keep it clean.

As he stood looking down on the sight, waiting for the two younger boys to catch up, Shane suddenly realized that there was no government or organization working here, to supervise a collective group of people to accomplish anything. Yet, people had triumphed, year after year, for generations, working together to improve their special place, without as much as a committee meeting. He was amazed that it could even be possible, when these same people struggled and argued at home, and made little improvement in their collective full-time community lives.

Heath and Hunter caught up, and Shane pressed on, down the mountain, to the big pool, where they crossed the river's wide, lazy, shallow spot to their campsite. Half way across, Heath yelled out and pointed to a water snake swimming in the pool between them. Shane just laughed and said, "Buck up, man, it's only a water snake!"

Hunter placed a hand on Heath's shoulder, and spoke something to him that Shane couldn't hear. Heath rushed ahead, after the snake crossed in front of him, to be closer to his older brother. Hunter 'stood guard' between the snake and Heath. When Heath caught up to Shane, he put his hand on Shane's shoulder, seeming to gain some confidence. He then waited for his friend.

Arriving at camp, Shane found three of the men already seated at the fire pit. The fire had just been lit, and a lazy drift of smoke worked its way upward and then nowhere, seemingly disinterested in the freedom of direction allowed by the lack of a breeze. Shane asked Hunter and Heath to get cleaned up for dinner. Shane had already bathed in the lake, while Heath and Hunter swam, and he was ready to make his move when his dad returned from their tent.

Shane walked to the fire, listening to a friendly argument that had erupted over whose fish was heavier. It seemed that length didn't matter, as only heavier weight was needed to win the bet between these friends. Shane heard his dad walking up behind him, laughing at the group. He said, "Believe it or not, two of you are tied at 2 pounds 7 ounces. Hard to believe, since one fish is 2 inches longer than the other, but I put them on the fish scale twice. Looks like you two big winners have to split the $12 pool today!"

The three men left to go check the weights for themselves, involved in a friendly debate on whether one fish held more water than the other, and, how emptying both fish of water, might produce a more decisive result and define a clear winner.

Shane moved in close to his dad. Patrick could always tell when something was up with Shane and asked, "So, what's going on?"

Shane eluded the direct question, saying, "What do you mean, dad? I haven't even said anything yet!"

Patrick laughed and put a strong arm around his son. He said, "I know myself pretty well after all these years, and yet, I think I know *you* about as well as I know myself. You always try to work into a seat next to me when you need to talk, while we're up here in the woods. Why don't you just ask me whatever you want, whenever it enters your mind? Why does it have to be here at the fire?"

Shane looked incredulous. He said, firmly, "The fire pit is where *the men* talk about serious things. The days are for fun, and the nights for idle talk until we all go to sleep. But the fire pit is where we always talk about the problems we face in life, or what bothers us. It's what we've always done!"

Patrick smiled, and affirmed his son, saying, "Shane, you're right. I hope you know how proud you make me. What do you want to know, son?"

Shane asked, "What's the "blowback" you and Kent were talking about at the lake? And what danger does our family face?"

Patrick stared at his eldest son, trying to contain his emotions. He was proud of Shane, fearful for his family, angry that his family was in danger, and irritated that his son had to worry about danger that came from one of his own decisions, being involved with this case. But above all, he was committed to take care of his family, and keep them safe. Patrick was slow to answer, and when he did speak, his words were guarded.

"Shane, that's just work stuff between Kent and I…it's really nothing for you to worry about."

It was a feeble attempt at best. Shane was too smart to accept such a meager explanation. He immediately looked hard at his dad, and said, "I'm not Heath. I'm not a little kid, dad. I can handle the truth, and right now *the truth* is what I need to know."

Patrick released a heavy sigh. He gathered his thoughts, and said, "The *truth* is that I am working on a case involving some very powerful, and very dangerous, people. Kent is working a connected case, involving some of the same people. And we're trying to identify all the people involved, the crimes they have committed, and then decide on how to proceed. The *truth* is that we're both scared, for ourselves and our families, but we will take precautions to make sure everyone stays safe. I don't want you to have to worry about it, Shane."

Shane asked, "But, dad, why are *you* involved in this case? I mean, why did it have to be you? There are investigators and cops for all that, aren't there?"

The three fishermen came walking back to the fire pit, still debating about who won the bet. Patrick looked at his son, and placed a hand on his shoulder. He said, "Do you remember meeting my friend, Scott Mayfield, the Attorney General?" Shane nodded, remembering him from a party at the Beckett home earlier in the year.

Patrick continued. "Scott asked me, as a personal favor, to take the role of special prosecutor, to review this case and identify suspects and charges for prosecution. I'm working with a small task force of very dedicated people, who have completed the preliminary investigation, and put together an introductory report. It's pretty scary stuff, Shane, but I am working out a plan to protect us all, especially you boys."

Patrick thought hard for a second and continued. "And, more to your point *why me*…these people's bad acts will impact all our lives, if men like Scott, and Kent and I stand idly by and do nothing. Some of these evil schemes are hard to believe, but could work, and change the way we all live…for the worse. A good man must stand up for what is right. Freedom and justice don't come easily, or without sacrifice. If people don't fight against evil, evil will always triumph. I hope you always remember that."

With that, the fishermen's debate engulfed the campfire area, as others from the group joined the debate, having left their tents, one by one, to join the fire. In the end, it seemed that both fish, once *certified* as dry, still each weighed 2 pounds 7 ounces, and the pool had to be shared between the winners, after all.

Everyone was happy, laughing and telling stories about the bigger fish that got away, except Shane. He figured he had to accept his dad's explanation for now. He thought he would work out something he could do to help protect his family, when they got back home. His mind began to fill with images of criminals, threatening to hurt his family, and he knew he couldn't let that happen. But he had won a victory, and had won a temporary seat next to his dad at the cherished fire pit.

Patrick leaned over, and whispered to Shane, "I will never leave you without a plan, and hope for the future, to understand this all. I will find a way to explain it to you, when the time is right. I promise, son." Patrick placed his hand on Shane's shoulder. The two stared hard at each other, until a smile formed on Shane's lips.

"I love you, dad."

"I love you, too, son. I always will!"

Shane wrested himself away from the image of his father, and the men at the campfire. This time, he literally forced himself to awaken from the dream. He didn't want to forget the dream, as people often do when they gain full consciousness. It was still dark. Lying face up, he struggled to focus on something in the room and keep the conversation fresh in his mind. He remembered, and decided to tell Kate, to make sure he remembered for good.

He turned toward her, knowing she was sleeping, as her head still rested on his chest. The movement dropped her head to the bed, but she didn't move. He shook her shoulder forcefully, saying, "Kate, wake up…hurry, Kate, and wake up!"

Kate sat up quickly, struggling to awaken from a deep sleep. She didn't know why she was struggling, or what the reason was, but she focused on the urgency in Shane's insistent voice. She looked quickly around the room for some perceived problem, asking, "What is it, Shane?!"

Shane rattled off quickly, so he wouldn't forget, "Its Kent Murray, the DEA agent, my dad's friend, Kent Murray! I remembered the conversation. How could I have forgotten it? Kent knows about the investigation. He may have some missing pieces. We need to find Kent Murray, and if not, then Scott Mayfield's family. Kent and dad investigated the same people. I need to ask Pete. Maybe he knows where Kent is now!" Shane got up out of bed and frantically began to dress.

Kate said, "Shane, honey, its 4:00 in the morning. Maybe, we could let Pete and Tasha sleep a little longer…you think?" She patted the bed, after she turned back the covers for him.

Shane looked out the window to the dark valley below, illuminated only by a moon sliver and star light. He smiled, and said, "Oh, sorry. I just got excited. I finally remembered it!" He got back into bed, as Kate smiled up at him, and immediately reached to snuggle up next to him.

"We can't forget it. Will you remember in the morning?"

"I'll remember, dear. *Trust me*. I'll remember. Kent Murray...4:00 in the morning!" Kate snuggled back onto Shane's muscular chest and melted her body into his side. Within a few minutes, she was fast asleep.

The excitement of the revelation had jump started Shane's system. He tried to get back to sleep for what seemed like an hour, but was only ten minutes, according to the digital clock on the nightstand. He couldn't sleep. He held Kate for a minute longer, and asked, "Are you awake? Please, Kate. This is important. Can you be awake?"

Kate moved up on top of Shane and kissed him deeply, her tongue finding the back of his mouth. She said, "Does that answer your question? What do you think?" She arched her back above his chest.

The night moon and starlight in the room painted accentuating shadows onto Kate's beautiful breasts, which now dangled enticingly down to him, her large, erect nipples brushing and teasing his chest, ever so softly. They enjoyed another long kiss, and Shane was instantly rock hard. Shane caressed Kate's smooth back and bottom, while his tongue continued to explore her mouth, neck and her ears. He inhaled the fragrance of her hair, until he could barely constrain his throbbing penis. He wanted to savage her, and thrust himself deep inside her beautiful, tasty, wet pussy. He restrained his entry for a little longer, as the anticipation and passion built.

Ardent kisses became more daring, while hands caressed and explored more aggressively. Finally, Kate relaxed her legs and moved further on top of him. Shane reached down between her thighs, and stroked the pubic area she had shaved the night before. He slid two fingers inside her, smoothly, as she was already wet with anticipation. She moaned softly, with the collective voice of both angel and seductress. Shane's body tensed as he felt his blood surging.

"Deeper, deeper," she groaned. "Let me come to you now," she whispered.

Shane kissed Kate's neck, and used his tongue to trace her luscious body from her lips down to the breasts that called to him like sirens of the sea. She moved up on him, and presented a breast, sideways, just above his face. He seized the swollen orb in his mouth, sucking the hardened nipple. He teased and held it in his mouth, and then ran his teeth over it playfully.

"Harder! Bite them...gently!" Kate demanded. She used her hand and pushed the breast deeper in to Shane's mouth. She pulled the back of his head toward her to force the breast in further, while using her body to push from the other side. "Harder!" she demanded.

He willingly complied, moving from one nipple and breast to the other, until he himself was ready to explode, but holding back. He withdrew his fingers from inside Kate, and explored her sweet spot with his fingertips, softly pressing, stroking, rubbing, using just one finger and his thumb.

Fully aroused, their kisses became deeper, and even more intense. He suddenly drove his fingers deep inside her and began alternating thrusts and withdrawals. He settled in to an age-old rhythm, until Kate cried out, arching her back further. As her body tensed, he felt her strong orgasmic contractions grip the fingers still deep inside her. The spasms relaxed briefly, and then came again, in waves, each lasting a shorter time.

Kate smiled down into Shane's eyes, and then, suddenly, took control, firmly grabbing his erect penis, guiding it up inside her. She moved on top of him, undulating back and forth, up and down, grinding herself into him, until she came again, this time with more violent, but briefer, contractions. She was a woman possessed with passion, pressing down on Shane's chest with both hands, while he strained to kiss and suckle her breasts, moving from one to the other with his tongue and hands.

Shane tried to give equal attention to each breast, as he flicked his tongue around areola, sucked each nipple, and lightly chewed the tip. Kate's nipples became increasingly engorged and fully erect, as both Shane and Kate became even more aroused. Finally, he held a nipple between each thumb and index finger, and gently twisted, while rubbing the tips.

At last, with Kate riding on top of him, moving feverishly, using her last ounce of strength, he felt complete release as he exploded in a series of throbbing waves, emptying himself into her, as she came to her final and strongest orgasm.

Their sexual movements slowed and diminished, as the both gradually relaxed. Their movements stopped, and they both enjoyed the exquisite oneness of complete fulfillment. Kate lowered her lips to meet his. They kissed softly, lingering in and over each other's mouths for several moments. Kate lowered herself down on Shane, coming to rest on his chest. They lay quietly, breathing slowed, listening to their combined heartbeats.

Suddenly, and completely without warning, Kate rolled over and off Shane, in one quick move that allowed her to land, out of bed, and on her feet, arms raised over her head.

"What the hell?!" He exclaimed.

Kate laughed, "You get me up at 4:00 in the morning, buddy… now *you* have to get *me* coffee!" With that, she ran to the bathroom, calling behind her, "And I get a "10" for the dismount!"

Shane stretched lazily, thinking how lucky he was to have a woman like Kate. She was everything he had always wanted, and more. She was incredibly athletic, smart as a whip, talented, loyal, committed, and a passionate lover. And, she was *all his*. She was his…girlfriend? He smiled, and couldn't help but think their relationship would lead to something more. "Girlfriend" sounded too…unattached, uncon- nected, and unimportant.

At least, now, he allowed himself to hope for a future with her. He knew he had more to live for than ever before. He got up and gingerly pulled on his briefs, careful to avoid the slightly tender souvenir of his and Kate's passion. He threw on a robe, and quietly descended the stairs toward the kitchen, trying to be quiet and not wake anyone in the house. To Shane's surprise, he found all the lights on in the kitchen and heard voices as he approached. He could hear the espresso machine, as Sam and Jesse chatted in the background.

When he turned the corner, and walked into the kitchen, Shane's eyes met Jesse's.

"I can't believe *you're* up this early, too, but I'm glad!" Jesse said.

Shane, immediately interested, asked, "What's up?"

Jesse answered, "Before I start to explain what we've found, can I get you anything?" He nodded toward the espresso machine and smiled, anxious to ply his trade.

Shane said, "Oh, please, yes…that's why I'm here. Could we please have two lattes, and do you have caramel?"

Jesse said, "Shit, you're *both* awake? I hope the noise we made down here didn't get you both up!" Shane just grinned and shook his head, deterring any explanation.

Jesse continued. "Okay, good! We do have caramel, and I'll make two. You better get Kate, so I can tell you both what my team found!"

Shane nodded, realizing that Jesse had some important news. He ran back up the stairs to get Kate, ascending them two at a time.

Arriving in the room just as Kate came out of the bathroom, Shane saw that Kate's expression was questioning, seeing there was no coffee in his hands. He said, "We'd better get dressed and go down to meet Jesse. He got up early, too. He's making caramel lattes, and he's found something!"

Kate began to dress. She said coyly, "I bet he didn't wake up like we did, though! And I'm hungry now, by the way. Just so you know, these sessions with you always make me hungry! I could even swear I smell cinnamon rolls." She laughed. Shane just smiled, feeling a little proud of himself.

Within a couple of minutes, they were downstairs, meeting Jesse in the new "war room." Jesse handed them their drinks, made with whipped cream on top, supporting caramel and unsweetened dark chocolate sprinkles. He motioned to an office space his team had set up, with individual work spaces, each equipped with computers and surveillance monitoring equipment. He said, "Please, sit. I've got fresh cinnamon rolls there, too. Baked them this morning when I couldn't sleep."

Kate teased, and said, "So that's what woke me up! I thought I could smell fresh baked cinnamon rolls!" She cast a sly look at Shane, as she brushed his leg with her foot, and said, "It would have to be something especially sweet and tasty to get me up and going at this hour."

Shane reddened slightly, though he thought, or hoped, Jesse didn't notice. He cocked an eyebrow at Kate to stop her, knowing it wouldn't work. They both enjoyed these teasing games they played, although he wouldn't admit it, if the question came up.

Kate asked, "How long have *you* been up then?"

Jesse answered slowly, as he sat at a machine next to a computer. "Maybe three hours now. I had to work out something that was bothering me about a file on the flash drive Shane found. I think most clearly when I cook. So, a tray of cinnamon rolls, a couple of hours and three espresso macchiatos later, Sam and I figured it out."

Jesse moved around the machine to an attached computer, motioning them to take two chairs to his right. He spun the screen around, so they could see what he was reading. He explained, "We haven't had nearly enough time to begin to digest all this information, but I found one file, in the first ten master files, that didn't make sense. It's Number Nine, not that I know why or if, that's important yet. The file contains nothing but scores of quotes, mostly from famous people. There is no internal reference, or explanation, as to what relevance it might have when combined with thousands of pages of documents and investigation."

Jesse opened the file. The first quote was by Abraham Lincoln, and read, "In the end it's not the years in your life that count. It's the life in your years." Jesse looked from Shane to Kate, and found only blank stares.

He said grinning, "That's the same thing I thought." They all laughed.

Jesse continued. "But then, I remembered a book I had read years ago. It was a spy novel…you know a conspiracy-theory type of story. Anyway, the main spy kept a series of quotes in a journal he used, to take notes on the case. After he was murdered, his partner studied his work to look for clues to his death. He found the quotes, and finally figured out they must be the key to the real information contained in the pages of his journal. Finding the key broke the code, which led to the discovery of the missing investigation, that solved the case. Pretty cool, huh?"

Kate and Shane returned blank stares to a beaming Jesse. Shane raised both hands and tilted them outward, asking for an explanation.

Jesse nodded, as he accessed software on the computer, "So, I ran the quotes through our version of EDA."

Jesse looked from Shane to Kate for approval and understanding, but realized he still wasn't making progress.

He sighed, and continued. "Many software companies have developed code breaking software. We use a version *similar* to what the Central Intelligence Agency and the National Security Agency use here, in the United States. It's really just an updated version of the Enigma Decipher Algorithm, or, EDA, developed about five years ago."

Jesse looked from one to the other of them, hoping for a glimpse of acknowledgment that they were beginning to understand his explanation. Seeing nothing, he said, in a speaking-to-children voice, "You know, an advanced code-breaking software."

By the change in their expressions, Jesse could see they were finally catching on to where he was headed, so he continued. "During World War II, the Germans had come up with this machine, an ingenious invention, to code and decipher communications. The Allies eventually captured one, and used it to decode German communications… and help win the war. It was one of the game changers for our side."

"After the war ended, both the U.S. and the Brits continued to work on code breaking machines, so they would never encounter a similar problem in the future. Eventually, with the advent of computers, software, algorithms, data analysis and the like, the code-breaking software programs were born, and now continue to be upgraded."

Kate and Shane were nodding their mutual basic understanding, so Jesse continued. "Think of it like computer viruses. Some programmer invents a computer virus, and then another programmer comes up with an anti-virus. It's the same with codes and encrypted communications, only on an exponential scale now, with governments hacking each other's systems for intelligence. Everyone wants to be ahead of the other guy."

Jesse's face lit up, as he began to talk excitedly, about a subject he loved. "Imagine a U.S. intelligence agency sending a file to the Secretary of Defense. They know, when they send it, that our enemies, like the Iranians, the Russians, the Chinese...hell, even our allies, like the Brits, are trying to intercept it and decode it. So, our government uses protected secure servers that are constantly monitored for hacking, viruses, Trojans, worms, virtually every kind of known threat... then, they *encrypt* the file, so if someone does get past the security protocols, or the information is stolen, the unintended reader can't read it without the correct key...the *cypher*."

Jesse continued at an excited pace, now on a roll. "So, the software becomes more and more complex, as cypher technology is constantly changing, evolving to a higher level. You can conceal an important message, report or document, among gigabytes of worthless information, so the average reader could never find what he or she is searching for, without the correct cypher. It's really cool stuff, actually," Jesse beamed, as he sat back and clicked the mouse, in triumph.

The first page of quotes was instantly transformed into a guide with instructions for the reader to assemble a series of documents, attachments and reports, using different cyphers to decrypt each document, in order to decipher the actual report.

Jesse clicked the mouse again, and pointed to a sentence in a report. "Look at that!" he exclaimed. Individual, non-contiguous words were highlighted in the sentence with numbers following each word.

Jesse shook his head and said, "Man, for their day, these guys were good, really good!"

He turned to Kate and Shane, expecting admiring smiles, but once again was met with blank stares. He sat forward in his chair and said, confidently, "We can break this code with time. So far, it appears that the real report and attachments will be revealed by deciphering all the documents that we are directed to search. Using words, or letters from words, in the exact order the cypher tells us, should reassemble the information, so we can create the real report and attachments! It's very complex, but achievable, now that we are beginning to understand the process."

Shane said, "How long will this take…just a guess? I don't mean to press you. I'm just trying to plan my moves with Grant and Roberts," he explained.

Jesse nodded in understanding, and said, "Time is controlled by the speed and success of our software, and the number of people and computers we have working on the project. Once the convoy arrives, we'll have the people we need to speed up the process. Until then, it will just be me, Sam, and two of my team. In the end, maybe no more than two or three weeks, if all goes well…and *if* we can identify the correct cypher."

Shane and Kate finished their lattes simultaneously, and Shane rolled the empty cup in his hand, looking down at the few drops remaining, as he thought ahead.

Jesse stood up, holding out his hand, and offered, "Another?" Shane smiled and handed him the cup, and he and Kate followed him to the kitchen.

Jesse worked his magic with the espresso machine, while Kate and Shane stood silently behind him. Jesse was consumed in thought. He turned and handed the latte to Shane, and took Kate's now empty cup to repeat the process.

He looked at both of them, studying him carefully, and said, "You know, I really love coffee, espresso machines, and cooking of all types. It *could* be my life. But there's one thing I love more. Do you know what that is?" Both Kate and Shane stared at him intently, and shook their heads back and forth.

Jesse continued, as he turned back to the machine. "It's unraveling a good mystery. And coded communications are among my favorite parts of a good mystery. I want to run something by you both. But before I do, let's put this whole thing in perspective, and think about it for a moment. Let's all take a hard look at the complete picture."

Jesse was quiet for a moment, while he steamed the milk and added caramel and chocolate drizzles. He plopped a moderate spoonful of whipped cream on top of the foaming liquid in the cup, and topped that off with the appropriate sprinkles and more drizzles.

He turned and said, "I know it's unconventional, but I like to experiment. What did you think?" He motioned to the latte as he handed it to Kate.

Kate expressed a sigh of relief. She replied, "Oh, thank God, you weren't asking me what I thought about the decryption. I'm afraid that's out of my league! The latte is wonderful. I would never have thought about adding the whipped cream and sprinkles with drizzles of chocolate *and* caramel!" She sipped the latte and smiled, getting a little whipped cream on her nose. Shane smiled as he watched her. He thought how he even loved the way Kate ate and drank.

Jesse smiled too, as Shane wiped the whipped cream off Kate's nose. They walked to the war room, so Jesse could begin his recap. They all sat deeply back in a leather couch and matching chairs that surrounded a fire place, with only dying embers remaining for heat. Kate looked at the smoldering fire and realized she was cold. She pulled a blanket over her as she sat next to Shane, and prepared to listen to Jesse. She thought he looked a little too concerned, and found she was almost dreading what he would say next.

Jesse began. "In summation, what we know, so far, is that some 13 years ago, an ongoing criminal conspiracy, involving drugs, money laundering, government corruption, drug cartels, misappropriation of millions in public funds, and multiple murders, was discovered and investigated by an honest Attorney General, using a task force of specialists, who did their work in secret. Eventually *your* father, Shane, reviewed the final draft of the case at the AG's request. His assignment was to identify the people, and specific crimes that could be charged, linking everything together, through a well-documented investigation. Correct, so far?" Shane nodded and sipped his latte.

Jesse continued. "Kate, your father was competing against a known, sophisticated drug lord and murderer, who owns dozens of businesses and corporations, for a government contract worth hundreds of millions of dollars. Before your father could modify and submit his final bid, both he and his assistant were murdered, and buried alive under the basement floor of the project they were bidding to win. I'm sorry to bring this up to both of you, but my point will be clear in a moment." Kate nodded, and Jesse continued.

"Shane, your father encrypts the entire case file with, what was then, state-of-the-art technology, probably obtained from the military, and secretly saves it on two flash drives that he hides in his old classic car. He tells no one about this, not even Pete, who he trusts with his life. Instead, he has Pete store the car in a different city, locked away in a storage unit. He then writes a letter to you that only you and he understand, knowing you will look at the tire, find the photo, disassemble the walking stick, and find the flash drives, once Pete delivers the letter and car to you *years* later."

"He also knows that no one else will understand the message in the letter, if they find it. And he knows that Pete will never sell the car, so no one but you will find the flash drives. He does this knowing it's his long-shot, backup plan to eventually expose the truth, should he be killed. And your dad's plan worked. You do find the drives, many years after he dies. Good so far?" Both Shane and Kate nodded again, sipping their latte in unison.

"But, it is also important, Shane, that, *before* your father could finish his task and provide a recommendation for indictment to the AG, both he and your mother were murdered in a staged traffic accident. As we now know, that accident was staged by the drug lord's criminal organization, with assistance provided by one of the AG's own investigators. The investigation into that accident was lost, by persons unknown, working in law enforcement or government." Jesse looked from Kate to Shane, and they again nodded in agreement with the summation, to this point.

Jesse continued. "The AG is then murdered, when he is given an experimental drug, *after* trials on the lethal pill had been stopped, due to serious side effects that included death. The drug induced a massive heart attack. The AG's task force was disbanded, and all records of the investigation were again, lost by persons unknown, working in government or law enforcement."

"The huge government contract *your* father was killed over, Kate, was awarded to the drug kingpin murderer that arranged for *your* parents' deaths, Shane. *And,* we now know, this piece-of-slime dealer has acquired numerous law enforcement officials and politicians through the years, who are all bought and paid for, to assist him and his organization with all kinds of criminal acts, including murder."

"So, Shane, you become a police officer, work a series of assignments, and eventually become a highly sought after, independent contractor, used by security services and law enforcement to investigate cases they aren't equipped or trained to handle, or when they need an undercover operative from *outside* their own organization."

Jesse paused, and said, "By the way, my guess is, that if your father knew you very well, he would have figured you would go into law enforcement." Shane nodded in agreement.

Jesse added more. "The current Sheriff of Carson City, Nevada, who was formerly a Special Agent in Charge with the FBI, had been frustrated in his attempts to investigate the same organization, and a series of murders they probably committed, while he was a Fed. His attempts to investigate this group resulted in him being pulled off the case by his own bosses, *and* his wife coincidently vanishing off the face of the earth, maybe as a warning to him."

Jesse didn't stop. "He became the Sheriff to have a free hand at investigating the old cases, and to hopefully find out what happened to his wife. He then hired you, and brought you in from the outside, so none of his people would realize you were investigating the drug lord, his crime organization, and his corrupt circle of friends. Unfortunately, the Sheriff trusted his Undersheriff with some of this information, and we now know that the Undersheriff is also on the drug lord's payroll, having participated in the murders of both Kate's father and his assistant."

Jesse's eyes stared a thousand yards ahead, as he focused on his recap. "That miscalculation of trust, on the Sheriff's part, resulted in you being set up to be taken out by a professional hit man. You were nearly murdered!"

Kate squeezed Shane's hand under the blanket, as her whole body shuddered, and she shook her head, looking down. Tears had formed in her eyes, and she didn't want either Jesse or Shane to notice them. Shane was aware of the change in Kate's breathing, and tightened his grip on her hand, while avoiding her eyes, out of respect. He didn't want to see her cry, or precipitate the release of any more of her tears.

Jesse continued. "We now know from our surveillance and phone monitoring investigation that this same Undersheriff that set you up, called someone in the crime family, who called Hector to tell him you were at the location. Someone made a call to the hitman, while he was lying in the field, *before* the Undersheriff got out of his car to meet you. Someone told the hit man to 'take out both targets.' But, before he could shoot you, and the Undersheriff, an unknown sniper took out the hitman…and completely vanished."

"And now we know that the Undersheriff is reporting to an informant on the inside who isn't giving the Magadinnos all the information, meaning that the informant and the Undersheriff are working for both the Magadinnos, *and possibly* another unknown person or group. In addition, we have a mole in our group, and we have no clue to *his* ties."

Jesse looked up and got the head nods acknowledging the accuracy of the recitation. He continued. "To complicate all of this, if it isn't complex enough, even with all the bugs and cameras on the inside of the compound, we don't have a clue who the informant is, or whether he or she is inside the compound, or not. And, we have no idea who, from the compound, is communicating with the friendly sniper, who saved your life."

Jesse stopped and took a long drink of his own macchiato, pleased with his rendition of the current state of affairs in the case. "Damn, I know I drink too much of this, but I dearly love it!" he said. Looking from Kate to Shane, he asked, "So, does that about sum it up, or have I missed something?"

Shane looked at Kate, and said, "Just one thing. A DEA agent, named Kent Murray, told my father he was working a parallel investigation involving drugs, cartels and corrupt politicians, also focusing on some of the same suspects as my dad's task force, at the same time my dad was working on this case. His superiors pulled him off the case. He told my father the order to cease and desist from the investigation came from DEA's top command. He was worried about my family's safety, in addition to his own."

Jesse rubbed his face with his hands. "*Great*, they own people *that* high up!" Jesse said sarcastically. "Just great!" He stared at his empty cup. "So, we are dealing with massive corruption involving multiple law enforcement agencies, government officials, drug cartels, unknown informants, professional hitmen, a friendly sniper, a mole in our group, and even an outlaw motorcycle gang that is being worked into the picture to move meth. Does everybody else see how dangerous this case has become?"

Shane said, "It was this dangerous all the time, even way back when our parents were murdered." He squeezed Kate's hand and gave her a smile. "We're just now piecing it together and figuring it out. It's a *massive* case. So, what are you thinking, Jesse?"

Jesse said, "I need to ask permission to pull one more person in to help us get the information out of your dad's files, as soon as possible. Whoever we're dealing with knows some of our moves, even before we make them. We need to tighten this up fast and get on a level playing field. I want to bring in my military trainer, who taught me cyphering techniques…a real expert in the science."

Shane asked, "Who is he, and where can we find him?"

But, before Jesse could answer, a voice from the stair landing half way down to the war room, said, "He's a she, and she's at home with Jesse's kids."

Jesse, Kate and Shane all turned to look, and found Pete and Tasha standing there, leaning on the stair bannister. They had been standing there the entire time, silently taking in the briefing.

Tasha stood, pale and wide eyed. Pete looked at her in surprise, and said, "I told you it would be dangerous!" He then turned to Jesse, as he walked down the stairs, and said, "Excellent summation, by the way. And I think you should bring Tracy into help. Everyone says she's the best around with encrypted data and data mining."

Pete then turned to Shane and Kate and said, "We couldn't sleep. We smelled cinnamon rolls."

Everyone laughed, got up and walked to the tray of cinnamon rolls, while Jesse brought Pete and Tasha up to speed on the developments with the flash drives.

Kate and Shane chatted alone about what their plans should be for the day. Shane suggested they take in some sights while they waited for the convoy to arrive. He wanted to de-stress and think, and just enjoy time with Kate…completely uninterrupted. He didn't want to think about Heath, hit men, moles or encrypted data files.

13

"In preparing for battle I have always found that plans are useless, but planning is indispensable."
(Dwight D. Eisenhower)

eath slept through the day and night, and continued to sleep far in to the late morning the following day. He had the first long good sleep of the last several months. His phone suddenly interrupted a seemingly bottomless deep sleep and if not for the persistence of the ring that finally roused him, he thought he may have slept all day.

But it was Bobby, and Hector was pressuring him to find out about what the Sacramento area dope dealers knew about Big John's murder…and now their hitman's murder. Heath gave Bobby a false excuse that he had made calls late last night and his feelers were already out, but Bobby said Hector wanted all Heath's sources contacted, and an answer back today, no later. Heath had agreed, reluctantly, to himself. But, he had agreed.

Heath showered quickly, changed in to a fresh set of clothes, and drove to a chain coffee shop not far from the motel. He walked in

371

and ordered a large Mocha with double shots and double chocolate. Once he became sober he developed an instantiable desire for sweets, and the mocha routine was his morning treat. Today he also ordered a companion chocolate muffin with nuts. Heath didn't want to return to his motel room and spend the day on the phone making calls, so he drove to Mills Park. The weather promised to stay warmer and drier today, and he craved fresh air, and fresh scenery.

While he waited for the comely young barista to fill his order, he watched her as she moved and noted that, although she was not a ravishing head-turning, eye-popping beauty, she was in fact *very* attractive. With long flowing black hair, large blue eyes, flawless olive skin, and a well-defined body that displayed all the right curves in all the right places, this 20-something server could offer the hope of love to any lucky partner.

Heath was instantly reminded of just how isolated he had become in life. He hated his solitary existence. He had no partner, no real friends, and a strained relationship with any family he had left. His thoughts soon drifted back to his wife…or *ex-wife*, now happily paired with another man…and his daughters. He cringed and shut his eyes tightly, at the thought, and remembered.

Still, the picture in his mind remained. The picture of his ex-wife with another man, and the man raising his daughters. *His* twin baby girls, who were now growing through life without him. A wave of anguish overcame Heath. He wrenched his eyelids down harder, as if doing so would allow him to block the pain the picture triggered. It didn't work in the least.

"Headache?"

Heath heard the words coming from somewhere behind the picture of his family with the *substitute* man, an image now lodged on the backside of his brain. The picture began to fade, as the question now registered and struggled to take first position in his mind, replacing the pain the scene had created.

Heath forced his eyes open and blinked twice, realizing a lone teardrop had rolled down each cheek on his face. The young, toned, olive-skinned beauty stood staring at him, her head cocked, with a look of concern one seldom saw in strangers.

"Shooting pains." He offered the explanation apologetically, instantly realizing no apology was needed. He was embarrassed by the young woman's concern, caused by his own lack of control.

"We're not supposed to…but I have Acetaminophen…if you would like to try it. I can't take bad headaches for very long without some pharmaceutical assistance, myself!"

"I'm sure it will be fine in a minute," Heath countered. He flashed a reassuring smile, as his eyes flickered down, belying the smile.

"You don't have to be the macho man with me. We haven't even met, so you have no image to protect…yet!" The beauty smiled and revealed the whitest, most perfect teeth Heath had ever seen. She grabbed a necklace absentmindedly with her left hand, and toyed with the gold Christian cross that dangled from a matching gold chain. As she stared at Heath he looked down at the cross. And as he did she looked down and realized she had pulled it from its resting place in her blouse where it had been nestled between her firm breasts.

"A gift from my mom before she passed away. It was hers…I guess I touch it a lot without even realizing I touch it."

"Nice…very nice." Heath smiled back.

Another customer moved in behind Heath, impatiently waiting to place his order. Heath ignored the man, and held out his hand. He said, "I'm Heath."

"Jessica," the beauty offered as she took his hand. "Have a seat and I'll bring your drink and the rest of your order." She motioned to a free two-top table against the wall to her right. Heath complied, sitting down next to, and not far from another two-top where two young men sat debating. His attention was immediately drawn to their spirited debate.

"James, most of Hollywood is behind them, our President is behind them, and almost the entire party is behind them. Our country has enough money and resources to take them all in, feed them, clothe them, house them, educate them, provide them medical care, and help them integrate in to our society. It's our responsibility, as a nation of compassionate people. We just need to take more money from corporations and the rich, to help the poor. And most of the *wealthy* in Hollywood support the idea!"

The other man countered. "What gives those pampered, west-coast Hollywood elitist actors, artists, and all their coastal elitist friends the remotest idea that they alone, have the gift of superior knowledge, *and* that they possess an inherent right to lecture *me* on how I should think, vote, and act, as a citizen of the United States...or even as a person?! These assholes are no different than their Ivy League professor buddies, who sit in their gilded halls of *pseudo-knowledge,* and lecture the children of the rich and famous, indoctrinating generations of empty-headed, impressionable, naive young minds. They brainwash the youth to believe in social systems, that *if* implemented, would destroy the very way of life that allows these same tenured, myopic, idiotic educators to bloviate. The *same* way of life, that allows the pampered darlings of the wealthy to continue the very privileged existence they were born in to, without straining to make a living!" The angry young black man in his thirties was well built and fired up. The veins in his neck began to thicken and stand out, as his anger flared. Heath considered him carefully.

"Communism, socialism, fascism, dictators and war-lords of all shapes and sizes...it's all been tried and failed, hundreds, if not thousands of times throughout history! And yet these simpletons in our own country try to lead us down the merry path of fools toward destruction, beseeching us to try these same old tired and failed systems again!"

"And they use podiums created by lefty liberals, for lefty liberals, at events like the *Oscars* or *Golden Globes*, or even worse the *SAG Awards*, where they pat themselves on the back for getting paid millions of dollars to act. Act, Mike! They reward themselves because they **PRETEND** to be someone they aren't! These same poor excuses for human beings seem incapable of learning from the lessons of the past, even as they watch the societies they worship fail, time after time."

"And by the way, exactly how do the liberal elite magically acquire all this impressive knowledge, that seamlessly transforms a pampered A-list star, in to a world renowned expert on social issues, environmental science, poverty, law, warfare, interrogation techniques, women's rights, race relations, and the grey lines separating free speech from the need to classify and protect sensitive information... just to name a few of the skills presumed by the coddled famous. Skills they acquire, by the way, at the very moment they make it big?! And damn it all to hell, and shame on us, for listening to this chorus of fools, broadcast by the leftist media who worship these sons-of-bitches."

This man was now on a fast roll, and rapidly continued venting, while his friend sat looking down at his coffee cup. The friend stared hard, as he rolled the cup back and forth. He strained to see, as if the cup were bottomless, and he was trying to decipher a defense, located at the furthest depth of the container…a defense he could barely see with the naked eye.

"They turn to *Scientology*, or eastern religions, and haughtily feign enlightenment, only to discover there are no better answers in those realms, either. And yet they still can't shut their pie holes. They continue to preach and chastise the working class, and then run off to Saint Barts, where they board their designer yachts, attended by throngs of servants, so they can rest up for their next public appearance."

"Yet another appearance, Mike, where the liberal media once again welcomes them with loving outstretched arms, and film them admiringly, as they continue to vomit forth their diatribe. Once again, they graciously *consent* to instruct the rest of us peons on how we should think and act, to prove we are *for* the working class, and by that proof, worthy to survive, and breath their precious air."

"Hell Mike, we **ARE** the damned working class. It's only the freeloaders, and the lefty liberals who love the adoration of the freeloaders, who are *for* these crazy ideas. Fuck them! Fuck them all!"

"James, you voted for this administration, just like I did. He's leading us in the direction *we* chose!"

"Mike, you and I didn't choose this path! And I'm tired of the Liar-In-Chief lecturing me on what it means to be an American, and telling me how I need make sacrifices, as he takes his entourage and seventy-five secret service men on paid overtime to protect him, on one of his many vacations. He's either an idiot, a liar, or one of the craftiest men in our history! Either way, he's one of the biggest single problems our country has faced, in decades!"

Mike raised a hand to protest and countered, "He said he's socially liberal, but fiscally conservative. You should like that!"

The angry man cut him off, and snapped, "Bullshit! Socialists *all* say that crap. It's a tired old leftist party line. Like they told us we have plenty of money, while we can't even meet the obligation to pay the *interest* on our country's loans. And, they spout this B.S. while the liberal administration increased the national debt more than any other president in history, while it left the country less able to defend itself against enemies from within or without…*and*, while it racially divided the country, sending us *backward* fifty years, as it reignited race wars. All bullshit, smoke and mirrors."

"James, that's all wrong. This administration is offering a hope for a positive change in *everyone's* lives. It's about social justice, inclusion, health care, and equalizing the plight of less fortunate nations, forced to deal with the massive economic force the U.S. represents. The left offers hope to the world and is *committed* to remaking our country for the better."

"More bullshit, Mike! Socialism does massive damage, and when criticized, claims the other side was responsible for the real damage. They say they just tried to *save* us all from ourselves. Leave us the hell alone. Take the Hippocratic Oath! *First do no harm!* You don't pass a 2,500-page law, taking away people's right to buy medical insurance as they choose, and take away their choice to keep their doctors and preferred plans, only to later *read* the law you passed, and discover the harm you've done. Years after you did it, you finally begin to understand the mess you've created as the system crashes and burns! And then you won't even admit the problem! And that's only one example. Stupid, stupid, politically motivated bullshit!"

The man's friend said, "If you talk to someone on the far left, they *will* defend these actions and state the facts a little differently than their opposition, you do realize. That stupid law got medical insurance…for 12,000,000 people that never had it, *before* the law!"

"Hell Mike, Liberals can't defend their actions or lack of actions, so they continually revise history and lie. Don't you understand that their *only* defensive solution is to alter history? By lying about the facts and pretending that it's just all better now, they justify their own failed policies. The deductibles and costs are so high for those 12,000,000 people they can't afford to use that insurance! Fuck that bullshit."

"And if we're discussing the mistakes of the *ruling* left, I'm sick and tired of the absurd political correctness destroying our country, as we take an ostrich-like, head-in-the-sand posture while refusing to honestly confront our problems and our enemies. Now our government even apologizes for the actions of those who erode our civilization, and threaten our way of life. Our President is an idiot, or a traitor, who is intentionally trying to destroy our country, to level the playing field with other emerging nations, much to the detriment of his own citizens." The man finally paused, as his peak pet peeves seemed to have been stated.

The man's tablemate, Mike, leaped at his obvious chance to interrupt the pace and object. "But James, you can't think that way. You're ivy-league educated. You're successful. You've worked in government. For god's sake, you're even a registered Democrat! And, lastly, you're a black man!" he protested.

"That's exactly the problem the socialists have created, Mike. Thanks for proving my point. As you pointed out so eloquently, I *am* a black man and I *know* I'm black. And I have my own mind. And I *can* think any way I choose…and I choose *my* way."

"You see my friend, identity politics only serves to divide the nation by defining and juxtaposing the identities that wrestle each other for power and control, and in so doing encourage more division and opposition. Black lives don't matter anymore than the lives of any other race. But *saying* they matter more, creates division and invites bigotry and hatred. *All* lives matter. All men, women, and children matter. We can't *divide* to achieve harmony…we have to *unify*, and eliminate division, to create harmony!"

"That's where the hate crime enhancement went wrong, and damaged our chance to solve different crime problems. Why should it be a worse crime to kill a person if you're motivated by your dislike for the victim's sex, religion, creed, race, sexual orientation etc., than it is to just kill them? They're fucking dead, Mike! They don't care if you killed them because you didn't like them or not. I think they assumed that you didn't like them when they died."

"You see? We lose touch with the *crime* of murder, when we focus on it being worse if a person murders a member of some protected *group*. And someone else is always left out of the protected group status, and *their* assailant doesn't get the press or prosecutorial attention that they should…so *that* group is divided out, and angry. We need to focus on the crime itself, and then suddenly we're back to the same justice for all…no division."

"Mike, someday I hope you'll understand that I can be a black man, and a Democrat, *and* a conservative. I can fight for what I think is a correct social agenda, and not feel any guilt when confronted by a party-line spewing, ultra-left, progressive liberal. My life and my mind are formed from the union of *my* being, and the sum-total of *my* experiences and judgements. I don't have to agree with the first black POTUS because he's half black and identifies only with *that* half, any more than I must agree with my mother's pro-life viewpoint, because she's a woman, or because she's my mother. I'm an American, and I'm free to choose, and free to be me."

"If we could all set aside the division, and work together, we would all be solving the problems that face us, just as the founders believed we could. And then, we would really *all* be a lot better off in every way."

Mike laughed. "Well you have a point there. But to work together we would have to rely on receiving factual information. And to do so, news would have to be just real *facts*, instead of politically, emotionally and racially choreographed opinions and conjectures. And even then, we would have to rely on honest discussion and debate, instead of name calling, and shout-down techniques! It's sad to say, but we've strayed so far as a nation in to our separate polarized divisions, I really don't know if we can ever get back to sanity and reality."

And with that the two men both smiled at each other and clinked their cups, and the tension was dissolved.

Heath realized he hadn't even considered politics for years, and yet it remained an important part of many people's daily lives. He had been watching the men, somewhat mesmerized, as they shared very different opinions, yet retained their friendship, and a mutual respect. They reminded him that he had one more void in his abnormal life. As he contemplated what had transpired, Jessica sat his drink, a chocolate muffin and a small plastic sleeve containing two capsules in front of him. She grinned.

Before she left she said, "Nice to meet you Heath. Here is a card with our web site listed. You can take a survey on the site, and receive a free drink with your next drink purchase. Once you complete the survey you can print out your coupon, or bring it in on your phone app."

Heath took the card. On the back Jessica had included a note of thanks, her name, and a phone number. Heath looked up as she walked away. He couldn't help but focus on her tight butt and shapely calves. He smiled and nodded as she looked over her shoulder at him. After finishing the muffin, he took the coffee drink and walked to his car to drive to the park.

Heath parked where he could keep watch on the main arteries that fed the park with walkers, bicyclists, motorists and the occasional police unit. He had come here in the past and had watched Nevada Highway Patrol and Carson City Sheriff's Office vehicles park side by side, and head to tail, as they chatted through open driver's door windows. Some came here alone to eat their lunches, or take a break. Oddly enough, Heath felt comforted knowing that law enforcement was here, and *where* they were, for two very different reasons.

As he sipped his Mocha, he thought how odd it was that he had always been a supporter of the police, even those that arrested him. It was the criminals you couldn't trust. The cops were just the good guys doing a job that nobody else wanted to do, to keep society from falling in to anarchy. Anarchy was a horrible place where no one was safe...*and* no one had any rights. And even more difficult to understand, was how quickly the average citizen turned on the cops. In prison Heath had learned that the average career criminal respects the cops. He may try to *kill* them to avoid arrest, but he respects the job they do, for the most part.

Heath always found it odd that the biggest critic of the police was often the smart ass, know-it-all college kid with no life experience, or the institutionalized radical college professor, who also had no life experience apart from college. They thought they knew much more about the cop's job and law, than the police did after years of training and experience.

Then there were the soccer moms whose kids were detained for smoking dope or underage drinking, who couldn't believe that their little Johnny or Jane could possibly do anything wrong. They would threaten to sue the cops or have-their-badge for even talking to their smug little shits. They just couldn't seem to admit there was a real problem with their own little angel. Once again the cops were just doing their jobs, which seemed to be fine with everyone, until they themselves were the subject of law enforcement.

Heath knew lots of stories from prison about how mommy and daddy had protected their darling little dummy, and fought against holding their child accountable for anything they ever did wrong. The stories were repeated each week at visitations throughout the nation's lock-ups. He saw families with the same sad eyes, who came to visit their inmate loved one in the "joint." They still just couldn't believe that little Jonny had killed those four teenagers, in a drunk driving traffic accident, and that he was now serving four concurrent sentences of 10 years in prison, for four vehicular manslaughter convictions. The parents didn't understand how they couldn't have known their child had a drinking problem. They still believed "if only" they had received some warning they would have helped the little drunk.

But hadn't little Johnny been arrested or written citations for Minor in Possession of Alcohol seven times in his last three years in high school…and hadn't the first ticket come after three warning phone calls from the same deputy? But no, they couldn't listen to the cops. The parents believed they knew better. They simply knew little Johnny was being picked on, maybe even "profiled." After all, this *was* the entitlement generation. There was no accountability for bad actions, and everything was free! Heath shook his head and laughed out loud after his sipped the mocha. Some people were so stupid, he thought.

A sheriff's unit pulled in ten parking spaces away from him toward the highway and backed up to wait for another unit. Heath instantly felt safe. He grabbed his cell phone and began making calls to dope dealers. Heath used all his vehicle mirrors and windows as his eyes swiveled back and forth to make sure no one walked up on him while he was talking. After his forth call, another sheriff's unit pulled straight in next to the first unit, so the deputies could talk window-to-window. Heath relaxed even more. He felt nothing bad could happen to him, with two police units right there at his side.

The cops talked for about 20 minutes, when suddenly the first one to arrive activated the unit's overhead lights and drove out quickly. When the officer arrived at the main highway he activated his siren, and sped off eastbound. The dealer on the phone asked Heath if the cops were there for him.

Heath said, "No, one of them is going to some emergency call, probably to bail someone out of a jamb they got themselves in to. Whoever is involved will probably end up hating the cops, saying it's all the cop's fault, and suing them over whatever happens. And they'll probably get a settlement!" The dealer laughed, and the conversation continued.

This dealer was an old-time doper from the bay area, who had settled in west Sacramento. He had gone to prison only once, in his youth. But once he was out of the joint and off parole, he had opened an auto body business, employing only ex-cons who had gone straight. The business was successful, and eventually he got married and began raising a family.

This guy never used any "product," but eventually couldn't resist getting back in to the business for the thrill of the deal, and the easy money, of course. Prison had taught him to be more careful. This dealer later taught Heath valuable lessons about dealing drugs, when they first met. In prison, Heath reflected on those lessons, and how he should have paid more attention, and not made the mistakes that sent *him* to prison.

The dealer never worked with anyone other than longtime associate dope dealers, and he never took delivery of any "product." He facilitated deals, bought and sold, and only took delivery of money. He referred to himself as a "broker" and had used his lifelong network of large dealers to establish himself as a major player. He always knew who really needed product, and who had an oversupply, and needed to sell. He skimmed a chunk of cash off of each sale, and people on both sides were happy. He had become an institution in the business. He was truly "networked."

Heath actually like this guy. But as with all the other calls Heath made that day, "the broker" had no information about the two murders. And Heath wasn't surprised in the least. He swallowed the last sip of his now-cold coffee. The sensation of hunger temporarily satisfied by the muffin, had already returned. In fact he was *very* hungry. More importantly, he was restless, and tired of being alone. He again thought of Jessica.

Two and a half hours later Heath ended the last of his calls. He sat in his pick-up staring out at the grass. About 20 little kids had gathered to play soccer, while a few parents directed them on a field, a hundred yards away. Heath smiled remembering being a kid, and loving to play catch, with his dad and his brother. Even their mom had thrown the baseball with them when they were young.

But it was football that Heath and Shane loved. Their dad loved to toss the ball with them, but their mom could never get the hang of throwing a football. Her hands were too small, and they always teased her when the ball drifted away a few yards and thumped the ground, off to the side, when she attempted a pass. But she was a good sport, and would always try one more time, then just laugh, and give up.

Heath had loved his mom above all else. He still missed her. The hole she had left in him when she died, was sometimes just filled with angry, unbearable pain. To make matters worse his heroic dad and saint of a mom had died together, the same day...the day that ruined his life.

Heath made the phone call to Bobby, reporting that he had contacted everyone in Sacramento he knew, and that no one had any information. He said he had pressed all his contacts to pressure their sources, hoping some information would surface. He promised to call Bobby as soon as he heard anything.

Before he hung up he suggested to Bobby that the family try and use other contacts, outside the dope world, intimating that maybe these hits had come from someone other than rival cartels. Bobby had listened, but made no commitment to relay *that* message to Hector. He seemed to be scrutinizing the conversation, but for what, Heath couldn't guess.

Heath decided to go for a drive and see some sights. He would drive to Virginia City to see if he could find one of the old famous saloons that had been there since before the turn of the century. He thought the drive would do him good. And he could think about Jessica while he drove.

He dreaded that he would actually have to go back to the doctor's house tonight. He couldn't be absent for two nights in a row he thought. That would be too risky. But before he made it out of Carson City, Bobby called again. Bobby told Heath that Hector wanted to talk to him right now. Heath pulled in to a convenience store parking lot off Highway 50 East, so he could to stop and focus on the call.

Heath recognized Hector's voice when he said, "Heath is that you?"

Heath replied, "I'm here, boss."

Hector said, "Bobby says none of your contacts in the whole Sac area has heard a word? Not one word? No bragging? No calls to suggest the business needs to go back to the former contractors?"

Heath assured Hector there was no news. He said, "Hector, I pressured all these guys. I talked to one guy for almost half an hour. I told you about this guy, 'the broker,' who knows everyone and everything, and *he* knows nothing about this. They're all as mystified as we are! No one knows anything, and if they do, they aren't talking. And…you know, even *that* possibility just doesn't make any sense. Who could they be so afraid of to keep them from talking to *us*, if they did know something?"

There was silence on the phone. Hector asked, "So Heath, tell me what do *you* think? You're a smart guy, and you know the game."

Heath had no choice. He had to tell Hector the same thing he had told Bobby, or he could put himself in a bad spot. He hoped Bobby had relayed his thoughts from the prior call.

Heath said confidently, "I think if it was a rival contractor we would have heard something by now. The guys we know in Sac are big enough players that they don't like being threatened, or pushed around. At least *one* of them would tell us, if they knew something. So my hunch is that this problem didn't come from our competition. It must have come from somewhere else, outside our world of business."

There was an eerie silence on the phone. Heath listened closely to monitor any whispering or background conversations, but he detected nothing. Hector finally said, "That's what Bobby told me you thought. Any ideas who?"

Heath said firmly, "I haven't got a clue, but then I'm new to our group, and don't know the history. So, I'm thinking enemies, or revenge, or maybe someone trying to re-order the game and power structure, within the organization. I don't know who, but that angle seems to make more sense to me than some of our competition."

After another silence, with some whispering in the background that Heath couldn't make out, Hector said, "I think you may be right my friend. This doesn't make any sense to us on this end either. Nothing going on at the doctor's house?"

Heath lied, "I've seen nothing at all, ever since I've been there."

Hector immediately replied, "I want you to take some time off, and relax. No need to come to the doctor's house tonight. Go get a steak dinner. Relax and have some fun. You've done a great job. And if you need a girl, we can send one your way!"

Heath said, "No, thanks. I appreciate it. All I need is a steak, and some sleep. What do you want to me do tomorrow?"

Hector said, "Bobby will be in touch in a few days. Take some time off. You've earned it. Stay out of sight in case we need you again. We're still looking at our own people, and don't want them to know about you. But Heath...if you hear anything, and I mean *anything*, you call Bobby, as soon as you hear. Okay?"

Heath assured Hector he would call immediately if he heard anything, and ended the call. He drove out on to the highway, and headed east to Virginia City, or "VC" as the locals called it. He thought he really needed some "R and R," and was glad that he wouldn't be interrupted by phone calls, or have to yawn through another boring shift at the doctor's house, looking all night for something that wasn't there, and would not appear. He knew he would never be calling Bobby with information on the shooter. After all, he *was* the shooter!

Within minutes he was turning off Highway 50 East onto State Route 341 to Virginia City. All Heath could think about was a steak dinner, a stiff drink, and a pretty girl to look at, while he ate. He wished he knew when Jessica was off work. He could anticipate the steak and drink, but he craved the site of a pretty face, and a nice body. He hoped he wouldn't be disappointed.

As he drove up the grade to the little mountain town he thought how he really needed to make a plan. He had to find a way out of this whole situation for himself, and he had to find a way to continue to protect his brother and his daughters. But the two didn't seem to fit together. He decided he would just sit and relax, eat and drink, and people-watch, while he made a plan. He needed a good plan. But *Shane* had always been the planner. If only he could talk to Shane, Heath thought.

Long before Heath had left his motel room that morning, Shane and Kate had finished their cinnamon roll and second latte. Once Jesse finished briefing Pete and Tasha, everyone wanted to go explore town and have breakfast at a local restaurant to experience the local color. Kate and Shane were still hungry and agreed to join them.

The new lovers showered and were dressed and ready in 30 minutes. Kate pulled on a light purple jacket over a lighter colored purple turtleneck sweater. Both the sweater and the jacket seemed to form fit Kate's lovely curves and flat stomach. Jeans that fit her like a glove completed the presentation. Shane couldn't take his eyes off her. She was form fitted like *Annika Hansen* who played *Star Trek Voyager's, Seven of Nine*, yet Kate was even more alluring, more beautiful, and more voluptuous...if that was possible!

Shane watched as if in anticipation of some major event, as Kate applied purple lipstick, and then accentuated her eyes with a purple eye liner, blended with nearly black accents. She then finished her eyes with a faint greenish blue upper eyelid color, she feathered out and in to black, to make her large beautiful eyes appear even larger, and more striking. Shane began to sweat as his heart pounded harder. An erection in his jeans began to surge.

After a few touches of mascara to lengthen her wonderful eyelashes, and darken the color to an even darker black, Kate completed the masterpiece, adding a few strokes of dark brown eyebrow pencil, to her luscious thick eyebrows. Shane marveled at the resulting artistry, that stared back at him through the mirror. Kate was super-model material, drop dead gorgeous, he mused. As an added benefit, she had completed the perfect canvas with the speed and skill of a master makeup artist, in less than ten minutes.

Kate wheeled around as if in a rush, not realizing the effect she had produced on Shane, and said, "Ready? Not much of a makeup job today. But, I'm famished!"

Shane wanted to throw her down on the bed and repeat the earlier engagement, but he settled for a quick kiss, and followed Kate out the door, appreciating every movement of the perfect body before him. He quickly adjusted himself, to avoid obvious detection. They met Pete and Tasha at the bottom of the steps. Shane wondered if they could read his mind, see his bulge, or detect pheromones he must be releasing. He slightly blushed at the possibilities.

Tasha said, "I'm still so hungry after the cinnamon roll. I'm afraid I rushed through my make-up this morning." Looking back at Pete as they walked, she said flirtatiously, "I hope the boss doesn't fire me!"

She and Kate laughed and chatted, as Pete looked to Shane and whispered, "Fat chance of that!" They both grinned at each other. Shane hadn't seen Pete look so happy in years. Tasha was after all, beautiful, smart, loyal and very nice…a rare, and almost unattainable character set for a modern-day person, Shane thought.

As the two women walked out the front door ahead of them Shane grabbed Pete around the shoulder with his strong right arm and said, "Pete, I'm so happy for both of us. I just want you to know how much I love you. You mean the world to me, and I promise you, when this is over and we're all safe, I *will* be an even better…son to you, and to Tasha."

The word "son" made Shane's voice crack, and tears filled his eyes, as he whispered the few words that followed. He couldn't control the flowing tears, as suppressed emotions from his very soul gushed forth in a tidal wave.

The wet flow just kept coming, streaming down his face. Suddenly he couldn't speak. He could barely breathe. He lost his ability to utter any sound, and the words he mouthed formed in pained shape only, without as much as an accompanying gasp of breath.

The feelings he longed to express were now contained in lengthy emotion-filled sentences, comprised of important silent words he wanted to say, but was unable to speak. His mouth stopped trying, as the unspoken words stacked up in his mind, like logs jamming a raging river at a narrow bottleneck. The effect was overwhelming.

Shane stood in the doorway helplessly overcome with emotion, and not really understanding why. He knew how much Pete meant to him and he couldn't bear the idea that Heath had hurt Pete so badly. And even worse, he himself had confronted Pete about Heath, and hurt him even more, just days before. Shane felt overwhelmed with guilt, with love, and with the need to make amends. He knew he needed Pete to understand his true feelings.

Pete sensed Shane's emotions, and instantly understood. He grabbed Shane in a bear hug, as sympathetic tears filled his own eyes. He choked out, "Shane, my boy, I do understand. You mean more to me than any three sons I could have ever hoped for…I don't understand how you could *be* any better. What could possibly be bothering you?"

As the two strong, brave men stood in the doorway hugging and crying over their combined love and respect for each other, two stunned women looked back from the pick-up they were about to enter. They were both at a loss to understand what had transpired to change the mood so quickly, in the short journey between the landing, and the front door.

Tasha asked Kate quietly," What could have happened in the time it took to walk a few steps to the truck? It must be something terrible." She and Kate both froze in their tracks, afraid to approach their men and ask, and yet not wanting to get in the pick-up, and act disinterested.

As the men slowly recovered, chests heaving, both struggling to control their breathing, they walked past their mates to the truck, drying their eyes, each with an arm still around the other's shoulders. The two women got in the back seat, figuring the men would want to continue talking, and the explanation would follow, without asking.

When they arrived at the pick-up, Shane struggled to say, "Pete, I'll drive, and you navigate, so I can learn the towns." With that the two men got in their seats and buckled up, without another word. Shane drove off slowly and carefully down the long drive, not even looking in the mirror at Kate. In the back seat two women glanced at each other with anticipation, expecting the worst news to come at any moment.

At the end of a mile Pete turned around and reached back for Tasha's hand. He said proudly, "God, I love this boy and this family!" He then took Kate by the hand and said, "Do you know how lucky we all are to have each other?" Both women remained quiet for the explanation.

He then smiled proudly, released Kate's hand, turned back around, and said in a calm voice, "Okay Shane, this road will lead to the highway going in to Joseph. I'll let you know where to turn to go the back way, along Alder Slope. It's a pretty drive, and we'll see some deer and maybe some elk, if we're lucky."

The men looked at each other with huge grins, as the women looked at each other, as if studying one another's face for the answer. No more was said, and the women figured whatever it had been, the crisis was over. Tasha whispered to Kate, "Do you find that sometimes men are difficult to read or understand?"

Kate laughed quietly and whispered back, "Yes, and they say we're the emotional ones!" She then grabbed her cell phone and dialed a number, asking a friend to join them for breakfast.

Arriving in Joseph, they passed the 1917 Lumber store and came to a stop sign at the highway. Shane asked, "Since we've been here I haven't seen a stop light, only stop signs...so are there any traffic signals here?"

Pete said approvingly, "Not a damn one! Isn't' that great?!"

Shane said, "I know where we are now. *1917 Lumber* is the place that sells lumber, building supplies, and those smokers you have at the estate and ranch. Jesse uses those to smoke all types of meat and to barbeque just about anything. Where do we want to eat? I'm starved!"

Kate was still on the phone and said, "Are you sure? Okay then, we'll be there in 10 minutes!" She ended the call and said, "Honey, turn left. We've all been invited to breakfast!"

Within two minutes they were out of Joseph heading back to Enterprise on the Wallowa Lake Highway, which Kate said was also known as the Joseph Highway, and also known as Highway 82. She said, "I think it's an Oregon thing!" and they all laughed.

Less than a mile and a half out of town, they turned left onto a dirt lane, and continued up the drive about a mile, to the two-story house perched on a hill. The sign at the entrance to the driveway read, "Creek-View Bed and Breakfast."

As he parked Shane said, "Isn't this where your friend lives who taught you about mushrooming?"

Kate nodded and said, "You'll love her. She's fun and wonderful, *and* a great cook!"

Shane replied suspiciously, "I hope she's got a lot of food ready. I'm starved from the…stress of the morning!" He smiled at Kate, who returned the smile, knowing exactly what had made them both so hungry.

Pete added, "We seem to have had a lot of…stress too, last night and again this morning so we're starved!" He smiled proudly while Tasha blushed, as they headed from the pick-up to the front door.

Kate placed an arm around Tasha and said, "I couldn't be happier for you two!"

Just as they arrived at the front door the door suddenly swung open, and a man in his fifties pushed the storm door open with his shoulder while he wheeled two .22 rifles out with his right hand. Leaning against the door he said, "Hi, I'm Carter, Mary's husband. She said you'd be joining us for breakfast."

Shane stared at Carter, not knowing what to do, while Kate took Carter's hand, and pulled him in for a hug, rifles and all.

Carter returned the hug, released Kate, and leaned back against the door with his shoulder. He cradled both rifles in one arm and held the door open, while he offered his free hand to Shane. "Glad to meet you all. Go right in. I'm stocking up the truck for some ground squirrel shooting later. I'll be right back."

Carter then shook each person's hand, as they walked in and said their name. A large wide smile never left his face. They instantly knew his greeting was sincere, and that he was genuinely glad to receive them as guests.

Kate walked in to the entry like she was arriving home, and immediately exclaimed, "Bentley! Bentley!" A medium sized handsome dog, with pointed, sound-tracking ears that stood halfway up and then flopped over, and a crooked tail, raced to greet Kate. He jumped up and down, and spun around avoiding hitting her, obviously excited to see her.

As he wriggled in circles, to Shane's amazement, the dog began talking, as if murmuring, "Where have you been, I've been looking for you, forever!" He continued to "talk" to Kate as she greeted him and petted him. He then fell over on his back, and presented his belly for rubs, which Kate generously and vigorously supplied.

Kate had dropped to her knees in the entryway leaving just enough room for Shane, Tasha and Pete to come in, and wait behind her, as she nuzzled and kissed the dog like a long-lost friend. Carter's wife Mary walked in from the kitchen and said, "He remembers you, every time!"

Kate jumped up and hugged Mary, finally turning back to the others, and introduced everyone, first to Mary, and then to Bentley. Shane stooped down to pet Bentley's short, yellow lab-like coat. He was instantly sniffed, and then licked in the face by Bentley's long black tongue. Shane loved dogs, and was fondly reminded of how much he had wanted his own, for so long.

Mary said, "I heard you all met my gun-toting husband. Come on in. We were going to have a Bloody Mary. Can I get you each one, or something else?" Everyone opted for a Bloody Mary, and Mary directed them to the couch and chairs in the living room, within sight of the kitchen, as she went to get drinks.

But then, one-by-one, as company often does when faced with a host departing for the kitchen, Kate, Shane, Tasha and then Pete followed Mary to the kitchen, and stood at the center island as she prepared the drinks. Mary just grinned, as if she expected everyone to end up there. She was genuinely excited, and happy to see Kate, and meet the rest of her crew. Her hospitality and friendliness were infectious, and she flowed through the kitchen making drinks and preparing food, as if she was a magician, mastering each task as though it was simple and effortless, even as the results proved outstanding. Shane wished Jesse was there to appreciate the art of Mary's movement and delivery.

As Carter returned through the front door, Bentley made the rounds from Kate to Tasha to Pete to Shane. Finally, everyone was sufficiently licked and sniffed, and had returned the affection with appropriate hugs, pats, and comments. Satisfied that everything was under control and had met with his approval, Bentley walked to the door to be let out onto the deck, where he would assume the position of protector of his realm, and watcher of rock chucks, deer, and red-digger ground squirrels.

The adults stood around the center island in a circle, talking excitedly, and getting to know each other, as Mary prepared the fare to be served, and Carter made sure the drinks remained full. He poured refills from a pitcher of Bloody Mary's pre-made earlier that morning.

While everyone had tasted a Bloody Mary before, no one could recall one so tasty. As with all her recipes, the hostess was coy about her secret ingredients, but eventually confessed to using a slice of bacon, *Absolut* vodka and her own blend of spices, to complete the drink, and coat the rim of the glass. The flavor was exceptional.

Shane looked at his watch and the time was exactly 8:30 in the morning. He was finally really relaxing, enjoying being a normal person with people he loved, *and* he was even making new friends. He felt blessed. He was de-stressing and convincing himself that life could be good, normal and safe.

But he wondered where Walter and the convoy were now, and what Heath was doing at that very moment. A nagging feeling that something was about to happen haunted the recesses of his consciousness. He pushed the worrisome thought further back in his mind, until it was out of sight. He was going to enjoy himself today.

As Shane sipped his Bloody Mary, the convoy was closer than he imagined. They had driven for several hours to reach the outskirts of Treasure Valley, near Boise. They had gassed up in Parma, in southern Idaho. The town was small and not far from Interstate 84 where they would continue their journey due north, another four hours, to the ranch. The convoy's counter surveillance team had trailed at a respectable distance, to ensure they were not followed.

The group had taken a route through Nevada to Oregon, driving from Carson City through Reno, Winnemucca, and finally McDermitt, where Highway 95 entered Oregon, at the city limits. They had driven northward, through desolate, unpopulated stretches of sage brush and high desert. Cell sites in the area were sparse at best.

The country was monotonous and unspectacular, until the highway crossed the Owyhee River at Rome, and finally reached prettier country, with more water and the accompanying greenery, near Jordan Valley. After Jordan Valley the highway eventually dropped in to the Treasure Valley, west of Boise. Walter had always loved Boise, "a good-sized, clean, small, yet big city," he boasted.

The little towns along the route had been perfect places for the convoy to detour and wait, while counter-surveillance teams ran through their routines, to assure they weren't followed. The teams then rushed forward to rejoin the group. At Jordan Valley, and again at Parma one counter-surveillance team had deployed a drone, to watch all roads entering the area, for any suspicious vehicles following them. At the same time, all convoy vehicles were re-scanned for GPS vehicle tracking devices, while the lead vehicles were fueled, and the rest of the team took a break. The sky was also continually monitored by a team member.

Prior to leaving on the trip, Tom had taken everyone's cell phones, and locked them in to a portable lead lined safe, with all cell phones turned off. If anyone attempted to track their movements by cell, it would be impossible...no towers to ping, and no signals could escape the safe.

Communication between vehicles in the convoy was accomplished using portable handheld radios, set to scrambled frequencies Tom and Jesse had programmed at the last minute, before the group had departed from Carson City. The channel selected had also been programmed in to one radio given to Kate and Pete, which had accompanied the group flying to Joseph.

The cadre wanted to ensure as best they could that no one would know where they were going, as they worked on unraveling the mystery contained in the AG files, Shane's dad had sacrificed his life to preserve. They were committed to not repeating a mistake like the one they made with Wesley.

The convoy made their final counter-surveillance check in Parma, before they drove on to I-84 to travel north, as planned. They would continue through Idaho, and once again enter Oregon at Ontario, and continue to the ranch. So far everything had been fine.

But Lee and Tom were disappointed they had discovered no one following the convoy. They had developed a plan to capture and interrogate anyone following them, or conducting surveillance on the group. They planned to extract information to discover who may be monitoring their moves. But the well-developed plan had so far produced no results. They continued on toward the ranch with dwindling hopes of success.

As the convoy left Ontario, Carter served the breakfast guests their second Bloody Mary in a fresh glass, with a celery, bacon flavored and season-salted rim, another secret to Mary's success as a mixologist. Mary continued chatting with the group around her kitchen island, as she effortlessly assembled the ingredients for the main course. An enticing sweet aroma escaped the oven, teasing the already hungry crew.

The kitchen and house were welcoming and comfortable, and the view of the surrounding mountains was spectacular. The day was warming up nicely and although it was just early May, the weather was nice enough to eat on the deck. Mary had Carter set the table for the group outside, while she worked on finalizing the breakfast. He seemed to take direction well, even when chastised for a small error in concentration, as he visited with the guests.

A smoker on the deck offered up the aroma of smoke-barbequed pork. The guests moved to the deck, and sat in padded Adirondack chairs, taking in the sights, sounds and smells of the area, as Bentley curled up at Kate's feet. Bentley remained content, but watchful and alert, as if he too was expecting trouble. Shane smiled down at the dog, and reached to continue petting him, as Bentley remained on guard for strangers. Shane thought he needed a dog like Bentley, and Kate smiled, apparently reading his mind.

Shane finally leaned back in the comfortable deck chair, sinking deep in to the plush cushions, allowing his shoulders and mind to fall in to a mesmerizing state of relaxation. He looked skyward and watched a flock of geese squawking, as they flew northeast, directly overhead, not 50 feet above the table. The birds were in tight formation, and paid no attention to their admirers below.

Shane closed his eyes as the morning sun bathed and warmed his face. When he opened them, movement in the pasture to his left alerted Shane's eyes. He gazed over at a pair of spotted twin fawns, as they bound toward their mother, who had just stood up after a nap in the field. He thought to himself what a perfect place this truly was, and how many such places must exist, scattered throughout the country. The United States held many such gems within its borders.

Shane was now finally really relaxed. Kate seemed to sense his mood, and reached for his hand to squeeze and caress, as she sat next to him. Bentley moved toward Shane, and collapsed on Shane's feet, as if protecting him while he rested. Shane smiled, knowing he had already bonded with Bentley, his new and loyal friend.

Mary brought out an air pot of coffee with accompanying cream, sugar, honey and flavored creams, while Carter took a perfectly smoked pork loin off the smoker, to carve. Mary reminded him to let the loin rest for a few minutes, to seal in the juices before he began carving. Carter just smiled and nodded to the guests, as he disappeared into the kitchen, with his wife in pursuit, chatting out more instructions.

Kate stroked Shane's strong hand with her own soft hand, playing with each finger as she settled into the scene, and appreciated the beauty of the area once again. But before she could get more comfortable, Mary returned immediately with bowls which she placed in front of each guest, on different colored placemats.

Each bowl presented vanilla yogurt, topped with baked pears, basted in a mixture of brown sugar, orange juice, butter, cinnamon and cloves. The guests all immediately came to attention, as the aroma of the hot pears and spices hit their noses. They all took a spoonful, blew on it to cool it down, and took a healthy bite. Each guest was instantly rewarded with an explosive medley of sweet and citrus blended flavors that delighted their taste buds.

As Mary directed Carter to carve the loin into slices of perfect thickness that would meet her exacting standards, she stirred black beans one last time, before creating her trademark dish, Huevos Rancheros.

On warm corn tortillas, Mary spread a thin layer of sour cream, sprinkled on a blend of three Mexican shredded cheeses, and topped that with hot black beans infused with diced peppers and onions. She topped the bean blend with more shredded cheese, and covered the affair with chopped fresh baby spinach, and a small dollop of sour cream.

She then crowned the dish with one perfectly round fried egg, taken hot off the egg pan. She garnished the presentation with red, orange, and yellow bell peppers, sliced in thin wedges, placed alongside sliced tomatoes, avocados and limes. She then sprinkled finely grated parmesan cheese over the entire plate and added a dusting of finely chopped fresh Cilantro.

Carter added a healthy slice of smoke-barbequed pork loin, and delivered two completed plates to Kate and Tasha, who had both just finished their yogurt and pears.

Mary carried out the last two plates, and served Pete and Shane, as Carter topped off the Bloody Mary's one more time. Before sitting to join the guests at breakfast, Mary positioned a tilted sun umbrella to block the warming sun, shining in Shane's eyes. She then sat with her coffee, and talked about her first adventure with Kate, on the mushroom trail, in the high country.

Kate and Mary laughed and teased each other about mishaps along the trail, as Shane, Pete and Tasha listened to the conversation intently. Meanwhile, the creek rushed past the house thirty yards below the deck, and the occasional flight of geese barked and squawked directions to each other, as they appeared briefly overhead. The leaders of these squadrons occasionally relinquished their positions to rest, as they allowed a new leader to cut air for the group.

The effect of the meal and the ambiance was mystical. Shane relished the scrumptious meal, while he looked out over horse farms in the green agricultural valley, and wondered if he had made wrong choices about where he had lived, until now. He knew he could fit in and be very, very happy, right here in this sparsely populated county. It was his kind of place. And Carter and Mary were his kind of people.

Kate was teasing Mary about sharing her last *warm* beer when they had first met. Shane watched closely, and noticed that Kate really enjoyed the company of this generous and kind woman, who had become a fast-friend. As he studied Mary, he thought how many similarities there were between Mary and Kate.

Mary was a ¾-size version of Kate, smaller, about twenty years older, and beautiful in her own right. He could tell Mary was fun loving, and like Kate, was also talented, smart and athletic. He realized for the first time in a long time, that he had never developed friends like this, and he suddenly had a longing for stability and a more normal life.

He also realized that Kate needed that too, and he silently began to dream of an exit plan from this dangerous, nomadic profession he had chosen. He yearned to embrace a more traditional and rewarding life with Kate, family and friends. He was suddenly reminded of what he had always really known, that work comes and goes, but family, friends and *living* life are what is important, in the little time we are granted on earth.

Carter returned with his own plate, and sat at the table, taking the only vacant chair. Shane asked him about the history of the valley, and received an articulate and well-organized briefing of the people, places and events that had created the history of the area. Shane felt an instant kinship to Carter, who appeared to have a somewhat similar history, from the little he shared on their first meeting.

At the end of the discussion, Shane felt he could lean back and go to sleep in the chair. He was completely safe, relaxed, and stuffed with good food. The Bloody Marys had worked their magic too, and the warmth of the day called to him like a mythical seductress, urging him to release all of his worries, if just for an instant.

And as he rested and sank further into peace and calm, he thought to himself what a good day it would be just to sleep right here on the deck, in the sun, with the sounds of the creek, geese and neighing horses in the background. He leaned his head back and closed his eyes as Tasha and Kate helped Mary clear the plates. Normally he would have helped, but he had to stay here and keep Carter and Pete good company…not saying a word, with his eyes closed. He thought, "Someone has to be gracious."

Fifteen minutes later Kate was shaking Shane's shoulder and saying, "Are you already asleep? I guess I'm going to have to be gentler with you next time!"

Shane opened one eye and said, "I'm just baiting you for more attention, my love." He smiled up at her, receiving a warm kiss.

Kate said, "Carter and Mary have invited us to go red digger shooting with them on their ATVs today. Do you want to go, honey?"

Shane grinned and said, "I will as soon as I can move. I'm stuffed after all that great food. I shouldn't have eaten the second slice of pork Carter put on my plate …but man it was so good!"

14

"It is a mistake to try to look too far ahead.
The chain of destiny can only be grasped one link at a time."
(Winston S. Churchill)

Pete and Tasha left in the pick-up to tour more of the county, while Shane and Carter loaded the ATVs on to the trailer. Kate and Mary cleaned the kitchen and started the dishwasher, as Kate filled Mary in on her new love. They chatted on like two sisters who needed to catch up after a several months' absence from each other's lives.

Finishing before the girls, Shane returned to the deck, and laid back even deeper in his deck chair. He basked in the warm sun that had just managed to sneak past the shade. He thought to himself, "I really need to get back to work and make a plan. I need a good solid plan with contingencies. Maybe tomorrow. Maybe then, I'll make a plan." He slowly drifted off to sleep holding on to the feeling of the warm sun on his face, for as long as he could be conscious of its presence.

As Shane slipped in to unconsciousness the convoy drove north on I-84, headed to the ranch. Walter and Juanita drove point in their SUV, and talked openly about how they had waited too long to express their feelings for each other. Walter had been a true gentleman, never imposing on or abusing the friendship and trust Juanita had placed in him. But through the years, even though he had fallen in love with her, he had also never told Juanita the truth, or made future plans *with* her.

Walter was more than a decade older than this woman he cared for so deeply. He thought he could never hope to conquer her heart, even though he had correctly read the cues and looks of interest she didn't hide.

For her part Juanita had come from a poor background, with little hope of success in life, until she met Walter and his wife. Through the years, she learned to admire the unusually kind, gentle man, who gave her opportunities beyond her wildest hopes. And through the years of service she provided to Walter and his family, especially as she watched him care for his wife, Juanita's loyalty, friendship and devotion had turned to love. She still remembered the very day she realized she had fallen deeply in love with Walter, long after his wife had passed. Yet she remained silent.

She had watched with admiration during those most difficult last two years, as Walter had done everything possible to make his wife comfortable, and keep her included and relevant, in family life…even as his wife slowly slipped away, fighting an aggressive cancer. Juanita had been there to help, comfort and console the couple through their struggles, individually and collectively.

She had dreamed about one day finding a man with half the character, compassion and loyalty she found in Walter. Her feelings of friendship and admiration grew to include concern, commitment and a deep love. Many months after his wife was gone, Juanita told Walter how much she admired him for who he was and how he treated people. But she stopped far short of telling him she had fallen in love with him, out of respect for his station in life, and with the knowledge of her place in the home…even though he was not one to believe in positions and titles.

She explained to him that she had never known someone with a capacity to love like he did. She told him she had never seen anyone care so much about others, and she wanted him to know how wonderful it was that he had gone to such lengths, for all the important people in his life, including her.

As they had driven on that day together, completing errands as they did each Thursday, Juanita began to explain to Walter how she felt. Walter had taken her hand and held it tightly as his eyes glistened with tears. And then, Juanita began to feel the fear of rejection as she approached the opportunity to use the word love…and she stopped.

She had wanted to tell him right then and there that she had fallen deeply in love with him. She yearned to do so. Her insides were nearly bursting with the desire to reveal, and the need to conceal, her expression of love. In the end she contained the critical information that fought to escape, and she never told the man she loved her true feelings. But as she stumbled through her words, all that came out, was that she could never repay him for everything he had done for her.

Juanita remembered how Walter had just smiled, and released her hand with a simple squeeze, as he quickly recovered from the emotions of the moment. He had remained quiet for the remainder of that trip. He had misunderstood her preamble to a declaration of love. He had believed at that moment, that Juanita just cared for him as a close friend.

And she had immediately known that she had waivered and faltered, at the most opportune moment. But, she had been embarrassed, afraid that further explanation would result in her love being totally rejected, and a friendship destroyed. And she couldn't place him, or her heart, in that position, to take that chance. She thought she would rather continue as a friend, and not risk the loss of the friendship.

So, on that day long ago, Juanita had vowed to herself to remain in the role Walter had created for her, that of a friend and confidant… an employee…just to be near him. She had reeled herself backward, along with all her hopes, plans, and dreams of love, settling instead for a business and friendship relationship. She would remain hopelessly committed in love, to a man she would never pursue.

When she thought about it later that night, she didn't really believe that Walter could feel the same about her, anyway. He was the man a thousand women could fall head over heels for, if they took time to know him, and his heart. After all, she realized as she watched him closely, Walter was still well built and attractive. Time had altered his once spectacular body, as time always does, and the loss of his wife and son had aged and changed him. Deep pain could now be seen in his gentle eyes.

But many of these changes were for the better, she thought, having molded him to be even more generous and loving than he had been before, when he was consumed by business. Walter now *always* focused on plans for loved ones, that would secure both their safety and their future. Family and friends were always more important now, than any business, for this man. Juanita loved that trait in Walter.

And so, it had remained for Walter and Juanita, until Kate changed everything, and gave her the push she had needed for years.

When she told Walter that night at the estate that she was done hiding her love, she made her true declaration of love to him. For the first time in years she felt totally free to be the woman she always knew she could be. She told Walter how long she had loved him, and declared further that she had to confess her affections now, regardless of the outcome. She told him she hoped for everything with him, but expected nothing in return.

When she finished her explanation, Walter had immediately embraced her, literally smothering her with kisses, while professing his love for her. He was gentle, passionate and affectionate all at the same time. Afterward they had talked for hours about the events that led to them fall in love with each other. Walter confessed he remembered the conversation in the car, after all these years, and confided he had also been ready to declare his love to her, that very day. But he had misread her feelings, and committed to himself to love her as best he could, while they remained separated by their respective chosen places in life. He had also feared rejection, and losing *her* friendship.

That night at the estate after they had finally shared the *truth* together, they joyously recalled other times when each of them had *almost* mustered the nerve to confess their true feelings to the other. They recounted and lamented over the days that had been wasted... days that had slipped quickly away, one by one, until years of happiness together as a *couple* had been squandered.

They had made love in Walter's room at the estate that night. Afterward, both realized even more clearly, all that had been lost. The intimacy, deep commitment, and love they had both yearned for together...those together-years had been wasted. They spent the rest of the night in each other's arms, holding on tightly, trying to somehow make up for that missing time in their lives. They finally decided they could only make up for lost time, by spending as much quality time together, each day, as was possible. They pledged that they would never again be too cautious to express love, and they would *never* take each other for granted.

On this drive up with the convoy, just two days later, Walter had taken advantage of the down time in Jordan Valley, to drive them to a bluff overlooking the area. While they admired the beauty of the valley, Walter knelt on one knee, looking up to his love. He asked nervously, "My love, Juanita, will you do me the honor of becoming my wife? Will you marry me?"

She immediately accepted as she pulled him up and kissed him repeatedly, saying, "Yes, yes, yes!" in between kisses. "I love you. I have loved you for so long!"

Walter, the self-made billionaire good-guy, and Juanita, the sweet, talented, loyal employee, were now fully committed to enjoy each other completely, and would waste no more of their lives apart. After her acceptance, Walter had apologized that he didn't even have a ring, but vowed to take her to a custom jeweler he knew, as soon as they arrived in Joseph. Afterward, as they drove on toward their destination, chatting about their future, they made and shared plans…plans they had waited for years to build together, and had already secretly made apart, in their previously trapped, and isolated minds. And neither let go of the other's hand while they drove.

While the convoy pushed onward passing Baker City, only two hours from their destination, Franky and Hector were both coming out of a private meeting in the office at the compound. The double doors had been locked so no one could enter. They had spoken for more than an hour, finally coming to agreement on a plan to go forward, and solve the mystery of the murders.

They had shared their plan and refined it together, Franky the "Don," and Hector, the heir-apparent. As always Franky was in the lead, but he was proud of his son-in-law, his "tigre pequeno," or "little tiger" as he liked to tease Hector. Hector always smiled at the teasing, while inside he churned with rage. And he hid the rage very, very well. Hector had polished his acting skills to perfection.

The two men then left to drive to the Reno airport together, to board different flights, so each could go their separate way. Hector told Franky he was off to San Francisco to meet with members of two Mexican cartels and local leaders of MS-13, to make sure they were not involved in the murders. Franky told Hector he was off to meet with an old trusted FBI agent in Las Vegas, who had been on his payroll for years. Franky would press the FBI agent for answers about the murders, to see what the "Feds" had to offer. If needed, Franky promised he would threaten the agent. The tactic had worked in the past, he bragged.

Franky had little hope Hector would be successful, but he had all the faith in the world that his federal sources would be able to discover what was going on with these murders. Franky made detailed plans to demand several answers from his paid employee. His "Fed" would provide him all the resources he needed to get results, he thought smugly to himself. He chuckled, "That's what I pay him for! And the little bastard won't fuck with me!"

Arriving at the airport they each grabbed their carry-on and walked to the sidewalk in front of the airline entrance. Before they wished each other well on their separate missions, Hector asked Franky, "Do you believe in God, Franky?"

Franky laughed and said, "Of course, I believe in God. I'm Catholic, remember?"

Hector frowned and looked serious. He said, "That's not what I mean. I mean apart from making an *appearance* when you go to church to attend the mass, or going to confession where you can't really reveal *all* your sins to the priest, or donating some money to make sure your conscience is temporarily relieved…do you really *believe* in God?"

Franky momentarily returned the serious expression, but the moment passed quickly. He said, "I don't worry about it much. I'm busy doing what I need to do here on earth, where I don't see *God* helping me to get by. Name one thing this *God* did for me to help me get to where I am now! I did it all on my own! Why do you ask me this now?" He appeared agitated.

Hector looked up at the sky, where the moon was still visible in the fleeting daylight. He said softly, "I questioned if God was real, only once in my life. But then I regained my faith. And after I did, my son was born, and I saw God's forgiveness, a promise He kept to me…maybe more of a gift than a promise, really. You see Franky, I believe we all have to pay for our sins eventually, either here on this earth, or when we see God after we leave this place."

Franky looked at Hector intensely for a moment, and then did what Franky did best. He pushed any thoughts of responsibility or accountability completely out of his mind. He laughed, slapped Hector on the shoulder and said, "You do that, and let me know how that works for you! I already chose my path, a long time ago. You see Hector, my conscience is clear, because it doesn't even *exist*. I'll meet you back at the house tomorrow."

Franky's expression had turned from worried concern and near anger, to joy, in a twinkling. With that he turned and walked toward his flight, whistling a happy tune as he walked.

Both Franky and Hector had previously made several phone calls to precipitate their separate meetings. They both made the phone calls in secret, and both had kept the contents of the calls from one another. As they now bordered their separate flights, both men replayed the conversations they each had spoken separately, in their own minds.

Both were confident their plans would be successful, as they settled into their first-class seats. Franky had champagne to remind him of success, while Hector drank tequila to remind him of home and family...and to celebrate a victory that he believed would soon be won.

As their planes took off on separate paths, both men believed that their *life* plans had come together very well. But both Hector and Franky had withheld important life-changing information from each other today, information that would now alter both of *their* lives, and the lives of their families forever.

And yet, as confident as each man was of success, both still quietly worried about their own plan being *completely* successful. As they took off in different directions, they each focused on different concerns. Time promised to disclose any measure of success or failure, but each now wondered if their own plan would proceed uninterrupted. Plans were important, but were often altered by people, timing, and unforeseen factors. As they flew, both men measured the risks they had independently taken.

Franky had made secret plans to turn over more control of his organization to Hector. Papers had already been signed and notarized to give Hector control of most of Franky's companies and corporations.

Franky had also secreted more than one hundred million dollars in to seven offshore accounts in the Turks and Caicos. And only he and his girlfriend knew he had built a fortress of a compound, disguised as a large beach home on one of the islands there, in the paradise that awaited.

Franky's new home was located on one of the less populated but more exclusive islands in the archipelago, east of Cuba and south of the Bahamas chain of islands. It was the perfect place for Franky to hatch his exit strategy, and enjoy life as a mega-millionaire. He planned to simply disappear with his new love, telling only Hector where he was located, and then only once he was settled in, and safe.

Franky knew his own wife would be devastated, but he had left her enough money to keep the compound going, and she could live in comfort there. She couldn't know about his hot young girlfriend. Hector would take care of Franky's daughter and grand-babies, and maybe bring them to the island to see him, a few times each year.

As his flight proceeded onward, Franky day-dreamed about the snorkeling, boating and fishing he would finally be able to enjoy, while he left Hector behind to run all the businesses, assume all the stress, and take all the risks. Hector would send Franky millions each month to add to his nest-egg. And when Franky grew weary of the islands, he planned on traveling to Europe or wherever he wanted to go, with his young bombshell of a girlfriend at his side. *She* would never nag him and push him to bend to her will, because she would always be *just* a girlfriend, and not a wife. And if he tired of her, or she lost her figure or good attitude, he would find a new girlfriend. He smiled, knowing he had planned this very well.

In the future, Franky planned on just enjoying the good life, the fruits of his years of laboring over countless schemes, crimes, and murders. He had finally reached his retirement goals and his secret plans were set. He smiled wider as he thought about the painstakingly detailed plans no one knew about, that included his new boat, and his young tight girlfriend. Both were already waiting at the island compound...the bombshell and the boat. He imagined what his young lady was wearing today, as she dressed for the pool, and he laughed out loud. He planned on being with her in less than a week. He couldn't wait!

Hector's flight landed ahead of Franky's. He was met at the airport by a driver in a waiting limo. They spoke no words as he handed the driver his single carry-on. Hector knew he wouldn't be staying long. In fact, he would be taking a red-eye back to Reno to tonight. As he approached the right rear passenger door, the driver placed his carry-on in the trunk, and suddenly, the car door opened from the inside. Hector stepped in without hesitation or concern of who was waiting inside the limo. He closed the door, knowing two of his partners would be there, patiently waiting for him. One of them handed him a glass of tequila, which he took and immediately raised in toast. The other two men raised their glasses in response.

Each man took a long drink. Hector finally said, "He's on the plane."

The large muscular man sitting furthest from him, asked, "Everything is on schedule then, according to plan?" Hector smiled and nodded as he released a long deep sigh of relief. He sipped his tequila thoughtfully.

The man seated next to him asked, "He expected nothing then?"

Hector smiled, and said, "Not a *damn* thing. The bastard will deliver himself up for slaughter like the arrogant prick he's always been...thinking he is *"the only man,"* untouchable as always. In the end his own ego and greed betrayed him. He could have had it all and kept it all, except for that one major defect."

The large man raised a bottle of reserve tequila to top off Hector's small glass. Hector pushed his glass toward the pour as the man shook his head slowly. He said, "No, Hector, Franky couldn't have kept it all. We all knew ten years ago that Franky would eventually betray us, not just with money, but with our plans, our Primary Objective. We knew there would come a time he wouldn't follow the guidelines of The Committee. Franky got too big for himself, and definitely too big for his place in an organization like ours."

The large man poured the drink and continued. "No one, by themselves, is bigger or more important than the group. That's the reason we established The Committee almost thirty years ago. We can all enjoy the money, the power, and most importantly, the *control* we want. We have planned and refined the system, over all these years. But we can't *ever* allow one person, or one faction, to jeopardize the Primary Objective. It's *the reason* we will always be in control, and we will eventually eliminate all the fighting, and all the risk. Franky forgot that, or he never understood it. He made himself dispensable, disposable, and far too risky for our group. Our ways are the new ways, and he was a dinosaur…an ugly old T-Rex that everyone hated and feared." Hector nodded in agreement and sipped his tequila.

The large man continued, "It's why we brought you in to the cartels years ago, and set you up to move in to your position with Franky. You marrying his daughter was the icing on the cake of our plans. We couldn't have even hoped for that a few years ago. But when you came up with the idea of bringing your *sister* in to play the girlfriend role, we knew it was time to move on Franky. He had already set you up to take over his entire syndicate, and your sister reported on all his moves in the Turks and Caicos, right back to you, and from you, to us. Franky created the perfect opportunity for us, with his own deception and disloyalty."

The smaller man leaned back in his seat, looked down dejectedly and sighed, saying, "I must admit, Franky was very useful in the beginning. But, he was *never* a real team player. He was a vindictive murderer, really, a sadist and psychopath. He was a *useful* psychopath though, at the time we really needed him. Franky cleared out a lot of initial opposition for the group in the cartels. But it only emboldened him over the years, to think he was the invincible and central figure to our committee. And now this thing with Brian Grant, and the undercover cop. That sped up his demise, and sealed his doom."

He continued, "The Committee officially ordered him to wait until we had the 'undercover' identified and investigated, so we could formulate a workable plan to take care of the problem on our own, without any obvious public murder, and *after* we knew for sure what we were really dealing with. We needed to interrogate the cop and learn everything, as usual."

"Franky stepped out of bounds, left the reservation, showed his true colors. He was all for himself, and never really believed in the master plan. We can't allow that. There is far too much at stake. For God's sake, we're almost there! Franky put us all at risk of discovery. A very public murder with two unknown players and an Undersheriff… one of our own bought and paid for Undersheriffs. What a mess. Now Franky has to pay the price for his arrogance."

Hector nodded, sat back and sipped his drink. The large man looked at him and asked, "How are you doing…any regrets?"

Hector shook his head said instantly, "About Franky, not one. Franky created his destiny with me when he killed my parents, thirteen years ago. My mom and dad were forced to work as unwilling mules for the Sonora cartel at the time, as you know. They had us kids to raise, and they weren't about to try to run and hide from the cartel, and get us all killed. So, they went along, unwillingly."

"Franky had my mother and father killed, so he could steal a small shipment of less than 100 kilos of meth, just to send a message to the rival cartel. He never even knew my parent's names. But everyone in my village knew who Franky was, and we all hated him. Most of all, my sister and I hated him all our lives, and vowed one day we would find him, and exact our revenge."

Hector took another long sip of tequila, rolling the liquid over his tongue. He like both the tingling feeling, and the taste. It brought back memories of sipping tequila with his dad, when he was only fourteen years old.

Hector said slowly, "When you both approached me several years ago, with the plan to place me in the cartels, and your long-term *plan* for me to befriend Franky, and work my way in to his organization, I couldn't believe my luck. I knew then I would finally have a workable plan, to exact my revenge on the little, arrogant prick. And all I had to do was stay true to the plan, take my time, and pay my dues. But when you offered me a position in The Committee, and explained the Primary Objective, I knew there was no going back. I knew this is what I was born to do." Both other men smiled approvingly.

Hector continued thoughtfully. "The hardest part, and really my only regret, is having my little sister play the role of Franky's girlfriend. She was only 10 years old when he killed our parents. She jumped at the chance to play a part in this plan. Now she's a beautiful 23-year-old young woman. And the thought of her having sex with that monster disgusts me. But I can't imagine what it did to *her*. I promised her she would see the pictures of Franky, to know he was dead for sure when it was done. How will it happen?"

The large man said, reassuringly, "Franky will be picked up by his trusted FBI contact and controller in about half an hour. As he sips his champagne, he'll be driven to what he thinks is a secret meeting place to meet a few key members of The Committee. Northeast of North-town Las Vegas there's a dirt road leading to the Valley of Fire. Ever heard of it?" Hector shook his head as he sipped his drink.

"It's an especially isolated, unforgivably hot, hell-hole of a place in the desert. Perfect for Franky to meet his end. He'll get out of the car, sipping his champagne, and be knee capped immediately by the passenger, riding up front, with the chauffer. The assassination will be filmed. If he resists, he'll be bound by his companions in the limo, who will explain to him, as he pleads for his life, why he has brought this upon himself. Violations of Committee rules will be *formally* read to him, while his lies in agony on the ground. Then he will be unceremoniously executed, with a bullet to the head. After that, he'll be burned, and finally, buried in a pit, covered in hot, sterile, desert sand, consigned to remain there, for eternity."

"We will text your sister the video clip as promised, to the stolen smart phone we provided you to give her. She can watch it as many times as she likes, before she takes the battery out of the phone, and dumps it in the ocean as planned. The stolen phone that sends the clip will also be destroyed as planned, burned and buried with Franky, in the hole that was pre-dug for him, at his place of death."

The large man leaned over toward Hector and assured him, "It will all be over very soon. Your sister will call you and verify the plan is complete, after she receives the video. Then you will step in to place, and take over all of Franky's businesses, and keep the money he stole from The Committee, he placed in his off-shore accounts. That's your reward and reparations for your family's pain and suffering… and your bonus for becoming a Committee member. We always take care of our own!"

The large man handed Hector an envelope, and said, "Here is a list of all of Franky's account locations, numbers, codes, and instructions for wire transfers, along with a signed and notarized affidavit, giving you complete control over all his accounts, companies and property. Any necessary forgeries are impeccable, completed for us in the FBIs own laboratory by members of our group, who are experts in the field. Our best legal analysts have confirmed everything is in place. You will take over Franky's position in The Committee as soon as his position is officially vacated."

The smaller man seated to Hector's left said, "We hope you and your sister enjoy your new island retreat. As agreed it will make an excellent alternate annual meeting site for our Committee's senior steering group."

Hector nodded, and assured his companions saying, "You will *never* have to worry about me, like you did Franky. I'm completely committed to the Primary Objective and The Committee." Both men smiled their approval. They all three raised their glasses and toasted again, as they arrived at the real site of the only Committee meeting scheduled for this evening.

Hector and his partners walked in to the lavishly appointed meeting room that could host at least 100 people. Hector and his companions arrived at the well-stocked bar, and ordered their drinks. The room was buzzing with activity. Hector grabbed a water to drink first, discovering he was suddenly incredibly thirsty. He realized how nervous he had been earlier in the day talking with Bobby, and then Franky.

As his companions introduced him to the group, one person at a time, Hector couldn't help but think how much he appreciated when a good plan fell in to place. Everything had finally come together, and today he would be free of the monster that had plagued his life for 13 long years. He reminisced about all the sleepless nights during those years. They were nights filled with nightmares, fears, rage, and plans that had nearly consumed him. But today, Hector thought it was finally going to end...his plans had really come together.

At the same time Hector was being introduced to the senior senator from Nevada at The Committee meeting, Pete and Tasha stood on a hill overlooking Wallowa Lake. They had hiked to a bluff above Lake Shore Drive, and stood beside a small waterfall, as they both marveled at the spectacular view.

Their hike had disturbed an osprey from its nest, located high above them, in a dead Tamarack tree. The bird screeched as it soared and called to its mate, who returned from its flight over the lake to check out the problem. As Tasha and Pete stared up at the birds, the osprey pair decided there was no real threat. One bird returned to the nest, while the other flew off to complete its fishing duties.

Tasha told Pete she had made up her mind, and held his hand as she looked in to his eyes. She said softly, "I know you warned me about the danger the family faces, and to become part of it with you means I face that danger, too. I would die if anything happened to you, Pete. You and I both know I have been in love with you for years. I have become *accustomed* to the pain, of not being able to share my love with you, and I *could* live safely like that, for the rest of my life."

Pete tightened his grip on Tasha's hand, as he feared what was coming would not be the answer to his prayers. She continued, "Last night, after we made love, I was so happy, for the first time in years.

But then I couldn't sleep afterwards for a long time, as I went through all the 'what-ifs' and fears, over and over again, in my mind."

"This morning I was more confident, until we heard the briefing recap from Jesse. It all terrifies me. I'm not brave and strong, like Kate, Walter, Shane, and you are. When we hiked up here this morning I still didn't know what I was going to say. I knew if we discussed this you would promise to protect me. And you would protect me Pete, I know that…with your life."

"At the end of my heart lies a path to take, one with, and one without you. I can turn back now before it's too late and I may get hurt, even if it's only emotionally. The other path leads to a life with you, a man I have loved and wanted for many years. You know that Pete. I do love you so…but that life could lead to seeing you killed, or even us both being killed." Pete nodded and remained silent, releasing a long sigh that signaled defeat.

Tasha looked up at the male osprey, returning to the nest with a fish in its talons. She finally said, "Pete, I want us to be like them." She pointed upward.

Pete looked up at the birds, one repairing its nest from last winter's damage, and the other sharing a fish it had just caught in the lake below. The birds went about their business, working together, not worrying about the people below who possibly posed a threat.

Tasha said, "They don't let the worries and cares of life drive them apart. They just want to build a life together. None of us knows how long we really have. More than anything I know, I want us to try to live each day, to be as happy as we can. And now that I have just begun to really be a part of your life, I could never give it up!"

With that, Tasha kissed Pete, and they held each other more tightly than before. Pete breathed a long slow sigh of relief, and quietly thanked God for answered prayers. Tasha held on to him, and nestled in closely, as she quietly prayed that the good Lord would bless the plans they would make together. She also prayed for safe guidance through the dangerous times ahead.

She closed her eyes tightly, almost afraid to look and discover the danger that lurked. She hoped she could be strong enough to be a real part of the family. She prayed the plans the family had made for a normal life would really happen, and this case, The Case, would come to a triumphant end. A battle was brewing, and she must now play her part, whatever that part became.

As Pete held on to Tasha under the nest at Wallowa Lake, Franky's limo stopped at an unlikely meeting point in the Valley of Fire desert, where another parked car was waiting. Franky got out holding his champagne glass, now half full, after the fourth refill.

As he had been driven out of Vegas, Franky had thought once more through the plans he had made previously on the airplane…to voice a few additional demands he felt The Committee would automatically concede. They almost always conceded to his demands. He looked up at the burning remains of the setting sun, and marveled at how far he had come in life, even now, as he nearly controlled this secret society of powerful, important people.

But just as Franky finished that thought, stretched and yawned, a car door opened to his right, and his old FBI contact called his name. When he looked at his old trusted handler, he paid no attention to the passenger in the front of the limo who had quietly exited the car, just a few feet ahead of him.

Franky heard one pop from a revolver fitted with a silencer… and then another. He dropped to the ground in incredible pain, felt clearly, through the numbing effect of an entire bottle of champagne.

And as he fell to the ground, Franky dropped the champagne glass in his hand. The glass plummeted straight down to the soft sand beside him. The glass lay undamaged, but empty, having spilled all the expensive, golden elixir it had contained.

Franky stared at the ground, watching the tasty liquid disappear in a split second in to the parched porous dirt. He clutched his hands to both of his knees. Blood spurted from the holes in his knee caps, as his beating heart forced the warm, sticky, red liquid between his fingers.

He rolled over on his back and in disbelief, yelled, "What the fuck. You idiots. Don't you know who the hell I am?"

But suddenly the pain was too great to continue talking. It seized him in near waves of agony. He closed his eyes tight in anguish, unexpectedly unable to speak. He thought of all the times he and Big John had done this same thing to people. He had never realized how painful it was. But he still wasn't sorry for his victims…he had no remorse. And he was going to have these pricks killed!

When he managed to force his eyes open, he saw his old trusted FBI handler standing over him with a smart phone. Franky instantly knew he was being videoed. He writhed back and forth in excruciating pain, feeling his heart nearly beating of his chest. He felt rage beyond anything he had ever felt. The pain and injuries, however, left him incapable of acting to avenge the attack.

A man from the other car approached, and began reading him a list of violations of Committee rules. Franky now understood what was happening, and pleaded for his life, promising to fix everything, to make it up to The Committee. But the man just kept reading. So, Franky shouted over the list of charges being read, as if he could invalidate the words, as they were spoken.

Franky implored for mercy, and promised he would never stray from the Primary Objective again. But no one paid any attention to him. At the end of the reading of charges the man pronounced his sentence…a forced removal from The Committee, "with prejudice." Franky knew that Committee findings were never reversed. "Prejudice," meant death. At first, he pleaded harder, as he panicked. But finally, he raged.

With a strained breath, Franky cursed at all the people standing around him, all the "fools" looking down on him. Inside, Franky churned with anger. But, he was powerless to act on those same emotions that had always given him the strength of a ravenous lion. He was powerless, maybe for the first time in his life. He was no longer a fierce lion, king of the beasts of his realm, but just a mere mouse, afraid of the smallest of kittens surrounding him.

Finally fear took over, as the onlookers just stared at him, and the recording continued. Franky made one last plea saying, "We can fix this. You'll never find a replacement for me, who can give you everything I can provide! You'll see. You all need me!"

The FBI agent said in a calm clear voice, "Don't worry about that, Franky. We have already selected your replacements."

Franky screamed, "Replacements! What replacements!? *No one replaces me!*"

Another shot rang out. This bullet ripped through Franky's right hand, and continued through the already damaged knee it had been caressing and cradling, causing pain to swell in him, as he had never imagined. He screamed in anguish for nearly a minute until he was exhausted.

The man reading the chargers calmly said, "Mr. Magadinno, you are hereby forcibly relieved of your position in The Committee, with prejudice, as directed by Tier Eight. Within the hour you will be replaced at the induction ceremony now in progress, by Hector Alvarez. The Primary Objective will be accomplished without you, and all your assets are hereby awarded to Mr. Alvarez...and his sister, who even now is waiting at your island retreat...waiting not to receive you as *you* planned, but waiting on *her* new boat, to receive this video of your removal, as *she and her brother* planned."

Franky somehow managed to scream a near breathlessly weak expanse of air, forming only two words, "What?! Noooooo!"

But as he gasped for air and nearly passed out in pain, his old FBI handler calmly said, "Franky, your *replacements* are Hector... and his sister, Gabriela, who you thought was your girlfriend all this time. You see Franky, many years ago you had Hector and Gabriella's parents killed, to steal a meth shipment, and send a message to the cartels you were taking over. You must now pay, at least for *some* of your earthly sins. Hector requested you think about your faith in God...or should I say your *lack* of faith, before you die. I think he even tried to prepare you for that as he said goodbye, at the airport earlier today. But as usual, you won't take the hint from anyone!"

Franky's eyes flashed with surprise and rage as he thought about Hector and Gabriela setting him up, and he tried to remember their parents. He could not. He had killed too many people, for too long, to recall *anyone* that long ago. But before he could speak out, another bullet denied him the ability, as it penetrated his skull, forcing its selected path through his enraged, pain-filled brain.

Franky gasped and finally released the death grip he had held on his knees, as his body relaxed in to the bloody mass of dead monster flesh. He exhaled a lone final breath, and then breathed no more. As if having the last word, his body released all the urine his bladder had held. The yellow liquid immediately soaked through his thin slacks, soiling the virgin ground. Some of it spread to mingle with his spilled champagne, and the fluids were reunited.

Two men wearing green medical latex gloves, approached Franky and emptied his pockets. They picked up the lifeless monster. They unceremoniously threw his limp corpse in to the pit, that had been pre-dug, to be Franky's final resting place, in the Valley of Fire. The sand was soft, and the digging had been easy until a rock outcropping was eventually struck some five feet down.

The assassination detail then destroyed Franky's phone, by smashing it to pieces. They then placed it in a small vat of acid, covered the acid container with its lid and threw it in to the pit on top of him.

The gun used to kill Franky had been delivered to the assassination detail by a Committee member, who was also a member of one of the Mexican cartels. It had belonged to an officer in the Mexican Army, who had acquired it from the U.S. government in a program initiated by the ATFE, when they attempted to track guns in Mexico, by providing criminals guns.

The revolver had been easily smuggled back in to the country through the porous U.S. southern border, at a border crossing where the cartel instructed a Customs agent on their payroll to waive the car that smuggled the gun through the checkpoint. The U.S. Alcohol, Tobacco, Firearms and Explosives Agency that provided the weapon had already destroyed records of some of the guns lost in the failed operation, at the direction of the United States Attorney General, and this *was* one of those guns.

The now untraceable gun was placed in another vat of acid and covered. Even if later discovered, its serial number would be useless to any investigator. It was thrown in to the pit on top of Franky's still bloody immobile corpse.

Franky's personal items, and all his jewelry, were placed in yet another vat of acid, covered and thrown in to the pit with him. One of the men then lifted a five-gallon gas can, that contained a mixture of 4 parts diesel and 1 part gasoline, out of the trunk of the second car. He walked to the pit and poured the entire contents on top of Franky, his belongings, the acid vats and the gun. Another man threw a match in to the pit and the fire flashed and began to build.

Once the fire was good and hot, two 4-foot by 4-foot sections of plywood were lowered in to the pit and placed over the fire. Additional firewood retrieved from the trunk of the second car was placed on top of the plywood. The fire began to build even more.

A second pair of plywood sheets were lowered in to place, over the fire. Once they rested in the correct position, and had begun to burn through, the two men began to fill the burial pit with the mound of soft sand that had patiently waited to be returned to its hole, and final resting place.

The oxygen-deprived fire would smolder underground for days, destroying everything identifiable, except possibly partial dental records, should a fragment of skull or a few teeth be found, in any future excavation. No one could be linked to the assassination. Franky's dental records had already been removed by The Committee.

Hector and Gabriella's plan, aligned with The Committee plan, had finally been completed, and everything had gone according to that plan. Franky's plan had failed miserably and unexpectedly…but unexpectedly, only to him.

The assassination detail drove back to a swank Hotel in Las Vegas where they all parted company and cleaned up in separate rooms.

All the men involved later met for dinner and drinks of celebration. They spoke in hushed tones about their next assignment.

Even before they had arrived back at the hotel Franky's FBI handler sent the video text to Franky's sister who had been waiting in Franky's new 45-foot "fishing" boat, off the coast of the designated Caribbean island. Hector had provided her the coordinates assigned for her to receive the video, after he had obtained them from The Committee. The boat was still positioned over one of the deepest trenches in the area. The bottom of the ocean floor was some 2,000 feet below the water's surface, coincidently not far from shore, *and* near a good strong cell site.

Hector's sister sat waiting on the comfortable outside seats of Franky's shiny new toy. The phone beeped its receipt of the text. She shaded the screen with both her hand and her oversized floppy beach hat, and pushed the play button. She watched the video three times completely through, beginning with Franky exiting the limo door and being immediately shot, all the way through to his burning body lying in the covered pit. She took the phone apart in silence, removing both the battery and the SIM card. She stood up and walked to the stern of the boat, where she dropped the pieces in to the deep blue water one at a time, as the boat moved slowly away from the land.

Gabriella Alvarez, Hector's beautiful, sweet sister, walked in silence back to her seat and sat down, leaning all the way back on the overstuffed seat. She looked around, scrutinizing her surroundings, and eventually admired the beautiful boat, the only thing Franky had ever requested *and* allowed her, to decide on, and pick out, completely on her own. He had wanted a surprise, and she had granted his wish.

From her reclining positions, she looked down passed her luscious perky, barely-covered breasts, passed her flat and toned small waistline, over her hot pink bikini bottoms, and slowly down her thighs, to her long, beautiful sculpted legs. Her gaze finally rested on her artfully formed sexy feet, each toe adorned with hot pink toenail polish that matched her hand nail polish and lipstick. Each body part called attention to itself, and yet blended harmoniously with the others, to produce a hypnotic, euphoric effect on an admirer.

She was drop dead gorgeous, and she knew it. And she knew she had used her looks to help her brother exact the revenge they both had desired, on their tormentor. Gabriella now only hoped she could somehow forget Franky making love to her, and touching her with those awful hands…the hands of a monster…the guilty hands that had killed her parents, and so many other good and innocent people.

But their plan had worked. At long last the monster was dead. She stood and made the call to Hector, with her own phone, and said simply, "It's done. The monster is dead." As she ended the call she saw her reflection in a window of the cabin, where the captain and first mate waited for instructions. She said softly to herself staring back in the window as if talking to Franky, "This is my boat now, you rotten son-of-a-bitch!"

With a hand signal she motioned for the captain to take her back to the compound, and she laid back on the seat to enjoy the ride. Gabriella closed her eyes as the motion of the boat through the calm ocean gently rocked her up and down, back and forth, and side to side. She closed her eyes more tightly and tried to picture Franky…where he was…at that very second. Hopefully he had already completed his special journey to Hell, she mused.

She also hoped Franky had heard her calling to him from his special place in Hades. She prayed Franky would always be angry, seething with rage, and that he would remain trapped in his customized

Hell-cell, just so, nearly mad beyond description. She fancied him experiencing never ending surges of constant incredible pain, raging ferociously, totally unable to act on his unimaginable anger. She saw Franky lamenting his failed devious plans, consumed by hatred and lust, desiring her in every way, yet realizing she was unattainable, for all eternity.

An hour later, as she arrived at the dock of her new home, Hector's sister wondered where Hector was at that very moment and what he was doing. She walked slowly to her palace-prison fortress.

Hector in fact had just finished taking his oath of allegiance to The Committee, and was escorted to his own seat in this group. He received his "pin" from the ranking United States Senator from Nevada, who sat next to him at the table, all smiles, patting him on the back a little too often.

The pin displayed an American flag waving in the wind, suspended from a golden flag pole. The far-right upper corner of the flag had a very perceptible dark black spot located where the top folded red line ended, and the spot design began, signifying the wearer was a member of the secret society. Hector was instructed to wear the pin at all meetings with the group.

Hector studied the heavy gold pin. He focused on the spot, which revealed a five-pointed star surrounding a cross resting on its side, short end to the left, seemingly suspended in the center of the design and raised from the flat surface, to accentuate its presence. Hector was relieved to see the symbol did not display the pointed lines running from the tips of the star, crossing in its interior, point side down, and surrounded by a circle, like the satanic pentagram displayed.

Further examination confirmed the pin was fashioned of ceramic material with an 18-carat gold flag pole. The pin was more than twice the size of the average lapel pin, and displayed true artisan workmanship.

The business portion of the meeting was then called to order by the ranking member of The Committee present, the United States Assistant District Attorney. Hector was formally introduced, as the ranking Senator next to him stood with him, and officially "pinned" him.

With the brief ceremony complete, the business portion of the meeting was called to order, and Hector sat back in the plush chair, and relaxed. As the man spoke at the podium, Hector tried to imagine what his sister was doing and thinking at the very moment. She had paid a huge price to complete their plan, a plan that had not conformed to their timetable, or unfolded as they had originally intended.

To ensure the plan succeeded, both he and his sister had pretended to be people they were not, for more than a decade. And along the way, each of them had lost a portion of their self, and their soul, in the process. They were both changed, forever, from who they could have become.

The plan had changed radically through all those long years, he thought. His first plan had proved useless. But even though the plan had changed repeatedly in substance and form, he realized now that the *planning* had been indispensable.

Hector fondled his lapel pin, as he listened to The Committee chairman, and wondered what would become of him, and his beautiful, loving sister. He knew he must make another new plan now…a more complex and convincing plan…and he must do this very quickly. But *this* plan, he realized, may come together slowly, like a chain, only one link at a time. It would be more difficult, and take more time to construct, and would likely change even more, as it developed. And of course, in the current situation, it would involve *much* more risk. Hector again prayed silently, for safety for his family.

The senior Senator sitting next to him tapped him on the hand, leaned over, and said, "Your training will be scheduled soon. It will involve two weeks of isolation at our California headquarters. You'll learn our history, listen to the Plan of the Prophet, be versed in all aspects of the Primary Objective, and be trained in all pillars of faithfulness and allegiance required for membership in The Committee. Take this very seriously. Always remember what happened to Franky. You too must watch his video before you fly back tonight." The Senator leaned back in his chair and smiled. Hector prayed harder.

While Hector continued his silent prayers, Jesse found Shane at the ranch, as Shane checked the grounds around the house, before dinner. Shane recognized the look of concern on Jesse's face, stopped near a bench, and cocked his head to inquire, as Jesse stopped in front of him.

Jesse looked as if the weight of the world were on his shoulders. He said, "You probably never heard about a group called, 'The Committee,' allegedly formed by some politicians from different countries, during the cold war." Shane shook his head.

Jesse continued. "I want to tell you a story my grandfather told me, just before he died." They sat down on the bench together.

"Granddad was a very quiet man, who served in World War II, and then lived in Europe for about ten years. He met my grandmother there, brought her back to the states, married her, and bought a plumbing business. He was very successful, and eventually had shops in about a dozen different cities. He lived a quiet life, apart from traveling for the business, and making quarterly trips to Europe, to meet with suppliers he dealt with in high-end appliances."

"My granddad never spoke about the war, or told us why he stayed in Europe after the war…until he was dying of cancer. My dad and I were there with him, in his room at the hospital one day. He was in incredible pain, but for days, he had refused the pain meds that would help. He said he needed to be lucid, to talk to us, alone. He was a tough old guy!" Jesse looked down, fondly remembering.

"Anyway, he told dad and I that we could never say a word about this to anyone. And then he told us that when he was in Europe, he worked in Army intelligence after the war ended. The U.S. was preparing to pass the National Security Act, after the war, to make sure we would never be victims of another Pearl Harbor. They were forming the CIA, to ensure we stayed ahead of our enemy's plans. Eventually, Grandad agreed to be transitioned in to the CIA."

"The business, and the Europe trips to meet with appliance suppliers, were all a cover for his work at the CIA. Granddad told us he worked on only one *major* investigation for decades. It began during the cold war. It was an investigation involving a man known as 'The Prophet,' and a group called 'The Committee,' who were working toward a 'Primary Objective.' He said it was the only thing that ever terrified him."

"He told us that the motivation for the group was to manipulate public opinion, to facilitate control over, and direct the public, as the group worked to change how governments interacted. He said that the group was made up of a small number of politicians and officials in various countries. At that time, they were small enough that the group lacked the ability to implement the changes they planned."

"He and other Allied intelligence officers tracked the original members of the group, and attempted to acquire information on them and their plans, for years, with limited success. They never learned a great deal about them. Eventually, all the Allied countries terminated their investigations, one country at a time."

"He said The Committee's plans were unconventional, and involved developing alliances between cooperating governments and organized crime. In his last days at the Agency, no one else even *knew* about the investigation. Grandfather discovered that all records of the investigation had been sealed, or were missing. And then, just before he died, he said he had received credible evidence from a trusted associate, that the group was in place, and operating effectively, *within our own government.* They were still secretly working toward their goals, and they had grown in number, and in power."

Jesse looked at Shane. Shane nodded, encouraging Jesse to continue. Jesse said, "I never gave it much thought, after Grandad died. I was still so young, and my dad never spoke about it again. I don't think he wanted my grandmother to know anything about all this. But in the limited amount of information we have been able to decipher from your father's heavily encrypted case files, 'The Committee' is referred to multiple times…and now we just found it again, along with a reference to a 'Primary Objective.' I don't think this is a coincidence."

Jesse looked more serious than Shane had ever seen him. He said, "I hadn't put this all together until today. But I think this could be the same people my grandad spoke about. Nothing *ever* scared him. But he was *terrified* of this group."

The two men sat on the bench in silence, contemplating what they should do next. They now both realized that their long-term plans may have to change. They knew they should prepare, but they just didn't know *what* to prepare *for.* What they did know for sure, was what they *needed*. They needed the Beckett Cypher…and they needed it fast. With it, they could unravel the mystery, and put a plan together, one link at a time.

Acknowledgements

This book is dedicated to the men and women in law enforcement, and all their families. Millions of these dedicated men and women have served in this profession during my life time. I have had the honor of being trained by, serving with, and training, hundreds of these fine officers, some of who made the ultimate sacrifice of their lives to protect our cherished way of life. These men and women comprise the thin blue line that holds the space between anarchy and lawfulness, terror and security, and subjugation and freedom. These officers and support staff will always have my love and respect, and that of most hard-working good citizens. I stand with them, and salute them.

This first book in the series could not have been finished as it exists without the encouragement and help of two of my very closest friends in life, Tom and Marilyn Suarez. They were both tireless critics and editors, who offered many good insights, to help keep the story and reading experience on track. I owe them a debt of gratitude that good friends can never truly repay, to good friends.

I also credit my parents, Alma Juanita Rutherford Holub and George John Holub Jr., the best parents a young man could ask for, and those most responsible for shaping me and my values. I will love you always.

I wish to thank my loved ones and friends who have supported me this far during my time here on earth. I have learned and grown with our collective triumphs and failures. I hope this book makes you proud, or at least, leaves you entertained.

And lastly, I thank my biological father, Lee Cunningham, who, along with my mother, gave me the gift of life. I wish I could have known you, and listened to the music you made, with your band. I write these novels in our name.

A final comment. This book is a work of fiction, although mingled with real places, characters I have known, and actual events. As the series develops, crime, corruption, world incidents, politics, love and opinions are all expressed in many different ways, both as fact and fiction. My idea was to tell a story by painting a series of literary pictures, some real and some imagined. I encourage you to read the entire series, to experience all these pictures together, as they lead to a focal point. I hope your literary journey will be thrilling and rewarding. As with all such experiences, my highest and best hope is to stimulate the imagination, provide entertainment, and possibly induce a positive change, through reflection.

About the Author

Lee Cunningham's father was killed when Lee Jr. was just 6 months old, while driving from Nebraska to Idaho to reunite with Lee Jr. and his mother. Lee Jr. eventually became known as "Danny" a nickname given him by his eight aunts. Lee's mother relocated them to California, seeking a better career opportunity, to improve their lives. Struggling, as a working, single mother, she met and married George Holub, when Lee was  9. Lee's step-father adopted him when he was 12. Lee was proud of his new father, and had his name legally changed, to Daniel Lee Holub.

Lee attended the U.S.A.F.A., C.U. Boulder, and U.C.L.A., graduating with a degree in Zoology, minoring in English. His daring mother often ventured in to the California deserts, to help him collect rattlesnakes, for college research projects. His father taught him to fish, hunt, camp, and love the outdoors. Lee's parents taught him to respect and love his country and be thankful for life. He also always loved to write. His first success was an essay, published while he was in college.

In the year following college, Lee worked a drug case assisting D.E.A., and flew a Cessna 210 airplane from California to Bogota, Colombia, as an undercover pilot. He participated in one of the largest out-of-country drug sting operations of the time, when he was just 24 years old. Lee became enthralled with police work, was hired as a police officer, and graduated the L.A.P.D. academy, as co-valedictorian.

Lee worked in law enforcement in California and Nevada for 25 years, serving in both uniform and plain clothes. His work included assignments in patrol, a narcotics task force, a gang unit, and detective units, where he investigated thousands of cases, including homicides. He interviewed thousands of criminals, including some in prison. Lee served as a S.W.A.T. member and became a S.W.A.T. Commander.

Lee went on to work in Security Management at one of the world's largest gold mines. He and his team were responsible for protecting more than a billion dollars' worth of gold and silver shipments annually, while providing high level security for explosives and other sensitive chemicals. Lee trained and supervised a security team that won multiple Best-in-Security awards.

Throughout his careers, writing remained one of Lee's passions, and he planned this collection of novels, for years. Calling on all his training and experience, Lee Cunningham now offers his first series of fiction novels as *The Beckett Cypher* series.

Lee now lives in Florida with his lovely wife, his nearly "psychic" multi-breed rescue dog, a King Charles Cavalier puppy, and a grand-motherly Cocker Spaniel. He enjoys writing, traveling, experiencing the great outdoors, good food, family, friends, and pets.